'You say you don't believ̶ ̶ ̶ ̶ ̶ ̶ ̶ ̶ ̶ ̶ ̶ ̶
but you've just bought y̶ ̶ ̶ ̶ ̶ ̶ ̶ ̶ ̶ ̶ ̶ ̶ ̶ ̶
me the option, I'll work in your fields. I'll slave in your
fields until my fingers bleed if necessary, and I'll pay off
your damned debt faster than you ever dreamed possible.
For all your cant, Mr Savage, you've got yourself a
white nigra slave! On your conscience be it—if you have
one.'

She thought she saw a lessening of the anger and
something akin to respect flicker in those dark eyes, but
then Paul turned aside and a mirthless smile touched
his mouth. 'Very well. On my head be it. You have
spirit . . . for one who calls herself a slave!'

Beatrice broke in, almost in tears at the apparent
callous indifference to her niece's plight. 'And you, sir,
will you break her of that?'

His voice softened. 'I've neither the desire nor the
need to do so, Lady Davenport, but unless there is steel
beneath that silken skin, my country will do that for
me.'

'It didn't break *you*,' Melody interjected, 'and it won't
break *me*. I'll learn to weed and plough and sow, milk
cows, pick cotton, or whatever it is you do grow in that
barbaric place.' She faced her aunt bravely. 'I've often
doubted my strength at times, but this isn't one of them.
I shall survive, never fear, and then, God willing, I'll
come back to you, wherever you are, and we'll begin
again.'

Hazel Smith lives in Coulsdon, Surrey with her husband and fifteen-year-old son, fitting in her writing between a hectic full-time book-keeping job and keeping their ten-roomed house in an acceptable degree of chaos.

In her early twenties Hazel emigrated to America for four years, during which time she covered over ten thousand miles in her travels, working in San Francisco, Los Angeles, Las Vegas, Houston and Miami, with an unforgettable holiday in the Hawaiian Islands, and 'meanderings' in such opposite towns as New York and New Orleans.

Of New Orleans and San Francisco, which are to be re-visited in a number of her novels, she says, 'They fitted—instantly—like a warm and familiar cloak', and of American men, 'I met only gentlemen. The age of chivalry is very much alive and well in twentieth-century U.S.A.'

A Savage Pride is Hazel Smith's fourth historical romance and the first in the Savage family saga.

A SAVAGE PRIDE

HAZEL SMITH

WORLDWIDE BOOKS
LONDON . SYDNEY . TORONTO

First published in Hardback in 1987 by Worlwide Books, Eton House, 18-24 Paradise Road, Richmond, Surrey, TW9 1SR.

This paperback edition published in 1988 by Worldwide Books

© Hazel Smith 1987

Australian copyright 1987
Philippine copyright 1987

ISBN 0 373 50674 0

Set in Monotype Times 10 on 10 pt.
09-0188-141477

Typeset in Great Britain by Associated Publishing Services Ltd Printed and bound in Great Britain by Cox & Wyman Ltd, Reading

To Edna, whose letters painted an inspiring picture of a beautiful, Savage land and Alf, my New Zealand Research Department.
With thanks to a very special aunt and uncle.

PROLOGUE

A FINE SHEEN of perspiration clouded her high, unlined forehead as the birth pains reached their peak, and Lady Arabella Fortesque-Savage reflected almost dispassionately that at this time, as at all the other major events in their marriage, her husband was absent. She was beyond pain. Thirty-six hours earlier she had bitten her lip through, but now she calmly awaited death. It brought her some small comfort that the beautiful mulatto woman she called Nanny—a poor substitute for the plump, bustling angel of her childhood—hovered near by, loving her mistress enough to stay with her while her own octoroon daughter gave birth in the slave quarters.

There was a sudden commotion from below, a crash as the front door gave, and shouts and screams that resounded through the lower floor, and in that peaceful world she had reached—far above the bed on which it seemed another woman writhed helplessly—Arabella recorded the sound. 'My people . . .'

'Are free,' Nanny said softly. 'It is their time and yours to fight for what is coming; though, the Lord help them, their deliverance will be far longer than yours. Easy now, child. No time to talk. Breathe deep. In . . . and out again. Shorter now. We're nearly there. Yes, I can feel it. Shallow and fast. Push now. And now.'

And a pain ripped through her, and then another, wrenching a stifled cry from those full lips as the English lady refused to acknowledge any sign of weakness. Stars burst behind her tight-closed eyes as tissue ripped. Still she fought the agony and the swift approaching darkness as the coffee-coloured woman delivered the child with expertise and thrust it into the dying woman's arms.

'Is it . . . ?'

'A lovely daughter, Miz Arabella.'

Almost as an echo to her own torn flesh came the sound of splintering wood as the blacks rampaged below, smashing the beautiful panelled doors and the delicate gilt Louis XV occasional chairs that Arabella had brought from England and lovingly cherished. The mistress of the plantation they called St Clare knew in that moment that those cries, bestial in their hatred, would have heralded her death had not the baby dragged from her too slender frame already done so.

The slaves had finally torn free of their chains, urged on by followers of the slave preacher, Nat Turner, whose revolt eight years before in 1831 had led to the deaths of over sixty whites as well as many innocent negroes. In the years since, several outbreaks of this mass hysteria had exploded into violence throughout the South, and even now her husband was out combing the countryside with other vigilantes to bring in a group of blacks who had killed a planter's family to the east. It was ironical, Arabella thought, that he should be charging about the emerald hills of North Carolina while his own home was being ripped apart.

As the welcoming shadows enfolded her, the English lady looked back on her seemingly endless life with that once strong lion of a man she had married—a man who had turned brute on his home territory. She had been appalled at his cruel treatment of his slaves: the daily floggings for minor offences, the children sold away from their mothers, and, above all, his insatiable lust—his use of her and of any other young girl who, by her sheer presence, might flame his desire. She had attempted to rail against him once, saying that she was accustomed to respect and love. He had laughed at her, telling her that he respected her as he respected any other beautiful possession, and that if it was love she wanted . . . and then he had taken her, brutally, there in the hall where they had been arguing. She had never spoken of it again, enduring his lovemaking and glad of the times when his attentions turned elsewhere. If only . . . and bright as a morning star came the thought of the young Englishman, Alexander Davenport, an acquaintance of her youth, invited in a fit of despairing loneliness and who, incredibly, had fallen in love with an octoroon savage instead of herself. Tears came to her eyes as she remembered that the illegitimate fruit of that union, of that shocking, illegal union, was at this moment being born in a wooden hut on a bed of straw. 'It could have been mine,' her bleak thoughts ran. 'It *should* have been mine! It *must* have been a son! The son of an English lord and lady.' At that she remembered her first-born, the son that had so disappointed her husband by his fragile beauty and delicacy. 'Brett?' she asked of the woman washing her hands in the flowered porcelain bowl.

'I'll take him with me.'

'He's only seven. He'll be so afraid.'

'He'll be safe.'

Arabella nodded weakly, feeling the strength draining from her, hearing the plaintive mewing sounds from the infant in her arms, and her heart twisted as she realised that she would not even have time to feed her. She made a fluttering gesture, and at once Nanny crossed to her side, bending low. Blue eyes met brown. 'Save her,' Arabella murmured, holding the shadows at bay for just a moment longer. 'Whatever you have to do . . . save her', and was comforted by a brief nod before, finally, she allowed the warm blanket of eternal darkness to enfold her.

The negress bent and brushed full lips against her mistress's forehead. 'Could never do that when you were alive, Little Missis. Goodbye, and may the good Lord keep you safe.' The velvet eyes were damp as she gathered up the child and wrapped her in clean linen, carrying her in the crook of her arm as she made her way to the top of the stairs. 'Masta Brett! Where are you, child?' she called urgently, pitching her voice low so that the intruders would not hear.

Sounds of smashed bottles, mingled with laughter and

the occasional curse as shards of glass cut into bare feet, told her that they had broken into the wine-cellar. A frown touched the high brow, and her search quickened. She felt nothing but contempt for the marauding blacks, but, once drunk, even their leaders would have no control over them. 'Brett! You come out, boy! You come here this minute wherever you are, 'cos I gotta get this babe outa here.' No reply, but as she turned to search the other rooms, a tiny figure slipped from behind the long curtains at the end of the corridor and scampered into his mother's room.

'Mama! Mama!' he whispered, golden-brown curls gleaming in the light from the candelabrum. 'Nanny's got the new baby you told me about, and there are bad men in the cellar. Mama, I'm frightened!' His words trailed to a halt as he reached the bedside, and his long-lashed ice blue eyes widened in fear. 'Mama?'

She appeared to be sleeping peacefully, but there was a strange, unpleasant odour in the room and blood on the bed that the hastily thrown coverlet did not quite hide, and he was afraid to touch her. The sound of Nanny's low voice outside caused him to slide quickly beneath the bed. Nanny had always been a haven of safety, shielding him from his father's bullying, and that of his peers, who saw his delicacy as weakness, but this time he was determined to stay firm. He was not going to leave his mother to those bad men for anything!

The mulatto quickly searched the room again, but then made a decision, sacrificing the young master for this new, helpless babe. Wherever the boy was hiding, he would be safe as long as he stayed hidden and silent. She would take Missis Arabella's baby to her own daughter to suckle and return for Master Brett when the raid was over. She knew her people, and reasoned that they were interested only in looting and venting their spleen on a few sticks of furniture before making a fast escape to the North. The men of St Clare weren't killers, though any one of them would gladly have killed 'Bull' Savage, and the white woman would undoubtedly have suffered—and in her condition died—at their hands. 'They won't fire the house, and Mr Savage'll be back soon when young Cato finds him.' Swiftly she made her way downstairs and slipped out of the back door, across into the kitchen block, then ran across the field to the slave quarters.

Not all of the slaves had joined the revolt. One or two stood in awkward silence around the hut that housed her daughter, men too old to fight, too tired or too afraid to seek the Freedom Road. One approached, meeting Nanny a few yards from the doorway. 'She won't let us in. She done dropped her sucker a while ago, but she say she don' want no one but you.'

Nanny gave him a sympathetic smile. 'That's okay, Rufus. You wait here. There may be some way you can help later.'

'She ain't done no screaming an' hollering like my Bessie did when she had our Josiah,' the man put in worriedly, and Nanny's lips tightened.

'She's a Coramantin. She don't give vent to no pain.' In that, the negress reflected, there was little difference between her beautiful wild octoroon daughter and the aristocratic English lady she had just left. Both would bear whatever pain life inflicted on them with stoic indifference. With a sigh she promptly forgot the men and moved into the hut.

In the tiny room, Ereanora had given birth easily and alone. Her mother had been one of the new and quite illegal shipments smuggled into the country since the law of 1808 banning the slave trade from Africa. Ereanora was strong and proud and in her prime at sixteen, but picking cotton all day had taken its toll. She bit her lip, refusing to acknowledge the strange stabbing pains that had not felt at all like her mother had advised her, but then it was over and all she wished to do was sleep. As if in a dream she saw her mother enter, a bundle in her arms. Weakly Ereanora indicated the still carelessly wrapped girl-child that lay silently on the palliasse beside her, refusing to suck at her over-full breasts. 'She . . . won't . . . feed . . . '

One glance, and her mother's lips tightened. The soft velvet eyes closed for an instant as if in pain. 'It's all gonna come right,' soothed the beloved voice, the educated tones, copied from her mistress, reassuring Ereanora as no other could. 'See? I'll wake her. She's just tired after all that hard work. Babes go through a long voyage out and then all they want to do is sleep, just like you.'

Ereanora allowed the child to be taken, and then there was a cry . . . a lusty, hungry cry. The newborn babe was put to the breast and pulled eagerly. With tears in her eyes Ereanora smiled up at her mother. 'She's a fine healthy girl. I told you it would be easy for me when you had to go see the mistress. I told you I'd have me a fine healthy baby.'

'Yes, daughter,' the woman said, some strange, small catch in her voice. 'You were right. She surely is a fine healthy baby. You have done well, warrior woman! You couldn't do less. You are Coramantin and you must never forget it; the most prized of Gold Coast slaves, best in courage, hardest in work. We don't take no white man's beating with screaming and wailing. We look him straight in the eye, and we look at life the same way.'

Ereanora smiled and closed her eyes in acceptance. Only then, the lump in her throat threatening to choke her, could Nanny watch Arabella's child pulling at the full breast and her heart went out to her own daughter who lay, relaxed now, lips curved into a smile at the tiny pain that the hungry child caused.

'I'll be back right away,' she said softly. 'Just got one little thing to do, and then I'll be back.' Bending, she lifted that other bundle from the earth floor and shielding it from her daughter's sight, carried it outside.

The Big House was silent now, the marauders already satiated with their mindless vandalism and a surfeit of wine. Making her way up the stairway to the mistress's bedroom she wrapped the tiny body in an exquisite silk shroud, a length of dress-material found in one of the smashed drawers. 'No slave burial for you,' she murmured. 'You're a lady now, little one.' Her cheeks were damp as she prayed to the ancient gods in the language of her ancestors, but then she rose and took a deep breath. There was a future to plan, for, strong as was her love for the sweet and delicate Englishwoman who had treated her with nothing but respect and kindness, so was her hatred for her master.

'He'll not have her,' she muttered, thinking of the newborn babe now sleeping in her daughter's arms. 'Sooner be a slave than a child of "Bull" Savage. I'll get her out. Get her on the Underground Railway. Get her started with one of the "conductors".' While moving about the room she thought of the heroic network of men and women, black and white, Northerner and even Southerner, who helped runaway slaves to freedom. No railway of steam and steel this, but its tracks ran across woods and fields and rivers, its stations were houses, barns and churches belonging to the agents of the railroad. The way was long and fraught with danger, but each year thousands made that journey to the North, and Nanny was determined that her daughter and the child should join that number as soon as possible.

There was a momentary pang as she thought of that other child, a seven-year-old boy, golden haired like his mother, who could never pass for black and be smuggled away from his brute of a father; he would serve only to increase their danger. The baby, however, had hair as black as a raven's wing and the golden-olive skin of her father. 'She'll pass,' the woman nodded to herself. 'And, anyway, Mr Alex'll be back soon. Maybe he'll have an idea. He may be a whitee, but he sure loved my Ereanora like a gentleman should, not forcing her like the Bull once did, but loving her sweet and gentle.' And Nanny smiled as she thought of how lightning had flashed between them on their very first meeting, the proud octoroon in the field and the young English lord riding through. 'Lordy, that child would have been fine!' she murmured. But now there was work to do.

Two horses raced through the night: one a dun-coloured,

fiddle-faced mustang, its rider a slender, fair-haired youth whose language more than his spurs drove the horse on, the other a thoroughbred bay, beaten by whip and spur to greater effort than its gallant heart could endure. The mustang, dragged back on its haunches before a tiny wooden hut, was seized by waiting black hands eager to do some small service for their Ereanora and the young lord they had come to love and respect. The horse was gentled as its rider threw himself from the saddle and raced into the hut. It was rubbed down with cooling mosses and walked in soothing circles while being praised lavishly for its bravery and strength. The bay mare fell as her rider kicked free of the stirrups, taking the porch steps at a run, bellowing his anger to the skies, not glancing at the dying horse or at the splintered stairway and smashed furniture of the now empty house. Pounding up the stairs, he flung open the door of his wife's room, barely glancing at the shrouded body of Arabella, and demanding, 'Where is he? Where's my son?'

The beautiful negress he knew only as Nanny faced his anger with even eyes, knowing that he was not referring to that other child who still remained in hiding. 'It was a daughter, Master, but both she and your lady . . . I'm right sorry, sir.' She indicated the silk-covered bundle in the white wickerwork cradle.

His cry rent the heavens. 'Damn her! Damn her for not giving me a son! Damn her for being so weak!'

The brown velvet eyes were expressionless, yet some small unnoticed spark ignited deep in their depths. 'Master Brett is hiding here in the house, sir. I've not been here long enough to search all over, and my own daughter Ereanora is needing me now. She has just dropped Mista Davenport's sucker . . . '

'Yes . . . Yes. Get outa here. Damn her to hell! Couldn't she have gotten a boy? I could mourn a dead son, but a daughter . . . useless, whimpering thing growing like her mother. Bah!'

In the suffocatingly warm hut the young Englishman

gathered the woman he loved close to his heart. 'I'll never let you go, you know that.'

'You must, Alex,' she replied strongly. 'Look at your daughter. Look at her eyes.'

Not understanding, he obligingly pulled away the cotton wrapping from the baby's face. The child was well fed and content. She dribbled excess milk from rosebud lips and opened her long-lashed eyes. They were a brilliant sapphire blue. 'All babies' eyes are blue,' he smiled. 'We'll call her Melody for the sweet music we made.'

'Not a nigra child. Not even a white nigra. Not *that* blue,' Ereanora stated, ignoring the name he had given the child. 'She's white. Like you.'

'She's *our* child. My eyes, your wonderful creamy golden skin.'

'No!' Ereanora clutched at his arm. 'Take her away from here. Tell them anything. Tell them her mother died in the attack on the Big House. Take her with you, my only love. Make her white!' Weakly, hating her weakness, she fell back on the straw-filled mattress and closed her eyes. 'Please!'

The tall negress they called Nanny moved in from the night. 'Take her, young sir. Find some good white woman. All the troubles are over for now and the men are gone, but the troubles will come again *and* again before all the slaves are free. There will be plenty of killing, both black and white. You are from England. No slaves in England. You can make her white, a white English lady like the mistress. Look at her. She is *your daughter*! Will you leave her here to be a slave—maybe forced to marry some no-brain Congo nigra, or be sold as a bed-wench to someone like the master?'

Agonised, the youth searched the fine-boned features of the woman on the bed, herself a bed-wench, raped at thirteen by the very man he had spent the past year with. 'I don't know . . . Oh, my dear, of course I could take our daughter to England. I could make her safe and happy and pass her off as white and no one would ever know. But it's *you* I love!'

The brown eyes were as hawkish as ever. 'Then, for love do it! *I* am slave. If my daughter stay here *she* is slave. Now my daughter can be free . . . free English lady. It will be enough to make me live.' She clutched at his sleeve. 'Don' tell the Master. Go! Go now! Take her!'

Tears in his eyes, Alex acknowledged powers far stronger than his. One last time he took the girl, for she was little more than that, into his arms. 'I shall never ever find love again,' he said brokenly, vowing, 'She *will* know one day, I promise you. When the time is right I'll bring her back and I swear we'll find you.' Then, gathering the gurgling bundle close against his chest, he blindly ran out of that place and re-mounted the mustang. There would be a wet-nurse in the nearest town, or even a slave who would suckle the child as well as her own. Back in England there was Charity, a widow now, with a young son, free of a duty-bound marriage and awaiting him, as she had waited since they were fourteen years old. She would take his child and, for love of him, call it her own.

At the Big House an enraged, grieving man smashed his fist against the bedpost. 'Damn her!' he repeated. 'What in God's name is his curse on the Savage family that we can't beget sons that grow into men! I sire two stillborn and a pathetic porcelain lily, and my wastrel brother has to *adopt* the only man among us.' A movement from the side of the bed brought an oath to his lips, and tearing aside the curtains, he revealed the cringing shape of his son, Brett—the soft, delicate creature who reminded him too sharply of his fragile English wife. 'Why? Why you?' he cried.

The tears started in the wide, pale blue eyes as the child stuttered, 'I—I . . . tried to—to stay with her, Papa. I tried to hit them!'

The blue-black bruise on his cheek testified to the marauding negroes' contempt for a seven-year-old's bravery, but his father could not, in his self-guilt, see either. '*Hit* them?' He bellowed. '*Hit* them, you pathetic brat?' and with an inarticulate cry he spun away from the wide, shocked eyes.

As he stumbled down the porch steps he saw his house-
guest, Alex, race away along the road to the north as
though the hounds of hell were after him. They had spent
a good first month together, he remembered: downed a
few jars, got high a few times and gambled away a few
nights among the dimly-lit salons of Raleigh, the capital
city to the north. The boy had been a friend of his wife,
but he, Luke Savage, had soon put a stop to that! Oh,
he'd seen the sheep's eyes and the close conversations, but
he'd already sized up the Englishman and found him
remarkably easy to lead . . . until he had met up with
that coffee-coloured wench in the slave quarters. The boy
had fallen for her as if she was a white woman, even
though he had been told that she'd started out as a bed-
wench and was sure no virgin. Luke's thick lips curved
upward as he remembered the time he had taken her.
Man, had she fought him! But they'd not named him 'the
Bull' for nothing, and he was proud of it. She'd not
fought for long, though he'd near killed her, tearing her
up so bad that she'd been abed for over a week. He
frowned as he thought of Nanny coming to carry her out
of his room and staring at him long and hard from those
dark eyes. 'You come to no good end,' she had hissed.
'You die hard and violent like you live. You see.' Of
course he had flogged her for her insolence, but the curse
had stayed with him for many months, and still came
back occasionally to haunt him. He had put the child into
the fields after that and taken a more willing wench, but
to see his house-guest with her made his blood boil.
Hospitality and the fawning obsequiousness of his neighbours, not to mention the considerable sums of money
that young Alex Davenport had allowed him to win at
poker, made him put up with the boy, but he would not
be sorry when the little affair had run its course. The boy
had even offered to buy the wench—offered far more than
she'd bring elsewhere—but 'Bull' Savage hadn't finished
with her yet and wasn't about to see a nigger bitch-thing
who had rejected him being treated as some Queen of
Sheba by London society.

Of course he would sell the chit when he'd taught her a lesson—broken her of her newly-acquired airs and graces. She would bring a good price in New Orleans where her almost white skin would be highly prized. He would keep the sucker and give it to one of the Mandingo women to raise. It would be only one-sixteenth black, so he would have to sell it here in North Carolina, he planned, mildly irritated that the other States considered octoroons as black, but not their get if they were out of a white man. 'Matters not,' he muttered. 'I'll get top price in Raleigh.'

His quick temper rose again as he thought of the woman upstairs and her frigid indifference to his lovemaking. He had even forced her to watch once when he had taken one of the serving-maids, but she had not uttered a word, and the contempt in her eyes had cut into him like a knife. 'Forget her!' He cursed aloud, shaking his great head. 'Got to forget. Forget it all. Start again. Get to town. Get drunk. Forget them all, damn their hides!' He looked after the settling cloud of dust on the road. They had both been on the vengeance trail when they heard of St Clare's own rebellion, told by a hysterical houseboy bumping atop an equally panicked horse. They had turned for home and the thoroughbred had outrun the mustang—but at least, he reflected bitterly, the mustang was still alive!

'Must get away! Think it over tomorrow.' The carriage— The carriage was untouched. Quickly the man dragged out the ancient grey mare that the houseboy had ridden, now recovering in the stables, and forced her between the shafts. From the porch a small, high plea rang out as he climbed aboard.

'Don't leave me again, Papa!' A tiny shape hurtled down the steps and clambered aboard as, uncaring, the man applied the whip brutally to the still sweating back.

They would have made it, too. They almost made the lights of the town, of safety and freedom . . . and drunkenness and forgetfulness. But the slaves had taken a few moments to linger on their all-too-short freedom

trail that had ended with their being cut down by the
same group of vigilantes with whom Luke and Alex had
been riding. They had taken time to stretch a rope across
the road at fetlock height—to catch a lashed, terrified,
blindly careering horse and send it over, screaming and
threshing in splintered shafts.

Almost in slow motion the carriage toppled sideways,
and the man and child, like broken dolls, were tossed just
as carelessly through the air. Within that moment in space
the man had time to reflect on what a fool he had been,
but as his features twisted in remorse his body crashed
into the giant oak and his neck broke cleanly. The child,
however, was still wandering up the rutted road towards
home when the coloured woman found him at dawn.

Gently she gathered him into strong arms. 'It's gonna
be all right, Masta Brett.'

The child gave a frightened whimper, bravely stifled.
'It's all dark, Nanny. I can't see. It doesn't hurt much
any more, but I just can't see!'

'I'm here now. It's all over and you're safe. No one will
hurt you, either of you, again.' But she didn't explain,
and the seven-year-old clinging to the comfort of a familiar
haven didn't question . . . not then.

CHAPTER ONE

THE LONDON PAVEMENTS were silvered by the light rain that had fallen for the past few days, accentuating the mood of the girl at the piano and the haunting strains of Chopin's Nocturne in E flat. The light from the candelabrum shot fire from her blue-black hair and drew a softer gleam from the black glacé-silk crinoline, but it was her eyes that one noticed first—long lashed and slightly elongated like a cat's, and of an incredible sapphire blue— misted now with tears. She stiffened as the door of the music-room opened, but refused to turn.

'A little heavy, isn't it, Melody, my dear?'

'It was one of Hugh's favourites.'

'Your husband has been dead for just over three months. I consider it unhealthy for you to carry out this daily resurrection.'

'I find comfort in the piece.'

'I'd rather you found forgetfulness.'

Her fingers left the keys, clenching in her lap as she fought the urge to run. 'Forgetfulness? After only three months, Luther?'

Luther Hogge came to stand behind her, thick fingers curling over her shoulders, and she shuddered, yet the hands remained, even tightening fractionally. His nails were spatulate, always beautifully manicured, and on the third finger of the right hand a large square-cut emerald ring, its setting ornamental enough for a woman, yet Melody had seen a servant's cheek cut to the bone by that self-same ring when he had dared to answer back. The backs of his hands showed a sprinkling of black hair that thickened as it went up his arms. She had seen him once with his sleeves rolled up, and the thought that this curling black mat might possibly cover most of his body . . . 'No!' she choked out, answering her own thoughts as well as his suggestion.

'Then take the comfort instead, but not that of the Nocturne—one of his waltzes perhaps.'

Holding herself as rigid as possible, she shook her head mutely, wanting to scream at him to leave her alone, but her fear of him went far deeper than her revulsion at his touch. He was a big man, his figure testifying to his gargantuan appetite, and the florid complexion to a more than passing acquaintance with the brandy bottle. She felt herself turned on the stool to face him. His fingers slipped to her arms and she was lifted to her feet. 'Melody . . . ' The voice was silky, the smile that of a friendly wolf, but his eyes, black as jet, burned with his hunger for her as they roamed over the averted profile.

When she was drawn closer until her slender form touched that corpulent stomach, she was unable to hide the anger and revulsion any more, and dragged free. 'No, Luther. I'll not accept your comfort or anything else you offer, and you should know better than to offer it.' She closed the piano with a little bang to emphasise her point, moving to tidy the pile of music on top, putting its width between them.

His smile faded and there was a warning note in his tone as he stated, 'I've denied you nothing since I inherited this house and everything in it from your late brother.'

'Not everything,' she shot back. 'My brother may have owned the house and furniture after Father died, but that was *all* he owned. When you persuaded him to sign over his inheritance to you, I wonder if you knew that he would join Sir Hugh Rose's force in India and die in putting down the resistance at Jhansai.'

The black eyes glittered at her accusation, but the feral smile returned. 'If the boy insisted on doing his patriotic duty in some far land, it was only right and proper that he should leave a Will appointing some responsible person to protect and care for his dear sister. And who better than an old and trusted friend of his father?'

Melody's hands clenched spasmodically on a piece of sheet-music, quite ruining it, and her eyes shot sapphire flame. 'You were a business associate only, and a poor one at that! Father never would have made a fortune—he loved his horses far more than the wheeling and dealing on the floor of the Exchange—but we did well enough before you came. How was it that within a year his investments began to fail? He was always a bit of a dreamer, always talking of taking me to America to trace some friend or other, but he never used to be as nervous and insecure as he became. He never turned to anyone for advice, so why to you? What power did you wield, Luther, to bankrupt him?'

The threatening tears almost choked her as she thought of that terrible night when Alexander Davenport had left the house for the last time, a pale and broken man, saying that he needed to be alone for a while with his thoughts. He did not return that night, nor the next, and it was almost a week later when his body was found—washed up on a mud bank downriver.

Luther heard her words, their bite going deep, but he forced himself to relax, biding his time. He allowed his gaze to wander over the lovely features before him, lingering on her mouth. His eyes moved downward to the soft swell of her breasts revealed by the slightly décolleté neckline of the crinoline, and his breath caught in his throat. He moistened suddenly dry lips with the tip of his tongue and his voice came thickly as he chided, 'You're being deliberately cruel, Melody, when I have treated you with nothing but kindness and generosity. Since your father's . . . demise, I've taken over the debts and responsibilities gladly, certain that one day you would see me as head of this house and master of your home. I've bought you dresses and you've not worn them; jewellery, which remains in its box.'

'They were not suitable for a widow still in mourning,' she stated firmly. 'And you should have known that I could not possibly accept such gifts from any man to whom I was unrelated.'

'Just so,' he purred. 'I came to talk with you on exactly that subject. Let us go into the drawing-room, where it is more comfortable. I have ordered a fire lit, since we appear to be having a typical English summer, and firelight is appropriate for what I have to say.'

Melody felt a chill cut through her and stared at him—as a bird that is trapped by the mesmeric gaze of a snake. He crossed to her side, moving surprisingly lightly for a man of his size, and took one of the hands that twisted before her.

'Come, my dear.'

. . . His touch had repelled her from the first, the nightmare time when they brought the news of her father's death. Luther Hogge had exuded shocked concern and sympathy, was the epitome of kindness, but even in her innocence Melody had shuddered when he put those great arms about her and murmured condolences.

Times had changed, yet so slowly that none of them could give a reason or define any way in which their lives were less than before. Indeed, the investments that had ruined her father now appeared to prosper, and the family were given every opportunity to feel grateful to their generous patron who, by now, had become a very real part of the family. Yet slowly the house fell silent, the piano that she had played since childhood was closed, and laughter became a thing of the past. She noticed that her mother did nothing to reproach him, or argued with his decisions. Her eyes became over-bright, and she walked through the rooms as might a sleep-walker.

Melody remembered the first time she had run into the drawing-room with a particularly diverting piece of gossip from her maid and had found Luther sitting on the couch beside her mother, a possessive arm about the slender shoulders, those bloated fingers over her breast, and her mother's eyes had been vacant—she had not even drawn away at Melody's stammered apology. The man had risen easily and crossed to where she stood in the doorway, his lambent gaze moving over her face. 'You will knock from now on,' he had instructed smoothly, his voice soft with menace. 'And not even by that look I see in your eyes will you again question any action of mine. Do you understand?'

Coward that she was, not comprehending pure evil, she had fled; from then on avoiding the man as much as was humanly possible.

Her mother became sick—from a broken heart, said all who knew of the love she and her late husband had shared—and her husband's sister, the Lady Beatrice Davenport, arrived. Her presence had been like a gust of pure cool air that swirls through an old house, blowing away cobwebs and dust as it goes. Even the shell of the woman that had been its mistress brightened for a time and even gave an order or two to the staff, but the 'medication' that Luther had introduced her to had too great a hold, poisoning her body as well as her soul, and at Easter it was lilies that were brought to the house rather than daffodils.

. . . 'You are dreaming again,' that hated voice continued, as he drew her from the music-room and across the hall, but following her train of thought, Melody prevaricated, 'I feel that any serious discussion—and I see by your tone that it *is* to be serious—should wait until Aunt Bee is well enough to join us.'

His slight frown reminded her that, in talking of her aunt, she was introducing a subject that he did not care for, but his tone was still silky. 'Yes, indeed . . . your Aunt Bee. What a pity she is laid so low with a mere chill. I do hope it's nothing more.'

Melody froze, turning to face him, remembering how he had recommended an infusion of herbs at the onset of her aunt's cold, remembering how he had been the one to introduce her gentle, fragile mother to an infusion of poppy-seed 'to comfort her in her grief and bring her sleep', but Luther's smile was bland. 'If your aunt's cold continues we must bring in the doctor, but I don't think we need disturb her just now. What I have to say is best said between the two of us, for, while I am sure she had your best interests at heart, I find her constant domination of you a little difficult to bear at times. Of course she is an excellent chaperon, but since she has neither personal income, nor a husband to support her, she is most fortunate that I am a patient and tolerant man. However, my tolerance of women like Beatrice Davenport is not infinite.'

'You have little choice,' Melody flared spiritedly. 'You're a powerful and affluent man, Luther, but Aunt Bee has the ear of far higher patronage than ever your influence can extend to; patronage that might ask questions about my father's death . . . and that of my brother.' She flinched as his hand whipped upward—but was then lowered again with considerable effort.

His thick lips parted in that feral smile. 'Please forgive that little display. I didn't mean to frighten you. I feel the need to remind you, however, that the lady is under my roof and has fared very well from my hospitality. In fact her figure, once the toast of London, now borders on the obese, and I feel she might do well to partake a little more frugally of my table. A woman of her weight and age should take more care. I'm sure she is quite aware that the staircase in this house is abysmally ill lit, and a woman of her size, should she trip over a carelessly dropped object and lose her balance, would have considerable difficulty in regaining it . . . But we weren't speaking of that. You mentioned the questions that might be asked concerning my totally innocent presence in a house whose owner had an unfortunate accident while walking the Embankment at high tide, and the quite terrible death of his only heir while in the service of his country.'

Melody felt the chill deep inside. There had been no ambiguity in his meaning. He was telling her that Aunt Bee was alive only on his sufferance, but his gaze held none of the threat in his words as he met her horrified eyes. 'Why, Melody, you look quite pale. Come and sit down. I'll ring for a glass of Madeira.'

Numbly she allowed him to seat her on the low couch by the fireplace and a moment later saw the maid, a new and slightly slovenly individual, enter with a tray bearing a bottle and two glasses. 'Where is Jessie?' she asked.

'I had to let her go, I'm afraid. She was quite insufferably rude to Cook.'

Melody fought back her rising anger. 'Jessie has been with us since I was a child! She's the most placid of souls. It must have been the new cook's fault; the old one got on very well with her. *All* our staff used to get on well together. Jessie was the last, apart from Simpson . . . People I've known all my life, and now replaced by your . . . puppets.'

Ignoring her last words he gave a nod, draining his glass in one draught and pouring another. 'Good butlers are hard to find,' he agreed. 'The others, however, were totally inefficient and of no more use than pampered family pets. The household runs far more smoothly now, and nothing happens here, no movement, no gossip, of which I'm not advised.'

Melody took a sip of the Madeira, forcing herself to control her fury, but seemingly unaware of it, he continued smoothly, 'But I didn't bring you here to talk of servants, past or present. What I have to say is of a far more personal nature.' He drained his second glass and then came to sit beside her on the couch, and for once she was glad of the wide-hooped crinoline that kept him a good three feet away. 'Melody, you know . . . you must know why I've been so generous to you over these past months; why I've gone out of my way to ease your burden of grief. I feel that the time has come for you to repay . . . no . . . accept my little kindnesses. You can't be blind to my feelings for you.'

She sprang to her feet, sickened by the naked lust in his eyes. 'I never asked for your . . . kindness, and certainly not your gifts, which I have never accepted.' She was aware of his eyes following her as she crossed the room to stare out at the rain. 'I'm not a child to be bought with baubles, Luther.'

He rose at the vehemence in her tone, his eyes dark, his patience running thin—the spider tired of waiting for the

fly to ensnare itself. Yet he kept his voice even. Luther
Hogge never raised his voice, and many broken men had
cause to regret the deceptive mildness of those pseudo-
educated tones, for he had clawed his way up from the
gutter, suffered the jeers of his compatriots over his name
and his obesity, and paid them back a thousand times
over. Now, presented with the greatest challenge of his
life, he decided to prove his power once and for all.
Melody and her aunt were alone and almost penniless in
a house that he owned lock, stock and barrel, and were
totally dependent on his charity. It was a heady feeling,
and it seemed unbelievable that they should still deny his
omnipotence.

'You don't understand, my dear. I'm not simply asking
you to marry me. I'm offering you a more than respectable
position in society among people who will look up to
you, even fawn upon you, knowing that you are my wife.
I'll buy you dresses and jewels such as you have never
dreamed of. We'll go to soirées, and entertain the cream
of society at the lavish dinners we'll give.' He came as
close as he dared, not wanting to frighten her, simply to
prove his point. 'You can't deny me, Melody. I've waited
so long. It has been increasingly difficult for me over the
past year to treat you as a child, and it cut me deeply
when you ran off with that insipid little Dutchman. The
son of your piano-teacher! How could you! Ah, but it
proved then that you were ready for marriage and I knew
that all my waiting was at an end. Nothing could come
between us.'

'Except my husband!' she stated coldly, averting her
face in disgust, feeling his Madeira-laden breath on her
cheek.

'You weren't in love with him,' Luther argued, his
anger and frustration coming through. 'You were in love
with love, with Chopin and Beethoven and pretty words
in a foreign accent.'

'I'll not even deign to answer that,' Melody retorted,
though in her deepest conscience she knew she would
have been unable to. Hugh had brought sweetness and

gentleness and kindness into a life that desperately lacked those qualities: he had been comforter, confidant and friend, and for that she had warmed to him. Of passion, of hunger, of wanting with a fire that turns the blood to molten lava she was entirely innocent, but as surely as she had loved her brother, Harry, so she had loved—and in the same way still loved—Hugh Van der Veer. 'It was because of you and you alone, Luther, that we felt the need to elope. We knew what pressure you could have brought to bear, knowing how strongly you would have disapproved.'

'Your aunt and his parents also disapproved.' Anger seethed in his words as he remembered her rejection.

Melody shook her head. 'I could have made them see reason in time, when they saw how happy we were together. You were different. You would never have allowed us to live in peace, I know that now. But, now, Hugh's dead and I blame myself. Had we not gone away, he would not have been killed.' Tears misted her eyes. 'It was such a perfect little inn!'

'It was a sordid, run-down rest house!' he snarled. 'And that squalid little chapel was even worse . . . ' He broke off sharply, but her incredulous gaze had already swung to his face.

'You . . . were . . . there?' She began to tremble.

'The boy was a penniless piano-player, a student fresh from studying in Vienna, a virtual stranger. You will forget him when we're wed: I'll see to that!' He experienced a momentary pang of remorse for his stupidity as he saw the horrified realisation in her wide eyes.

'A footpad on the road, they said. Hugh was shot in the back!'

Still sure of his power, he reached to touch her arm. 'Melody, my dear, I'm sorry you had to find out like this, but the boy had to go, of course.'

Quite unaware of those thick fingers on her arm—the horror momentarily numbing her mind—she spoke as if in a dream. 'You killed Hugh!' The truth was manifest in the involuntary tightening of his jaw and the narrowing of his tiny eyes. It crashed in on her then. '*You* killed him!'

He caught her before she fell to the ground, and he lowered her. Her head had fallen back over his arm, presenting him with the white column of her throat, and the black eyes glittered as he fought his hunger, but the temptation of that alabaster skin and the full curve of her breasts was too much. With a groan he rained burning kisses on her face and lips and neck, drinking his fill of the unconsciously acquiescent mouth. There was a fire in his loins, and he knew that he could never let her go now. He had killed for her once, and no one—no one—would ever be allowed to stand in his way! To touch, taste, possess, to use to the limits of his considerable knowledge! He plunged his hand deep into the low neckline, curling his fingers over warm satiny flesh . . . then withdrawing on the instant as she gave a low moan.

He was sweating profusely and the ache in his loins had become an inferno, but as she regained consciousness his tone was smoothly conciliatory. 'My dear Melody! A shock, of course. I *am* sorry that it had to come out at this time, but now there will be no secrets to mar our marriage.'

'I'll go to the police!' she cried, struggling to her feet, refusing his hand. 'I'll see you hang!'

'No, I think not. As my wife, you'll not be able to testify against me, and, in the remote possibility of their becoming interested, I have too many friends in high and low places to be called to account for any of my past actions.'

'Your wife? After this?' She gave a choked cry from the heart. 'You could have bought him off—he was poor enough to be tempted, heaven knows! You didn't have to kill him!'

He nodded, regretful but unrepentant. 'I did, I confess, give bribery a passing thought, but he was the kind of fool who might possibly have refused. He would most certainly have taken the night to think it over . . . your wedding night,' he emphasised. 'Your elopement turned my world upside down. I'd been so certain of you. Oh, I'd seen the long looks and heard the whispered conversations when you thought no one was taking heed, but I'd put it down to the petty infatuations that all young girls go through. Even Beatrice was fooled, and that, in all honesty, does you credit—to have hoodwinked the two people closest to you. Though when you left that pitiful missive begging for her understanding and forgiveness, she did not appear as shocked as she might have. I, on the other hand, felt as if my heart had been cut out. I was too late to stop the wedding, of course, but with judicious distribution of largesse managed to have my message delivered to the inn while you were changing. I bargained on the fool's sensitivity and guilt over the elopement, so when he was told that his mother had been knocked down by a runaway carriage and was critically ill, I knew that he would leave immediately.'

'He promised he would see her in safe hands and be back later that evening,' Melody whispered. 'I waited and waited.'

Luther felt his hands itch to reach for her, to plunder those trembling lips, to draw out the memory of that slender, honey-haired youth. Even now the thought of him caused the thick fingers to clench at his sides. 'You waited until dawn,' he remembered. 'You paced back and forth across the lighted window, too upset to draw the curtains, and I waited with you, careless of the cold or the rain. I had taken few chances, as footpads and highwaymen abound on that road. One more unfortunate traveller barely raised eyebrows.'

'You took no chance at all, shooting him in the back!' The contempt broke through her pain.

His eyes glinted, but his tone was still equable. 'You'll learn not to speak in that manner when we're wed. You must understand, Melody, my dear, that no one will ever be allowed to come between us. No one will possess you before I do. You will know nothing of love that I do not teach you, own nothing that I do not buy for you, and, I promise you, you will find me an experienced teacher, a

generous donor. You will be mine—all of you—your
virgin innocence, your beauty, your amazing intelligence
that was the only decent thing your father left you, and,
in time, even your love, of that I'm certain.' His tone
changed subtly. 'Can you believe that there are some
women in our society . . . yes, even in ours . . . who
are quite literally prisoners in their own homes? Why, I
have heard tales from men in clubs even as respectable as
White's who confess to keeping young women such as
yourself in back rooms until society has altogether
forgotten their existence, dressing them in naught but a
silk robe, keeping them simply for their nefarious
pleasures.'

His meaning was not lost on her, and trembling uncontrollably, Melody choked out, 'I'd die first!'

'Oh no, my dear.' He drew closer. 'If such a man
possessed you, a man a thousand times removed from
myself who is eager only to love and protect you, you
would be tied hand and foot to that too wide bed you
occupy until you had learned to please him in every way
conceivable—by which time dying would not enter that
lovely head.'

She could feel his breath on her cheek and closed her
eyes, fighting loathing and nausea, but then he suddenly
moved away to pour himself yet another glass of Madeira,
draining it as he had the previous two, as though his
barely veiled threat had never been made. 'I do appreciate
that my proposal may have come somewhat precipitously,
Melody, but I'm glad now that you can consider it with
no dark secrets to worry you. Later you will come to
understand the depth of my love. You may even find
some womanly pride that a man is willing to kill for you,
but of course I can understand your present confusion of
feelings.'

'Confusion of feelings!' She stared at him, her fear and
disgust in every line of her frame, in every spark of the
thickly-lashed eyes. 'I'd take a nun's vow rather than a
vow of marriage to you!'

The obsidian eyes narrowed. 'You are over-wrought,

my dear, and don't know what you're saying. It has all
been a great shock, but I'm sure that by this time tomorrow
you'll have reconsidered your future. I do beg you to give
it considerable thought. In fact I would request that you
don't leave the house until that time. I have a heavy
schedule in the City tomorrow and would be most upset
if I had to return before time and go out to find you—as
I found you before. Dear Melody, you must try to think
of what is best for you and for your aunt.'

'Marriage to a murderer?'

'That is history. Had Van der Veer never appeared,
you would have married me.'

'Not in a thousand years! I loathed you from the first,
and now added to that is my undying hatred.' Her head
came up as she fought to control her fear. 'If you force
me to become your prisoner, I swear I shall spend the
rest of what will be a very short life fed only by that
hatred. There would be nothing you could do that would
keep me alive in the hell of a marriage with you.' Spinning,
she ran for the door, hearing his growled command for
her to stop, but wrenching the heavy door wide, racing
through and slamming it behind her. Her breath coming
in panting gasps, she stumbled up to her aunt's room,
seeking the comfort that had supported her throughout
the past long months. As she reached the top landing,
however, her steps faltered. 'No! I can't!'

She knew she must never tell her aunt of Luther's
terrible crime, for nothing in the world would prevent
that staunch little woman from leaving her sick bed and
confronting him with it, and force alone would keep her
from going to the police. With her new-found knowledge,
she was certain that, however indirectly, Luther was also
responsible for the deaths of the rest of her family and
she vowed to protect her aunt at all costs. 'But I need her
so!' Her mind rebelled as the panic rose within her, and
with a trembling hand she knocked quickly and went in.
'Aunt Bee, we must get away from here,' she cried.

Beatrice Davenport lay swathed in blankets, her face
pale and clammy, her eyes red-rimmed and streaming.

'Easy, child, you'll catch this foul cold of mine,' she said
with her usual practicality, then she took in the girl's tear-
washed features. 'Whatever's the matter, lovey? Has the
Hog been upsetting you again? I know he's a boor, or
boar, whichever, but thanks to that hen-witted nephew of
mine we are somewhat dependent on his charity. Oh, why
did I not marry one of the dozens of millionaires who
asked me?'

Melody gave a sob, quite unable to react to the humour
in her aunt's remark. 'Please don't mention marriage!
Aunt Bee, what am I to do?' It was all too much, and
with a choked sob she flung herself across the bed to be
gathered to that opulent bosom. 'The Hog's asked me to
marry him. I can't! I just can't!'

Beatrice's grey eyes snapped, and her lips pursed tightly.
'No, of course you can't. It's unthinkable! You've another
nine months in mourning, at least! I was almost banking
on his adherence to social etiquette to give us time to
think, but I was afraid something like this would happen.
His anger when he found that you'd gone off with the
Van der Veer boy was that of a madman, not some
concerned relative or family friend. Heaven knows he's
never been either, far from it! I've kept my peace, but I've
seen his eyes devouring you when you play for us in the
evenings. I wonder whether that was why he began
encouraging you to play again after so long—so that it
would present him in a better light. I know how much
the piano means to you, even though you use it to mourn
poor Hugh rather than to build a new life. There is time,
however, and I'm only glad that you can lose yourself in
music. Glad, too, that you can't see that monster watching
you when you play, his beady eyes glittering in the
candlelight. It's obvious that he has only one thought on
his mind, and it isn't music!' With a snowy handkerchief
she dried Melody's damp cheek and forced her to
straighten, smoothing out the great bell sleeves and fussing
with the too severe chignon. 'We shall think of something,
sweeting, never fear. I haven't spent a fair proportion of
my life fending off the unwelcome attentions of a great

variety of men without some lessons being learned!' She patted her own honey-brown hair that even at fifty held no trace of grey, and gave a reassuring smile. 'It's late, and you need your beauty sleep. Tomorrow is another day, and I'm sure it will end quite differently. Go on. Shoo!'

With a tremulous smile Melody kissed the softly-scented cheek and slipped through the adjoining door to her room. Beatrice had insisted on the arrangement after the death of Melody's mother, and it left them two small rooms that had originally been designed as a suite. The indomitable woman had told Luther, 'As Melody's godmother and only living relative present, I take entire responsibility for her moral welfare. Since you now live in this house, it would not be fitting for you and my niece to occupy adjoining rooms.' He had been forced to agree, hiding his fury behind a bland smile.

Dawn brought an improvement in the weather, but not in Melody's mood. She had slept not at all, alternating between fury and tears, plotting Luther's downfall and planning a future, and as she hurried to her aunt's room she found herself praying that she would discover plans with more substance than her own.

Huddled beneath the blankets, Beatrice gave a low groan as Melody pulled back the curtains. She sneezed, and raised reddened eyes and a waxen face. 'Not good,' she remarked, seeing the reflection of her worsening cold in her niece's worried eyes.

'Oh, Aunt Bee, you look awful!' Melody declared tactlessly. 'I'll send for Dr Goodhew right away. Luther should be gone by now, but I'll find Simpson rather than trust one of the Hog's lackeys.'

Hurrying downstairs and passing the dining-room, she was dismayed to see Luther, obviously having risen later than usual, seated before several piled dishes of food and consuming the contents with noisy enjoyment. She prayed that he would not see her, but her heart sank as he called her name. For a moment she was tempted to pretend that she had not heard and run to the butler's pantry where

Simpson could usually be found at this time, but knew
that the Hog would follow her and question her intentions, so with a sigh she turned back.

He had risen, wiping his mouth with a fine linen napkin,
his dark eyes assessing her mood and seeing mute testimony to his power in the averted eyes and the fingers that
were twining about each other before her. So she had
slept badly, he guessed. The lovely eyes were darkly
shadowed and the skin drawn tight across the fine bones.
'Melody! It's a rare pleasure to see you down at this time;
I'm quite delighted now that I overslept. Usually you
contrive to remain in your room until I'm gone. Where
were you off to in such a hurry?'

His jackets, Melody noticed, were always made a
fraction too large for him, as if he was proud of his size,
equating grossness with powerfulness. The urgency of her
mission forced her forward a pace. 'It's Aunt Bee. Her
cold is much worse this morning, and I was going to send
Simpson for the doctor.'

His eyes took in the high-necked close-fitting bodice of
the black bombazine dress with its pagoda sleeves, their
flounces matching the pinked and stiffened flounces on
the skirt, and he gave a slight frown. 'That dress is almost
five years out of fashion. I must insist that you change
into one of those that I have bought for you before my
return this evening, and it's hardly the done thing to send
a butler on such a menial errand when you had only to
mention it to me and I would have sent for my man from
Harley Street when I reached the office.'

Desperately improvising, Melody said, 'But I thought
you had already gone, and surely Dr Goodhew is our
family doctor . . . ' Her words trailed off before the look
in his eyes.

'By this evening I am sure that you will agree to become
a very dear, very cherished, part of *my* family, and
therefore will accept my judgment in all things. I shall
send one of the boys for my own doctor who, I can assure
you, is far more qualified than that bumbler Goodhew.'
His eyes narrowed, though the voice remained suave. 'I

should not wish to be embarrassed to find that you have
gainsaid my wishes and brought in any other doctor prior
to the arrival of my own. Your welfare and that of your
aunt will always be my prime concern, my dear, but you
really must curb this tendency toward independence.'

She could only shake her head in mute denial and leave
him there, running back to the sick-room before he could
say more.

The doctor, when he arrived, was a plump, florid-faced
egotist, puffed up with his self-esteem to the degree that
he barely looked at the woman in the bed and not at all
at Melody hovering near by. He decreed that the patient
must stay abed for at least two weeks, that the windows
must be kept tight shut at all times to keep out the
poisonous miasmas of the London air, and that three
times a day she must take the medicine he had brought
with him.

The minute he left, Beatrice took one sniff at the
medicine and declared it more noxious than any fumes
that London might offer, instructing Melody to take it
out. 'I shall deal with my own ailment, since no on else
seems able to,' she decided. 'Instruct the kitchen to boil a
chicken until half the water is gone, then chop the chicken-
meat finely into the broth and have them bring it up to
me piping hot. I must sweat this chill out, and don't you
dare tell me that ladies aren't supposed to sweat . . . If
it worked on your father's horses, it should work on me!
Bring me some mulled wine, too, with plenty of cinnamon.
I'll be on my feet in no time. We have plans to make.'

'No, Aunt Bee, you mustn't consider moving,' Melody
protested, pushing the determined little woman back on
to the pillows. I'll have the broth and wine brought to
you, but there's no question of your getting up.' She gave
a deep sigh. 'I shall have to solve my own problems for
once: I have relied on you for far too long. I must grow
up some time, and it appears that now is the time.' 'If
only you knew it all,' her sick heart finished.

Yet, as the day progressed, it seemed that her problems
were insoluble. Only one decision became more certain as

the hours flew by all too quickly: she could never marry Luther Hogge and submit to the attentions that even to think of brought the bile to her throat. She had overheard the maids talk and once seen the coupling of her father's stud stallion to one of his mares, and putting two and two together made her ill with terror. And yet, she reflected, no such fear had touched her when drawn into the gentler embrace of Hugh Van der Veer, even though at the time she had thought of him more as a friend than a lover.

A smile touched her lips as she thought of his shy approaches and the worshipping looks in the pale blue eyes on the rare, secret occasions they had met after her lessons with his father. It had taken him almost a year to declare his love, afraid of her rejection, yet half expecting it, knowing that his family were far beneath her social level. Buoyed up by a bottle of wine, he had declared his love one evening when he had come to take her lesson as his father had had to visit a sick friend. There had been no lesson as, uncharacteristically, he had seized the startled girl in his arms, placed a fervent kiss on her lips, then apologised profusely and blurted out that he would kill himself if she did not marry him. Missing her parents, lonely, and afraid of Luther Hogge's increasing attentions, she had agreed, sure that love would follow.

'It would have been so different,' she whispered, and the tears came readily to her eyes as they had so often of late.

'It does you no good to weep,' came that hated voice from the doorway, and Luther entered, flinging his great-coat and hat on a chair before crossing the room to confront her, his constant smile as complacent as ever. 'It makes your eyes red and your features puffy. The correct colour of your eyes, my dear, is that incredible sapphire blue that should never go with black hair, and your features should be as smooth as the finest silk. Now, shall we go out to dinner for a change? I have given the servants the evening off so that we may not be disturbed when we return, or interrupted if we stay.'

'I—I'm not hungry,' she murmured, regretting the cowardice she had shown in changing into one of the more acceptable dresses that he had bought for her, but praying that, in attempting to please him in this one small thing, she might obtain a 'stay of execution'. The pale grey silk made her look fragile and delicate as porcelain, and above the deep décolletage the necklace of creamy seed-pearls glowed with their own luminosity against her skin.

Her loveliness caught at his throat, and her name came out thickly. 'Melody . . . ' He coughed, and continued, 'You wish to eat later? Very well, we shall talk first.' Before she could protest, her elbow was taken firmly and she was led into the study. 'This seems as appropriate a place as any to discuss our business . . . or is it pleasure you have chosen? A marriage that will be a battleground, or the slow, yet willing, surrender of the Ice Maiden?'

Vainly she tried to shake free of that deceptively casual grip, aware that there had been no wavering of his resolve, and telling him, 'I could never surrender to you, Luther! If you force me into marriage by whatever foul means, you'll be a murderer twice over.'

His smile tightened a fraction. 'Oh, I doubt that, for there are ways of forcing you to eat and denying you access to anything that might be used as a weapon; and should you attempt to run, you know that I would follow you, to the ends of the earth if need be, and find you— and make you wish you had stayed.' The voice became ugly. 'You've teased and tantalised me long enough, playing the innocent. You're not a child any more, Melody. It's about time I showed you what it is to be a woman.'

Before she could guess at his intentions, he had pulled her round, jerking her hard against him. Hard fingers curled into her hair and her scream was drowned by his thick lips covering hers. Half fainting, she brought her hands up, fingers curving, fighting as a trapped animal might, and her nails tore eight deep furrows across his cheeks. With a curse, he flung her away so violently that she crashed against the desk. 'I'll teach you, you bitch!'

The pain brought terror, and a desperation such as she had never known and, with it, memory. Stumbling round the desk, she pulled open the top drawer and grasped the sinister little pepper-box pistol her father had always kept there.

At the sight of the weapon in her shaking hands Luther Hogge hesitated, eyes narrowing into slits. 'You little fool! Give me that thing.'

'I've never fired a gun,' Melody confessed, wishing that her voice was steady and her hands steadier still. 'I know Father kept it loaded, and I know I have to turn the barrels after each shot. I will not marry you, Luther, and if you don't leave at this moment, I swear I'll use this. I'd rather kill you or myself than to submit to the nightmare you offer!'

But he had recovered now, and was able to put down the uncertainty that had knotted his stomach and caused his palms to sweat. Her beauty blazed with her anger, the flashing eyes lightning bright, the loose chignon unpinned by his rough fingers and falling in a midnight cascade down her back. God, how he wanted her! Keeping his tone conversational, he said, 'That toy hasn't been cleaned in over a year. It's old, and the springs have lost their tension. In all probability the shock of your first discharge, which will undoubtedly miss if you continue to shake so, will jar open the pan-covers and dump their priming on the carpet. Now, hand it over and we'll say no more about it. Your spirit does you proud, and I admire you for it. Come, let us talk sensibly about our forthcoming wedding. I admit that I may have been too harsh with you, carried away by your spirit, your beauty. I was wrong to try to frighten you into marriage. I've never known a woman like you . . . ' He was edging forward, watching her eyes, and, as they flickered, he lunged.

There was a sharp explosion, and he gasped in shock as the first bullet tore a fiery path across his cheek, but then he was on her, maddened by the pain and the fury that she had dared to attack him. Brutal fingers tore at her dress while the other hand crushed her to him. He

would take her! Here and now! The pistol forgotten, he
lowered his burning, bleeding head to her breast—and
there was another dull roar as the barrel she held against
his side discharged its lethal contents into that gross
frame. Luther Hogge reared back, disbelief in his eyes as
the searing agony ripped through him. For a second he
swayed there, one hand pressed to his side, the dark blood
oozing through his fingers. 'No!' Melody whispered. 'No!'
And, incredibly, he straightened. The great arms came
up . . . and in terror she fired again, the bullet knocking
him backwards to crash through a delicate Hepplewhite
chair and fall to the floor. His body jerked once and then
was still, his blood crimsoning the carpet.

Melody swayed, her head spinning with the crash of
gunfire and the horrendous, unbelievable result. She took
a step forward, the pistol dropping from her nerveless
fingers. She had to get help, had to act. Another faltering
step, then another, brought her to the crumpled figure on
the floor. So much blood! That terrible face! Forcing
down her nausea, she reached down trembling fingers to
touch the outflung wrist. She could feel no pulse. A moan
was torn from her throat and the room danced a slow,
sickening gavotte about her. 'Dead!' she whispered. 'Oh,
God, what have I done!'

A few moments later Beatrice Davenport, struggling up
from her sweat-soaked pillows at the sound from below,
found her niece standing in the doorway, dress ripped to
the waist, her hair a tumbled mass down her back.

Melody hung there, ashen faced. 'Aunt Bee . . . I
must go . . . *now*. I don't know where or how, but I
must—must go!'

'Melody, child!' Pushing aside her weakness, Beatrice
went to her, but was prevented from taking her in
comforting arms by the wild, bright look in her eyes.
'What has happened?' She spoke very gently and with
extreme care.

Holding tightly on to consciousness, Melody enunciated, 'I have just killed Luther Hogge.' And then, very
slowly, she slipped to the floor and into darkness.

CHAPTER TWO

WHEN THE DARKNESS receded and unwelcome reality broke in upon her, Melody opened her eyes with a sob, finding herself supported by Aunt Bee's comforting arms. 'It's going to be all right, child. Come now, get to your feet. Carefully.' Urged over to the washbasin, Melody allowed cool water to be splashed over her face and neck and dabbed on the deep scratches Luther had left when he had torn open her bodice. 'We must dress for travelling,' Beatrice stated, thinking logically even in such a crisis. 'We can take nothing with us apart from a few necessities and what little we have in cash and jewellery. We must be away from here before the servants discover him.'

She staggered as she turned too sharply toward the wardrobe, and Melody caught at her arm. '*You* can't travel. You should be in bed! There is nowhere we can go together. I can't ask anyone to shelter a—a murderess. I must just . . . disappear. Oh, Aunt Bee, you don't know the half of it! He killed Hugh. It came out inadvertently, but I almost believe he meant me to know so that he could gloat over my helplessness. I've never hated anything or anyone before. I've loathed him as one might a great fat slug, but I've never *hated* him until that moment. It's been festering like a wound, and I've been unable to eat or sleep because of it. I'm certain that he caused Papa to take his life, too, so that he could control us, and then persuade poor Harry to go to India after leaving everything to him. I suspected it before, but was too afraid of him to say or do anything. I thought I could escape with Hugh. And then, when he touched me . . . and tried to—to . . . I was sick with fear, but in that instant I

wanted him dead! Not now. Not now that I can think
and feel again. What am I to do? There's nowhere . . . '

Beatrice gave the distraught girl a firm shake and, in
spite of her illness, was at that moment the stronger of
the two. 'The man deserved to die, and there is a place
we can go, but only temporarily, since the gentleman's
name cannot possibly be linked with mine. It never has
been. Hurry and change, and all will be made clearer
later. Move, child, there is no time to waste in standing
there trembling.'

Melody drew a deep ragged breath. 'I—I must think.
Must pull myself together. If there is a place, even for
tonight . . . I have so little to pay for lodgings . . . '
Her eyes fell on the box of jewellery that Luther had
bought for her, exquisite pieces worth several thousand,
but put down the temptation. 'No, I'll take nothing of
his, *nothing*!' Then, as her aunt was turning over the
contents of a large chest, 'I must keep that, though—
Father's old valise.'

'That hasn't been unlocked for years; it's just some old
souvenirs of his travels and some sentimental rubbish. My
brother was a great magpie.'

'Then I can't leave it behind if it meant so much to
him. There is Mother's jewellery too, though there is
nothing of real value since she only ever wore that pearl
necklace that Papa bought her on their tenth anniversary.'

'Yes, she would have wanted you to have those few
pieces.'

'Oh, there's so much to think of, and no time at all!'
She sank on to the bed, burying her face in her hands,
whispering, 'Why did you trust such a man, Papa? What
hold did he have over you?'

'No good wrestling with shadows, child,' that beloved
voice said. 'We've much to do, and only a few minutes to
do it in. We generally complement each other, I with my
practicality and you with the spirit and strength of will
I've only ever seen in my own youth—most irregular in a
female! Come on, now! Put on this black cashmere and
consign that wreckage you're wearing to this old valise—

we'll dispose of it later. Hurry!'

Less than an hour later they were pulling up before a tall, classically beautiful, terraced house—typical in design of Thomas Cubitt, who followed the simple lines of Nash—on the north side of Eaton Square. A liveried footman answered their summons, and a delicate eyebrow was raised as Lady Davenport instructed him to pay the cabbie, then swept past him as though she had every right of entry.

Embarrassed and uncertain, Melody followed as she flung open an ornately carved door and announced, 'John, I need your help!'

The room's occupant rose with a startled exclamation from his high, wing-backed chair. 'Dammit, Beatrice, do you have to scare me half out of my wits each time we meet?'

When Melody recognised the tall white-haired aristocrat, she realised why Aunt Bee had been so careful to protect his reputation, and felt faint that she should expect favours from such as he.

He had crossed the room and had his arm about the older woman, supporting her to a chair. 'My dear, you look ghastly!' Then he turned to Melody, his brown eyes twinkling kindly. 'You must be Mrs Van der Veer. I feel that I know you already through Beatrice's high praises. Please allow me to offer my condolences on the death of your husband. Nasty affair! Our countryside must be better patrolled. But now a sherry, I think, while I ascertain the cause of your aunt's precipitous arrival.'

Melody shook her head bleakly. 'Thank you, no. I fear that I am the cause of all this . . . or Luther Hogge is, at least . . . the late Luther Hogge, that is . . . I mean . . . ' But she could not continue, the tears choking her, and turned from him, covering her face with her hands. She was led to a large couch, and a moment later a glass was slipped into her hand.

'Drink this, my child, you obviously need it. Now, Beatrice, what's all this about?'

Melody coughed as the fiery brandy burned her throat,

but felt immediately better and was content to allow her
aunt to summarise the past events.

The man cursed beneath his breath as the grim tale
came to an end and paced the floor, brown eyes crackling.
'I never knew your husband, Mrs Van der Veer, but I
certainly knew your father. It seemed inconceivable at the
time of his death that he should, whatever his state of
mind, be walking by the river.'

Melody raised puzzled eyes. 'I don't understand.'

'He hated the river, calling it, with good reason, the
London Sewer. People like ourselves may have the luxury
of water-closets, if you'll forgive my referring to such an
indelicate subject, but the vast majority still rely on street
pumps, and most waste goes direct into the Thames. Your
father was a fastidious man and, if I remember, they
called '58 the year of the Great Stink. The stench from
the river was so bad that the curtains of Parliament had
to be soaked in chloride of lime, and there was even talk
of moving the Law Courts to Oxford. He wouldn't go
within a mile of it, had he a choice.'

Melody felt a hand clutch at her heart. 'You
think . . . '

'That if you hadn't . . . executed . . . Luther Hogge,
I'd have done my damnedest to have seen him hanged for
a double murder!'

'So he never committed suicide. Thank God!' Beatrice
breathed, and only then did Melody realise what shame
his supposed action had brought upon the family. To her,
his death was the worst tragedy of her life, but to her
aunt it was something even more.

The man put a reassuring hand on Melody's shoulder
and turned his bright eyes to Beatrice with a smile. 'Of
course you were right to come here. I'm honoured that
you should turn to me before any other; though, knowing
you, it was a considered choice.' He went to her and in a
totally natural gesture raised one finger to brush a wisp
of hair from her temple. 'You've always come to me with
your insurmountable problems, and by so doing have
introduced me to more stimulation and, at times, outright

danger than the normal man dreams of! Now, however, you must accept the attentions of my redoubtable Mrs Fullerton and my doctor, in that order.' He made to ring for the housekeeper, but Beatrice forestalled him.

'In a moment, John, but there's more, I'm afraid. You must both be apprised of some salient facts that may change our whole future, and then I'll collapse quite happily into whichever little corner you choose while you resolve the best way out of this. First, of course, Melody and I must leave the country.'

'No!' cried Melody. '*You* can't. It's unfair! Your whole life is here . . . ' She was stemmed in her flow by a firmly raised hand, and a smile.

'A woman such as I can adjust to the most surprising of circumstances and locations so long as she's with those she loves. Now . . . ' and the grey eyes became serious, 'I must give you another shock, so you must be strong, my dear.' Beatrice took Melody's hands in a firm grip, sitting close beside her. 'Your father, my brother Alexander, was a gay and carefree man in his youth. He loved parties and travel, and the family was fortunately in a position to humour him for the most part. You must remember how he was always insisting that one day you must go to America? Just over a year before you were born he went there at the invitation of a young English friend, Lord Fortesque's daughter, who had married a Carolina cotton-planter for some inconceivable reason. While there, your father apparently fell in love with a young girl, Ereanora, whom we presumed to be a member of the family, though he refused to give any details. She must have been a niece or some close relative, for he said she had lived all her life on the plantation, but, apart from saying that she was the most beautiful creature he had ever seen, he was delightfully vague about the whole episode.' She looked momentarily uncomfortable. 'To his disgrace and hers, the girl had a child. Ereanora, poor creature, died in childbirth, he said, and her death quite desolated him.' Melody felt the colour drain from her face as she correctly guessed her aunt's next words. 'He brought the baby back to England with a nurse he'd hired on the way home. He couldn't, of course, raise a newborn babe alone, and would take no help from the family after their shocked reaction. However, he had always been fond of our neighbour's daughter Charity, a widow at that time with a young son, who had openly adored Alex since they were childhood friends. True to her name, the woman you came to know as your mother took on a man who had disgraced the family name, and his child. She brought you up as her own, and in return your father adopted her son Harry, later willing his entire estate to the boy . . .

Which, in part, is why we're in this fix now. The point I'm making, Melody dear, is that you do have relatives, and from your father's vague descriptions, affluent and hospitable people, in North Carolina. Were the facts—of your parents' deaths and that of Hugh—made known, I'm sure they would take you in. Even if your father left under a cloud, twenty years is a long time, and I'm certain that your beauty and charm would win them over, should there be any lingering doubts. After all, blood is blood, and you are the daughter of an English lord, which should count for something in a country that has none!'

Melody had sat as though carved from stone, barely hearing her aunt's words, her childhood memories of her 'mother' now clouded by the fact that the fragile beauty she had loved was in fact not her mother at all . . . and yet . . . 'And yet she loved me, made our family a close unit, held us together with her gentleness and understanding, and never once let me even suspect that I wasn't the most cherished of daughters.'

'And so you were. She was truly content with your father, and adopting a baby only a few weeks old made it hers almost as much as his; a man, you must remember, whom she had always loved, even though she had married another in compliance with her family's wishes. The Fortesques and Davenports both had an eye to increasing their fortunes, and old George Stapleton was an exceedingly . . . comfortable . . . man. I believe there was a time when I gave that a passing thought myself; but at sixty-seven then, he would never have lasted through even *one* polka, and one must always get ones priorities right! But now we must be serious. You have a family of sorts to go to, and we must make all haste.' Beatrice rose shakily, and immediately the man was at her side, one arm about her waist, his expression chiding.

'When will you cease to pack so much life into that stubborn little frame, Beatrice?'

'Not so little now!' She gave a choked laugh, covering her mouth, then allowed her hand to wipe the perspiration from her forehead with a carefully casual gesture.

'Little is a state of mind, I accept that,' he humoured her. 'But in spite of a delicious degree of extra cuddliness you are still a little woman, Beatrice Davenport. Will you now allow me and mine to take over for a while?'

She gave a sigh, then an answering smile. 'I do confess to a certain small tiredness and a very slight headache. So, if you insist, you may call your Mrs Fullerton to see me to my room. I'm sure I can now leave Melody in your more than capable hands.'

Within minutes Melody found herself alone under the searching gaze of the man whose job it was to read souls, who now suggested, 'We must talk, and it will be easier if you call me "John Brown", as your aunt does.' He continued, after some thought, 'I have a great deal of influence, Mrs Van der Veer, and of course, should you choose to remain in this country, I shall bring all of it to bear, but you must understand that I'm not above the law—though there have been some who have had cause to wonder!' Then, with emphasis, 'If you remain in England, you will certainly stand trial for the murder of Luther Hogge.' She shuddered, not doubting her companion's influence, but also not underestimating the power of Luther's friends. As though guessing her fears, John Brown said, 'My lawyers will naturally plead self-defence, but the prosecution will undoubtedly accuse you of enticement and a dozen equally unpleasant things.'

'But that's not true!'

'Of course it isn't,' he pacified her, taking her clenched

hand between his and gently easing open the tight fist. 'But it is their job to win their case, and much depends on the mood of the judge . . . and whether he was an acquaintance of the dead man. I know of Luther Hogge— though, thank heaven, by reputation alone—and can surmise how far his tentacles can spread—a judge or two would not surprise me in the least, but neither would a king or two in the underworld "rookeries" around St Giles or off the wharves!' He looked down at her palm, lost for a moment in his own dark thoughts. 'A long lifeline at least,' he mused. 'I have some small faith in palmistry . . . However . . . '

Melody gave a small start of surprise. 'How strange . . . Something I had quite forgotten. Last year . . . ' she shook her head with an embarrassed little laugh, 'Aunt Bee took me to Brighton to cheer me a little. We went to a gipsy fortune-teller, who told me that I would cross two great waters . . . Of course I've always believed that one's future is to a great extent in one's own hands. It's not that I disbelieve, it's just that I have a little trouble in believing all that I should.'

'Your fortune-teller undoubtedly told you also that you'd meet a tall, dark and handsome man.'

'Two,' she blushed, wishing she had not revealed what was only a foolish holiday memory. 'One as bright as day, she said, and one as dark as night. Of course I was already acquainted with Hugh then, so perhaps he was the fair one.' She shook her head. 'Oh, why am I talking such rubbish! I must leave, and leave at once. But what of Aunt Bee? She can't travel as she is, and I feel I must leave immediately. Could you possibly find some family that would look after her for a while, at least until she can resume her former life . . . before she became a nurse, confidante and guardian angel to me? I know she wouldn't stay here, for your sake rather than her own.'

John Brown nodded. 'She has always considered others before herself, and I can't see her changing now. Of course, I can do as you suggest and make travel arrangements for a single berth on the next available steamer or clipper ship to New York, where I can recommend hotels and contacts that would be only too glad to entertain you and escort you south. I could also put Beatrice in touch with friends who would be only too glad to entertain her for as long as she wished to stay, though, knowing Beatrice, that would not be for long. But I wonder whether you shouldn't consult her first. I've known Beatrice for many years now and never yet have been able to change her mind once it was made up, nor divert her from a course of action once begun. She accompanied you here because she was quite certain that she was needed. I can't see her allowing you to travel several thousand miles alone.'

'I'm not afraid,' Melody stated, but then with a shaky smile she amended, 'Well, maybe just a little.' She was warmed then by the understanding hand that covered hers. 'But it would be totally selfish of me to ask for her company on such a venture. She has been like a mother to me since my own . . . since Charity died, and I love her far too much to ask.'

The gentle gaze saw far deeper than her tone divulged, searching beyond the tightly controlled features and level eyes that bespoke a strength of character of which even she was unaware. 'I shall make all the necessary arrangements then, never fear, and I shall do what is best for both of you. Trust me. Now I suggest that you allow my Mrs Fullerton to show you to your room and bring you a well-laced glass of milk. No objections, now! You've been through enough today.'

Melody hesitated, then ventured, 'My Aunt Beatrice came to you instinctively, without thought or consideration . . . '

With a nod he agreed, 'Of course. It was on my return from a trade mission to Japan that I first met her. My wife had died the previous year in that terrible cholera outbreak of '49.' He had taken her hand again, turning the palm upward, spreading the fingers, gazing not at the soft silken skin but beyond at his own memories, the girl's hand, for that moment, only reminding him of another's.

'Do you know that when it began in the November of '48
they had only fifty or so deaths that first week—though
no one really counted the numbers who were lost under
piles of filthy rags in the "rookeries". In the last three
months of the epidemic a year later the deaths had totalled
almost thirteen thousand . . . in just three months!' He
gave her a crooked smile, returning to the present. 'I was
concerned with only one, but men in my position have
access to all sorts of useless information, you understand.
What was I saying, yes . . . Well, one cannot mourn
for ever. Life has a way of continuing—around you or
over you—and I had reached the stage where I had
decided to join the human race as slowly and carefully as
possible. It seemed a safe beginning to escort some pretty,
mindless little butterfly to the opera. I have no idea what
we heard, I know only that during the interval there was
a sudden commotion outside our box, and as I rose to
investigate, the door was flung open and Beatrice—a far
younger, but no less dynamic Beatrice, burst in carrying
a short-sword. You can imagine *my* feelings, and my poor
companion was too terrified even to scream. "Are you a
gentleman?" this creature challenged, and I still remember
her words, and while I spluttered something unintelligible,
she continued, "If you are, then teach *this* one to be!"
And she propelled a sheepish young lord into our box
with her fingers tight about his lapels. Apparently the
poor boy had escorted her to the opera and had become
quite incensed when another of her male acquaintances
had accosted them. The boy had drawn his sword, at
which point Beatrice, instead of obligingly swooning, had
boxed both their ears, taken the sword, and stormed in
on me. The long and short of it was that I left the young
lord being comforted by my pretty little angel and escorted
this remarkable woman home. It was as though a whirl-
wind had entered my life and blown away all the cobwebs.'
He gave a disbelieving shake of his head. 'Each time I
saw her, there was something new. She knew more political gossip than any of my contacts produced. She
challenged my beliefs and demolished my pomposity.

Then of course there were the quiet times, and instinctively she knew when I needed those, too. I went to her, never knowing whether she would be alone, and once, when I objected, she told me that there was no greater gift than freedom of spirit. She was always her own person. She never asked anything of anyone that they could not give, and demanded the same respect.'

Melody watched the emotions moving over the patrician features and asked, unnecessarily, 'You loved her . . . love her?'

John Brown's kindly eyes crinkled at the corners. 'Of course! One could not help oneself. But only as one loves a shooting star. Women like Beatrice never grow old, and one cannot consider growing old with them. While they pass through your particular space, however, it is like all the fireworks you've ever seen bursting into light at the same time. I shall miss her when you leave, but perhaps we shall keep in touch.'

The subject of their departure brought the present to drop its chill cloak over them, and Melody gave an involuntary shudder. 'I mustn't detain you . . . Mr Brown; you've been too kind already.'

'Kindness, I've learned, is like a ripple on a lake, spreading out from its source, touching others who touch another with the blessing. Talk with your aunt tomorrow, but now you really must try to sleep.'

Melody took her leave, and went to her room to change into the voluminous gown that Mrs Fullerton had acquired from an unsuspecting young kitchen-maid. Tired and confused, she settled to sleep, but the shadows cast by the moon through the swaying trees outside her window appeared to take phantom shapes and danced a fearful gavotte of death. She buried her face in the pillow and wept for the horror of that day and the dread of the next until, exhaustedly, she finally slept.

The morning brought little peace, however, only a respite from the nightmares that had tossed her back and forth, knotting blankets and tumbling pillows to the floor. Pale and drawn, the lovely eyes red-rimmed and darkly shadowed, she made her way to the breakfast-table where her aunt and John Brown were talking quietly and earnestly.

'You shouldn't be up, Aunt Bee!' she protested, hurrying forward, but received an admonishing look.

'I undoubtedly feel a great deal better than you look, so I suggest you fill your plate and we'll get to practicalities.'

'I'm not really hungry. Just a cup of tea, I think. I can't seem to think straight even this morning. I do apologise . . . not much sleep.'

John and Beatrice exchanged glances, but it was left to Beatrice to say, 'It's all right, child, you don't have to do any thinking just now. We are going to Carolina together. John has made all the arrangements.'

Melody's eyes flew to those of the quiet man, and he gave a nod of agreement. 'I also sent one of my most trusted men round to your house, Mrs Van der Veer. Luther Hogge is no longer there.' And, at her low cry, 'No, I don't think he's alive. The butler appeared agitated, but not frantically so, and seemed evasive, my man said.'

Melody let out her breath in a relieved sob. 'That's Simpson. He's Papa's man, and must have arrived home first and hidden the body, to cover up for me. He must have guessed what happened. I dropped the gun, you see. He hated Hogge. Does that mean we have more time?'

John spoke regretfully. 'I'm afraid not. There are others who will be expecting Hogge today, and enquiries will be made almost immediately. He is far from an insignificant clerk in the City, and certain wheels will not turn without him. The cogs that drive those wheels may well be as affluent and corrupt as he, but I'll wager many are even now wondering whether his disappearance is accidental or designed. The sooner you make your exit from that particular stage, the better.'

Melody felt the taut fear clutch at her heart again and pushed her cup aside. 'If anyone finds out it was I who . . . Will they . . . Could they . . . possibly find me even in some country plantation in America? You said that people will be looking for him. Will they use detectives or the police straight away?'

'Don't worry! Should your disappearance together with his give cause for conjecture, it will undoubtedly be of the basest nature and not at all associated with his demise. For others, I shall put the word about, quite indirectly, of course, that you are shopping for some new dresses in Paris and staying with friends of Beatrice. You *do* have friends in Paris, of course, Beatrice?'

Something flickered behind the grey eyes, but then she smiled. 'Not the kind I'd introduce Melody to, but no one here will know the difference! If you could make it Italy, though, I do remember a penniless count who thought I was a millionairess. He was trying to re-build his villa—naturally!'

'Naturally,' John agreed, and they exchanged understanding smiles. 'However, I feel that Paris is more appropriate.'

'Didn't you like my Italian count?'

'I disliked all of your beautiful young men!'

'But they weren't half as understanding as you, and not one of them gave me so many years of friendship.'

'I don't seem to recall that you went to them for understanding and friendship, but you're right: I would sooner be today's reality than yesterday's dream. As such, I can give you a new start, and even in a place like Carolina there must be at least one or two millionaires, even if only in dollars!'

Then those kindly eyes swung to Melody, who was staring unseeingly at her fingers. The nails were slowly gauging weals into her skin as the hands turned and twisted. 'Mrs Van der Veer,' he said gently. No reply. Lost in her nightmare world, Melody re-lived the feel of Luther Hogge's skin as she tore at his face. 'Melody!' The voice that had cut across the apathy of many a sitting in the House cracked the ice about her heart, and she looked up, startled. 'I'm sorry . . . I . . . What was it you said?'

His face had changed, become firm, lost the jesting

humour of his repartee with Beatrice. 'I have arranged for you both to take a ship to New York on the morning tide. You must make an effort to sever all ties here. There can be no final farewells to friends, since you are supposed to be returning in a few weeks, but if there are any social arrangements you need to make or notes that you can write to alleviate suspicion . . . '

'Yes . . . Yes, of course.' Then a vestige of her spirit returned, and she raised a smile. 'I wish we could have found time to become better acquainted: I find I like it when you call me Melody.'

'Then John and Melody it shall be. I'll keep in touch, never fear. In the meantime, your aunt has looked into that battered old valise of your father's, though nothing there is much help.' He brought it from beside his chair and turned its contents on to the cloth.

Beatrice gave a sigh. 'Most of it is years old. Alex was a sentimental romantic and I must confess he had a strange sense of value, but none of this is worth anything, and very little tells us what we are likely to encounter. I had hoped for a sketch, a family portrait.'

Melody glanced over the insignificant pile of memorabilia and gave a puzzled shake of her head. 'This looks like a native bead on a piece of leather. Here's a child's toy, carved with "To Unc.A. Love B." I wonder who "B" is? One of the members of the family? A child then, and a little older than me now? Here's a strange one. Looks like a page torn from a diary. "All over. Learned they sold her. Must go. Can't. Never again. Must tell Melody not to . . . " And then it's torn. Tell me not to what? I don't remember anything so important. And what was it that was sold and all that about going? What and where?'

'It's ancient history and shouldn't bother us now, my dear. What of the rest?'

It was an inconsequential assortment to have been kept for so many years: a bone-handled knife, an ivory comb, a doll that Melody had discarded with her babyhood. 'Don't dwell on it,' came John Brown's gentle voice, breaking into her reverie and easing the sudden choking

sensation in her throat. 'You may not know what lies
ahead, but have no fear of the shadows you leave behind.
I'll keep in touch as I've promised.'

'I hope so. I'm not an explorer by nature, and it will
be good to have some slender thread to tie me to home.
Now I think I'll go and write those letters. You and Aunt
Bee will have a lot to talk about.' Her smile embraced
them both as she left the room.

'Do we have a lot to talk about, John?' Beatrice asked,
rising to go to his side, running one soft finger along his
jaw as he looked up.

'No, my dear. Goodbye is only one word.' He, too,
rose then, smiling down at her. 'But I wonder if your
niece would be terribly shocked if she realised how many
ways there are to say it!'

Beatrice arched her eyebrows in mock surprise. 'With
my cold, you shouldn't be suggesting protracted farewells!
I should be in bed.'

'Precisely what I had in mind, my dear!'

Melody spent the remainder of the day in her room,
unable to eat luncheon and accepting only a small slice
of ham with buttered bread at dinner. She found that
there were few letters to write. She had lost touch with
friends over the past year, and those who had called were
politely but firmly discouraged from returning. Finally
darkness fell, and Beatrice came in to say goodnight. She
appeared brighter than the previous day, and Melody
wondered at the sparkle in her eyes and flushed cheeks,
but, lost in her own fear-filled world, could only attribute
it to her aunt's cold and felt even more guilty.

A second dream-tossed night brought her no better rest
than the previous one, and when she appeared downstairs,
John came to her with a concerned frown, taking her by
the shoulders. 'You really must put what has happened
behind you. You'll become ill if you don't eat or sleep.
Come now, I want to see you with a good breakfast
inside you before you leave.'

'I'll try, but truly I don't feel hungry. I'll be all right

once we are away from England. I worry about you, too, and the thought of someone connecting you with me. It would quite ruin your career, and I couldn't bear that.'

He gave a crooked smile and patted her cheek. 'Many people have attempted to ruin me over the years, and failed! It's the price of success, and I envisage no change of pattern in the future. I've always believed in making good friends on the way up as insurance against meeting one's enemies on the way down. Now . . . allow me to help you to some of this ham and some eggs. You will offend the cook if you refuse, which is even worse than worrying me.' Gently chiding, he led her to the side-table, and under his ministrations she found that she was more hungry than she had imagined.

Beatrice had already eaten, and had packed their meagre possessions—a little jewellery, some borrowed dresses, and five hundred pounds that John had insisted on their taking 'as a loan'. It seemed all too short a friendship, but Melody felt that she had known the man all her life, and it seemed the most natural thing in the world to brush a shy kiss on his cheek at their departure.

The brown eyes twinkled. 'Duels have been fought over such gestures, my dear, so you must be careful to whom you give such largesse!' He turned then to Beatrice, and their gazes locked. There were no words, no touch, only a nod and a smile before he handed them into the carriage.

'He took a great risk in helping us as he did,' Melody remarked worriedly as they started for the docks.

Beatrice smiled. 'I've kept him from becoming old and staid for many years now. The occasional risk, the rare encounter with danger is all part of that "other life" that we share. Don't worry about John, sweeting, he has undoubtedly enjoyed every hour of it!' Her eyes sparkled. 'Certainly a few hours, at least!'

CHAPTER THREE

THE CUNARDER MADE relatively good time to New York, but having ploughed through a storm in the Irish Channel and bucketed her way across a rough Atlantic swell, Beatrice was forced into her bunk and kept there for the entire crossing. Melody, on the other hand, found her first sea voyage a source of exhilaration and wonder. When allowed, she would wander the deck and throw her breakfast rolls to the ever-hungry sea birds. John Brown had ensured them a first-class berth and the close regard of the captain and his first mate, so her forays into the intricacies of the ship were well attended, and both men grew in stature before her intelligent questions and genuine interest.

The money and papers that John had given them worked magic on the sour-faced Customs men, and within minutes of arriving in New York they found themselves in the milling throng on the docks. 'I'm so glad we brought no more than these two cases that John provided,' Melody remarked. 'I'd hate to have to trust these porters. I'm so looking forward to getting to the hotel and putting what little we have of value into the safe and then setting out to replenish our wardrobes. I can't wait to get rid of these awful dresses.' Her eyes slid to the many-flounced, round-hooped crinoline in dark grey that John's sister had given to her, together with two others equally unfashionable. She had been glad of the family's generosity, not daring to return home for her own things, but felt distinctly uncomfortable in dresses made for a woman twice her age. Aunt Bee must have felt even more ill at ease, Melody appreciated, since the only person approaching her size had been John's housekeeper!

As they made their way through the crowds, jostled by
newsmen eager for the latest tidings and people awaiting
friends and relatives, Melody scanned the throng for a
cab to take them to the Hotel Brevort at 8th Street and
5th Avenue that John had recommended.

'Excuse me, ladies.' They turned, to find a dapper
young man at their elbow, his wide smile revealing two
gold teeth. 'You are obviously strangers here, and possibly
a little lost. I'm afraid it is quite impossible to find a cab
in this crush, but if you care to walk a short distance
there is a rank that few know of.'

Melody assessed him, not quite able to put her finger
on what disquieted her, not thinking at that time to ask
why a cab would wait a block away when all the fares to
be had were right in the dock area. 'Thank you, sir, but
we are only going to the Hotel Brevort, which I've been
told is quite close by. We are in no hurry and can wait
for this mêlée to subside, when I'm sure the other cabs
will return.'

The smile broke out again. 'Why, you would be wasting
your money! I know the Hotel Brevort well. Splendid
place . . . Splendid. Just a few minutes' walk if you
take the short cut. Please allow me to take your cases and
escort you. A cab from here would have to take you all
the way around those storehouses, a dozen blocks and
more, then he'd turn and bring you back on a parallel
street that you can reach by simply walking between those
two buildings. You can see the street beyond from here.
There . . . Those lights beyond that cobbled lane.'

Still Melody hesitated, but a glance at her aunt's over-
tired features, accentuated by her traumatic voyage,
decided her. 'Very well, so long as you are quite sure you
know the way.'

'Lived here all my life, ma'am,' he assured, swinging up
their cases with some difficulty and staggering ahead. The
two women exchanged glances, then hurried after him.
He entered the narrow alley, chattering continuously,
extolling in hearty tones the virtues of the city and telling
them who was playing at which theatres, but half-way

along he fell silent, slowing his pace, and finally stopped
before an unlit doorway.

'What is it?' questioned Beatrice, all tiredness forgotten,
feeling a warning prickle at the back of her neck. 'This
most certainly isn't the Hotel Brevort! Do you mind if we
proceed?'

'Proceed as far as you wish,' he said, the voice totally
changed, with a roughness and a menace in it that were
quite unmistakable. Gone were the pseudo-educated tones
and bright attentiveness, and even his upright frame
seemed to have developed a distinct slouch. From the
shadows a deeper shadow detached itself, then another,
and as they reached the circle of light from a dim lamp
over the doorway, Melody felt herself go sick with fear.

They were sailors, unmistakably half-breeds, and of the
lowest order, their features criss-crossed with scars from
years of gutter fights and pub brawls, their smiles revealing
blackened and broken teeth. 'Now, ladies, my friends will
relieve you of the luggage and, of course, any money or
jewellery you might be wearing . . . or hiding. Then
you may proceed at your leisure.'

'How dare you!' Beatrice snapped, swinging her reticule
at the young man's head, but found it wrenched from her
hand and thrown to one of the others.

'Don't be stupid, you old goat!' he hissed. 'We've no
call to hurt you. Most of those I lead down here come to
no harm at all, so just you relax and pay up.'

'Let them have the cases, Aunt Bee,' Melody urged.
'Don't give them any reason to hurt you.' She fought
down the urge to lash out herself, knowing that her aunt
was still weak from the journey and could suffer badly if
these ruffians lost their patience. Handing over the small
pouch of coins at her belt, she prayed that they would
accept it and leave. 'It's all we have. All our possessions
are in the cases there.'

Fetid breath assailed her nostrils as the largest sailor
thrust his face close to hers, grinning widely. 'That may
be, missy, but I'm just going to have to make sure you
ain't lying. You could be carrying a fortune beneath those

furbelows.' He snickered meaningfully but as his fingers closed over the high neck of Melody's bodice, Luther Hogge's face swam before her.

'No!' The scream ripped up from her throat, carrying all the horror of a nightmare re-lived, freezing the men for an instant, and in that split second, as before, her hands came up, talon-curled, and raked at the man's face.

He staggered back with an oath, then lunged forward, no longer smiling, no longer aware of anything but his prey—the kitten that had suddenly turned tigress. But he never made more than two paces before his head exploded beneath a smashing blow that drove him to his knees. Another roundhouse took the other sailor in the temple, crumpling him into the gutter.

The giant figure who seemed to have approached invisibly turned to the young man who had led them into the trap and lifted him almost gently by his lapels until his toes barely touched the ground. ' 'Tis tired I am of following you, you pathetic excuse for a wharf-rat! You'll lead no more helpless ladies down dark alleys, I'll be bound.'

'No—No, I promise,' babbled his victim. 'I know you warned me.'

'Twice.'

'Yes . . . Yes, twice. I'll not do it again.'

'That's right, me lad. You'll not do it again, because no self-respecting woman or man will ever look at you again, least of all trust you.' Almost casually he smashed a back-hand into the other's face, breaking nasal cartilage and several teeth, and tearing open one cheek with the large ring he wore. Sobbing and cursing, the once attractive young man was allowed to stumble away, covering the pain-filled wreckage of his face with his hands. Slowly, then, their rescuer turned, and Melody found herself looking at an older man, his thick mane of iron-grey hair bordering a face as scarred as those of her assailants, yet with eyes of a clear bright blue that gleamed with the sheer joy of battle. The eyes turned to Beatrice, who had been equally abused, and bore a rising lump on her cheek to prove it.

With her resolve unshaken she pushed herself away from the wall and attempted to straighten her torn dress. 'Who are you, sir, that we may introduce ourselves and thank you properly?'

'I'm an itinerant, ma'am. A vagrant, a professional wanderer.' He made a low, courtly bow. 'Patrick O'Shaughnessy by name, ma'am, and your servant.'

A tiny smile touched her lips, but her voice was reproachful as she took in the rough garb of a stevedore, which detracted not at all from the wearer. 'You could surely have saved us without *quite* demolishing the opposition so completely? That young man will never be the same again.'

'I hope not,' he growled, glaring down at the two groaning bodies, and giving one a kick as it attempted to rise. 'I've been all sorts of a rogue myself in my time, but never preyed on the old, the young or the helpless. This trio specialise in all three. I've given them fair warning over the past months, but enough is enough. Now . . . I'll see you to wherever you're going, and then bid you goodnight.'

'No need, Mr O'Shaughnessy,' Beatrice stated firmly, lifting her case with considerable difficulty. 'We are in your debt for your timely rescue and sincerely thank you for that, but we can make the rest of the way alone, thank you.'

Ignoring her, the man adjusted his scarlet neckerchief and turned that bright regard on Melody. 'Is she always so independent?'

Melody, having put down her fear, though recovering far more slowly than her aunt, felt herself inexplicably drawn to the man. 'Always!' she confirmed.

He gave it a second or two of thought, then nodded 'Good' and swung off his jacket, putting it about Beatrice's shoulders before she could protest. 'Not a word,' he ordered. 'You aren't fit to be seen on the streets, and I'll not escort a woman in a torn dress unless I've torn it

meself!' He lifted up the two cases as though they were
empty and started off up the alley.

'Just a moment!' Beatrice protested, and he came to a
halt and set down their cases.

Again he looked over her head at Melody. 'Will you be
doing me the favour, ma'am, of telling your sister that
she has the prettiest mouth imaginable, but that it's far
lovelier closed.'

'Sister!' exploded Beatrice, while Melody choked on a
laugh. 'I'll have you know, sir, that *I* am Lady Beatrice
Davenport and this is my niece, Mrs Melody Van der
Veer, and it should be patently obvious to anyone with
half an eye that I'm far too old to be her sister!'

Only then did he give her his full attention—as if she
had not been the subject of it all along—and let those
wicked blue eyes fall slowly from the top of her head to
the lowest flounce of her crinoline. 'No, ma'am,' he said,
'it's not that obvious. But perhaps it is in the well-lit street
ahead or, even better, in the clear fresh dawn when I'll be
taking you to see the sights of our fair city.'

'You'll be doing no such thing. You are a stranger, sir,
and a most impertinent and quite outrageous one.'

'Indeed I am,' he replied, quite unrepentant, and turned
away again, swinging up their cases with an ease that
quite belied the grey hair and weatherbeaten skin.

Melody flung a look at her aunt and discovered a tiny
curve to the pursed lips, but catching her regard, Beatrice
snorted, 'Vagabond!' and marched after him, shoulders
stiff beneath the enveloping jacket.

True to his word, he found a carriage and escorted
them to the hotel several blocks across town, pointing out
the sights along the way and completely ignoring Beatrice's
firmly averted profile. On arrival, he strode to the desk
and ordered two rooms with an authoritative air of
command that, even seeing the rough garb, the clerk did
not question. He took their room keys, carefully noted
the numbers, then handed them over with a bow.

'Your jacket, sir,' Beatrice said stiffly, making to remove

it, but was prevented from doing so by firm fingers on the lapel.

'I'll collect it after breakfast, milady. I'll not have you walking through the hotel in a torn dress.'

'But you'll have me walking through wearing your jacket, which will surely arouse as much speculation.'

'Speculation, ma'am, will do no harm at all.'

Still she felt the need to protest. 'We came for only a day or two on our way south. We may not be at the hotel tomorrow.'

Melody saw his face drop, and something within her prompted her to say, 'We have to send news of our arrival first, and also make arrangements for our journey, which could take all of a day, and then there is shopping and surely a little sightseeing . . . '

He threw her a grateful smile, revealing even white teeth. 'Sightseeing, is it? Well, I may be able to help you there. I've been in this fair city for almost a year now, working my way to the gold mines of West Nevada, around Virginia City, where I'll be making my fortune.'

'You're persistent, Mr O'Shaughnessy,' Beatrice interrupted, 'but just now we are far more interested in a cool wash with water that isn't out of a barrel, and a lie down in a bed that doesn't move.'

Instantly he was contrite. 'Forgive me, milady, I'm a selfish, thoughtless boor. I'll leave you be and call on you at nine-thirty tomorrow to escort you around New York.' With another bow, negated by a quite outrageous wink, he left them.

'Of all the . . . ' spluttered Beatrice, for once lost for words, but Melody had caught her aunt's flush and looked after the broad shoulders with closer regard.

'Of course, he is quite old,' she ventured. 'Past the age for the kind of life he's living.'

Beatrice turned abruptly to precede the bellboy who had come to take their luggage. 'Age is not always a matter of years, child,' she lectured. 'It's not how long you've lived, but how you've lived that counts.'

'Oh, Mr O'Shaughnessy certainly has lived!' Melody

smiled, but with a muttered imprecation that might have meant anything, Beatrice cut a swath through the other guests and refused to comment further.

True to his word, Patrick O'Shaughnessy was awaiting them as they emerged from the dining-room, the bright red neckerchief tied in a rakish bow. Before Beatrice could speak, he said, 'You were quite right, milady. You could not be mistaken for Mrs Van der Veer's sister in this light.' Then, irrepressibly, 'Your hair is like a bright new penny, while hers is like a raven's wing. Quite different parents, obviously.'

'Mr O'Shaughnessy!'

'Your servant, ma'am. Now, is it a telegram you'll be wanting to send and a few fripperies you'll be after buying?'

'I'm sure they'll arrange it at the desk.'

He turned to Melody. 'Will you be good enough to tell this stubborn woman that there is no way she'll get rid of me other than by giving me her note to send.'

'I can hear and speak for myself, Mr O'Shaughnessy, and I can't think of one good reason why I should give you this note and reveal our destination to a complete stranger, when all I wish is for you to leave us alone.'

There was the slightest edge of irritation to her words, and with an instinctive sensitivity underlying the soul of a rogue, the man retreated a pace. 'You're a cruel woman, milady, but I'll do as you bid. I'll even get a runner for you and bother you no more.' So saying, he turned and crossed to the desk, parting the throng as if they did not exist, and returned with a young man in tow. 'Now, boyo, you'll take this note with all haste to the telegraph office and not stop for a breath. Right?' Taking the note from Beatrice's surprised fingers, he scanned the address and handed it to the boy with a coin. 'I'll trouble you no more today, ladies, since that is your wish, but I'd advise you to take care if you wander abroad. Keep to the main streets and take no short cuts. Now I'll bid you a good day.' Sweeping off his cap he left them there, too surprised to speak.

Then Melody broke the silence with a choked giggle. 'Oh, Aunt Bee, your expression!'

'The—The scoundrel!' Beatrice spluttered. 'He saw the St Clare address after all!'

'Did you think to keep it from him? He has taken a liking to you, Aunt Bee, and that sort isn't easily discouraged.'

'*That* sort isn't even the type I'd dream of encouraging in my worst nightmares! A self-confessed itinerant, a vagabond, a man who lives by his fists and his wicked Irish wit. If he dares to turn up at St Clare, I'll tell the servants to throw him out!'

Melody kept her peace, but privately thought that it might take more than an irate butler to keep Patrick O'Shaughnessy at bay. 'Come on,' she said placatingly, 'let's explore, anyway. Thanks to John's generosity we can replace these awful dresses and at least give my relatives the impression that we are in need only of their hospitality, not of their charity!'

As it happened, the combination of John's generosity and Beatrice's title was effective beyond their wildest dreams. The socially conscious shop assistants and store managers were only too eager to relieve the autocratic Lady Davenport of her money, and the two women found doors opened to them which remained firmly closed to the casual shopper. Haute couture gowns, the latest from the House of Worth, were displayed before them: silks and satins dripping with embroidery and beads, rich velvets trimmed with heavy blond lace, mantles bordered with gold and silver.

'Just what we need for a few weeks on the farm!' Beatrice remarked drily.

The moment it was noticed that Melody was in mourning, the multi-coloured garments presented to Beatrice were always accompanied by black velvet ball gowns . . . 'Of course you won't feel like dancing, madam, but simply to be seen . . . ' and silk day dresses with the strange watermark that had recently become popular, and satins shot with midnight blue . . . 'In this progressive society, madam, unrelieved black is not at all the thing for one as lovely as yourself.'

By the late afternoon, the two women wanted nothing more than a quiet room and a chance to lie down for an hour or two. Having their purchases sent ahead, they returned to the hotel.

'We'll make travel arrangements in the morning,' Beatrice stated, easing her feet on to a low stool.

A tiny feeling of doubt clouded Melody's eyes. 'Should we not await an answer to our telegram before leaving?'

'Not at all. If we are welcome, then we shall spend a long and leisurely holiday there. You never know, it may turn into something more permanent. Your father was there for a year. If we aren't welcome, they will be too polite to turn us away. I'm told that the Southerners are known for their hospitality and courtliness, so we shall simply spend a day or two there, and leave.'

'For where?'

Beatrice smiled, and patted her hand. 'John will think of something, never fear.'

They dined late, and Melody was considerate enough to suggest an early night. The strain of the past events, her aunt's delicate health since the rough sea journey, and a long day's shopping had taken their toll, and she bore lines of tiredness round her grey eyes.

'Tomorrow we'll hire a carriage and see a little of the city,' she promised as she brushed Melody's cheek with soft lips. 'Goodnight. my dear, and, you'll see, everything will turn out for the best.'

'Of course it will,' the girl agreed, although in her heart she felt only the lead weight of her terrible crime, and she knew that sleep would come only with exhaustion.

As dawn threaded pale fingers between the curtains, a soft knock brought her to instant wakefulness.

'Mrs Van der Veer, it's your maid. There's a gentleman downstairs with a carriage who says he's here to take you and Lady Davenport for a drive.' The girl's puzzlement came through, and Melody's lips tugged upward in a disbelieving smile.

'He wouldn't! He wouldn't dare! Aunt Bee will demolish him!' Then, 'All right. We'll be right down.'

This time the stevedore had changed his garb for a broadcloth suit and fine linen shirt, but the familiar red neckerchief gave the whole outfit a distinctly foreign flavour, and many a censorious stare was passed by the conservative clientele of the Hotel Brevort. His lined and weatherbeaten face was carefully expressionless, but the irrepressible blue eyes twinkled as Beatrice Davenport bore down on him. In spite of her frown, he noticed that she was dressed for travelling, as was her niece, who trailed behind her trying not to smile.

'Do you always wear that abominable scarf, Mr O'Shaughnessy?' Beatrice challenged the moment she was within earshot. 'Has it some sentimental value?'

'Bless you, no, ma'am,' he smiled. 'It's simply a handy colour and size to mop up the blood that invariably gets spilled when men see my size as a challenge.'

Beatrice's frown deepened, but did not quite reach her eyes. 'You are indeed a violent man, Mr O'Shaughnessy.'

'Oh, no, ma'am, *I'm* a peaceable man. I just take exception to disbelievers!' He gave the scarf a twitch, setting it askew and lending it a slightly drunken tilt that caused Melody to choke on a laugh, covering it with a cough. 'Apart from which,' he was continuing, 'it's a sorta symbol; my mark. I like to be known, you see, and around the docks I'm called Red Pat. It appeals to my vanity to be remembered.'

'And there is no doubt at all that you have been blessed with a superabundance of *that* quality . . . not to mention pure gall!'

Melody came forward then and extended her hand. 'Are you going to take us sightseeing, Mr O'Shaughnessy?' She found it taken in a surprisingly gentle grip, and the grey head bent as he carried it briefly to his lips.

'It would be a pleasure and a privilege, ma'am.'

'So early?'

'We'll go to the Heights, where the millionaire merchants watched their clipper ships coming around Red Hook.

They named it Clover Hill, but I prefer Ilpetonga, which is what the Canarsie Indians called it before they sold it in the 1630s. The word means a high sandy bank, and they lived there in community houses, some as much as a quarter-mile long, would you believe. It's real pretty just after sunrise when the sun filters through the fog and the sea is like midnight velvet.'

'It is your persuasive tongue that's like velvet,' broke in Beatrice tartly. 'Do you have more of this useless information to hand?'

He turned that full, bright regard on her and smiled, instantly shedding ten years from his age. 'Volumes of it, milady! I spread my free time as evenly as possible between the library and Sam Fraunces' place in Pearl Street—the one he named Queen's Head Tavern, but is still just Fraunces' Tavern to everyone who's anyone. I was fifteen before I was taught to read by a Jewish merchant in lieu of wages, and I still figure I got the best of the deal. Now, ladies, your convenience awaits.'

Later, Melody remembered more of the small things of that day, rather than the sights. She remembered the strangely crisp muffins that he bought them for breakfast, steaming hot and covered in maple syrup, and accompanied by strong sweet coffee. Then the incredible conglomeration of people in the East Village, where among the predominantly Polish, German, Italian and Jewish community there lived also Ukranians, Russians and a scattering of others, so that in the whole neighbourhood bounded on the west by the East River, English was the foreign tongue. They saw Castle Clinton, the round brownstone fort built as a defence against the British fifty years before, and now used as the principal immigrant depot. Melody shuddered as she thought of the thousands of lost souls fleeing from their native lands, driven out by religious persecution, or the horror of the potato famine that had devastated Ireland in the three years from 1846. There were dreams of a new life in the New World—that ended here, to be followed by the crammed and terrible ghettos on the Lower East Side where, but for John and

Beatrice, she, too, might have paid for her crime.

She remembered the way O'Shaughnessy had shielded them from the worst sights, but had not painted an entirely false picture by showing them only the red brick, white-trimmed houses of the new aristocracy that lined the north side of Washington Square. He had a story for every occasion and proved a witty and erudite raconteur, and she saw Beatrice visibly softening as the hours sped by. He took them to dinner, not to Delmonico's with those who paid exorbitantly to see and be seen, but to a hotel dining-room at the corner of Fulton Street. Mr Sweet had opened trade in 1845 with the ships' captains that came to anchor at South Street, so that the fish and delicate spices he used were the finest in the city. The cooking was plain, but even Beatrice, after one wary sip of the thick crab chowder, raised an approving eyebrow.

By the end of the unhurried meal, she complimented him, 'You have a discerning palate, Mr O'Shaughnessy.'

He nodded with a wide grin. 'I'm also a large man with an appetite to match; a plain and simple man who enjoys plain and simple food. A lobster should look and taste like a lobster in my humble opinion, not be tortured into a tasteless cream and piped out to look like a rose! Now—is it a night of diverse dens of iniquity, or a concert at the Academy of Music?'

But Beatrice shook her head decisively. 'You have done enough for us, Mr O'Shaughnessy, and, I must confess in spite of my initial reservations, proved yourself a perfect guide and undoubted gentleman. Now, however, we must return to our hotel. There are arrangements to be made, train timetables to consider, and an early night for an early start tomorrow. It will be a long and tiring journey, and we are not at all sure what we shall find at our destination, or who.'

He raised thick eyebrows. 'You don't know the people you're going to?'

'Only that they may possibly be relatives of Mrs Van der Veer, if any of the original family are still in occupation, that is, and have not already sold the plantation.'

She smiled a trifle wearily. 'If that is the case, we shall have an equally long and tiring journey back.'

He looked grim. 'If you'll pardon my presumption, milady, you'd do better to wait for an answer to your telegram. These are disquieting times. The feeling in the North is running high in favour of emancipating the Southern blacks, and equally high in the South for retaining the only way of life they know. There is something called the Underground Railway from South to North, run by men who put their very lives in danger to help the runaway slaves to reach the dubious freedom of the North. There are a lot of opportunists on the roads south who pretend to be one thing and act as quite another. There are rogues and vagabonds and the blacks themselves, who are often at starvation level, living off the land and not too particular how. To put it as gently as I can, ma'am, two unescorted ladies are vulnerable to all kinds of danger . . . as you've already discovered.'

Helping Beatrice with her cloak, he hesitated, then suggested, 'If you were prepared to wait a few days, I could accompany you . . . Don't refuse right off, for it could have its advantages. I've a business deal cooking that should bear fruit in less than a week, which may put me well on my feet again, but I can't leave before then. What do you say?'

From where she stood, Melody caught the hesitation and the tiny smile that curved her aunt's lips, but Beatrice again shook her head. 'We'll not be beholden to you, Mr O'Shaughnessy.' This, she thought, said far more than the words conveyed. 'We'll do very well for ourselves, but thank you for your concern.' From that decision she would not be moved, turning at the hotel with a warm smile, and reiterating, 'I cannot allow you to accompany us, sir, but it would be most welcome to have a familiar face to see us off on the first leg of the journey. I hate to be the only one not waving at stations.'

'I'll gladly do that, and I can think of no man who won't pity me for letting you go and envy me for having known you.'

'Rubbish!' commented Beatrice, but she was smiling as she made her way into the hotel.

Keeping to his word, he was there with the carriage as soon as they had finished breakfast, loading their considerable stack of luggage aboard, and then saw them to the station. As expected of a large city, the station was a scene of total confusion, with people seething in never-ending movement, porters with overloaded carts shouting for gangway, steam hissing loudly from train wheels and black smoke billowing from their stacks, coating every-thing in an almost invisible layer of soot. It was quite impossible to talk, and, once, Beatrice had to lean close to the man to make a laughing comment in his ear, but finally it was time to take their leave.

'I'm not a letter-writer . . . Beatrice,' he said seriously.

'Nor I . . . Patrick. Goodbye, and thank you.'

'I move around a lot. I may see you again almost anywhere in the world.' He turned to Melody and took her hand. 'Take care of yourself, little one, and take care of this impossible woman too.'

'I shall, and I do hope that we meet again.'

Final farewells were said, and they settled into their seats for the first short leg of their journey south. 'I hope he does well from his business deal,' said Melody. 'He can't be very well off, but it was good of him to give us yesterday.'

Beatrice smiled a small, secret, smile. 'At least it will cost him none of his meagre finances. You remember my having to shout into his ear? Well, during that little exchange I managed to slip a hundred-dollar bill into his pocket. He's a proud man, that crazy Irishman, and he'll want to kill me when he finds out, but I'll not take any man's last dollars when I've more than enough for both of us.'

Melody laughed in disbelief. 'You are absolutely incre-dible, Aunt Bee. It's a good thing we'll be well away when he makes the discovery. I've a feeling he has a wild temper to match those wild vagabond looks.'

'Yes . . . well . . . I've other things to think about

than some Irish gipsy.' But seeing beyond her aunt's carefully casual expression, Melody knew that Patrick O'Shaughnessy would not be forgotten so easily. 'I wonder what St Clare will be like?' she mused. 'I know nothing of cotton.'

CHAPTER FOUR

ST CLARE, when it came into view, was a keen disappointment to Melody, though Beatrice declared charitably that it had an air of 'genteel dilapidation'. The cotton-fields through which they had passed bore a poor crop and, although this was September and the pickers should have started their second picking, with two or three to achieve before early January, there looked little enough for even one more. The field hands were listless and the mounted overseer equally so, barely acknowledging the passing carriage.

'I'd like to see Simpson's face if he saw this rabble,' Beatrice exclaimed. 'He'd soon whip them into shape. Do you remember that awful tweeny that dreamed only of the stage and didn't believe in doing more than she need . . . Oh, I'm sorry, my dear. How thoughtless! Please forgive an old fool.'

Melody smiled, and patted her aunt's hand as the carriage they had hired bumped over the rutted ground. 'It's all right, Aunt Bee. We shall always be doing and saying things that will remind me of home. Let's try to look ahead if we can. It's not such an awful place. Oh, it could use some repairs to the fences, a gardener to cut back that rampaging honeysuckle, and some paint on those columns that support that overhanging part of the roof, but it has good lines, as though someone had cared for it some time. Note that huge portico—one could sit and rock there in all weathers.'

As soon as they pulled up before the rambling two-storey house, the front door was opened and a huge negro emerged, followed by a young boy who took the horses. The man shambled down the steps, moving with the same studied indolence that had been apparent in the field hands. His expression was one of total indifference, though the tone was polite enough as he came to the door of the carriage.

'Lady Davenport? Mrs Van der Veer? We been expectin' you these past two days or so. Please come in this way. Mastah Brett in parlour.'

The two women exchanged glances. What kind of plantation-owner would tolerate apathy bordering on pure idleness from his field hands and complete indifference from his butler? They had heard tales on their interesting, though fortunately uneventful, journey south of field hands being harassed continually by the overseer's voice and whip, of floggings for the slightest sign of negligence, and yet here, it seemed, the slaves ruled the plantation as they chose.

With mixed feelings they followed the negro into a dimly-lit room to the right of the large square hall, and this time Beatrice's surprise emerged as a positive snort. Though warmed by a glowing wood fire and aglow with the light of an exquisite crystal chandelier, the room was virtually empty of furniture. Two high-backed armchairs and a long couch clustered for company about the fire, while an empty table stood forlornly by the window and, on the opposite wall, a small bureau held a number of carefully positioned letters and papers. All this they took in at a glance as the butler announced them, and a man rose from one of the armchairs, turning with a smile of welcome. He took a white-painted cane from the chair side and held it before him, its brass tip tapping lightly on the wooden floor as he came forward.

Hearing Beatrice's indrawn breath, Melody found that she could not even achieve that as she came face to face with the most incredibly handsome man she had ever seen. Yet handsome was not enough—he was almost beautiful, for in spite of a firm jaw he had a broad, smooth brow over which golden-brown curls cascaded, a patrician nose and full, sensitive lips. But then there were the eyes—blank-expressioned and sightless, but wide and long lashed and a brilliant ice blue.

Melody's gaze flew to her aunt's face, finding an echo of her own shock there, but almost immediately an overwhelming pity engulfed her. He was whip thin, his leanness accentuated by the slim-fitting white shirt and figure-hugging black trousers, but when he moved, hardly needing the cane as he made his way confidently across the room to stand before them, there was no suggestion of weakness, and she found herself revising her first assessment. Whatever else she had expected it was certainly not this, and she was quite unable to speak as hesitatingly she placed her hand within the outstretched one and found it carried in firm fingers to his lips.

'It is a very great pleasure to meet you, Mrs Van der Veer. Welcome to St Clare.'

Melody felt her initial doubts subside. No resentful ex-colonial or hypocritical host gushing false welcomes, but a young Adonis out of very girl's dreams who simply happened to be blind. For an instant the smiling, sensitive looks reminded her of Hugh, and she felt a pang of conscience that, for that instant, she had hoped this man was not a relative, but all she could think to say was, 'How did you know that I was Mrs Van der Veer and not Lady Davenport?'

He laughed, releasing her hand reluctantly, explaining, 'My mother defied the law by teaching her maid to read and write. She is still with us, and I have cause to be grateful, for she reads all my mail and can even write simple letters for me. Lady Davenport mentioned in her telegram that she was your aunt. When you crossed the hall there was a long, light tread and, forgive me, ma'am, a slightly heavier and shorter one, indicating a difference in your heights, at least. When I took your hand I felt long fingers and slender bones, and if I'm not mistaken you are less than a head shorter than I? Your aunt mentioned also that you were in mourning and in need of a period of rest. A lady in mourning would not wear the satin petticoats that rustle as delightfully as your aunt's. There is also no subtle scent of lip rouge, as again befits a lady in your circumstances. Are you answered?'

'Fully,' Melody smiled, impressed.

'I'm glad. Now, you must be tired after your journey, and although I am impatient to know all there is to know about you both, I shall curb my own curiosity for the present and call for Celine to show you to your rooms. Nanny is away for a week or so, so I'm afraid you'll have to use her grand-daughter Celine, who is rather new to house duties, but appears willing to learn.'

Disbelieving, Melody asked, 'You still have a nanny?' and relaxed at his laugh.

'Oh, no, not your typical English nanny at all, but I've never called her anything else. She was my mother's maid, as I said, and given to Mother when she first arrived from England. Nanny has been midwife, nurse, confidante and housekeeper combined ever since.' He pulled the bell-rope, and almost immediately the double doors opened behind them and a young girl entered.

She was a year or two younger than Melody and almost white, with high-piled black hair and large, liquid brown eyes. Melody again flashed a glance at her aunt to find the same 'What next?' query reflected in the raised eyebrows and tight lips. It was not that the girl was beautiful, but that, as a house slave, she flaunted that beauty so obviously. And then Melody realised. The heavy perfume, the rustling satin petticoats and tinkling ear-hoops would all be too much for a normal master, but for a blind man who relied on scent and sound and touch . . . She nodded to herself, correctly interpreting the lambent gaze that was fixed on the master's face.

Brett did not turn toward the girl, but only made a slight gesture that encompassed the two women. 'Celine, these are Lady Davenport and Mrs Van der Veer. They will be my house-guests for as long as I can keep them here. You will show them to the guest-rooms in the East wing—the sunrise is lovely at this time of the year—and help them to unpack. They will wish to freshen up before luncheon, so I trust you to see to that in Nanny's absence. They are honoured guests. Do you understand?'

Melody caught Beatrice's frown and had herself wondered at the unwarranted sharpness of his tone, but dismissed it as a flight of imagination.

The girl Celine gave a deep curtsy, swishing her skirt back as she sank to the floor. 'My pleasure, Mastah Brett, I see to the missis and the lady jus' lak they gran' ladies.'

Melody waited in vain for Aunt Bee to snort, 'We *are* grand ladies, you young chit!' but that lady was still staring at the girl in mild shock, so with murmured thanks to their host for his kind hospitality, she followed the girl up the high, curved staircase. There were deep gouge-marks on the polished wood, and touching them, Melody raised an enquiring eyebrow to her aunt. Beatrice shrugged and gestured to similar marks on the walls. It seemed strange to the women who were used to walls crammed with portraits of ancestors and assorted relatives that these held only the lighter-shaded rectangles where paintings had once been.

At the top, the girl turned to the left and opened an ornately moulded door which looked, from the quality of the wood, as though it had been replaced, and again Melody felt the puzzle deepen, but with a smile Celine announced, 'This room best for the Lady Da'enpaw. Bigger!' She moved on down the corridor, hips swinging insolently. 'And this for Missis Vander. Darker room to go with black dresses and misery feeling.'

Beatrice could contain herself no longer. 'You insolent little baggage! I've a mind to tell your master of your rudeness and demand he send you back to whatever field hand's hovel you came from. Now apologise to Mrs Van der Veer this minute.'

The girl had paled and lowered her gaze, but the set of her lips was mutinous and for a moment Melody thought that she was about to refuse, but then she muttered a barely audible, 'Sorry, Missis.'

'I'll accept your apology,' Melody said, 'but I feel that you also owe one to the Lady Davenport, don't you?'

The girl shot her a look of pure hatred before she turned to repeat her apology in the general direction of the older woman. 'Kin I go now?'

'As quickly as possible,' agreed Beatrice. 'You can send a more amenable servant with the water, and unless your attitude changes, my girl, I strongly suggest that you stay as far away from us as possible for the duration of our visit. Do you understand?'

'Yes'm.' The girl nodded, spinning away with a toss of her head and retracing her steps, almost bumping into the butler who had appeared at the top of the stairs with some of the luggage. 'You clumsy scrub nigra, you!' she shrilled, pushing past him.

'You is a nigra too, girl,' he countered. 'You might make like you white, but you just a freaky white nigra and get sold, sure as day follers night, when the place gets took over.'

The girl froze, half-way down the stairs. 'I don't never get sold! Mastah Brett he keep me for hisself. He never, *never* sell Celine!' Turning, she ran down to the hall and disappeared through a door, slamming it after her.

Slowly the man shook his head at the two women who had frozen in amazement at the exchange. 'That Celine she some high-tone wench, but nuthin' gonna make her white! No white man never gonna marry no black girl even if'n the law do gets changed. The sun itself go out afore *that* happen.' Still shaking his head, he took the cases into the first room and returned to the hall for the others.

'I don't believe it!' Beatrice exclaimed. 'I just don't believe it!'

Melody gave a gurgle of laughter. 'I should be furious if the situation weren't so unreal. Whatever have we got ourselves into, Aunt Bee?'

'No idea, child, but I intend to make the very best of it. From what little I can see, my room at least seems quite charming, even though it's hardly overcrowded with furniture, to be as charitable as one can, and our host is absolutely delightful. I suggest we wash and change and join him for luncheon. The air is warmer here in the

South, so the glacé silk might be appropriate for you, *and* it rustles!'

Melody smiled. 'I've no intention whatsoever of competing with a servant-girl, and if Brett is a distant cousin, I've no need to.'

'I wonder . . . ' Beatrice murmured, but said no more and turned to her own door.

The room that Melody had been assigned to was large and square, but its very size accentuated the lack of furniture, and her spirits fell a little. The curtains on the four-poster had once been a rich blue and gold, as had the matching ones at the window, but now the years of neglect had left them faded and limp. The bed-linen was clean, but of a cheap quality and even patched in places. 'Why?' Melody wondered aloud. 'Could it be that St Clare is not a thriving plantation after all? So much could have happened since Papa was here. Where are the family? Is that what the butler meant by his remark to Celine, that Brett is going to have to sell his slaves to keep the house?'

A knock at the door revealed a large negress carrying a jug of water. Wordlessly she transferred its contents to the pitcher beside the washbasin, then equally silently left. Not once had she raised her eyes to Melody's face, and the girl found herself fuming again. Poor Brett! What a misery his life must be, surrounded by such sullenness within and apathy without. But then perhaps he was unaware of it. If he knew only Celine, who obviously loved him, and her grandmother, who appeared as all the saints rolled into one, it was possible that the plantation and the house were run entirely without his knowledge. Washing and changing quickly, Melody hastened downstairs, eager to find out more about her host and his strange household.

Since there was no one to greet her in the hall, she went to the same room to which she had been shown on her arrival, and as before, Brett rose from the high-backed chair at her entrance. 'My aunt takes far longer at her toilette than I,' she apologised, going forward. 'But at least she isn't helpless without a maid, as are many of her generation.'

Holding out his hand with a welcoming smile, he led her to the chair beside him. 'I shall instruct one of the wenches to wait on her.' Crossing to the bell-cord he pulled it sharply, and as before, Celine appeared, hesitating as she saw Melody, her eyes worried.

'You want me, Mastah Brett?'

'Celine, Lady Davenport has no maid. You will give her a hand with her dressing and whatever else she wants. You'll wait on both her and Mrs Van der Veer while they are here.'

There was a flicker of relief in the dark eyes as she realised that Melody had not told him of the incident upstairs, but at the mention of being hand-servant to the two women, her lips set and her gaze was hostile. Melody met the stare levelly, and it was the brown eyes that fell first as the girl muttered, 'Yassuh', but at that moment Beatrice appeared at the door and with palpable relief she hurried away.

More sensitive to the vibrations in the air than Melody had given him credit for, Brett gave a tight smile. 'Celine has been spoiled just because she is Nanny's grand-daughter. A touch of the lash would do her good occasionally. It will benefit her greatly to have a mistress keep her in hand, however temporarily.'

'Is there no—no one . . . no lady of the house?' Melody ventured awkwardly, and he gave a shake of his head.

'I'm not married, Mrs Van der Veer, nor are there sisters, aunts or other female relatives to keep the girl in order.' He put aside the cane and turned to Beatrice, holding out an arm. 'Allow me to escort you into luncheon, ma'am, and you too, Mrs Van der Veer. From the proximity on our introduction, I am led to believe that you do not favour those unbelievably wide hoops, so I am confident that we'll be able to negotiate the doors. Shall we try? Then I can tell you more about St Clare and my family, or lack of it, as we eat.'

Unable to resist, Melody let her fingers rest on his arm, finding surprisingly hard muscles beneath the black jacket, and the trio edged carefully through the double doors, across the hall and into another brightly lit but equally stark room.

There was a central table of dark oak, a refectory table of a bygone age, with ornately carved legs and a sectioned top that could be wound apart with a handle to allow the central section, stored on runners beneath, to be slipped into place. There were six high-backed matching chairs, and a long sideboard in the same design sporting a meagre array of porcelain and crystal. No other furniture or ornament was in the room, and Melody mourned the friendly clutter of her own dining-room with its multiple side-tables, oddly matching chairs and over-filled what-nots gracing each corner. There were no clocks, cande-labra or assorted silver on the bare mantelshelf, though the fire glowed brightly enough. No family portraits, no mirrors, graced the walls, and the floor was bare of rugs.

'Please be seated,' their host urged, and the two women took the places indicated, one at each side of him, as he allowed the negro butler who had followed them in to seat him at the head of the table. He said nothing more until a simple brown soup of indeterminate origin was served, then with an apologetic smile explained, 'It's not *Sáumon mayonnaise*, but I fear you have found me in somewhat embarrassing circumstances.' He hesitated.

In her usual forthright way, yet with a gentle tone, Beatrice stated, 'You have no money.'

His smile was one of relief, and he nodded. 'It isn't a thing one usually confesses at a first meeting with strangers, but if we are to be relatives, or friends, I feel that I must be honest with you.' He made a graceful, yet vulnerable, palm-upward gesture, and Melody's heart went out to him.

Since their first meeting, something in the finely drawn features had reminded her of Hugh, causing a deep warmth within her that made her reach out now and briefly touch his hand. 'Please don't think of us as

strangers. I know my father remembered St Clare with
affection, and apparently he stayed here for a year or so.
You may not recall him—his name was Alexander Davenport, Aunt Bee's brother—but anything you can tell us
about your family and St Clare would be of inestimable
value to me. We found a toy among his souvenirs carved
with the initial "B". Would that remind you of anything?'

His eyes lighted up, and he nodded with a laugh. 'Of
course! Uncle Alex! I gave him a wooden horse of mine.
I fear I remember very little of his stay with us, but he
would talk to me as if I was a young adult and take me
for rides around the plantation. I don't remember his
leaving; it must have been just before my parents'
deaths . . . ' The smile died from those incredibly blue
eyes as if a light had been extinguished behind them as
his thoughts turned back the years. Almost absent-
mindedly he took a spoonful of his soup, then pushed the
plate away, possibly aware that Beatrice had already done
the same after the first taste. He waited until a young
negress had replaced the almost untouched plates of soup
with others containing brittle slices of roast pork, turnips
boiled to a mash and potatoes cut into tiny slivers and
fried in pork fat until crisp, a concoction that made even
the adaptable Beatrice push aside her plate with a grimace
of disgust.

Brett's meat had been pre-cut, and he toyed with his
food with an apparent lack of appetite. It was no wonder
he was so thin, Melody thought, if this was his usual fare.
Was it that he was too poor to afford better, or simply
another example of the indifference of his slaves that had
been evident elsewhere?

For several minutes he stared unseeingly at his plate,
then moved it aside. 'As you so succinctly put it, Lady
Davenport, I have no money . . . I have *less* than no
money, for St Clare is barely surviving on a mountain of
debts. Please allow me to explain. My parents died when
I was seven, my mother in giving birth to a stillborn
daughter and my father in the same carriage accident that
blinded me when the carriage turned over and we were

both thrown from it. My father's brother, James Savage, and his wife Barbara came up from Atlanta with their adopted son Paul to take over the running of the plantation and my guardianship. They were city people, however, with no knowledge at all of cotton, so were soon heavily in debt. The land had looked good then, so they borrowed money, not to pay off our high mortgage but to buy more slaves to work the fields. There was a bad frost that year and most of the crop was lost. They just hadn't begun picking early enough. Then there was a cholera epidemic, and instead of confining the families who had it, they made the healthy members work in the fields instead of taking care of their own and perhaps pulling them through. They lost half our slaves that way, but borrowed again to replace them. And so it went on. Mistake upon mistake, frost and disease, bad overseers working against them, and their own ignorance unable to turn the tide. I shan't bore you further, but when I came of age they gladly returned the running of St Clare to me, together with all its debts, and only then did I realise how bad things were. Being blind, I had to employ an accountant, who found glaring discrepancies and even false entries that they had made to conceal the truth from their creditors.'

Beatrice and Melody gazed at each other, but remained silent.

'I had no choice but to borrow again to pay off the original creditors who, by then, were baying for blood. The man that was recommended to me was a wealthy Mississippian with a thriving plantation of his own who was looking for new land. He gave me barely enough to pay off the debts and took St Clare as collateral, giving me a year to pay the debt plus interest. I have been using half the profits, what little they are, to live on, and the rest to pay off this Mr Wilkinson, though of late there has been barely enough to pay the interest. I have only a few weeks to go before he calls in the debt and St Clare becomes his, as well as whatever there is of value; goods, furnishings and, of course, the slaves.'

'But that will leave you both penniless and homeless!'

Melody exclaimed, horrified. 'What will you do? Where will you go?'

'I haven't decided yet, but I fear the decision will have to be made soon. I can't possibly feed the land—cotton is such a hungry plant—and I don't have time to change to tobacco as my neighbours have. I'm advised that at the end of the month Wilkinson is taking the journey up to assess the situation for himself.'

'But can no one help you? What of your aunt and uncle, or the son you mentioned?'

He gave a nod and a mirthless smile. 'My uncle and aunt are little better off than I, but Paul may be able to help. He became my staff as well as my eyes in the three years he was with us. I think he hated his parents, even though they adopted him—"for appearance' sake"—he used to say. There was certainly no affection there. I believe he disliked me, too, at first, as he dislikes any weakness, physical or mental, in anyone. Of course he is eight years older than I and tended to regard me as a baby. I was only ten when he left, so he was probably right to treat me so.'

'It seems he got out in good time,' Melody remarked drily.

Brett shook his head defensively. 'Of course Paul was quite unaware of the financial situation when he left home. He any my uncle had a fight, quite literally, over Paul taking the part of a negro whom my uncle was going to have flogged. Paul, I'm afraid, sympathised with those fool Yankee Abolitionists in the North, even though he was born and raised a Southerner.'

The two women exchanged looks, and it was predictable that Beatrice's own strong views would war with her desire not to offend her host . . . and win. 'We all have our opinions on the subject of slavery, Mr Savage,' she said quietly, 'but as an Englishwoman I am heartily grateful that my country abolished it over fifty years ago.'

Surprisingly he smiled, unoffended. 'You've met Celine. Would you consider her better off here or in some mud hut in Africa? They're slaves in their own country, too, and suffer far more than they do here. They're born to be slaves.'

'That hardly makes it right,' Melody interjected.

'But what would they do if we freed them?' he argued. 'Most of them would starve. Thomas Jefferson himself said, "in reason they are much inferior to whites, in imagination they are dull, tasteless and anomalous". He himself was a slave-owner, as was George Washington and a great number of other presidents we've had. Our economy runs on the institution of slavery. Slaves don't feel the heat of the fields, nor do they appear to need as much sleep as we do, therefore they can work from dawn until dark if necessary.'

He stopped speaking as the little negress came in to clear the barely touched meal, saying as she left, 'Of course I don't make the mistake of many of my neighbours, who treat the house-slaves as if they don't exist, talking quite openly in front of them. To know the family business gives them a degree of control that no white in his right mind should condone. There was a rebellion here at the time my mother died, and much of it was facilitated, so I'm told, by the house-slaves knowing when the master was going to be away. I remember very little of it myself, but they did terrible damage to the house. In some ways, I'm almost glad I can't see it. However, we mustn't discuss such matters. Let's go into the drawing-room; it's more comfortable than here.'

The change of venue also enabled Melody to change the subject. 'But what of this cousin, Paul?'

Brett called for coffee before settling into his chair, and leaned that bright head back against the faded upholstery for a moment, closing his eyes as though weary of the burden he carried. 'I don't know what happened to Paul after he left home,' he said eventually. 'He simply disappeared for several years with no contact or word at all. Then we received a letter that he was in New Zealand, where he was going to buy some land and set up a farm. That must have been about ten years ago, for the following year he came home to buy rifles and explosives, as well as farm equipment. It seems that they were having trouble with the natives there—something about a treaty that the whites had broken. Paul seemed sympathetic to them, but of course he would be. He could still get himself killed whether he agreed with the cause or not. We just couldn't make him understand that if the natives weren't using the land to its full potential, the settlers who wanted to farm had every right to take it from them and make it pay. They would have given the natives work on their farms, I'm sure, but Paul didn't seem to think that was as important as the natives keeping their own land, to cultivate or not.'

The same little negress who had served the dinner entered at that moment with cups of steaming coffee, thick and black and sweet, regardless of how anyone preferred it. Beatrice took hers, raising her eyes to heaven in expressive surrender.

Brett was continuing, 'The difference in our ages didn't seem so great then, with Paul at twenty-six and I at eighteen, but he had changed terribly. He was scarred physically. Nanny said that he had a knife-wound or similar along one cheek, but his real scars went much deeper. His voice, once pure Southland like mine, had become harsh and clipped, and somewhere along those lost years he had forgotten how to laugh. Yet I think we found something to respect in each other in spite of our idealistic differences, and while he was here we found a kind of affection that made parting difficult. That is why, when I found I could trust no one around me to give constructive advice and help, I asked him to come back. He arrived three weeks ago, and almost predictably, advised me to leave St Clare to Wilkinson and begin again elsewhere. But St Clare is all the home I've known, and leaving it, however run down it may be, isn't an easy decision. Paul's gone to Raleigh to raise money; I don't know how, or dare to ask. He isn't a man one can question too closely. He talks very little, but still gives one the feeling of security, and with Wilkinson breaking down the doors, I need that just now. I fear, then, that

our acquaintanceship is on borrowed time, though I beg
of you to stay for as long as you can.' He smiled, erasing
the lines of strain that had crept about his mouth as he
spoke. 'However, since we are acquainted, we must make
every effort to enjoy ourselves while we may. Now you
must tell me about yourself, Mrs Van der Veer, or may I
call you Melody—such a rare and beautiful name—on
the possibility that we *may* be related?'

Melody found herself drawn to him even more now
that she knew the adversities that he had overcome and
the trials that he was still facing with as brave a face as
possible. His views on slavery were, she was sure, born
only of a biased education and she could readily forgive
him that, vowing to use every minute to change those
years of misinformation. 'I'd like that . . . Brett. Now,
where shall I begin?' Carefully eliminating the last few
terrible days before their departure, she told him of her
childhood and her life up to her mother's death, finishing.
'Then Luther Hogge took over completely, apparently
believing that the house and everything in it, including
myself, would naturally belong to him. He was a hard
and evil man. I could never have contemplated a life with
him and committed what was, to him, a most heinous
crime by running off with the son of my piano-tutor.' A
lump rose in her throat, and for a moment she could not
continue.

Quietly, Beatrice ended the story by saying, 'Young
Hugh Van der Veer was killed . . . murdered . . . on
their wedding night. Luther Hogge waited a bare three
months before proposing to her in such strong terms that
we were forced to leave. So here we are, wanting nothing
more than a short rest-period before taking up our lives
again.'

'How terrible for you,' Brett commiserated, reaching to
put a warm hand on her arm in a brief gesture of
sympathy, and Melody felt a sense of loss as it was
withdrawn.

Beatrice, who had been observing the two closely,
asked, 'Is there no chance of your going to live with this

cousin in New Zealand?'

Brett smiled, turning toward her voice, and once again Melody found difficulty in accepting that he was blind. He shook his head firmly. 'I have some small amount of pride left, Lady Davenport. I couldn't become a dependent relative, not even having the distinction of being a blood relative, on a man who has carved a totally self-supporting life out of a wilderness. I should be of absolutely no use to Paul, and I know that the strain would tell on us both.'

Beatrice met Melody's frown with a direct look. 'That is what *we* were prepared to do,' the look said, and Melody felt her face flush. Rising, Beatrice decided, 'I beg you to forgive me, but I should like to rest before dinner . . . The journey, you understand, and there is a letter I must write to say that we have arrived safely.'

Reading her thoughts, Melody vehemently shook her head, rising with her aunt and accompanying her to the door. 'You can't!' she exclaimed, *sotto voce*. 'You mustn't involve John again; he has already done too much.'

'We are of absolutely no use here, sweeting,' Beatrice stated in the same low tone. 'John will find us another refuge, but here at St Clare we are only a drain on young Brett's already overloaded reserves. Whether you are related or not, neither one can help the other. We have a little money left, a few hundred, and of course a few pieces of half-way decent jewellery, but we shall need those if we are to begin again. John would of course send more should we need it, but I certainly won't ask him to bail out a useless and dying plantation, even if he were so bad a businessman as to agree. No, we must write and ask him to suggest other accommodation, perhaps with some friends of his in New York as he first suggested, until we can find some way of earning our keep, and leave this as we found it. I don't mean to be hard, my dear, only practical.'

'Then you must do as you see fit,' agreed Melody with a lift of the chin, 'but I'm staying for as long as I can. I won't leave him like this.' Then, seeing her aunt's surprise at the unaccustomed independence, she added, 'Just a few days, *please*? If I have to go to New York and find work eventually then I'll do so, though in all honesty I am fitted for very little, apart from some figure-work and perhaps work as a governess. I must try to give what support I can. You must see that.'

Beatrice saw far more than Melody realised, and gave an internal sigh. 'Very well. A week. No more. It will take the letter a further two weeks to reach John and possibly the same time to receive an answer. Five weeks, my dear, and a week after that St Clare will be sold anyway. No one can recover from a situation like this.'

Melody turned her head toward the forlorn group of furniture round the fire. She could not see that bright, golden-brown head, but knew every curl of it as if it were her own. It should not have been so when they had only just met, but every feature was carved on her mind's eyes as though she had known him all of her short life. 'We can't just leave,' she decided. 'Even simply to show him that someone cares . . . ' She gave a decisive shake of her head. 'I won't leave yet.'

Beatrice watched her return and sink into the chair to Brett's right and lean towards him, saying something that brought a chuckle. A slight frown touched her woman's smooth brow. Perhaps five weeks was too long. Melody was totally vulnerable just now, and Brett equally so. Two lost, bright and beautiful souls who would naturally gravitate toward each other—and possibly fall together. With a slight tightening of her lips, she determined to write that very afternoon. 'I'll not put *my* faith in some unknown Savage,' she muttered, making her way upstairs.

CHAPTER FIVE

MELODY SLEPT LITTLE that night, but for once her dreams were not of Luther Hogge but of the pale-skinned Adonis sleeping at the far end of the house. She had seen his room. 'Wander as you please,' he had said and, warily at first then becoming bolder, she had explored every nook and cranny of the rambling mansion. He had told them of the negro rebellion, not showing hatred of the band who had changed his whole life, but rather according them the shrugging acceptance a parent might feel for a recalcitrant child that throws the occasional tantrum under discipline. Except, Melody thought, studying the gashes on once beautiful woodwork and noting replaced doors, these children were more like feral beasts, dragging down everything in their path, and she shuddered with an instinctive loathing of mindless violence.

She had found Brett's room on the ground floor, unaware as she opened the door that it was a bedroom. She had stopped in the doorway, skin prickling warningly. It was dimly lit, with curtains drawn, and for the moment it took her eyes to adjust, her nostrils caught that familiar heavy scent. 'Celine?' No sound, yet as she crossed to part the curtains she was quite certain that the girl was near. 'Celine?' she repeated. 'I know you're there. I wonder if Mr Savage is aware that you sneak into his room when you've duties elsewhere.'

The room was as spartan as the others, though the bed-linen was of the finest and the curtains of the four-poster were richly embroidered, as were the edges of the pillow-cases, the letters 'B.S.' entwined in a dozen different forms. The work was exquisite and executed with a patience born only of love. As Melody stared in fascination, the curtain at the head quivered and the servant-girl stepped forward, eyes wary, body rigid as a cat's that treads unstable ground. For several seconds they stared at each other, and in that moment Melody felt an atavistic antagonism rise within her, alien and nameless.

'I'm cleaning,' Celine stated, head up, arms stiff by her sides, shoulders back, full breasts thrust forward beneath the thin cotton blouse.

'Obviously,' Melody agreed, finding a derisory sneer in her voice that startled her. What am I doing? she asked herself. Why on earth am I standing here disputing territorial rights with a slave? 'Please don't let me stop you. Perhaps you'd like me to order one of the other servants to assist you—and to bring some cleaning materials with her!'

Celine's eyes flashed fire. 'Just finished.' And, hips swinging, she strolled out. Melody swallowed hard, fighting the urge to aim a totally unladylike kick at the retreating *derrière*.

Exploratory mood broken, she paused only to re-close the curtains, wondering why it mattered, before returning to her room. That day and the next she wandered further afield, finding censure in the dark eyes all round her. 'Do they think I'm going to take over St Clare and make them work for a change?' she wondered aloud to Beatrice on their third evening. 'Heaven knows the place could use a little honest toil! I know nothing about cotton, but whole patches appear to be over-ripe and untouched, while the areas they pick are barely ready. They just won't move a finger more than they have to, and that so-called overseer is as idle as the rest. He's either sitting on his horse making lewd comments to the young girls, or lying in the shade of some tree scratching his over-fed stomach. Do you think Brett even knows what's going on? He seems worried about the decline of St Clare and its insurmountable debts, yet he seems unable to do anything about it. At least he could hire another overseer.'

The subject of their concern chose at that moment to appear at the drawing-room door and the conversation was changed, but still Melody fretted. Something in her mood must have communicated itself to the extraordinarily perceptive man, for when Beatrice had retired, he asked, 'You aren't happy here, are you?'

'Oh, I am!' she assured him, turning from the window. She had been staring out at the tiny patch of neglected garden and had not noticed his approach. He reached out to touch her arm, and his foot kicked a stool that she had brought in from another room and forgotten to replace. With a startled exclamation he stumbled, but she had already caught his hands to steady him. 'I'm sorry!' they both said simultaneously and then laughed, taking a step apart.

'No,' Brett objected, still smiling. 'I shan't apologise.' He took her hands again, his own strong and warm. 'Can we not . . . Shall we not assume that we are related? Surely no harm can come of it, for if you are a distant cousin there could be no possible objection to our holding hands, and if you are not, then it is only your objection I need care about. You don't object, do you, Melody?' His grip tightened a fraction. 'Say it!' he commanded.

Melody felt shaky and a little breathless before that smiling regard. 'No . . . No, Brett, I don't object.'

His sudden laugh was light and carefree, as if all the worries that must surely beset him were driven off by her small surrender. 'Good. Then I shall take your hand as often as I please.' But just as swiftly his face became serious, and he reached for her arms so that she faced him. 'Since we have progressed so far, so very far, I shall ask a favour that I would not have dared when we were strangers . . . Have we ever been strangers?'

She felt the same strange closeness. 'It is almost as though we knew each other before . . . in some other life.'

'I would have seen you then. Allow me, please, to see you now. Not with my eyes, of course, but in the same way that I might have seen Paul's scarred face had he allowed anyone as close as this. The sense of touch becomes so acute with blindness that my fingers can tell

me as much as, possibly more than, another's eyes . . .
If you'll allow the imposition, that is?'

Heart beating a little erratically, she lifted his raised
hands to her face and closed her eyes as those gentle
fingers moved, butterfly light, over her cheeks and
forehead, nose and chin, touching her eyebrows and lids,
and moving across her slightly parted lips—and returned
there to linger for a moment before touching her hair and
over her ears to her neck. She felt a tremor run through
the hands that rested for a further moment against her
skin before dropping to his sides, and they were both
breathing a little faster as he murmured, 'I never realised
that you were quite so lovely.' He gave an uncertain smile.
'I don't know whether I want Nanny to return or not. If
we are related, I don't think I want to know. If we're not,
then I want to know right now.'

Melody shook her head, fighting for composure. 'Aunt
Bee will stay awake until she hears me in the next room.
I must go up.'

'Just one thing, and I'll let you go.'

She turned back, drinking in the absolute symmetry of
his face. 'Yes?' Already she knew what he would say.

'Do *you* hope that we are not cousins?' Then, with a
devastating smile, 'Answer me, or I'll stay down here and
freeze in the night air until you do!'

She smiled at his silliness, but then answered in all
honesty, 'I hope that we are not related at all,' before
hurrying to the door.

As she opened it, there was a swish of silk and Celine
stepped aside, defending her presence from Melody's frown
by saying, 'I came to see if'n the mastah wanted hot
chocolate or a brandy afore bed.' She swept past Melody,
crossing the room with that hip-swinging stride before she
could think of a suitable retort. 'You need Celine to bring
you anythin', Mastah Brett?' she purred. 'You need me
for . . . anythin' at all?'

'No, you can go to bed now,' he said, smiling toward
Melody who had lingered in the doorway. 'Goodnight,

Melody. Rise early so that we can spend a longer day together.'

'I'll do that,' she promised, meeting the coloured girl's glare with a sweet smile before going to her room.

The incident was repeated several times over the next few days, however, with Celine behind every door, an equally plausible excuse on her lips, and Melody found herself setting ridiculous traps for the girl—entering a room where Brett was and indulging in light conversation, then going back to the door and flinging it open. Celine was always there, and finally she could stand it no longer and voiced her objections to him.

'I know she thinks a great deal of you and obviously feels it her duty in Nanny's absence to remain as close to you as possible, should you need her . . . ' Then she trailed off, bogged down by her own diplomacy.

Brett's winged brows drew together in a frown. 'If Celine has caused you or your aunt one moment of discomfort, she must be punished for it.'

'Oh, no! I didn't mean you to punish her . . . perhaps just a word . . . ' But already he was tugging at the bell-pull—unnecessarily, thought Melody with an internal sigh, going to open the door and admitting the hovering Celine.

The girl stood rigidly throughout the whole of Brett's tirade, which, because it was conducted in the softest of tones, was even more terrifying. 'And if you ever,' he finished, '*ever* give my guests cause to mention your name with anything but praise, I swear I'll send you back to the fields.'

With a rustle of crimson silk, Celine ran to throw herself at his feet, clasping him about the knees. 'Oh, please, Masta! Please . . . You can't. I been good to you. So good to you.'

Brett's normally pale features had iced into pure alabaster and his blue eyes glittered diamond bright, although his tone changed not at all, and Melody realised for the first time what it would be like to cross this man. 'You've served me as I would expect any nigger wench I took out of the fields to serve me. You do as you're told.

The instant you do anything to offend me, you go back to the fields until you're sold down-river. Do you understand?'

'Mastah Brett!' The plea emerged barely above a whisper, and Melody's heart went out to the abject mulatto, the tears flowing unchecked down the ivory cheeks, the long-lashed dark eyes in anguish.

'Brett, she meant no harm, I'm sure. She was perhaps a little too assiduous in her duties, trying too hard to please you, that's all.'

His features softened then and his mouth curved upward. 'You aren't accustomed to slaves, Melody. You mustn't allow them any leniency at all or they'll begin to think they can exert some degree of control; they'll begin thinking for themselves, and that would be detrimental to the plantation. In many ways they're like children, in many others just cattle.' He shifted irritably and Celine fell away, remaining on her knees as he walked over to where Melody stood. 'Don't worry, gentle Melody. I'll not punish her, since you ask it.' He raised his voice very slightly to address the kneeling girl over his shoulder. 'Get back to work, Celine. I'll ring for you if I need you, but from now on you'll remain in your quarters when you're not cleaning, and you'll make sure that the rooms you clean are well away from myself and my guests. Do you understand?'

'Yes, Mastah Brett. Thank you, sir.' Slowly she got to her feet and crossed to the door, eyes averted for once, features pale.

Melody waited until the door had closed, feeling distressed and uncomfortable. She herself had been surrounded by servants all her life, but Brett's attitude to his slaves brought a chill to her spine. The servants in the London house before Luther had replaced them had been family friends, although not of the same social standing. Their families were asked after, and time off was gladly given for nursing and visiting. As a child, Melody would sit in the kitchen being fed scrapings from the bowl of cake mixture, or would follow as close as a gipsy's lurcher

dog on the heels of anyone who would gossip to her. She
had seen her father put a grateful hand on a man's
shoulder for work done above and beyond the call of
duty, and talk to the ostler as an equal and with respect
over a sick horse. Brett's admission that not only were
his people totally inferior but barely even human gave her
a new insight into the fundamental differences in their
beliefs and the knowledge was upsetting in the extreme.
But already he was smiling that devastating smile and
causing a drum-roll in her heart.

'Come, take my arm, and I'll escort you to your room.
I want you to be happy here, Melody. We have so little
time together that we mustn't waste a moment of it in
bothering about a house-wench.'

She took his arm, still unhappy. 'I can understand
needing workers on a plantation, but is it necessary to
make them slaves? Why blacks and not white people? Oh,
I know you've said about them withstanding the heat, but
Aunt Bee and I saw enough poor shanty people on our
way down who were working their meagre vegetable
patches in the heat of the day. I'm sure they would be
only too glad of work.'

His smile faded, the lips tightening a fraction. 'Those
are just white trash, Melody,' he explained with the
patient tone one might use to educate a child. 'They don't
want to work . . . and I'd have to pay a wage even if
one or two honest ones could be found. They could never
work as hard as the nigras. I've been told that a prime
field hand can pick fifty pounds of cotton a day—twice
that if driven by a good overseer. Our blacks are fed,
housed and clothed, which, as I've explained before, is
more than they'd get in their own villages.'

'But many of them have never seen Africa. They're
born into slavery over here—in a country where all men
are supposed to be equal.'

He made to turn away, and Melody knew that he
considered the subject unworthy of her. 'The blacks aren't
men, they're a commodity. It's the system,' he said shortly.
'It has always been that way, and I see no reason to

change it. Please, my dear, try to accept what you don't understand. You're new to this country and know nothing of its politics or economic growth and very little of its people, so how can you judge with more than your emotions . . . gentle and sweet as they are?'

Taking pity on him, realising that his blindness went far deeper than his lack of sight, she changed the subject, to his palpable relief, and allowed him to accompany her upstairs.

At her bedroom door he turned her to face him, hands curved lightly over her shoulders. 'Don't be angry with me, Melody. I know you are, I can feel it. If I were a real man, I could take you into town, wine and dine you, and make you forget St Clare and the Celines of the Southland.'

'Don't, Brett, please! I'm not angry, truly I'm not. Our ways are just different, that's all. As for your not being a real man, there are many with all of their senses who could never take your burdens as bravely as you have. I'm perfectly content to be here with you, and I've never needed wining and dining. Tomorrow, if you like, I'll take you on a short carriage-ride round the plantation and describe all that's happening. Would you enjoy that?'

For an instant there was a tightening of his jaw, then he agreed, 'I'd love it. Tomorrow, then.'

'Goodnight, Brett.'

As he turned toward the stairs, Melody went to bid Aunt Bee goodnight—then spun in horror at a cry, in time to see Brett miss the top step and tumble, arms and legs flailing, to the bottom of the long staircase—where he lay quite still. She screamed his name and went racing down to him. Doors opened, and both Beatrice and Celine reached them at the same time.

'Don't move him!' snapped Beatrice, dropping to her knees beside the unconscious man.

'It's all my fault!' Melody cried. 'He wanted to see me to my room. We were talking about taking a carriage-ride tomorrow. I should have made certain that he was safely touching the balustrade before I left him.'

'Mastah Brett *never* goes upstairs,' Celine hissed, but backed off before Beatrice's glare.

Swiftly Beatrice examined the limp form for broken bones, and finding none, ordered, 'Celine, I'll need two strong men to carry Mr Savage to his room. See to it immediately. Melody, I think he's just stunned, but there's a nasty cut on his forehead. Get some water and cloths from the kitchen.' Then, observing the girl's stricken expression, she gave her a smile and a little push. 'Go on, child. He's going to be all right.'

Even before Celine had returned with the men, Brett gave a deep groan and opened his eyes. 'It's all right, Mr Savage,' Beatrice reassured him quickly. 'You've had a bad fall, but you've not come to any harm apart from a cut on your forehead. Celine has gone for a couple of men to take you to your room, and Melody will bring some cloths and water to bathe that cut. Celine said that you never go upstairs. While I applaud your gallantry in seeing my niece to her room, you were rather foolish to do so if you weren't accustomed to it, don't you think?'

Brett nodded, wincing a little as the movement shot a burst of pain across his eyes. 'Foolish. Very. Can't go on that carriage-ride tomorrow. Not now.'

'You most certainly can't. Here are Celine and Melody. Come on, now, you just relax and let these men help you to your room.'

He nodded acquiescence, biting his lip as the negroes lifted him, yet Beatrice thought for one moment that a tiny smile had touched his lips—a grimace, undoubtedly, she corrected herself.

Melody waited on Brett for the next two days, still blaming herself for his accident, while he spent every moment assuring her that it was only his clumsiness that was to blame. Celine stayed, as bid, in her own quarters, and it was probably only a worldly-wise Beatrice who identified the soft sounds that emanated from the ground-floor room—directly beneath her own—when all the house was still.

On the third day, Nanny arrived home and immediately

took charge. She was a tall, strikingly beautiful negress, still slender and unbending in spite of her seventy years. Because of Brett's absence, it was Beatrice who greeted her in the hall, a moment or two ahead of Celine.

'I'm Lady Davenport,' she introduced herself, going forward with a social smile. 'And you must be the redoubtable Nanny whom Mr Savage has told us so much about. My niece, Mrs Van der Veer, and I arrived last week for a short holiday, as I believe you were aware.'

The woman put down the large portmanteau that she had brought from the carriage, and inclined her head. 'I read your telegram and I'm pleased to make your acquaintance, Lady Davenport. I trust you've been well taken care of in my absence.'

Beatrice raised an eyebrow at the educated tones, and in pleased surprise replied, 'Yes . . . Yes, thank you. Mr Savage had an unfortunate accident three days ago, though he isn't badly hurt. He fell down the stairs after foolishly escorting my niece to her room, and has spent a couple of days in bed under her care.'

The black eyes sharpened, and without another word the woman swept by Beatrice, heading for the room where Melody was reading to the man in the bed. 'Well!' Beatrice murmured, abandoned in the centre of the hall. 'Not exactly your usual run-of-the-mill servant!' Following her, she was in time to hear Brett's glad exclamation, 'Nanny! You're back!'

Nanny gave a brief nod in the direction of the seated Melody. 'Mrs Van der Veer, your servant, ma'am.' Then, 'Mistah Brett, you've no sense at all going up those stairs, whatever the reason!'

'It was my fault,' interjected Melody. 'I should have made certain he had reached the balustrade.'

At the door, Beatrice shook her head. There was something about the woman that one could not help reacting to. She simply assumed command, making all about her feel like naughty children, and, she realised, she had done so for at least twenty years.

Seeing the man's high colour and the look he flashed

his companion as he reached for her hand, the negress gave a tight-lipped smile. 'I see you've been well taken care of, but I'm sure Mrs Van der Veer would like a rest now. Celine can take your place, ma'am, while you take some tea, and I'll have the kitchen fix some sandwiches.'

'No, Nanny,' Brett stated firmly. 'Celine has other work to do.'

There was a moment's hesitation as she studied his face, and something flickered behind the almost black eyes, but then she gave a nod. 'As you wish, Mistah Brett. Perhaps Mrs Van der Veer would like tea brought here?'

'Oh, no, that's all right.' Melody's throat and back ached from the hours of reading, seated on the low, backless stool. 'I'll take it in the drawing-room. You don't mind being alone for a while, do you, Brett? I'll return immediately.'

His thumb stroked the palm of her hand, sending shivers down her spine. 'You've been so good to me since my fall, how could I possibly object? But don't stay away too long, will you? St Clare seems so empty when you move away from me: I never noticed it before.'

Melody blushed, casting a quick glance at the impassive negress who preceded them out. 'What do you think of her?' she asked Beatrice as they reached the drawing-room and the tall figure had disappeared in the direction of the kitchen. 'She gives me the shivers!'

'She's more of an old-time nanny than I believed possible,' Beatrice smiled. 'And obviously resents *anyone* becoming closer to her protégé than she is herself. Don't forget, sweeting, she's had him to herself since he was seven, and my intuition tells me for a while before that, too. She showed obvious shock at his rejection of her suggestion of bringing in Celine. She is unaccustomed to such behaviour.'

Melody agreed, privately wondering how much of herself Beatrice recognised in the strongly protective negress, and answering both trains of thought, said, 'It's about time someone made her realise that children grow up. He needs rest, of course, and some nursing. After all, he was badly hurt by his fall . . . '

Beatrice gave a sigh. 'Melody, my dear, Brett was *not* badly hurt from his fall. He was extremely lucky to have suffered only a cracked pate, but that's all. His enforced bed-rest is, I suspect, a great deal to do with the constant loving care and attention he has received since.'

'Aunt Bee, you're being unkind!'

'Perhaps.' Beatrice subsided as the tall negress entered with the tea. 'If so, I freely apologise, but I feel that the young man could easily be up and about tomorrow if left to his own devices. What do you think, Nanny?'

She straightened from the low table on which she had placed the tea-tray, and her eyes met the cool grey ones with a level look. She hesitated, then gave a nod. 'Mistah Brett always did like fussing, and he don't look too bad to me. If you say he's not bad hurt and no bones are broken, I figure that he could get lonely enough to leave his bed for dinner tonight. I'll suggest it to him.' She moved gracefully to the door, then turned. 'My granddaughter, ma'am . . . Has she given you cause for complaint? I haven't seen her since I arrived, yet when I left I told her to take real good care of Mistah Brett.'

Melody spoke before her aunt could, correctly assessing the pursed lips. 'Celine was a little *too* assiduous in her duties, that is all, giving us no privacy, and Mr Savage felt compelled to speak to her about it. She is simply unaccustomed to guests, and didn't realise that she need not be on hand all the time.'

Nanny inclined her head, her gaze flickering over the girl before her with a new assessment, taking in at a glance the gleaming sable hair and thickly-lashed sapphire eyes, the exquisite bone structure and slender yet fully curved figure that even the black mourning dress could not conceal. With complete understanding she said, 'I apologise for my grand-daughter, Mrs Van der Veer, and to you also, Lady Davenport. I shall speak to her myself.'

It was as well for her that neither Beatrice nor Melody overheard the conversation that did transpire when she confronted Celine in her own room, stalking in without warning and stating, 'You are one prize fool, girl! You want Mistah Brett, and you act like field trash! Look at you! You think satin cast-offs from that no-brain Atlanta belle that thought herself missis here, and cheap perfume from the pedlar-man, gonna get him? You think acting like a bitch in heat's gonna get him?'

Celine flounced away, expression mutinous. 'Welcome home, Gramama,' she said, then gasped as her wrist was caught in fingers of steel.

'Now you listen to me, girl. You listening?'

'Yes . . . Yes . . . You're hurting me! I'm listening.'

'Then you hear, and you hear good. You're going to be nice to these white folks. You're going to be so nice that they'll let you back to wait on them.'

'Who wants to!' Celine objected.

'You do, fool! That white girl thinks she's a relative of Mistah Brett, though she sure don't act like one. Well, there *are* no relatives of Mistah Brett alive. Something's wrong there, and I mean to find out what they're up to. If you can get into their rooms and look through their luggage, you may find something. You can find out just who they really are and what they want here.'

Celine grew very still, and her wrist was freed. She nodded slowly, then looked up, meeting her grandmother's sharp gaze. 'You think I can still get Mastah Brett to marry me in spite of that blue-eyed cracker? You think he'll ever take me north and free me?'

'First off, fool, that Mrs Van der Veer is the furthest thing ever from a white cracker. She's a lady born and bred, and, as such, is a mighty powerful force. Second, Mistah Brett won't marry a slave-girl if he can find a dozen more like her! He's got to love you, girl; be so crazy about you that he don't care about your colour. Already he relies on us both for his very life. If St Clare is sold as they say, he will have to sell the slaves as well. He must need *us* so much that he couldn't even think of doing that, not to us. I've been Mistah Brett's whole family since before you were born. If those white folks leave, we shall be all that he has or needs of family again.

That white girl's real pretty, and the old woman too clever by far. You've got to be more pretty, and I've got to be more clever. You got it, girl?'

Celine was smiling too now, and gave an eager nod. 'I'll be so sweet those two whities won't know up from down,' she agreed, heart lifted. 'And I'll have eyes like a hawk and ears like a jack rabbit.'

Her grandmother gave a dry smile. 'Sounds revolting, but I take your meaning. Now . . . I want that hair done like that Mrs Van der Veer does hers, back in a knot, real prissy like.' She grinned then, patting the girl's cheek. 'It'll take Mistah Brett more time to get it loose on the times he needs to, and a little sweating and waiting doesn't harm any man. You still pleasuring him, girl?'

Celine shuffled her feet.

'Well?'

'Sure . . . sometimes . . . '

'Much?' When there was no answer, 'Now look here, girl, I didn't get you into this house for nothing. I didn't make Mistah Brett examine you himself, just as he would any bed-wench on the auction block, every inch of you, for nothing. They don't do that to the frozen white women they marry, with skins like the belly of a dead fish and hearts as cold. *You*, girl, can be Mistah Brett's bed-wench for now, and then, when he can't get you outa his blood, his wife, if we play our cards right. You listening?'

'Yes, Gramama. I'll be just like you say. I'll be quiet and sweet and as helpful as you please, so those whities will be turned face about. I'll watch and I'll wait. You'll see.'

The negress gave her a long considering look, judging the gaudy dress and abundant jewellery and finding them wanting, but finding no fault at all in the fine bones, full lips and wide-spaced liquid eyes, and she gave a deep sigh. 'How my sweet mistress got herself something as plumb pretty as Mistah Brett outa "Bull" Savage, and how your mammy got herself something as pure female beautiful as you outa that whitey no-account baccy-planter Bull rented her out to, I'll never know either. But you children surely belong together, *that* I know. Now you wash that face of your'n and get a high-necked clean cotton frock on, and we'll take the future right from here. You listening, girl?'

Celine's velvet eyes were soft with dreaming. 'Yes'm,' she murmured, and, satisfied, Nanny turned away.

CHAPTER SIX

WHEN CELINE APPEARED early the following morning, no one could have been more surprised than Beatrice, who took in the downcast eyes, demure cotton dress and neat chignon with something akin to disbelief. The girl stood, head lowered, waiting to be addressed.

'Wonders will never cease!' thought Beatrice in amazement. 'Yes, Celine, what is it?' she said.

'Kin I take a minute o' your val'ble time, Lady Da'enport?'

In spite of her instinctive distrust of this miraculous volte-face, Beatrice's tone was gentle. 'Of course. What can I do for you?'

Finally the large eyes were raised to her face. 'My gramama she tell me she gonna whup me real good if'n I don' say how sorry I is. I know I done been a terrible wicked girl, but I's changed, lady, truly I is!' The full lips trembled. 'I just don' know what come over me acting just like I was something important in the house. I's just a low no-account house-wench, missis, and if you say I should be flogged, then I'll go to Mastah Brett right this minute and tell him to have it done.'

'Good grief!' exclaimed Beatrice, torn between laughter and horror. 'What in heaven's name should I want you flogged for?'

'Then you'll forgive me? Let me wait on you?'

'Well, I wouldn't go quite that far . . . '

'Oh, please, lady? I kin iron real good, and even if'n you don't want me anywhere near you like you said, I could do your pressing like it's never been done afore.'

Capitulating in the face of such apparent remorse, Beatrice gave a brief nod. 'Very well then, just the ironing—but I don't want you to think this allows you back in my good graces. You'll do my pressing, hang the dresses in the wardrobe and the linen in the drawers, but nothing more. Is that clear?'

'Yes, missis. Oh, thank you, missis!' With a radiant smile, the girl sped out.

'Well I never did!' remarked Beatrice. 'On the other hand . . . ' She gave a grim smile. 'It's been a long time since I believed in miracles. That chit's up to something!'

Outside the door, the 'chit' was leaning back against the ornate panelling with a wide smile. 'Got you!' she muttered, eyes gleaming, and, head high, she returned to her room, hips swinging in her habitual slumbrous rhythm.

Beatrice was still in doubt as to her sincerity, and decided to ask Melody whether she had approached her, but before she could put her thoughts into action, the door opened and Melody entered, hurrying forward to take her aunt's hands. 'He's getting up, Aunt Bee. Isn't that marvellous?' She gave an abashed smile. 'I swear if I'd had to read one more poem or one more chapter I'd have collapsed myself! I must confess I could never nurse a sick patient for any length of time; I just don't have the fortitude.'

'You'd be amazed at what you could do if you had to, my dear. I'm glad Brett has decided to leave his sick-bed, however, considering the extent of his incapacitation!' Forestalling the defensive gleam in Melody's eyes, she added, 'Not that he didn't suffer a nasty fall . . . Now, shall we go in to breakfast?'

As they reached the dining-room door, Brett appeared from his room at the far end of the hall, and at once his acute hearing detected the soft swish of their crinolines as they turned to greet him.

'Melody! And you, too, Lady Davenport. You can't imagine how good it is to be up and about again.' He tapped across to where they stood. 'I missed you yesterday afternoon.'

He reached out so naturally that Melody found his arm about her shoulders as if it had every right to be there. It was a comfortable arm, a light and warm arm, and she reacted with all the affection that she had so missed since Hugh, slipping her own arm about his waist and leading him into the dining-room. Beatrice frowned a little at the obvious closeness of the pair. She was concerned that John Brown's answer to her letter would not arrive in half the time necessary if these two were to be separated. There was something inexplicably wrong here, and every instinct told her to take her niece and leave—yet there was absolutely no reason why she should feel so.

'See how well I am?' Brett exclaimed, doing a little side-step and swinging the laughing girl with him. 'I think I need to get out and about more. Would it be proper, Lady Davenport, for Melody and me to take a long walk after breakfast?'

Beatrice could not restrain a smile at his eager desire to please her and uphold the proprieties. 'Don't ask me, young man! Melody is an independent young woman with a mind of her own. However, it may tire you after your protracted stay in bed. Why not take the buggy, as you intended before your fall?'

'What a good idea,' Melody agreed, quite missing the momentary stiffening of Brett's slim frame, but then he smiled and nodded.

'Of course. Excellent idea! I'll have Samson put in the two bays. They're as easy to control as rocking-horses, so you'll not even need gloves. Will you come with us, Lady Davenport?'

'No, I think not. I'm sure Melody would sooner have you to herself now that you're well again. With your permission, I'll browse in the library. I've noticed that there are still a few good volumes that have survived rebellion and neglect.'

Eager to be off, Melody finished her breakfast quickly and hurried Brett outside. With a practised eye she approved the lines of the matched bays, wondering whether Brett would have to sell these too, and hoping that it would not come to that, so that perhaps . . . someone . . . might stay to take him out occasionally.

Helped aboard by the impassive Samson, she settled
herself into the maroon leather seat.

'A nice sedate trot round the plantation,' she said,
smiling, as she took up the reins and felt the responsive
velvety softness of the horses' mouths.

'That'll be just fine,' he replied, but there was a tautness
in his tone that caused her to throw him a quick glance.
It was only then that she remembered the carriage accident
in which he had been blinded and his father killed.

'Oh, Brett, I forgot! How could I! I'm sorry. Do you
want to go back? We can take a short walk instead.'

'No!' His rejection was sharp, and he made a visible
effort to overcome his fear. 'No, it's all right. I must face
it sooner or later. It was so long ago that it's quite
ridiculous to feel this way. Go on, give them a touch of
the whip. It's a good road through the plantation, so I've
heard, and you can tell me just how bad the situation
is . . . and whether there is anything worth salvaging. I
need to face Wilkinson with all the ammunition I have to
salvage even a tiny corner.' He felt for her arm and gave
it a reassuring squeeze. 'It's just that, believe it or not, I
haven't been in any conveyance at all since my accident.'

'But your aunt and uncle?'

'I was obviously of no use to them in the running of
the place, and they weren't as sympathetic and patient as
you. They could not have imagined a need for me to
"see" my property. If I left the house, it was just to feel
my way to the edge of the portico steps. It was quite
recently that I found I could manage very well on my
own if I felt my way about with that cane I carry. It took
weeks of bruised shins, not to mention my bruised pride,
but eventually I found my way about the ground floor
quite adequately. So, you see, I'm becoming more
independent by the year. Let's be off!'

There was a false note in his command, but, glad to be
away from the claustrophic atmosphere of the house,
Melody chose to ignore it. Trailing the long whip over
the animals' rumps, she gave a sharp click of the tongue
and revelled in their immediate response, guessing that

they had received as little exercise as she, and were equally eager. Brett's knuckles grew white on the arm-rest, but he sat forward bravely, and as the gentle sway of the carriage settled into an easy rhythm, he slowly relaxed. 'There's an old oak on our left,' Melody informed him. 'It has a large white scar—probably caused by lightning. Do you get many storms here?' And later. 'We are coming to a bridge over the river. It seems quite safe, but looks as if it could use some attention. You might mention it to your overseer. The underbrush needs to be cut back here, too: it's spreading well over the edges of the road. No two carriages could pass on this strip. Oh, look! I'm sorry . . . some young rabbits playing at the roadside . . . '

The big buck jack rabbit broke cover, startled by the thud of the horses' hooves and the rattle of the strange vehicle that should never have been on that isolated stretch of road. With a flash of buff and white it raced across in front of the horses, ears laid back, and the offside mare panicked, shying sideways, causing her companion to veer with her. The rabbit froze, spun, and raced back in panic toward its young—too late—and was caught beneath the flying hooves. The mare felt the furry obstruction, heard the tiny scream—and bolted. Catching the terror of its stable-mate, the other horse gave a high-pitched whinny and both animals leapt forward in a blind stampede.

In the split second it had taken, Melody reacted, bracing her feet and clutching the reins more tightly. Her father's daughter, it was not the first time she had been in charge of panicking horses, in both Rotten Row and the streets of London that were permanently jammed with carriages and wagons. Calmly she called to the animals, easing them back, reassuring and talking to them continuously, her voice holding no trace of fear, only a sense of excitement at the motion, and tolerance for their foolishness. Sensing this in their driver and feeling the strong confidence in the hands that pulled them in without sawing at their sensitive mouths, the pair lost their

momentary fear. Slowly she brought the rocking carriage
under control, and the moment it had come to a halt,
leaped down and ran to the horses' heads, caressing their
quivering noses, pulling at their ears, scolding and cajoling
until their heads lowered and softly they blew into her
skirt in mute apology.

'I should think so too!' she laughed. 'Now you just
behave!' She looked back, and the smile died. Brett was
kneeling in the dust of the roadway, his hands covering
his face, his whole body shaking uncontrollably. 'Brett?
Brett!' She raced toward him, stumbling, regaining her
balance, then flinging herself down beside him to gather
him close. 'Oh, Brett! Oh, my love, I'm sorry!' Arms
strong about him, she cradled him against her, kissing
that bright hair, feeling with a pain as deep as his own
the silent, racking sobs of a man that stemmed from the
terror of a child.

Gradually while she rocked him the quivering eased, as
the man within won that hard-fought battle, and his hands
left his face and then came about her, absorbing her
comfort, until with a deep final shudder he raised his
head, murmuring her name, a mirthless smile betraying
his shame and embarrassment as he choked, 'What a fool
I am!' His hands came up to capture her face. 'Forgive
me for that.'

'No! Oh, no! You mustn't. You're good and gentle and
brave, and after all you've been through . . . It was all
my fault . . . my thoughtlessness . . . ' And then he
kissed her, gently at first, his lips moving over hers in a
kind of wonder, then with a groan crushing her to him,
plundering her mouth with a passion never before realised.

For one sweet moment Melody surrendered to him as
fervently as she had dreamed, returning his kisses, but
then harsh reality swept in. 'No, Brett! No, we mustn't!'
She pushed at his shoulders even while longing to cling
for ever, and with a shudder he released her.

'Melody . . . ' His voice made music of her name,
husky with yearning.

'We must go back.'

For a moment he bent his head, eyes tight shut against the hunger that threatened to engulf him, then nodded. 'Yes. We must go back. We must speak to Nanny. It can't be put off any longer.' Strongly then he turned to her, those sightless eyes searching her face as though he could see the tears misting her own. 'If what I feel is forbidden, then, God help me, I shall feel it still! But if we are *not* of the same blood, I'll hold you against all comers and never *ever* let you go!'

His intensity communicated itself to the unlit flame that was already within her, and taking his face between spread fingers, moving them tremblingly over that firm jaw, she said, 'Then . . . for what is . . . whether right or wrong . . . ' and she allowed herself one more kiss, feeling the warm softness of his lips as she skimmed them, clinging there for an instant before freeing him. Shaking, she rose and helped him up beside her. 'Come, then. Let's find out what the future holds . . . whichever way the path leads.' She felt a slight hesitation as they turned toward the carriage, and she tightened her arm about him. 'It's all right. I'll keep the horses to a walk on the way back.'

Little more was said on the long drive back to the house, though when his arm slipped about her waist, Melody only leaned closer and allowed it to stay. His silence gave her time to question her own emotions, and she was baffled at the conflict within her heart. Surely what she felt for him was far far deeper than her affection for Hugh, whom she had accepted only to escape the intolerable situation at home, knowing that love *could* one day develop out of warmth and friendship. There was a similarity between these two men, and even in looks there was a distinct resemblance. Could that be the cause of her confusion? She could not deny that Brett's kiss had stirred her far more than Hugh's ever could, and the arms that had crushed her to him had been fashioned from steel and sinew. There was a strength in the whip-thin frame and passion in the firm lips, and yet . . . somehow . . . it had not been enough. She cursed herself

for being a childish romantic. Undoubtedly she had been
reading far too many tales of heroines prepared to die for
their heroes, even at thirteen, like Juliet for Romeo.
Perhaps, as her peers had intimated, women could feel
not passion but only love for their children, and at best
respect and affection for their husbands, tolerating the
baser side of marriage with patience and fortitude. Melody
gave a sigh. Then what she felt for Brett must surely be
love, since it was so much stronger than her feelings for
Hugh, and her protective instinct merely a natural part of
that love, since that was the way of a woman. And
yet . . .

'We're here,' Brett stated with relief in his voice, breaking
into her thoughts, his hand going strongly to cover hers.

Inside, however, the house was strangely silent, and
with a sense of foreboding Melody called for her aunt. A
subdued Beatrice met them in the hall, giving Melody a
reassuring smile before saying to Brett, 'Nanny and Celine
both went over to Whitewalls. I thought you'd understand, so I gave them what they called "walk-about"
papers—just a note, really, saying that they had my
permission to go to that specific place. I'm afraid that
Nanny's daughter, Celine's mother, finally died. A runner
came when you were out, and I let them pack immediately.'

'Oh, I'm sorry. Poor Nanny!' sympathised Melody,
adding, 'Celine, too. It must be awful for families to be
separated like this.'

Brett frowned. 'No doubt, but my uncle must have had
a perfectly good reason for selling her away. It could be
something that my father had already written down and,
of course, it would have been honoured. I believe that the
particular breed she was tends to be somewhat trouble-
some, though I can hardly believe it, considering Nanny's
devotion to both my mother and me.' He brushed his
fingers through his hair, and the frown deepened. 'There's
no telling how many days they'll be gone. It was most
inconsiderate of Nanny to allow Celine to accompany
her: after all, she hardly knew her mother. Nanny apparently convinced my uncle that the child would be better

off here—her mother wasn't with the Hallidays at White-walls at that time, but rented out to a tobacco-planter down-river. Sometimes I wish Celine had been sold with her mother when the Hallidays bought her; she's little use here.'

Beatrice's voice held an edge as she said, 'Then I'm sure that we can manage well enough without her for a while. If you'll allow it, Melody and I shall take over the supervision of the place, beginning with the kitchens and luncheon.'

Brett gave a distracted smile, his thoughts obviously elsewhere. 'I don't like to impose . . . Melody, we must talk.'

'Later,' Melody promised, some inexplicable sense of disappointment clouding her previous mood. She was disturbed by Brett's apparently unfeeling dismissal of the dead woman and her relationship to the two people who had been closer to him than anyone before she herself arrived. Still, she realised, he saw them as slaves, rather than as humans with feelings and heartache, pain and grief, quite equal to his own. 'I think I should go to help Aunt Bee,' she stated firmly. 'The staff will be totally disorganised without Nanny, and the ride has made me quite hungry.' Then, seeing his stiff features, she relented a little. 'We'll talk after lunch. We'll find a quiet place, and talk all afternoon.'

He forced a smile. 'You're right, of course. Forgive me, I don't think much of food normally, and even less right now. It's rarely edible, anyway.'

'It will be today,' Beatrice promised firmly. 'Come, Melody, let's see what the kitchens will yield.'

Melody shot a look at Brett, but already he was making his way to his favourite chair. So, stifling a sigh, she followed her aunt into the kitchen at the back of, and adjoining, the main house.

As expected, the cook was producing nothing more than an inedible stew, completely ignoring the jars of dried spices. There was fat and flour in abundance, corn and potatoes in a cool corner, a cooked side of pork and

a fresh chicken newly slaughtered and left to hang. It
took little imagination to realise who was the better fed
out of master and slave.

Grey eyes icy, Beatrice took a quick glance round, then
fixed that gaze on the two women standing anxiously by
the cooking-pot. 'So!' They jumped nervously at the
ringing tones of Beatrice at her most autocratic. 'I see
you are preparing your luncheon.' Having the grace to
look even more uncomfortable, they said nothing as she
continued, 'It looks more than enough for the two of you,
so I assume that you will be feeding any other house-
servants as well. However, I shan't argue with your
master's generosity. Now . . . With Nanny away again,
Mr Savage suggested that I take over the household until
her return, so we shall start with *our* luncheon. Do you
know how to make dumplings? Never mind; you'd
probably produce something off a rock-pile! Bring me the
fat and flour, and some of that fresh parsley I see hanging
over there. We'll have creamed corn, a few potatoes lightly
boiled with a sprig of mint, those peas waiting for shelling,
and a large slice of pork apiece. You, girl! You can start
scraping the potatoes. Move, now! Melody, I'm sure there
is some wine hiding somewhere. Go and explore, there's
a dear. Oh yes, and look for some apples in the cellar for
a pie.'

Restraining the urge to laugh at the expressions on the
faces of the cook and her assistant, Melody turned for
the door.

So it was that Brett and his two guests sat down to the
best meal that St Clare had seen for a very long time.
Brushing aside his startled praises, Beatrice promised,
'You wait until you taste dinner!' But his reply was cut
off by a sudden commotion from the hall, and Samson's
voice raised in protest.

Almost immediately the double doors were flung wide
and the unfortunate butler propelled into the room, as an
almost forgotten voice bellowed, 'This puffed-up popinjay
dared to tell me to wait! Me! Patrick Aloysius O'Shaughnessy, who waits for no man!'

Brett had leapt to his feet with a startled exclamation, but at once Melody reached for him, catching hold of his sleeve. 'It's all right, Brett, this is an old friend. He always goes through life like this! How do you do, Mr O'Shaughnessy. I doubted that we'd seen the last of you.'

'Forgive me, Mrs Van der Veer; and you, sir, I crave your pardon for intruding on your privacy and assaulting your man, though he sorely deserved it.' He came forward with the sure stride of an avenging angel and took Brett's tentatively outstretched hand as introductions were made; then he peered into those ice-blue eyes and gave a nod. 'A double apology, sir; I never realised. I'll not trouble you for more than a moment. It was your other guest I came to see, Mrs Van der Veer's aunt—a lady I've followed all the way from New York City at considerable expense and no little trouble.'

After the first sharply indrawn breath, Beatrice had not stirred, or uttered a sound, and now she took a deliberate sip of her wine as he rounded on her.

'You're a proud and stubborn woman, Beatrice, but this time you've met your match!' And he flung a much folded hundred-dollar bill on the table before her.

The grey eyes were serene, and what Melody used to call her 'cat-that's-ate-the-cream' smile touched her lips. 'Do you really think so, Patrick O'Shaughnessy?' she challenged.

The thick brows climbed high at her words, but the eyes were twinkling. 'I know so,' he stated firmly. 'All it'll take is the time to convince you.'

'Do you need to?'

Melody knew by Brett's delicately inclined head that he had picked up the same vibrations that she had felt from the very first time these two had met, the same thrust and parry, yet with a strange underlying peace, a certainty in their exchange that she doubted even they were fully aware of.

'I need to,' Patrick declared.

'Then you're a fool!'

'That, too,' he admitted. 'But it was worth the journey

to hear it from your lips.'

'Mr O'Shaughnessy,' Brett broke in, re-seating himself. 'Since you and Lady Davenport appear to have certain differences of opinion to discuss, would you care to join us for luncheon? I'm sure Lady Davenport could conjure another portion from the same mystical source as our own.'

'Thank you, no, sir. It's sorely tempting, just to have a meal set before me by her own fair hands.' He gave Beatrice a broad wink in exchange for her glare. 'However, I ate well on the road, but I'd not say No to coffee.'

'Or something stronger?'

'Well, now . . .'

'Melody, could you find the brandy that is in the sideboard? The key is in the third small bowl from the right, the one with the chipped lid.'

Melody raised a surprised eyebrow, but rose obediently. She had been unaware that Brett drank: he had never revealed the presence of spirits since their arrival, yet when she opened the sideboard, it was to reveal several bottles, all half full or less. She brought the bottle of Armagnac to the table, together with two crystal goblets, and set them before the Irishman. 'Will you have one, Brett?'

'No, thank you, Melody. It's Paul who appreciated fine brandy, drinking it for pleasure, not to drown the pain that sometimes comes when one is alone in a dark world.' He gave a wry smile. 'Forgive my bitterness. I've not needed a drink for a very long time, but it has been known for the mood to come on me, and since I refuse to resort to laudanum for blessed sleep, the bottle does as well. It certainly turns the harsh blacks and whites into softer shades of grey. It never solves the problem, of course, but it's certainly an answer. Now, sir, please help yourself while I finish this most delicious dinner. Take a second, do, for I've no intention of wasting a single mouthful. I may never taste its like again.'

'Most civil of you, sir, with myself a stranger crashing into your home with all the subtlety of a stampeding buffalo and all. Your health, sir.' He poured a generous measure and raised his glass, the heavy lead crystal still appearing crushable in the great hand. 'And yours, ladies. May the wind be always at your back and the sun overhead.'

'An appropriate toast for a vagrant,' Beatrice remarked.

'I prefer the word vagabond. It has an air of the country about it.'

'Are you a country man, Patrick?' Melody asked, and wished she hadn't as his eyes darkened. His tone was gentle, however, as he gave a twisted smile.

'I was, as a child, and a few times since, but I've learned that there is more money to be made in the towns, more chance to own both people and property, with the latter a shade more expensive! You have no chances on a lone farm when the landlords move in.'

'Are you talking of the British in Ireland?'

'I am, but don't let it fret you. I've nothing against the British as a whole—only a fool hates a whole country because of a few bad representatives. When they formed the United Kingdom of Great Britain in 1801, however, they promised the emancipation of the Irish, and the farmer or the Ulster peasant was not asked whether or not he wanted to be conquered.'

'Surely not "conquered", when there was so much good done by the Union?'

'I'm sure Richard said the same of the Crusades, too, but I'd not question a Moslem, if I were you! With a split Ireland, with Protestants and Unionists becoming synonymous and the Catholics forming their own Home Rule bands, there was bound to be rebellion. Over the years that followed, the Protestants became England's garrison in Ireland, and I was too young to fight and too old to countenance being told what to do with my father's land. I left to find a bright new world . . . and found the ghettos of New York! But that was many years ago. There were rebellions in Ireland, of course, maybe there will always be, for the split grows wider. The worst, I heard, was the one in forty-eight led by William Smith

O'Brien, but like all the others it was all too easily put down—especially since the British were fighting a country they had already helped into famine.'

'You can't blame us for that!' Melody said hotly.

'Lord, no, dear girl, but you surely did nothing to prevent it or to help. If one sees a child dying of hunger in the gutters of Harlem, one can pass by and say, quite rightly, that it wasn't you who put it there. If you don't pick it up, you're guilty of a worse crime.'

'You must hate the British if you believe them guilty of leaving the Irish to starve if they could have helped.'

'No, Melody, m'dear. As I've said, I can't do that and call myself a thinking man.' But then he gave a wide grin, turning directly toward Beatrice. 'Their women are far too beautiful for any man to hate, so there must be some good in the country.'

Melody interpreted her aunt's twitch of a smile as she caught her lower lip between her teeth to prevent the instinctive question, so she asked it for her. 'More beautiful than the Irish women, or just different?'

'Well, now.' He gave it mock serious consideration. 'I would be a great diplomat, as well as a much travelled man, if I gave you a wise answer to that, or even a truthful one. But, in my humble opinion, all women have something of beauty about them, and I'll be led no further.'

Brett gave a laugh, coming to his rescue. 'Bravo, Mr O'Shaughnessy! A diplomat, indeed. However, if the ladies have finished their meal, perhaps we could continue this fascinating subject in the drawing-room. Knowing my guests better than I, you must, I insist, stay and tell me more. Any friend of theirs is most certainly a welcome guest of mine.'

'One could hardly call Mr O'Shaughnessy a friend,' Beatrice interrupted decisively, rising with the others from the table. 'We have only a few hours of acquaintanceship.'

The giant smiled at Melody over Beatrice's head. 'Would *you* not say we were friends, ma'am? I save your honour, if not your life, I wine and dine you, escort you about

town, offer to leave a town I've come to terms with just
to keep you safe on your journey here. Would you not
say those were the actions of a friend? Even when this
ungrateful, self-opinionated tyrant—though she has hair
like a bright penny, eyes the silver-grey of the mist over
the moors and a mouth that would corrupt a saint—even
when such a woman insults me by *paying* for her meal
and more, what do I do? I make a long and hazardous
journey to be by her side, just to tell her that I'm now a
temporarily wealthy man and have no need of her
misplaced generosity. Now isn't *that* the action of a
friend?' Those sparkling blue eyes turned to Beatrice, who
was biting her lip to keep from joining the laughter of the
others. 'If we aren't friends, Beatrice, me girl, then what,
pray, are we?'

'Sparring partners at best,' she retorted. 'You've a
smooth tongue, Patrick, but I'll not commit myself to any
rash statements just to please your already inflated opinion
of yourself. I see you're still wearing that terrible neckerchief, and have no doubt that it was well used on your
so-called hazardous journey south. I don't see how a lady
such as myself could even countenance friendship with
such a rogue.'

But then she laid her hand on his arm and gave him a
smile of such brilliance that even Melody was startled,
and the Irishman blushed to the roots of his hair as he
escorted her into the other room. He handed her into an
armchair and pulled up a stool, lowering his great frame
to sit at her feet. 'You shouldn't!' she began to protest,
but then thought better of it. 'You're a difficult man to
ignore, O'Shaughnessy.'

'Impossible,' he agreed.

Brett was in his favourite chair, and Melody sat on the
couch, placing herself at the end nearest to him and
wishing for the casual confidence that Beatrice and Patrick
exuded. If she could only have led him to the couch with
a light laugh, pulling him down beside her, prattling and
flirting as she had seen others do; but instead she had to
content herself with watching the way his head tilted just

so and the flash of even teeth as the Irishman made them laugh at his outrageous anecdotes of the journey south.

As the hours passed, the conversation turned to more serious lines—the disturbing talk of war. 'As if I haven't seen enough,' Patrick said grimly. Then, refusing to be downcast, 'I may even have met a relative of yours, Mr Savage. It's not a usual name. This was a certain *Paul* Savage—"Beau" Savage they called him, among less complimentary names. Not that he's so handsome now, since the knife fight after Cherubusco, but that's another story. He said he came from around here, anyway. Would you be knowing him, sir?'

Brett leaned forward eagerly. 'I certainly would! Paul's my adopted cousin, who came here when my parents died. His father was my father's brother, and they took over St Clare until I gained seniority.'

Melody liked him for not mentioning before a comparative stranger that it was Paul's father who had run St Clare into the ground, though its state could hardly have gone unnoticed. 'Paul left here when in his late teens,' Brett was continuing, 'and he vanished off the face of the earth for several years, turning up again in New Zealand, of all places. Did you know him well, Mr O'Shaughnessy? Were you his friend?'

The Irishman gave a bellow of laughter. 'Know him, begad! The man saved my life once, and near killed me in the attempt. Friends? Oh, yes, but much later. New Zealand, you say? So that's what happened to him.' He laughed again at their wide-eyed attention. 'He must have been barely into his twenties, with shoulders like a wild bull, but quiet-like—the kind of quiet that make most men uncomfortable. Well, as mayhap you've gathered, I'm not averse to a friendly scrap meself, but I took note of how bigger and far tougher men than I walked wide circles around this one, so I figured I'd best do the same till I got his measure.'

'You mentioned a place-name of which I'm unaware . . . a knife fight?' Melody asked, and received a grim smile.

'Cherubusco is in Mexico, ma'am, but we met before that—on a god-forsaken march from Vera Cruz to capture Mexico City.'

'The Mexican War!' Brett breathed. 'So that's why he was so changed.'

Patrick nodded. 'Enough to change anyone. Polk sent out a volunteer army by sea from New Orleans to Vera Cruz under Old Fuss and Feathers . . . Sorry, ma'am, General Winfield Scott to you. Volunteers they *may* have been—soldiers they *weren't*. Drunk half the time on aguardiente, filthy, flea-ridden, undisciplined . . . and this rabble was supposed to back up Zach Taylor's invading army coming in from the north. Well, you don't want to know about marching nigh on two hundred and fifty miles through terrain that God forgot, living off the country, combating yellow-jack as well as the enemy. It was after Cerro Gordo that I met your cousin, Mr Savage. He was as sick of the so-called Southern gentlemen around him as I—begging your pardon, sir, you being a Southerner yourself. But I never did see such pillage and wanton barbarity as each village suffered that we went through. Any Mex was considered to be the enemy, whatever age or sex, and if you don't already know it, your cousin never did worry about whether a man was white, brown, yellow or black. He was either deserving of respect or he was not. "You can kill an enemy," Savage'd say, "without either hating him or making war on his women and children".'

Brett gave a snort. 'Paul's Abolitionist cant was what made the rift between him and his family in the first place. He never did understand or accept the necessity of slavery.'

Patrick gave Beatrice a quick glance, and acknowledged her tight lips with a nod. 'Well, with respect, sir, considering I'm a guest in your house, I don't exactly hold with it myself.'

Melody jumped as Brett thumped a fist on the arm of his chair, tired of having yet another Abolitionist in his house. 'The Southland has a heart,' he argued with an intensity she never knew he possessed. 'And the Abolitionists are about to plunge a sword into that heart. The same sword has already divided other families than ours. Why, even our neighbour has lost a son—gone west for his beliefs, the fool, where there *are* no slaves, but for all that a man can work in the goldfields until he drops, doing the work of ten slaves, putting more into a day than the jackass he rides and coming out of it as poor.'

'Some do,' Patrick agreed. 'But some strike it rich, and even those that don't might consider it worth while just to escape an intolerable past.'

'You haven't told us how you met Paul,' Melody intervened, diverting the electricity that had crackled in the air a moment before.

Patrick accepted the diversion, giving a nod, his thoughts moving into the mists of time, bringing back the campfire and the pale-faced, slim young Louisiana gambler with eyes of ice who faced him over the deck of cards.

'I should never have gotten into the poker game in the first place,' he began, 'but when you're sick of the sight of fly-ridden corpses and the stench of blood and sweat and fear, anything that takes your mind off it is welcome. The boy with the old man's eyes was straight out of a New Orleans gambling house, but with the money of a good family backing him and their aristocratic blood in his every move. Even his clothes somehow appeared to stay clean, and I loathed him on sight. I'd spend every evening watching his play, and learning, planning my time. When that time came, there was quite a crowd watching the game—out under the stars, sitting on a fallen tree, its branches rotten and scattered about. Well . . . I'd had my fair share of that filthy liquor with the worm crawling in it—enough to affect my judgment as well as my concentration, though I'd never have admitted it at the time. When it came down to the two of us, I played wildly, I know that now, and of course he beat me easily. I was crazy enough to accuse him of cheating, he who had lived his whole life with the cards!'

Patrick's jaw tightened with the memory. 'He didn't even take offence, not then: he simply laughed at me. "I don't mind taking money off these ditch-digging, peat-bog peasants," he drawled, "but they're such damned poor losers, even those few who *aren't* too blind drunk to see their cards!" Well, it was like red rag to a bull. I leaped to my feet, calling him *and* his mother and father all the names under the sun, and threatening to tear off his arms and other parts of his anatomy, and . . . Begging your pardon, ladies . . . Well, then this quiet man came out of the crowd. "Back off, Irish," he said. The crowd had moved off when I'd got to my feet, and it was just the three of us, but I could feel all those eyes boring into my back. What I could *see* were two high-tone Southerners siding against a "peat-bog" Irishman, and I gave a kinda roar and lunged for the skinny runt, ready to tear *him* apart and then go on to the big man. But then, in that split second, two things happened that I hadn't counted on. The gambling man produced a squat, ugly little toy fit only for the ladies, but it was pointed straight between my eyes, and then something exploded at the back of my head.'

The Irishman gave a mirthless smile and a self-derogatory shrug. 'I found out later that your cousin, Mr Savage, had picked up a chunk of wood and hit me over the head with it. When I came to, it was just him and me all alone, with him bandaging my head and regarding me with a totally unrepentant grin. "What'd you use?" I says. "You coulda killed me!" "Maybe," he agrees, "but he *would* have killed you. All *I* did was to dent that thick Irish skull." Well, I can tell you I was a lot more wary of whom I crossed after that. I guess it was my shame that kept me away from Paul at first, but in time, through the battle of Chapultepec and on to Cherubusco, we found ourselves in each other's shadow and it was of some small comfort to me to have him on my side.'

'You mentioned something about a knife fight at that place,' probed Melody, and the Irishman gave another of those grim smiles that they had not previously associated with him.

'Not a fight, ma'am, not really. You see, there were all

sorts in that volunteer band—patriotic gentlemen, adventurers, and the occasional thing that had crawled out from under a rock at the scent of blood. The Bête Noire was one such—the "Black Beast" they called him, though his name was Pierre something-or-other. He was a Cajun 'gator-hunter from the bayous of New Orleans, and as stinking and ugly as the brutes he hunted. When he was sober he was mean, but on aguardiente he was a killer, and many was the man he'd beaten half to death or cut up with that great skinning-knife o' his. He picked on a young kid one time, a pretty young fop who never could keep his mouth shut about how much land his family owned and how many slaves. Well, we all know how children like to impress, especially when they're in an adult situation they can't deal with, and most of us would ignore him, but Paul was different, somehow. He had got it into his head that the right kind of education would reverse all this kid's teachings, broaden his horizons. He and the kid would argue all night long, being on opposite sides of the tracks, as you might say. Anyhows, the Beast began to hint at what the boy and your cousin were *really* up to out under the stars, and the fool kid lost his temper and jumped him.'

'I don't understand,' Melody said with a frown.

While Patrick had the grace to look uncomfortable, regretting his fool tongue running away with him, Beatrice merely patted her hand and told her, 'One day you will. Go on, Patrick.'

Looking relieved, he continued, 'Well, of course, by the time the fight, if you could call it that, was over, the kid was nigh on dead, and no one, not even his mother, would be able to look at him again without feeling bad. When your cousin came in from sentry duty and found out what had happened, he went straight to where the Beast slept, hauled him up and felled him with a right to the jaw, then hauled him to his feet again. By this time the brute had wakened and come to his senses. Within seconds they were rolling on the ground, punching and gouging like two half-wild animals. Paul rolled aside and gained his feet, then, as the Beast charged, he threw him over with one of those weird throws he'd learned, he said, from some Chinee cook on his travels. The crash shook the ground, and the man just lay there. O' course we was all gathered round by then and urging Paul to finish the animal off. We all hated him, you see, and most of us with good cause. But he, Beau Savage, just gave one o' them half smiles of his and walked over, holding out his hand to pull the other feller to his feet. "Leave a space around my friends and me in the future," he says, quiet like. Well, none of us saw the next move, but as he bent, the Beast came up with a knife from his boot and with a slash had laid your cousin's cheek open to the bone.'

Patrick's gaze returned from the past, and he gave a philosophical shrug. 'What happened next wasn't too pretty, so I'll not offend you ladies with it. The Beast died two days later, some sorta bleeding inside, they said, but there wasn't a man there who didn't welcome the news.'

There was a moment of silence as all in that room regained control of their errant thoughts, thoughts that had totally rejected the unbelievable violence of the men Patrick had described: men hardened to war, men released from that war as trained killers, not changed in character, but hardened, as one tempers steel into something far more deadly than the raw material.

Following that thought, Melody asked, 'What happened to you both after the war?'

Again that philosophical shrug. 'War isn't the way to make and keep friends, and Paul and I were too unalike for it to last. When we entered Mexico City in mid-September, we kinda lost touch. He just seemed to disappear. After the Treaty of Guadalupe Hidalgo in the February of '48, I moved north. America got the Rio Grande boundary, California and New Mexico, easy pickings for those who'd a mind to settle, but I'd seen enough dark skins and scrubland, and longed for clean sheets, blonde women and the soft fizz of good champagne.'

'And did you find them, Patrick?' Beatrice had a twinkle in her eye.

'I'm working on it, milady; always working on it. Mind you . . . ' Those wicked eyes roved over her face, and her hair, soft honey-brown in the firelight. 'I'm thinking of changing my mind about the blonde women!'

Even Beatrice had the grace to blush just a little, swiftly changing the subject. 'Your work, Patrick. Did you find work easily?'

He gave a slow shake of the head, spreading the huge hands palms upward, and gazing down at their iron hardness for a moment before answering. 'I had it easier than others, I guess. I was fit, healthy, and could turn my hands to a number of trades, quite literally. Being Irish, of course, was a two-edged sword. There were some who condemned us as robbers and illiterates, and others who saw us as cheap labour. I found work of one kind or another for enough of the time to keep from starving. It wasn't always pleasant and it wasn't always legal, I have to admit, but it was work. It did help that I'd been in a war that taught me the use of an assortment of lethal weapons.'

Beatrice knew that a small frown tugged at her brow, and had to say, 'Did you never question that path? There's surely something about those who live by the sword dying by the sword.'

His eyes cleared. 'Lord love you, ma'am,' he laughed, 'it wasn't a sword I was wielding, it was me shillelagh.'

Melody gave a choke. 'Your . . . what?'

'My shillelagh, missy: a fine stout oak cudgel that can crack a pate as if it were an egg . . . Oh, begging your pardon for my indelicacy.'

'Most . . . evocative, Mr O'Shaughnessy,' Beatrice remarked archly. 'But surely there is little future in . . . cracking pates.'

'Oh, I don't know,' he reflected. 'I once acted as chaperon and protector to a lady of considerable quality and affluence who suggested a more permanent situation after our journey from Washington to New York.'

'Was she beautiful?' Beatrice asked—immediately wishing her words had not slipped out, as that bright regard was turned on her in surprise.

He smiled then, a long, slow smile that washed over her, bringing unaccustomed waves of warmth that moved up from her toes. 'As I've said, ma'am, all ladies have something of beauty about them. This one had the prettiest hands under the sun . . . You're fishing, ma'am!'

'Rubbish!' she expostulated, blushing.

'Not at all. 'Tis a trait of the fair sex, and one which, thank the Lord, they never outgrow. The lady to whom I referred also had an insatiable curiosity about the other angels in my life . . . ' His grin became positively roguish. 'You'd think she would have outgrown it, her being all of seventy-two!'

This time Melody collapsed with laughter at her aunt's expression, folding up in paroxysms of giggles, her breath coming in gasps, taking several seconds to sober again.

Then Patrick's smiling eyes were on her. 'I've rarely heard such a wondrous sound,' he said. 'True merriment should always be so. You've a love of idiocy as strong as my own. I've a feeling we'll be true friends, and no one can pass over one of those . . . They're few and far between, like all rare treasures.'

Melody wiped her eyes and gave a final hiccup, covering her mouth with her hand as she caught her aunt's eye and suppressed the urge to dissolve again, but then Beatrice returned her smile.

'I'd allow this vagabond to talk all night if it would bring that light to your eyes again, sweeting, but I'm sure there are other things to do in this barn of a place. It must be near time to eat again, and I'm sure there will be nothing forthcoming without our supervision, so I suggest we leave the men to become better acquainted and take a look ourselves at the chaos of the kitchen.'

Reluctantly Melody followed her aunt from the room, feeling lighter in spirit than she had for weeks. 'I like Patrick around,' she remarked, and saw the slight curve that touched her aunt's lips.

'I wouldn't go so far as to say I *liked* him around,'
Beatrice judged, 'but he certainly brings a life to the place
that was lacking before. I suspect that is the way he goes
through all life. No one could possibly be quite the same
after having met him.' She gave her niece a sharp glance
over her shoulder, catching the grin. 'Not that I'm not
going to try,' she promised. 'The Patrick O'Shaughnessys
of this world may be impossible to forget, but equally
impossible to live with, so you can take that knowing
smile off your face.'

'Yes, Aunt Bee.'

'I have absolutely no intention of encouraging any
overtures of friendship from Mr O'Shaughnessy, despite
what he may believe.'

'No, Aunt Bee.'

'And the sooner we are away from his presence and
amid civilised people, the better.'

'Of course, Aunt Bee.'

'Melody?'

'Yes, Aunt Bee?'

'Be quiet, and take that silly grin off your face.'

'Yes, Aunt Bee.'

CHAPTER SEVEN

DURING THE WEEK that followed, it seemed to Melody that her terrible ordeal in London must surely have happened to someone else. It also became more and more apparent that she was rapidly falling in love with the man who could be her cousin. His natural vulnerability presented her with a hundred opportunities to touch him, to be close, and Brett, too, seemed to come alive under her ministrations.

Beatrice watched them together and worried, yet was unable to confide in anyone, and for the first time in her life she felt helpless, missing John Brown and his wise counsel. She knew that Melody must be warned, yet could not find the words that would prevent her from getting hurt. She had once tried to bring out their obviously opposing views on slavery, asking her whether she could ever live happily on a plantation whose very lifeblood depended on people who could be bought and sold like cattle, but the girl would not be drawn.

'People's views can change,' she had replied enigmatically.

Now, making little attempt to read the book she had found, Melody dreamed of what might have been, and, if this faceless Paul Savage lived up to the faith Brett had in him, what still might be. She looked up with a start at Beatrice's hand on her shoulder.

'Take care, sweeting,' she advised. 'He is very much like Hugh, and even more attractive, and you are terribly vulnerable just now.'

Melody felt herself blushing as her aunt read her innermost thoughts with uncanny accuracy. 'Don't worry, Aunt Bee, I shall keep a tight rein on every emotion—at least until I find out whether we are related.' But she knew that she lied, knew that already her heart was planning a future that might never materialise.

'And then?' Beatrice persisted. 'Can you really afford to consider taking on a destitute blind man and an unknown path ahead?'

Melody's full lips tightened a fraction. 'I'm not afraid of the unknown. Even to make a bare living with a gentle, considerate husband by one's side must surely be worth the challenge. I can accept hard work, and thanks to Father, I can tally accounts and run a household if necessary. I'm not much of a cook, but I can learn, and I can sew a little, even though I've never actually made a dress. I can ride, and know all about horses.'

'And cattle? And killing chickens? Slaughtering pigs? And planting vegetables, hoeing and weeding? How about chopping wood, building fences, drawing water—all the things your husband might do if he could see? That's the life a poor white can look forward to, with no servants or slaves because you'll not have enough to afford them. And you'll take time off only to bear a child each year until the body is too worn and the mind too numb to carry on; then to know that you still have yet another child to take care of, a beautiful, helpless, *blind* child! Much as he may *love* you, he'll be of no *use* to you whatsoever.'

'Aunt Bee, you're being deliberately cruel!'

'No, my dear, I'm being realistic. Someone has to burst that brilliant bubble you've been creating for yourself over the past week or so.'

Melody gazed into her lap, the tears close, knowing that she spoke the truth, her harsh words coming only out of love and a desire to save her from pain. 'Do I love him enough?' she murmured, searching her soul.

'Do you love him at all?' Beatrice countered. 'Or have you been blinded by his undoubted good looks and remarkably sweet nature . . . at least where you're concerned. He is a gem, my dear, and, but for his obvious misunderstanding of the basic rights of humanity, I'd adore him as a relative, but I'd never in a hundred years consider him as a husband.'

'It's true that he doesn't have a convenient fortune!' Melody shot back angrily, then clapped a hand over her mouth in horror. 'Oh, I'm sorry. I'm so very sorry. I didn't mean that! Please forgive me, Aunt Bee.'

The grey eyes that had turned icy at her remark slowly softened. 'Apology accepted. Of course, you were quite wrong. Had I needed only an offered fortune to marry, I shouldn't be in this present predicament. It's true that I shall probably spend the rest of my days as an unlovable, irascible old spinster, for I've long given up hope of finding that indefinable quality that I need in a man.'

'But surely dozens of men have asked you? Have you met no one, ever, who gave you a moment's doubt?'

Her face became sad for a bare, almost imperceptible, instant, but then Beatrice said, 'We all do foolish things in our youth; embracing danger as a game and believing ourselves invulnerable. There *was* a man—very much a man—who said he loved me. I certainly loved him, and even now a certain tilt of a head, a turn of a hand . . . ' She returned to the present with a fleeting smile that did not quite reach her eyes. 'He held the wrong political views for some, and was killed for them.' She said it quickly, her voice tight and encouraging no questions, but then her smile widened. 'Still, all that is history, and I've lived well since . . . '

Suddenly, with a clatter of riding-boots, Patrick burst in from his visit to the nearby town. He brought the fresh country scents with him, and his rugged features were wind-tanned from his gallop back.

Beatrice's eyes lit up at the approach of that giant frame, but her voice was as caustic as ever. 'You have a habit of charging about the house like a rampaging bull, Patrick! We were quite enjoying the peace your outings allow us, and here you dare to return hours early!'

A twinkle appeared in his bright eyes, lightening his previously serious expression. 'I can't object to being likened to a bull: 'tis me nature, you see. Neither can I make any excuse for disturbing your peace, since I came south to do just that.' Then he grew serious again. 'This time, though, 'twas more than my pleasure in disturbing you that made me cut short my visit—just as I happened to be partaking of some liquid refreshment, too.'

'You were in a saloon,' Beatrice remarked, cutting across his nonsense. 'And not the first, I'd imagine.'

But this time he would not be drawn into their usual banter. 'It was there I overheard your name, Beatrice.' Immediately he had their undivided attention, and Melody felt a prickle at the nape of her neck. 'Two men,' he continued, 'conspicuous by their anonymity, if you understand. Medium height and build, brownish hair and eyes, clothes off-the-peg of any store. They were talking quiet-like, so I caught only the odd word, but it appeared that they have contacts in London who are looking for you.'

'Are you sure it was Aunt Bee they mentioned, and not myself?' Melody had to ask, but was still not reassured by his positive nod of the head.

'It was definitely your aunt, and if they did mention your name, I didn't catch it. They were Northerners, too, and if they weren't Pinkertons, my name's not Patrick Aloysius O'Shaughnessy.' To Beatrice, he said, 'The Pinkerton detective agency is like an octopus with tentacles that reach out all over America. Some are bumbling fools, but the majority are dedicated and ruthless men. If *they* are looking for you, milady, it'll be only a matter of time before they find you . . . though I think you've a little longer now than you had.'

'How so, Patrick?'

For a second he had the grace to look embarrassed, studying his hands, but then looked up with a twinkle. 'The two I'm speaking of were of the former type, thank the Saints, and after a long and thoroughly trying search they were as eager as two speckled pups over a bone when I told them I'd heard of you . . . that I had kept company, very brief but pleasurable company, with a maid o' yours just the week before . . . in New Orleans.'

Beatrice gave a gurgle of laughter. 'Patrick, I have

hopes for you yet! By the time they've combed a town that size they'll be at their wits' end, and we'll be far away from here.'

Melody put her hand shyly over his, drawing a blush from him. 'We're again in your debt for a timely rescue, Patrick, and are more than grateful. Whoever instigated the search won't give up, but we *must* stay until Nanny gets back and I can question her about my background. You've bought us time for that.' She turned to her aunt. 'I'll go up to change for dinner. Under your tuition, the cook has actually begun to enjoy her position! I doubt that anyone has encouraged her to use her skills for a very long time, and there's nothing worse than an employer's lack of interest for encouraging laziness and apathy. I'll wear the taffeta, I think, and a little rose-water to celebrate your victory over the huntsmen, Patrick.'

Once in her room, however, Melody sank on to the bed and covered her face with her hands. Would the past never die? Would Luther Hogge's power continue to haunt her even after his death? 'Oh, hurry, Nanny!' she prayed aloud. 'I can't begin a new life without knowing who I am . . . And it will be an exceedingly empty life without Brett to care for, if the answer's not in our favour.'

Two days later her prayers were answered . . . changing her life in a way that none of that close-knit group could have visualised in their wildest fantasies. The two women were rocking gently on the porch, basking in an unseasonably warm sun, when Beatrice broke off the conversation and shaded her eyes with her hand as she looked down the long road.

'A carriage! I wonder if we're to be blessed with company, or simply with the return of the intrepid Nanny and her scheming offspring! I still say that girl is up to something with her newly-laundered looks.'

Melody felt her heart beat faster, but kept her voice miraculously steady. 'I could well do without Celine, but it will be good to have Nanny back and be able to resolve my position here, once and for all.' Then, as the occupants were recognised, 'It is Nanny! I'll go and tell Brett.' But for a moment, as she reached the silent dimness of the hall, she allowed her poise to drop, and her knuckles whitened as she clasped her hands before her. '*Quo fata ferunt*,' she whispered, quoting a favourite phrase of her father: As the Fates direct. 'Oh, please let them be directed towards me!'

When they arrived, Celine was ordered to her room, but Nanny was immediately summoned to the drawing-room by an impatient Brett, who, after briefly murmured condolences on the death of her daughter, said, 'There is something that only you can help us with, Nanny. Something of the greatest importance concerning Mrs Van der Veer.'

She gave a slight inclination of the head, waiting impassively, still mourning the death of her beautiful, proud daughter who had worked without complaint until her illness was too far advanced ever to be cured, simply because the people who had bought her had treated her with trust and respect.

Not quite knowing how to begin, Brett suggested, 'Pour brandy for me first; and something for the ladies, if they wish.'

Beatrice went to stand by the window, where she could observe both Brett and her niece. 'I think we may need a measure of the same, whether we want it or not,' she commented.

'Did I hear the chink of a glass?' Patrick asked from the doorway, striding in from his daily ride about the surrounding countryside, smelling of fresh breezes, the tang of his own perspiration mingled with that of his horse. He caught the atmosphere at once and immediately apologised, 'Sorry. Have I interrupted something? I'll take me drink and meself to the library.'

'No, please stay,' Melody implored. 'As our dearest friend, you have every right to know. Doesn't he, Brett?'

After only the briefest hesitation, he nodded. 'Of course. We were just about to ask Nanny about Melody's parents. If anyone knows, she will.'

Patrick turned to the negress, who had halted in her pouring of the brandy awaiting the newcomer's request. 'Bourbon for me, Nanny. Beatrice, is that a touch of brandy I see in your glass?'

'No, it's a very *large* brandy you see in my glass. Is that a touch of disapproval that I see?'

The Irishman gave a chuckle, taking his drink and crossing to join her. 'No, it's a large measure of admiration, but more of that another time. I'd hate to hold up the proceedings.'

Brett compelled himself to relax. 'Nanny . . . There is a possibility that Mrs Van der Veer and I are related through her mother's side of the family. Her father, Lady Davenport's brother, visited St Clare many years ago. You remember, the man I called Uncle Alex, who came shortly before . . . before my accident?' He gave a forced laugh. 'Quite a romantic story really. Apparently he fell in love with a young woman who lived here then, possibly a cousin or a house-guest, though I don't remember a lady being here for any length of time . . . One of Mother's friends, perhaps.'

'All we know,' Melody broke in eagerly, 'is that my mother had a most unusual name, Ereanora. *Did* you know of her?'

She had been watching Nanny's face with taut expectancy, but nothing could have prepared her for the change that her words wrought on the darkly aristocratic features. The black eyes flew wide; incredulity, shock—and something akin to pain—draining the colour from her face and leaving it a sickly grey-brown. Her hand closed over a chair-back as she swayed, searching the girl's face before closing her eyes spasmodically for an instant, murmuring, 'So you came back!' There was an electric silence in the room, a silence so intense that one felt that the smallest sound would shatter the crystals of the chandelier.

Then Beatrice gently asked, 'Who was Ereanora, Nanny?'

She never took her eyes from Melody, assessing,

deciding, then, with a small tightening of the skin over
the fine bones, answered strongly, 'Ereanora was my
daughter.'

For an instant time stood still; then, as realisation came,
something exploded inside Melody's head. Flashes of
multi-coloured lightning burst behind her eyes. She heard
nothing of the exclamations and disbelieving gestures of
the others. She knew that she was shaking her head, but
no sound would emerge from the parted lips, no scream
of repudiation, though deep inside, every nerve-ending,
every fibre of her being, denied such an awful truth.

Brett's face turned chalk white, then, with a gesture of
total rejection, he flung his cane towards the negress. 'No!'
he ground out. 'You lie! I could *never* love a nigra. I'd
know! I'd know!'

These were the last words Melody heard, as mercifully
she slipped to the floor in a dead faint.

'Damned fool!' Patrick stated uncompromisingly,
striding across to lift the unconscious girl in his arms. 'I'll
take her to her room. Beatrice, she'll need you.'

The woman's grey eyes were still shocked, and held
betraying tears. 'More than ever in her life before,' she
agreed softly. She cast a glance at Brett, who, after that
one brief outburst of fury, had stumbled to the high
fireplace and now stood, back towards them, head dropped
on his arm, slamming his clenched fist rhythmically against
the wood as though the very pain would negate the awful
truth. 'He'll need help, too,' she murmured. 'But it's only
a dream he's lost.' Opening the door for Patrick and his
burden, Beatrice thought she saw a flash of red silk
disappear through the adjoining door, but her mind was
too full to give it any thought. 'It would have been better
for her to stand trial for murder and be well defended
than to have come to this!'

'Murder?' asked Patrick, but gently, and with no
judgment in his tone.

Beatrice gave him a long look as he strode effortlessly
up the wide staircase. Then, with a deciding nod, she told
him the whole story as succinctly as possible.

'Poor lass,' he said, laying his burden tenderly on the bed, then he growled, 'I'd have killed the brute myself had I been there, with my bare hands, and taken pleasure in the act! Ah, but this little soul. What it must have cost her . . . And now this.'

Melody gave a low moan and then a sob as consciousness returned. The lovely sapphire eyes were bright with pain, and she mutely reached for her aunt's hand and found it firmly clasped.

'You'll be just fine,' Patrick assured her awkwardly, and Melody raised a bleak smile.

'You have no need to stay, Mr O'Shaughnessy,' she said gently, her quiet dignity tearing at his heart. 'I'll quite understand if you'd rather not acknowledge our acquaintanceship under the circumstances.'

His brows shot up. 'What is it you're saying? Did I hear you right?'

Melody lowered her gaze to her free hand that plucked convulsively at her skirt.

'Now you listen to me,' Patrick continued, his voice a quiet explosion of feeling. 'I've known some mighty high-tone women in my time, but nary a one had your beauty, or your brains, and not one of them came within a thousand miles of being as much of a lady. If it takes a smidgin of black blood to achieve that, then I'd wish the world were a great melting-pot so's we could all benefit. Isn't that right, Beatrice?' He turned—and stopped, puzzled by the strange light in those usually cool grey eyes.

A slow smile curved her mouth, taking his breath away. 'Whatever you say, Patrick.' She turned to Melody and gave her hand a squeeze. 'You're no different, sweeting, and neither are we. No one else matters.'

Melody felt the warmth of their loyalty, but it was from the heart that she spoke. 'I *am* different, and others do matter,' she murmured, holding back the tears, Brett's last terrible words still ringing in her head. She looked up, and met the Irishman's sympathetic gaze. 'You once offered to be our escort. Does that offer still hold?'

'You know it does. You'll not be rid of me so easily this time! I've nothing to hold me anywhere, and own nothing but what's in my bags, so I'll be with you until you tell me to leave.'

'Aunt Bee, do we have enough money to take some small lodgings in New York? Patrick knows the city, and until we decide on our future, it seems the best place to be. They don't mind . . . negroes . . . there!'

'Stop that!' Beatrice ordered sharply. 'Your mother was an octoroon, just one-eighth part black. That doesn't even make you coloured in any other State, so enough of lashing at yourself like this! We'll go to New York if you wish, and I can write to John from there. There's no need to give him any details; just that it didn't work out here. He'll find us something.'

'John?' Patrick queried with careful nonchalance.

'A friend,' Beatrice answered, giving him a direct look. 'An old and trusted friend who is very dear to me.'

A small muscle tightened in his jaw while he took count of his heart, but he met her gaze levelly. 'Close friends are God's own blessing. He must be quite a man to earn your regard. I hope you'll always have such people by you.'

Again that deep warmth lit her eyes, but she merely nodded and returned her attention to her charge. 'Are you ready to go downstairs again, sweeting?'

Melody put down the swift leap of panic and took a deep breath. 'It has to be done, doesn't it? We can't leave without thanking our . . . host . . . ' But her voice choked on the word, and, unable to say more, she allowed Beatrice to help her to her feet.

In silence the three descended the staircase, lost in their own thoughts: two conscious only of the girl between them, Melody summoning every ounce of strength and dignity she possessed to face Brett and the awful condemnation she was sure she would find in that perfect face. At the door to the drawing-room, she turned to lay a firm hand on her aunt's shoulder. 'I must see him alone, Aunt Bee.'

'I wouldn't think of allowing you . . . '

'Wait. I must.' She gave a tremulous smile. 'I should imagine that Brett's hurt is almost as great as my own just now. To support *me*, I have two loyal and wonderful people. He has no one. Allow me to talk to him, if he'll let me, and then we'll make our final arrangements.'

Brett had not moved from the fireplace but now stood, jaw tight, staring sightlessly into the flames. At her entrance, he straightened swiftly. 'Nanny? I don't want to be disturbed just now . . . especially by you. You've done enough.'

'It's not Nanny, but I'll go if you wish.'

'Melody!' The storm of emotion that raged across his face, the joy and fear and despair, set her heart racing. She wanted to run to him, to hold him close as she had after the carriage-ride, but then, remembering his last terrible renunciation, merely said, 'I came only to say goodbye. I know you'll agree that it's best. We shall be leaving tomorrow for New York.'

'No!' He stumbled forward, almost falling over a stool, kicking it aside, those incredibly perceptive senses lost in the trauma of the moment, coming to her with hand outstretched until she could stand it no longer and met him half-way. 'Oh, Melody!' It was a cry torn from the heart as he clasped her against him, holding her close, crushing the will from her as though by his very strength he could close the chasm between them. 'Forgive me. Please forgive me!'

As that bone-crushing grip loosened a fraction, she could raise her eyes to his face, drawn now with emotion . . . and was lost. Of its own volition, her hand crept to the tumbled hair, and her wrist was seized and brought to his lips. 'Say you won't leave! You've brought the only warmth I've ever had in a cold, lonely life. I couldn't take that again.'

There was a choking sensation in her throat. 'I won't leave you.' Then, more firmly, 'No one need know, and it's not as if I'm . . . really coloured . . . in colour, I mean. Brett, I do look white!'

He looked unhappy. 'You may be as white-skinned as I, but the books take no account of appearance.'

'Books?'

'The slave-log of St Clare. You will be listed as Ereanora's daughter, and, as such, a slave born into slavery and the property of . . . ' His face suddenly drained of colour, and there was a look of such fear on his face that Melody felt faint.

'Brett? Brett! What is it? What are you saying? I don't belong to anyone! I'm English. My father was an English lord.'

Slowly, as if in a dream, he shook his head. 'Your father and mother never married. They couldn't have here; so, according to the law, you take the status of your mother.'

'But that's wrong! That's terribly wrong! That means Celine and I . . . ' Her words faded as the horrified realisation dawned. 'No . . . it can't be! Oh, Brett, I must leave. You can't ask me to stay. Not now.'

'Celine doesn't know, and I can make sure that Nanny says nothing. Melody, I can't let you go.' One hand moved to the back of her neck as his other slipped about her waist. 'Please? It can be so good between us.' His voice was husky with longing, and as those perfect features moved closer, she closed her eyes a moment before his mouth found hers.

With a tiny sob, Melody clung to him. Wasn't this where she had longed to be? Had she not dreamed of those surprisingly strong arms about her, those mobile lips crushing hers, parting them as his tongue probed inward? Then why was her heart not pounding? Why was she not afire, or experiencing lightning flashes behind her eyes?

His mouth was withdrawn, and he looked puzzled. 'You do love me, Melody?'

Guilty and confused, she kissed him lightly. 'It's all too much for me to cope with now. Of course I love you.' She saw the joy wash over his face, but when he would have pulled her back into his embrace, she slipped free.

'Give me a little time, my dear. Let me talk to Aunt Bee and Patrick, and tell them we'll be staying.'

'Of course. You must be brave, Melody, and patient. We must both come to terms with the situation.' He gave a shaky laugh. 'Things aren't so different really. I was upset at first, of course. What man wouldn't be? Seeking to marry a young and beautiful English aristocrat, and then finding she's . . . Well, no matter. I would have made you mine, but find that you are mine already.'

'Brett, please!' Melody interrupted, something cold touching her spine at his words. 'I must find the others. I'll join you again later.'

Predictably, Beatrice and Patrick were totally against her decision and did all in their power to change her mind, but she remained adamant. 'I must face this. I must, to use Brett's words, come to terms with the situation,' she stated firmly. 'I shan't do that by running away. Brett has apologised for his words, blurted out in shock, and . . . Oh, Aunt Bee, I truly believe he loves me. He certainly *needs* me! I can't leave him now.'

The Irishman gave a disapproving snort. 'I sure hope the young man realises how lucky he is! Now, it seems, the first thing we must do is to get rid of any records connecting you with St Clare.'

'Brett mentioned some books listing all the slaves born. Shall I ask him for them?'

'No, little one. For all your trust and love, the boyo is still a Southerner. I'll find the books myself. This Wilkinson fella isn't due for a few days, so we've time enough to turn the place upside-down.'

But, as Melody had said so prophetically earlier, *Quo fata ferunt*—As the Fates direct. And the fates can be as capricious as they are often cruel. By mid-afternoon the following day, O'Shaughnessy still had not found the elusive ledger—and in a cloud of expensive Havana, Elliott Wilkinson arrived early at St Clare.

CHAPTER EIGHT

HE GREETED BRETT expansively, but the heavy-lidded eyes swept about the room with the swift assessment of an abacus—coming to rest on Melody, and only then lighting with genuine admiration. 'Won't you introduce us, Mister Savage, sir?' His accent dripped molasses, but not one person in the room was lulled into a false sense of security, and the air seemed to vibrate as Brett cleared his throat.

'Mrs Van der Veer and . . . and her aunt, Lady Davenport, from England. Their friend and escort, Mr O'Shaughnessy. The ladies are my—my house-guests.'

Beatrice saw the puzzlement creep over the man's face, and stepped forward with a completely natural laugh. 'Brett, you'll have Mr Wilkinson gaining all sorts of wrong impressions! It's my fault entirely that we are here at all, Mr Wilkinson. My dear departed brother, Mrs Van der Veer's father, knew Brett's mother, a sweet girl and a neighbour of ours before she came here to marry. Well, of course, being *such* dear friends, she just begged him to come for a holiday and meet her husband. He spent the longest time here and simply adored the place, so I couldn't wait until I'd seen it myself. Well, you know how the years just fly by . . . the London season, balls, the opera. Well, by the time we got round to it, we never dreamed that Brett's father had also died, or I'd *never* have intruded. But Brett has been an absolute treasure—the epitome of your justifiably famous Southern hospitality.'

Patrick O'Shaughnessy appeared to have developed a sudden fit of coughing, and Melody turned away to give her embroidery unwarranted attention, but the newcomer was obviously captivated.

'I do hope that we are able to make your visit as memorable as your late brother's, Lady Davenport. I myself am planning to stay a few days on some business that Mr Savage and I have to conduct—business that has suddenly become a very real pleasure, if you don't mind my saying so, ma'am.' But it was to the averted profile of the girl that those gin-trap eyes flashed.

'So kind,' Beatrice cooed. 'But business is just too much for my silly head. Come, Melody dear, we'll leave Mr Wilkinson and Brett to their . . . business. Perhaps a game of backgammon. You can watch, Patrick. I'll not play with you again, since you were so ungentlemanly as to win last time, but you have an amusing fund of stories that appear to make Melody lose her concentration, so I win either way.'

'My pleasure. Mr Wilkinson, your servant.'

'Until dinner, sir.'

The moment the door closed behind them, Beatrice dropped her empty-headed, simpering air like an ill-fitting cloak, and her lips tightened. 'The library. We must find that ledger, or there could be a number of awkward questions asked, and I've far less faith in Nanny's silence than Brett has.'

'Why don't we ask her if she knows where the book is?' Melody suggested. 'She seems to know everything else that happens round here.'

Beatrice looked uncertain, but Patrick gave a decisive nod. 'We need the woman's help, and her support. If Melody *is* her grand-daughter, as she says, surely she'll do all in her power to protect her, but whatever happens we must leave here tomorrow. There's a while left, so if you ladies can find an excuse for my sudden disappearance, I'll ride into town and make arrangements.'

'Go, then' Beatrice urged, cutting across Melody's automatic objection, her every nerve prickling with a sense of danger. There was no reason at all for her to feel the tight knotting of her stomach, but it was there, as it had been once or twice before in her life, and experience told her to heed its warning.

In the library, she pulled the cord to summon Nanny, and found herself fuming at the woman's slow approach. There was no need to hurry now, she realised. They were all equal in the slave's eyes.

'Yes'm?' Nanny asked, coming to a halt just inside the door, the fine features expressionless.

Beatrice took a deep breath, but it was Melody who moved forward.

'Nanny, I need your help.'

Dark brown, almost black, eyes met sapphire-blue, and there was a fraction of softening there. 'You must go from here.'

'We shall . . . tomorrow, but first I need more than just your word that I'm . . . who you say I am. There is a book, a ledger, with all the names. I must know whether *my* name is there. It's my future I'm fighting for, so I can't simply take your word for it. You must understand.'

Almost regretfully, Nanny nodded her head. 'Melody he called you. Melody for the sweet music he said they'd made. Lady Melody he called you. I was there. I told him to take you. Never even knew his real name. Just "Mistah Alex" everyone called him. Didn't act like no lord—just like a fine gentleman. No airs and graces like some of them pretend to have who come from your country. Yes, missy, I told him to take you and make you white. Saw him put you into his coat and ride off. You had the blackest hair and bluest eyes I ever did see. You were so beautiful, even then.'

Melody felt the tears pricking her eyes, but still she had to persist. 'Mr Wilkinson is here. He will be going through the books. If Mr Savage's brother Paul doesn't raise the money to save St Clare, the property will be sold. Brett will have nowhere to go, and as long as no one knows who I am, I can help him . . . stay with him.'

The fine nostrils flared. '*I* shall stay with him, like always. *I'll* take care of him, me and my Celine . . . like always. Best for you to go. Anyways . . . ' She turned, one hand on the door-handle. 'Mr Wilkinson, he took the books last time he came. He's already got a list of everything that's to be sold. Celine and me, we'll stay. You'll see.'

Melody felt the chill creep into her as Nanny—her grandmother—left, closing the door firmly behind her. She felt Aunt Bee's comforting arm about her and raised a mirthless smile. 'I tried!'

'Of course, but there comes a time in most battles when a strategic withdrawal is quite in order.' She put her head to one side at the sound of men's voices, and going to investigate, returned with a frown. 'Some friends, if one can call them that, of Mr Wilkinson. I think it best if we repair to our rooms until dinner is served. They aren't the kind of company I'd encourage you to keep, and, if my eyes are as good as I believe in assessing male attire, both were wearing guns beneath their coats.'

It was with relief, therefore, that Melody found only Brett and Elliott Wilkinson in the dining-room when she entered, and both rose, smiling. She noticed the lines of strain about Brett's mouth and her heart went out to him, so that when he held out a hand, she hurried to take it and to reassure him with a quick squeeze of the fingers.

'I see that you two young people have become real good friends.' Wilkinson beamed, but the smile somehow never reached his eyes.

'Yes, we have,' Melody answered, her quiet dignity forestalling further comment. 'Did I hear other company arriving, Brett?'

'Hardly company,' Wilkinson laughed. 'They're my men. We've a coffle coming down from Virginia for the auction.'

'A coffle?'

'Yes, ma'am. A string of slaves. They don't usually give any trouble when they've been pushed a few mile, but I'm after some prime bucks for my place and I've been told there are some Mandingoes in the bunch. Then again, much depends on what tomorrow brings, as far as St Clare goes.'

'But you gave me to the end of the week!' Brett objected.

'Well, sure I did, Mr Savage, but that's for the house and the surrounding five acres. You've already contracted the slaves and the rest of the land over to me. You got twenty-five half-way useless field hands out there with a half-dozen or so suckers. Ain't looked at your house-wenches yet, but that's what I'm here for. If your brother don't get back with cover money, I'll put your people up with the coffle that's due for auction. I've not seen anything that's any use to me, but I've loaned you a fair-sized amount, Mr Savage, so I'm looking for repayment, nothing more nor less. I'm not an unjust man, but I'm still a business-man first and foremost. I surely do appreciate your situation, and I've helped you all I can, but it's time for you to honour your debts. Your slaves belong to me anyway, but I'll have to take St Clare, too, if you can't raise enough.' He glanced at Melody, then took a step forward. 'You okay, ma'am? I declare, you're as white as a ghost.'

'Yes . . . Yes . . . Silly of me! All this talk of buying and selling people . . . '

'Why, ma'am, you can't think of them as people, not like us. They are just nigras.' He moved to pat her hand. 'I can tell you're a real English lady. We Southerners know it's a God-given right to trade slaves. Why, their own people do it all the time. They don't have real feelings like other folks . . . I guess it's the sun that does something to their brains over the generations.'

Saved from answering by Beatrice's entrance, Melody put down her sick anger and concentrated on her food, tasting nothing.

'Your . . . friend not joining us?' Wilkinson asked Beatrice.

'Not this evening.' She smiled into his eyes, and Melody wondered at the woman's acting ability, knowing her contempt for the man. 'Patrick is, as you say, a friend . . . Just a friend, who has friends of his own, and by all accounts a fair number of them. I believe that this evening's companion has a Louisiana accent and an affluent father—a lethal combination, wouldn't you say, Mr Wilkinson?'

'Not half as powerful a force as that right here, nor could she be possibly half as lovely,' he answered with a leer, and the subject was adroitly changed.

Somehow Melody got through the seemingly endless evening and the even longer night. She heard Patrick return just before dawn, and felt a small sense of relief. The very size of him would diminish any problem she might encounter from Wilkinson and his men, of that she was sure.

Breakfast was a restrained affair, with Patrick only having time for a brief word of reassurance that there was a fast carriage and pair awaiting them at a neighbouring plantation. 'The family there have already freed their slaves,' he murmured *sotto voce*, and at the moment their eldest boy is a conductor on this Underground Railway that helps runaways to reach the North. If you can't go as Mrs Van der Veer, then, B'Jesus, you'll go as a runaway slave, and we'll be with you every step of the way, missy.' He gave her an encouraging wink, conveying a reassurance that he was far from feeling, having already assessed the slaver's acquisitive and razor-sharp nature to perfection.

The man in question disappeared immediately after the meal to inspect the house and servants, with little respect for Brett's feelings or privacy. Conversation was strained, and conducted in spasmodic little bursts until Melody was forced to ask, 'Brett . . . is there any chance of your brother returning before the end of the week, and with enough to buy St Clare and its people?'

He gave a deep sigh, looking much older in that instant than his twenty-seven years. Slowly he reached into a pocket and withdrew a letter. 'This came yesterday. I usually ask Nanny to read my mail, but couldn't bring myself to do so in the circumstances.' Mutely he held out the envelope, and with shaking fingers Melody opened it.

There were just four short sentences, written in a

strongly slanted hand. 'All legal methods unsuccessful. You appear to have few friends and fewer sponsors. Have one final card to play and think I have a Royal Flush, but will return Saturday regardless. Promise Wilkinson anything until then.' It was not even signed.

Melody raised her eyes to the set faces about her, and her heart sank. To leave Brett to this, to allow him to face that unfeeling monster alone!

'We can do nothing,' Beatrice stated firmly, reading her niece's innermost thoughts with her usual accuracy. 'Much as we would like to stay, there is an obvious danger here, however small. At the very least, Melody could suffer extreme embarrassment if this man found out about her relationship to Nanny.'

'But he won't!' Brett insisted. 'No one knows. Nanny wouldn't say anything, and even if she did, who's going to take the word of a nigra against four whites?'

'Three whites,' Melody corrected softly.

'No, I won't have you leave . . .'

'Leaving us?' Wilkinson spoke from the doorway. 'Surely you can't be thinking of such a thing? I shall suppose it had something to do with my arrival.' He came into the room, a thick ledger under one arm. He had dressed carefully for dinner, his black evening dress a decade behind the times, but the thinning hair brushed forward to hide the receding hairline was oiled to a sheen, his nails manicured, and the slightly corpulent frame corseted tightly. The two women exchanged glances, as visions of Luther Hogge came sharply to their minds.

'I heard of some unfinished business in New York,' Patrick improvised with a dismissive gesture, 'and the ladies were going to leave in a few days anyway, so they were kind enough to allow me to meet my deadlines. Your own business is with Mr Savage here, and I'm sure you're as eager to see it concluded as I am mine. Did you find all that you were looking for? Mr Savage has allowed me the pleasure of riding over the whole of St Clare, not to mention a fair portion of the surrounding countryside— and most beautiful your Southland is too, sir. Should there be any way in which I can help you with your inventory before we leave . . . '

Wilkinson forced a thin smile. 'That won't be necessary, though I thank you for your kindness, sir.' He turned to Brett with a sigh. 'Your house-people are almost as useless as the field hands, though the buck called Samson should sell well, and that white nigra, Celine. She'll fetch a real good price.'

'No!' Brett leaped to his feet, knocking over a small side-table as he spun to face the plantation-owner. 'You can't sell Celine, or Nanny. They're all I have!' Then he blenched, and his unseeing eyes swung towards Melody. 'You said you were leaving . . . '

Wilkinson's sharp eyes missed nothing, as the girl's colour drained from her face and he saw the deep hurt there, Brett's betrayal burning deep. 'You've no need to heed Mr Savage's words,' he stated tersely, his contempt for the man coming through as he contemplated the impossibility of *any* white man not fighting to keep this incredibly beautiful woman by his side by whatever means possible. But already she was backing toward the door. 'All the slaves will be sold, Mrs Van der Veer, including the wench Celine. I'm running a business, not a philanthropic society!'

There was a muffled cry at his words, and the door beside Melody crashed open as Celine burst into the room. 'You don't sell me!' she cried. 'I hear at door. You don't never sell me. Tell them, Mastah Brett. You wouldn't *never* sell your Celine!'

There was an instant of shocked silence as she stood there, magnificent in her fear and anger, resplendent in crimson satin, full breasts heaving over the extreme décolleté neckline, and Wilkinson let his tongue touch his lips. Then those heavy-lidded eyes hardened. 'You don't belong to Mr Savage, wench. You never did. He contracted every slave in this here book as collateral for his *last* loan. I'll get enough for you to start next year's cotton crop, and maybe re-build a barn or two that the storms took last month.'

'I won't go!' Celine sobbed, but then her fierce eyes turned toward Melody, and at that instant the girl knew the depth of her jealous hatred. 'Well, what'll you get for *this* white nigger then? Tell me how many barns she's worth.'

Three people spoke at once, but Wilkinson's eyes only narrowed, hiding the shock of her words. 'Hold your lying tongue, girl,' he warned softly. 'You've already earned yourself a flogging.'

'I ain't lying, Mistah! This here high-tone white nigra is my half-sister. Didn't you hear Mistah Brett? If'n he can't have *her* in his bed, he'll come back to me. It's all the same. A white nigra is just like a real whitey, 'cept we knows a heap more tricks. You ask her her mammy's name. It's Ereanora, same as mine. It's in the book. Nanny's our gramama. You'll see.'

Panting, she turned her burning gaze to Melody. 'I was outside the door when you found you was black. I know why you leaving but you'll just be one runaway nigra slave if'n you leave now. You been tryin' to take Mistah Brett away from me with your soft voice and simperin' ways, but you don't get him *now*, Miss High-Tone!'

Brett's features contorted. 'I should have sold you down-river months ago, but as God is my judge, Celine, if your new owners don't kill you, I shall!'

Slowly Wilkinson crossed to the bureau and opened the ledger, and for one wild instant Melody felt the urge to flee in blind panic. But then her aunt's arms came round her, holding her tightly and stilling the trembling that shook her frame. 'It can't be!' Melody whispered in disbelief. 'This can't be happening!'

The slaver had turned, and there was an ugliness in his expression that caused Celine to take a pace back. 'Well, you sure had me fooled! All of you. Hiding the prize of the lot. What was it? Some kind of conspiracy? Something you'd planned even before I got here?'

'Now, just a minute!' Beatrice objected, stepping forward as if to protect Melody from his glare, but he stopped her with a dismissive chopping gesture of his hand.

'Enough from you, too. This here book says: "Melody. Female child. Beget of Ereanora." And we none of us dispute who *she* was. In Louisiana, I'd miss this bargain because it says your mammy was an octoroon, but here in North Carolina you're a nigra, and I'll make a fortune on you.'

'Over my dead body!' Patrick O'Shaughnessy growled, and leapt forward, but at a shout from Wilkinson the door was flung open and his two henchmen appeared, each carrying a long-muzzled revolver.

The Irishman spun, eyes blazing, but Melody cried out, 'No!' halting his projected charge. 'Please, Patrick. Not for me. They'll kill you!'

'There's a sensible wench!' Wilkinson said, breathing more easily, and to his men, 'Take him to the barn. I want him hog-tied until this business is over.'

Again Patrick made to attack, prepared to tackle even the deadly fire-power that faced him in defence of the girl he had come to regard as his own responsibility, but Melody ran to place herself in front of him, clinging to his arm. 'Patrick . . . You are more than a friend, and I'll not have you hurt because of me. You can be far more help this way. Please go with them.'

'I don't like it. I don't like leaving with you in their hands, the filthy meat-merchants! I'll get you out of this somehow.' But her eyes implored him, and with a shake of his craggy head he allowed himself to be led away.

'Now . . . ' Wilkinson loosened his collar. 'The others will be at the auction tomorrow. They'll be fed and watered and rested overnight.' He glanced at his host, standing as if turned to stone, knuckles white on the back of his chair, staring at the floor. 'Mr Savage will no doubt want me out of this house and I wish I could oblige, but unless he's willing for his fancy wench to be tied in the barn tonight with the others—and I've a feeling she hasn't seen the inside of a barn in many a moon—I shall confine her to her room and guard the door myself. I'll also be generous, and allow the other wench to stay in the house tonight with a guard at *her* door. Your choice, sir.'

Slowly Brett raised his head, and even Melody in all her agony of spirit felt her heart wrung for him. The anguish in those finely chiselled features was almost too much to bear. 'If Mrs Van der Veer has cause to complain of either your attention or that of your men tonight, Mr Wilkinson, I shall find a way of ensuring that you regret it for the rest of your life.' Then one fist slammed into his palm. 'Is there *nothing* I have to buy you off? The chandeliers . . . books . . . Whatever price you ask, if you'll set Melody free. You see? I don't even mention Celine or Nanny, and Nanny has been my eyes for the past twenty years. Is there nothing? No plea to your honour?'

For an instant Wilkinson's eyes had turned ugly at that initial threat, but then, almost against his will, they had softened a fraction, and his tone was almost regretful as he admitted, 'Mr Savage, you have nothing of more value on your whole plantation than this girl here, or any combination of goods that would buy her. Most of it is mine already, and the remainder will realise barely enough to cover your past debts.' He turned to Beatrice. 'I suggest you leave here, ma'am, and return home to England to save yourself further embarrassment.'

'Embarrassment!' Beatrice exploded. 'Mr Wilkinson, what I feel is disgust, contempt, a total loathing for you and your kind: men who regard human beings as nothing more than saleable meat. I feel a sick fear that a country as beautiful as this could ever be governed by such men, and spread its corruption through trade to others. And I feel anger—nay, fury—at my own helplessness and utter inability to relieve the horror of my niece's present situation. What I do *not* suffer from, *Mister* Wilkinson, is embarrassment! Now . . . with your permission, Mrs Van der Veer and I will go to her room, so that we need be contaminated by your presence for no longer than is absolutely necessary.' And, not awaiting his reply, she turned, and with one supportive arm firmly around Melody's waist, led her from the room.

Outside the door, the guards, who had returned from

immobilising Patrick, moved to stop the two women, but confronted with the flashing eyes of Lady Davenport, they hesitated.

'Let them go,' Wilkinson ordered sharply. 'But see they don't leave that room.'

Obligingly the men followed them upstairs and stationed themselves on either side of the bedroom door. 'Don't seem right,' one commented. 'Treating a little lady like you in this way. What you done to the boss, anyways? He's usually got an eye for a pretty face.'

'Not when it's coloured and smacks of profit,' answered Melody bitterly, pushing past him before the tears that threatened to choke her overflowed. Storming into that spartan room, refusing to allow her shock and grief to paralyse her, retreating into anger, she swept the dressing-table clear, dashing its contents to the floor with a crash. 'There must be a way! There *must*! This is not happening! This is the nineteenth century, and I am Melody Van der Veer. There must be a way out!'

'We have twenty-four hours,' agreed Beatrice, 'and we're not done for yet.'

Looking into those level grey eyes—eyes that had seen her through the deaths of her mother and father, the murder of Hugh and the repulsive attentions of Luther Hogge, not to mention his death at her hands, Melody felt a determination there that matched her own. 'Escape must be possible!' she declared, but with an evasive gesture, her aunt shook her head.

'Not by ourselves. I must find a way of freeing Patrick, and then it would mean despatching Wilkinson and his men—all well armed. There is, however, another alternative. Do you remember the address on the letter that Brett's cousin sent?'

'No, but . . . Yes, here it is. I put it in my pocket when Wilkinson came in.'

Beatrice scanned it and gave a decisive nod. 'Our Mr Slaver knows nothing of Paul Savage's possible success at raising the money for St Clare, so he will not be expecting any communication from that source. *You* are a prisoner

here, my poor dear, as is Patrick, but so far he has not
decreed that *I* should be—quite the contrary. I can't think
for one moment that he would doubt my helplessness,
one woman alone against three strong well-armed men! If
I chose to go for a short carriage-ride to calm my nerves,
and appealed to his chivalry, with suitable apologies for
my hysterical outburst . . . Well, it's worth a try!'

'But Raleigh's *not* a short carriage-ride,' Melody
objected, fearing for her aunt's safety in those troubled
times. 'Anything could happen to you alone on the road.'

'Nothing happened on the way south,' Beatrice pointed
out. 'This Paul Savage has indicated that he has every
likelihood of raising the money to save St Clare. My only
concern now is whether Brett loves you enough to put
the money to another use.'

A tiny spark of hope flared within her. 'You heard him
offer Wilkinson everything he had to save me. Yes, I
believe he does, Aunt Bee.' She looked down at her hands.
'I pray he does!'

Beatrice's heart went out to the girl, and she gave her
a quick hug. 'There's only one way to find out. I'll be
back in plenty of time, and if Paul doesn't have the
money, I'll find a way of freeing that battling Irishman
and we'll see the fur fly! I'll take some pieces of jewellery
and use them to buy weapons, or to lace a few drinks,
whatever it takes. We'll not be beaten, Melody child!
We're British. We've dealt with every kind of enemy under
the sun, and one insignificant little slaver won't stand in
our way, you'll see.'

Melody gave a wry laugh. 'What would England and I
do without you!' She received an encouraging wink, and
then Beatrice was out of the door, demanding to be taken
to Wilkinson. As she paced the floor, striding from the
window, which gave her a view of the road, to the door
and back again, suddenly her aunt came into view, driving
a light carriage pulled at a sedate trot by an ancient grey.
Their host was taking no chances, apparently, for this
group could never make the long journey to Raleigh and
back in anywhere near the time necessary, even though

she knew that Beatrice could make any horse perform miracles if required. But then, instead of turning north at the fork, the carriage turned east. Melody's heart skipped a beat as she suddenly remembered Patrick's assurance of a fast carriage and pair at a neighbouring plantation. 'Please let it be!' she prayed. 'Please let it be!'

She watched the carriage out of sight, and then caught her breath, for a rider had appeared down the road that Beatrice should have taken. He rode with a curiously rigid manner as though more accustomed to driving than riding. She could make out no features, for he wore a dark slouch hat, but she was certain he was not one of Wilkinson's men. He reined in before he reached the property, and sat looking at the house for several minutes. She gained an uneasy impression that he could see her at the window, and pulled back, feeling her heart beating erratically. She knew this was not Brett's cousin, for this man was spare of frame and wore his long coat untidily. Should she attempt to call for help? No; there was something forbidding about the lone rider. She turned again to the window. If only she could see his face . . . But he was gone. How could that be? Unless he was coming to the house. Giving a shiver, she was glad that she had not called out. He was undoubtedly one of Wilkinson's men, and help was the last thing he could have given. She simply had to wait . . . and hope . . . and pray that her aunt would make the journey safely . . . and in time.

During the next twenty-four hours, Melody's hopes turned to ashes and her dreams to despair. She refused to leave her room, even though her 'owner' had agreed to allow her to join them for her meals. Even Brett had come to her door with assurances that she would be treated as the lady she was, earning the contempt of the men stationed there who had been told that she was no more than a 'white nigra', but still she would not be moved. 'Unless you order me to,' she told him through the door. 'You can, of course, or you could have my master flog me.'

'Don't, Melody! Please don't say such things. No one shall touch you.' But this tone lacked conviction, and he had gone away.

Finally, as night fell, her tears dried and she formed a bitter resolve that if she *were* sold as a slave, she would kill herself before submitting to any man. She would go to the slave block head high, and show them that they were purchasing an English lady, not a cowering bitch-thing to be used and abused. She kept down the sick horror within her, feeling already light-headed from hunger, and when, at last, and without Beatrice, she was called below, she went down to the hall like Mary Queen of Scots went to the block.

Elliott Wilkinson watched her approach, and wondered, for the hundredth time, whether he could possibly be wrong. He had the evidence in the slave-log, and the sworn statement of Celine. Even Brett, while begging for her release, had not denied her coloured blood. Yet, seeing the grace and dignity in that exquisite form, he questioned. She did not look at him. Instead, those sapphire eyes looked through him, and he was disquieted by their blankness, not knowing that his charge had already entered her own unassailable world.

Melody heard voices, but not the content of their words; she saw faces, but the eyes, whether questioning or anguished, hate-filled or indifferent, stirred her not at all. She had changed that morning into severest mourning, but then realised the hypocrisy of using poor Hugh's memory to conceal her looks. 'I'm sorry, my dear,' she had whispered, dismissing that little lie once and for all. 'I truly did *want* to love you.'

Her dresses she had packed neatly into the trunk, folding Beatrice's rich clothes with equal care. She had felt that she would never need them again, realising with dread that her new master would want her in clothes of his own choosing, probably the crimson and emerald silks in which men appeared to prefer their concubines—if Celine was anything to judge by. 'Perhaps he'll be kind,'

she had dared to hope. 'Perhaps he will even free me
when he hears my story.' But she had known it was a
vain hope, and that any man who would pay a high price
for a female slave had only one future planned for her.

The old and battered valise of her father's that she had
brought from England was carefully packed with Beatrice's
things. She had lifted out the doll and held if for a
moment against her cheek before resolutely replacing it,
consigning her childhood innocence to the depths. The
scrap of diary she had read through once more, and a
shudder had run through her as she repeated the words;
'All over. Learned they sold her. Must tell Melody not
to . . . ' Its message finally, terribly, clear. If only he *had*
told her never to return to the land of her birth. If only
he had told her the truth—all of it—when she was safely
in the circle of a loving family. If only . . . She had
drawn a deep breath. The world could be lost in dreaming
of what might have been. She had touched the bead
necklace. 'I wonder what you were really like, Ereanora,
for my father to have loved you?' She had remembered
something she had overheard Nanny say when Samson
had offered sympathy on the death of her daughter. 'My
Ereanora never die. She always with me. Good reaches
out just as evil reaches out. Ereanora always find me.'
Melody had felt a prickle at the back of her neck. *Could*
evil reach out? And Luther Hogge's face had swum before
her. 'No!' she had said aloud. 'I won't think of that . . .
I won't think of—of anything that can harm me!' She
had closed her eyes and concentrated on a field—spring—
new grass rippling in a light breeze—she and her father
riding—laughter. Yes . . . that's better. They can't find
me there!

She had selected a gown of heavy black velvet with
seed-pearls, like stars in a midnight sky, scattered over
the skirt. A pearl necklace brought out the ivory luminosity
of her skin revealed by the low square neckline, and a
pearl comb held her high-piled hair. A full-length matching
cloak enveloped the whole, giving her an untouchable and
undeniably regal air, and it was this that gave Wilkinson

his deepest doubt.

Surely this creature could not be of the same blood as the screaming, fighting, foul-mouthed Celine that he had just had thrown into the back of the slave-wagon? Yet the one he knew as Nanny had been a different matter altogether, and it quelled his doubts as to this slave's colour. The grandmother's air of quiet dignity and concern over her English grand-daughter, as well as over her blind master, had brought back memories of his own mammy; a coal-black mountain of flesh who had comforted him through many a scrape. It had been partly this which had eventually persuaded him to leave the woman behind. He had no moral qualms about splitting up families, but a sympathy, as one gentleman for another, for Brett Savage's terrible disability, a disability he had staunchly refused to use in his vain bargaining for Melody's freedom.

Something in the bearing of the girl before him made him relent very slightly. 'This one'll go in my carriage, not in the wagon with the others.' He had expected some gesture, even a glance, of gratitude, but the creature seemed carved out of ice and had made no sign as she allowed the men to lead her out. Only once, when Brett stumbled from the drawing-room, throwing off the restraining arm of Wilkinson's guard to vow, 'I'll get you back. I'll free you somehow. I'll think of something,' had she shown any reaction.

She had turned then, and very quietly said, 'Think quickly then, Brett, for I'll not live a day past the auction block.' The watchers had felt chill at the resolve in her tone as she walked in silence, head held high, to the door.

CHAPTER NINE

THE AUCTION AT North Fork was a small affair, but it still brought plantation-owners from out of State, and the prices compared favourably with those of the well-known auctioneers Pulliam and Betts in Richmond, Virginia, though were nowhere near as high as Charleston's. Since the previous year, prices had been booming, together with the price of cotton, and a prime field hand could fetch twelve to fifteen hundred dollars, with children of ten to fourteen selling for around half that.

The people from St Clare were graded and dressed accordingly. The Number One hands were 'spruced up', their bodies oiled, teeth rubbed over with a whittled stick, and their hair given a brushing. The men were given a new suit of clothes, the women a starched cotton frock, and ordered to smile. The Number Two hands warranted no such care, being simply hosed down and dressed in linen shifts or 'cut off' trews and warned not to cause trouble, or they'd feel the lash.

Within the crystal cave that enclosed her mind, Melody neither saw nor heard the horror and degradation about her as slaves were stripped and minutely examined, especially the attractive females, as though they were cattle. The cries of children separated from their parents did not reach her, though the cruel practice occurred again and again, this being neither Louisiana nor Alabama, where a child under ten could not be taken from the mother.

Wilkinson had kept her in his carriage until the last moment. He had already reaped a high profit from Celine, whose crimson crinoline had been ripped to the waist in her struggles to escape the 'vendue table' or auction block.

Her hands had finally been manacled behind her, and as soon as the bidders caught sight of the full creamy breasts, the bidding had soared, eventually reaching almost five thousand. Kicking and fighting, she had been forcibly carried to the closed carriage of a man from South Carolina, and speculation was rife as to how he would convince his shrewish, frigid wife that she needed another hand-servant. The woman's cruelty to her slaves was legend, and even the most hardened man there hoped that the coloured girl would hold her tongue and her temper.

Wilkinson turned to Melody, and again the deep doubts assailed him. She had spoken no word since that icy promise to Brett on her departure, and seemed totally unaware of her surroundings. 'You're next, wench,' he said gruffly, hiding his discomfort. Almost against his will he came round and helped her down from the carriage, leading her forward between the rows of benches on which the planters sat. A murmur arose, and as Melody's mind registered the low, bestial note, something flickered in the sapphire eyes, yet she stood as though carved from stone as Wilkinson went to talk with the auctioneer.

As if from a great way off, she heard Wilkinson say, 'Up you go', and she was almost lifted on to the raised platform. The murmurs grew louder as each man there felt the same instinctive disbelief that had assailed Elliott Wilkinson. Melody stepped forward, heavy cloak drawn tight about her, high-piled hair rippling slightly in the light breeze, her gaze going out above the heads of the crowd to some distant pasture where she rode with her father and laughed at his jokes.

Sensing the crowd's unease, the auctioneer hastened to cry, 'A rare beauty, gen'l'men! A prize indeed! The finest you'll ever see. Now I know that there ain't one o' you good ole boys ever see'd a blue-eyed nigra afore, but we got one right here today. Accordin' to her master's records, this high-tone filly is the daughter of a genuine octoroon and a white man. Her great-great gran'mammy was a Guinea princess. Her daddy, they say, was an English lord, and you can see she's real honest-to-goodness nobility through'n' through. Now ain't Nature wonderful to create a blue-eyed white nigra? And ain't the Fates on our side to bring her right here today? Come, now, I know we can begin at two thousand and save time.'

The bidding rose to almost four thousand, and then, with a theatrical gesture, the auctioneer dragged Melody's cloak from her shoulders, shattering that crystal cave and bringing her mind to the full horror about her as the bidding rocketed.

'No!' But her horrified rejection emerged barely above a whisper as her hand flew upwards. At a sharp command, two men leaped forward to wrench her wrists behind her back, and she felt the manacles bite into her flesh. The auctioneer was taking no chances that this one would give trouble. Her anguished eyes swept the crowd, aware at last of the lust and brutality in the upturned faces.

'You sure she's a nigra?' called one man, and, sickened, Melody swung to meet his leering gaze—and beside him saw Beatrice Davenport. 'Oh, no!' Her mind rebelled as tear-washed grey eyes met blue. 'I don't want you to see this.'

'Two ways to tell,' the auctioneer replied. 'They got a blue line at the base of the nails, but there's a surer way, since this'n has had her blood pretty well diluted. Ya'll saw this one's half-sister a moment ago. You saw her stripped down and those tantalisin' dark brown peaks. Always dark brown in a nigra, no matter how white they looks.'

Melody could not tear her eyes from Aunt Bee's ashen face, for if she loosed that one thread of sanity she would surely lose her mind. But Beatrice had turned away, speaking urgently to a man beside her as the auctioneer called, 'Well, I kin see you won't be satisfied till I proves it, gentlemen.' She felt hard fingers pulling the bodice from her shoulders—and heard a voice call out.

'That won't be necessary!'

Melody turned to look at the man beside Aunt Bee, and she swayed as recognition blinded her like a lightning flash. Dimly she heard the auctioneer's denial and the ugly growl from the crowd cheated of their sport, then Paul Savage, for it could be no one else with that tall, arrogant stance and the scar crossing the hawk-like features, stepped forward.

Almost negligently he held an ugly sawn-off riot-gun in one hand and a large leather pouch in the other. A heavy Walker Colt revolver was strapped to one lean hip, and those who cared to look down noticed the handle of a long-bladed knife protruding from one of his unfashionably high boots. As he approached, the crowd parted before him, and as he walked between the benches, men slid a little to one side, though he looked neither right nor left. His gaze swept over Melody from head to toe, and a slight frown drew in winged brows. 'Ten thousand should satisfy your client,' he stated coldly.

'Why—Why, yes, sir,' the auctioneer babbled, never having seen so much money paid in his life for a slave, however beautiful.

'Then get those cuffs off!'

Within seconds, Melody was released. The stranger bent to retrieve her cloak, thrusting it into her trembling hands, and in that instant their eyes met. His skin was tanned to a rich mahogany, his hair the colour of finest jet and long enough to curl on to his collar, but it was his eyes, dark brown, almost black, holding an expression of such anger, that made Melody catch her breath.

But all he said was, 'Cover yourself. The carriage is over there', before he turned away, his broad shoulders cleaving again through the crowd.

Near to tears, Beatrice ran to enfold her niece in the heavy cloak, murmuring words of comfort and reassurance that the nightmare was over. 'We had to wait all through that awful sale,' she said, the agony coming through. 'We arrived only an hour ago, as we had to go to St Clare first. Brett is quite beside himself, insisting that his cousin buy you at whatever cost, even if it left him penniless. Oh, come, sweeting, let's get away from here.'

Then she stopped, as a figure detached itself from the

milling crowd and barred their way. 'Yes, sir?' The man was dressed entirely in black, and his cavernous features were thrown into shadow by his wide-brimmed slouch hat. There was something disquieting about him, something in his intent regard that caused her to add, 'We are, as you can see, in rather a hurry.'

He addressed himself directly to Melody. 'Are you Melody Van der Veer?' No title, no bow, no courtesy. There was something strangely evil in the sibilant tones.

With an effort, Melody brought her attention to bear . . . and then recoiled. It was the man she had seen from her window, the one in the slouch hat who had sat his horse and watched the house so intensely. With an effort, she said, 'I am, sir. Whom do I have the honour of addressing?'

The man gave a thin smile. 'My name doesn't matter, so you can just forget you've seen me . . . for now.' With a nod and a long look that sent a shiver down her spine, he turned and disappeared into the crowd.

Melody felt a sense of foreboding. Who *was* he? What did he want of her? 'He was watching St Clare, Aunt Bee. Could he be another of those terrible men following us? Oh, Aunt Bee, I don't think I can take much more!' Reaction set in, and she began to tremble, shaking like a leaf in a storm as Beatrice supported her to the waiting carriage. She did not look at the man who had bought her, but felt a strong hand beneath her elbow helping her in.

'I'll meet you at St Clare,' he instructed the driver, and she heard the snort of a restive horse and then hoofbeats, as he rode off without a word.

On the short drive back, the sinister stranger at the auction was forgotten as Beatrice told her of her search for their rescuer, not having found him at the address given, and being advised that he was not expected back until the following day. She told of the banks and bar-rooms she had stormed and the gentlemen and villains she had accosted, desperation over-riding both fear and caution. Her ordeal was plain in her voice, even though she kept her tone steady, and Melody took her hands.

'Dear Aunt Bee! What you must have gone through.'

'Nothing compared with your own nightmare, child, but it's all over now. This Paul Savage managed to raise over five thousand—some quite illegally, I believe—and brought another eight thousand of his own. His first loyalty, of course, was to Brett and St Clare, but dear Brett said that he would sooner lose everything to Elliott Wilkinson than have you sold into slavery. He blames himself for everything that happened, and curses himself for his cowardice.'

'So now I belong to this Paul Savage.'

'No! No, I'm sure it isn't like that. He's a strange, silent man, but I believe a good one in the little time I've known him. His views on slavery are well known. No, everything will be all right, you'll see. Here we are. Let's get this terrible business over and put it out of our minds.'

The carriage had stopped before the house, and immediately the door was wrenched open and Melody was swung out into Patrick O'Shaughnessy's strong arms. 'Thank God you're safe! I've cursed myself time and again for not taking that rabble apart, guns or no guns.'

Gently Melody disentangled herself from the bear-hug and touched the clenched jaw. 'They'd have had no hesitation in killing you, and I'd not have you harmed for the world. Is Brett inside?'

He nodded, and as she turned to hurry into the house, he held out a helping hand to Beatrice. 'You're covered in dust from your drive, since you refused to waste time even washing, and you look tired out. How many more times will you go gallivanting around the countryside unescorted, woman?'

Their eyes met, grey and blue, and read their mutual anguish, then Beatrice smiled. 'I do it only to plague you, Patrick, and force you to find me.'

'Will you always be such an irritating female?' he growled, his hand completely enfolding hers in a grip that told her far more than words could of the sick worry he had endured.

'Always is a long time, but I'll be as I am until someone changes me.' With an enigmatic little smile, she freed her captive fingers and moved toward the house. Patrick going to stable the horses.

At the drawing-room door, Beatrice hesitated before the tableau there, feeling the tension in the air. Brett sat upright in his high-backed chair, while Paul stood with his back to the half-closed window shutters, his broad frame silhouetted against the pale afternoon light. Melody had been standing beside Brett's chair, one hand resting on its back, but she hurried forward at her aunt's arrival, her eyes stormy.

'I thought you said this—this *Mister* Savage was an Abolitionist!' she exploded.

'I've never owned slaves in my life,' came the sharp rejoinder from the man at the window. 'But neither do I make it a policy to give eight thousand dollars of my own money to any stranger who may need it. My cousin may do as he pleases with his, the money I raised in Raleigh, although I always thought he had more sense. You, madam, legally belong to me—English lady or mulatto slave, it's all the same under the skin as far as I'm concerned. You can pay your debt now or work it off on my farm, either on the land or in my bed. The choice is yours.'

'How dare you!' Melody cried, eyes flashing, and Brett rose with a growl.

'If I could see, I'd make you take that back!'

He was met by an answering explosion, as the man came forward with the lithe stride of a tiger. 'Don't try my patience, either of you. Frankly, I've always preferred experience over enthusiasm in both situations, and you, Mrs Van der Veer, appear to have precious little of either. I can understand the need to travel several thousand miles, mortgaging my property to the hilt, making totally illegal deals with men I'd normally not touch with a ten-foot pole to save *your* home, Brett, but I'll not waste *my* money on buying you a pretty plaything!'

Brett grasped his cane, knuckles whitening, but Melody,

too, had sprung forward and now faced her enemy, her fury as great as his. 'You can't talk like that . . . ' She broke off with a gasp as iron fingers closed over her wrist.

Brutally the man raised her hand and prised open the clenched fist. 'These aren't the hands of a nurse using lye soap all day.' His other hand closed over her free arm. 'And there are no muscles here of a field hand or housemaid. What *other* work would you have done here? You aren't teacher material, even supposing my brilliant cousin needed one.'

Melody struggled to free herself—and was suddenly aware, at the same instant as he, that their bodies had come together in the conflict: velvet against steel, her pounding heart against his chest, his angry breath caressing her cheek. For that moment time stood still as their stormy eyes met, and lightning flashed between them.

'You'll not gainsay me, madam,' he said, his voice low and husky, and his hands dropped to his sides as he turned away, leaving her shaken. 'I've made my decision, and there's no more to be said.'

'Oh yes, there is!' Beatrice snapped. 'We'll pay back the money. It will take a couple of weeks to get a letter to England and the same to receive a reply. If you can bear to support us for a month in this God-forsaken place, you'll have your eight thousand, and you can name your interest.' She did not allow her uncertainty to show, the worry that had gnawed at her since receiving no reply to her previous letter.

Melody came to put a restraining hand on her shoulder. 'No, Aunt Bee. We can't put ourselves so deeply in John's debt when he has already done so much, even though everything in me cries out "Yes".' She took a deep breath. 'I'm growing up fast, Aunt Bee. It's my life. I'm the one who got you into this terrible position in the first place, the one who forced you to leave England. I'm the one who's . . . ' She choked on the word, but continued strongly, 'I'm the negress, and that alone would bring deep shame to the Davenport name were it known at . . . home. That is why my father kept it such a secret. This is something I have to come to terms with if I am to salvage any of the Davenport pride I once knew. Aunt Bee, a few days ago I was prepared to work in the fields for quite another cause, do you remember? When I left England, I left behind everything that was dear and familiar to me, except you. Now it appears I must let even you go, and nothing can be worse than that, so to travel to the other side of the world can't be half as painful as the pain I'm feeling now.'

They both stared at her, Beatrice in anguished disbelief, Paul with narrow-eyed speculation, and it was to him that she addressed her next words. 'You say you don't believe in keeping slaves, Mr Savage, but you've just bought yourself one. Since you've given me the option, I'll work in your fields. I'll slave in your fields until my fingers bleed if necessary, and I'll pay off your damned debt faster than you ever dreamed possible. For all your cant, Mr Savage, you've got yourself a white nigra slave! On your conscience be it—if you have one.'

She thought she saw a lessening of the anger and something akin to respect flicker in those dark eyes, but then Paul turned aside and a mirthless smile touched his mouth. 'Very well. On my head be it. You have spirit . . . for one who calls herself a slave!'

Again Beatrice broke in, almost in tears at the apparent callous indifference to her niece's plight. 'And you, sir, will you break her of that?'

Meeting those Atlantic-grey eyes levelly, he saw the turmoil there and his voice softened. 'I've neither the desire nor the need to do so, Lady Davenport, but unless there is steel beneath that silken skin, my country will do that for me.'

'It didn't break *you*,' Melody interjected, 'and it won't break *me*. I'll learn to weed and plough and sow, milk cows, pick cotton, or whatever it is you do grow in that barbaric place.' She faced her aunt bravely. 'I've often doubted my strength at times, but this isn't one of them. I shall survive, never fear, and then, God willing, I'll come back to you, wherever you are, and we'll begin again.'

'Paul, you can't!' Brett cried sharply, his voice vibrant with emotion. 'Melody wouldn't survive a life like that. You may be used to native workers, may have lost all idea of what a lady is, but you *can't* subject her to such work!'

'That's enough!' Paul rapped. 'I'll not have you debase yourself over any woman, however beautiful. Mrs Van der Veer's physical condition is, I can assure you, far more obvious to me than to you, and she doesn't appear to be the type to expire just yet. She'll go with me to New Zealand, and the life she lives there depends a great deal on her. I've never lost one of my people yet through overwork or harsh treatment, but there's no place at Windhaven for a simpering, swooning English miss, and *you* don't need one either.'

Melody's palm itched to slap that arrogant face and her fingers curled, longing to draw more scars to join the one that blazed across the bronzed cheek. 'I've never known what it is to hate a man completely until now!' Her voice was shaking with her fury.

Again that irritating half-smile lifted his mouth, though his eyes were cold as ice. 'I've never considered it a necessity for my servants, or anyone else for that matter, to like me, as long as they do as bid.'

The drawing-room door opened suddenly, precluding any response, and Patrick strode into the room. 'Thanks be to the Saints that we've put *that* affair behind us!' he said. 'How are you feeling, Melody child? Better, I see by your high colour. I presume you will be returning to New Zealand now, Paul, and taking young Brett with you. Then what are our plans, ladies?'

Her anger as high as that of her niece, Beatrice answered, 'We haven't been given a choice. Melody is to be taken to Mr Savage's farm in New Zealand as a—a field hand . . . since at present it seems he owns her, and I shall, of course, accompany her. I have enough jewellery to pay my fare and some lodging or other, I'm sure.'

The Irishman stared at her for a moment, then exploded,

'The devil you will! I thought you a man of honour, Paul Savage!'

'I'm also a man of business and don't take kindly to wasting my hard-earned money. Mrs Van der Veer will be treated as an expensive investment and as honourably as she herself wishes, which is more than she *would* have been. I've just over two and a half thousand left, and most of that will go on taking her and Brett back.'

'I've no intention of returning with you,' Brett interrupted angrily. 'I'll make my own way somehow, with Nanny as my eyes as she has always been, but I won't be a part of any household that treats a gentlewoman so.'

'You? Make your own way?' The contempt, and something more . . . something of frustration and concern . . . grated across Paul's tone. 'You've neither money nor sense, man.'

'He'll stay here,' Patrick suddenly decided, meeting Paul's glance levelly. 'We owe you eight thousand, Paul, correct?'

'Not you, Patrick.' Melody put him right. 'The debt is mine.'

'Your troubles have been mine from the very first time we met, remember?' He smiled, the blue eyes softening at the determination in hers. 'We three are more than friends, you said so yourself, and whether your aunt, bless her stubborn soul, objects or not, I shall assume part of that debt.' Then, turning again to Paul, both veterans of war, in every sense of the word, 'I shall pay off your eight thousand, and you'll not ask me how I made it. Agreed?'

'Agreed.' Paul nodded, ignoring Melody's gesture of protest.

'And Brett will stay with me. I have friends . . . Not the kind I'd normally introduce a gentleman to, but they'll take good care of him and ask no questions. He'll be comfortable and well fed, and Nanny shall go along as well.'

'Go on,' Paul prompted, the dark eyes narrowing, reading the Irishman's intentions long before he spoke.

'You have my word that he will be well looked after,

better than he has ever been before . . . equally as well as my two ladies.'

The threat was implicit, and Paul's lips tightened a fraction, but his tone was easy as he agreed. 'Then that's the way it shall be, but I'll meet these friends of yours, if you've no objection.'

'They live in Natchez. Out of your way, if you're taking the boat.'

'I can take a detour from New Orleans.' His tone brooked no argument. Almost as an afterthought, he added, 'They live Under-The-Hill, I take it.'

'I don't make the kinds of friends who might live On-The-Bluff.'

Melody had also understood Patrick's implied threat, and now went to put a hand on his arm. 'I can imagine the difference, even without knowing the town. In spite of all that has gone before, I'd not want Brett to—to . . . ' She floundered before the frown on Patrick's brow.

'Brett?'

'Yes, Patrick.'

'Do you trust me with your life, boy?'

The previously set features broke into a grim smile. 'If you mean that you are holding me to ransom so that Melody and Lady Davenport are treated honourably, I'll be a willing prisoner, whatever the state of my prison. However, I think you wrong my cousin. Although there can never now be friendship between us, I believe him to be a man of his word in spite of an unpromising exterior.'

'I don't need your reference, Brett,' Paul said harshly. 'The cards being on the table, as it were, I shall go ahead with my travel arrangements and you may make your plans to take Brett to Natchez. I shall, however, still wish to meet his jailers.'

Melody's eyes went from one to the other, and she felt her heart pounding at the contained anger and leashed strength of the two men. She knew that Patrick would not harm Brett, or let anyone else do so, for they had formed a strange kind of friendship in the short time the

Irishman had been at St Clare. For her own safety,
however, she was not so certain, and looked to her future
with dread. Voicing only a small part of the fear within,
she had to ask, 'Since you no longer have to pay for
Brett's ticket, will your travel arrangements include Aunt
Bee, or should she go with Patrick to sell some of her
jewellery now?'

Paul's gaze swept over the rich velvet of Melody's dress,
lingering only momentarily on the tiny band of lace that
edged the neckline and touched the ivory swell of her
breasts. 'I shall take care of your aunt's fare, accepting
that until you reach the farm you will need a chaperon.
You will also need something more appropriate for farm
life than the dress you're wearing. You may purchase that
in Wellington, our nearest large town, but I should not
wish you to discard the rest of your wardrobe. My
country is not totally lost to civilisation.' With a short
bow to Beatrice, he spun on his heel and left.

'*His* country!' Melody exploded. '*His* land!'

'A savage land, indeed,' Patrick agreed quietly. 'But I'll
have you both out of there before a year's out, and bring
you back to a country of peace and quiet and rare beauty.
You've my word on it.'

But not even the worldly-wise O'Shaughnessy could
have envisaged that in the terrible spring that followed,
the peace and quiet, as well as much of the rare beauty
of which he spoke, would be shattered, gone for ever, in
the wake of a shot that would echo round the world—
directed at an insignificant pile of brownstone called Fort
Sumter.

CHAPTER TEN

DURING THE LONG days and even longer nights it took them to reach Natchez, travelling by road and rail through country no longer threatened by Tuscarora or Cherokee, but still by road agents and robbers, Melody lost much of her dark despair.

The morning after the auction, Paul had found her in the library deep in a book of Shakespeare's sonnets. She rose immediately, pushing the book aside. 'I'm sorry. I understand it's not permitted for a slave to read.'

A muscle leapt in his jaw. 'I've told you . . . I have no slaves, nor would I even had slavery not been abolished in the colonies in '33. You're an employee, or will be when we arrive, and one who'll earn the regular wage for work done, forfeiting it until your debt is repaid. I'll have a contract drawn up tomorrow.'

'As far as I'm concerned it's one and the same,' she said bitterly. 'You bought me on the slave block; I belong to you all the time we're in this country and will be held in servitude in the next. You can wrap it up in any words you wish to salve your conscience. I'm still a slave.'

The gold-flecked eyes darkened. So battle-lines were drawn. So be it. 'I have no conscience, Mrs Van der Veer, in hiring a servant. As for the book, you may read what you will; in fact several of the old volumes were mine originally—something that Wilkinson, for all his faults, was gentlemanly enough to take my word on, and I shall be taking them with me, including the one you have there.' He crossed to take it from the table beside her, bringing him close, and instinctively she took a pace away. Sharply he said, 'You have no need to fear me, Mrs Van der Veer. If necessary I shall reiterate my words of yesterday: you and your aunt will be treated as honour-ably as you wish. I'll accept your state of mourning, *and* your desire to avoid my company—for the time being. I have no use for you until we reach Windhaven, so there is little point in jumping like a startled deer every time I come within ten feet.'

'And once we're at Windhaven?' Hating the fear that made her voice shake, she found herself unable to meet his eyes, and her fingers clenched as the silence drew out.

Then, softly, he reminded her, 'You made your own choice, Mrs Van der Veer, and only should you change your mind will I have use of you before. However . . .' He scanned the pages, then held out the open book to her. 'Since you regard yourself as a slave and, in fact are one until we reach New Zealand, you may find instruc-tions in this one . . . number fifty-seven, that begins, "Being your slave, what should I do but tend . . . "'

Melody's previous fear melted in the white heat of her sudden anger, and it was only when she took the book, flinging it on the chair and turning to him with blazing eyes, that she realised he was deliberately taunting her.

'You're even more beautiful when you're angry, but you'll find it an exhausting state to maintain for long.' And with that half-smile and a short inclination of the head that could have served as a bow, he left her fuming.

Her anger supported her through dinner—a scant meal since all the slaves were gone and, in their despair and anger, had destroyed most of the perishable food—but that night she had the first of the nightmares that would torment her for many years. She had retired early . . . 'With your permission, Mr Savage' . . . unable to use the word 'Master'.

'You've no need to ask. We've a long journey ahead.'

She had hurried to her room, leaving the others below, and exhausted both mentally and physically from her ordeal, fell into a fitful sleep, but found no peace there. She tossed and turned, moaning as the nightmare world of her dreams mingled with the equally nightmarish reality of her past.

. . . She was on the auction block with the sea of
faces before her, but this time she was naked to their
gaze, the raven hair that fell loose to her waist her only
covering. Suddenly from the crowd stepped Luther Hogge,
a scarred and shadowy figure shrouded in black, as
terrifying in death as he had been in life. In her dream
world she was unable to move, frozen by a force beyond
her understanding. She was screaming, denying his existence, but no sound emerged. He climbed on the dais and
came to face her, and he was smiling, telling her that he
was not dead and had come to claim her as a slave. She
felt those bloated hands on her body, moving all over
her, doing things that only in her worst nightmares could
she have imagined, never having known the near-rape
common to the auction block. And she screamed again, a
high animal cry that shattered the realms of darkness . . .

In the drawing-room, that agonised, inhuman cry
brought them to their feet. 'My God! What was that?'
Brett exclaimed, rising, but already Paul was up and
moving toward the door.

'No!' Beatrice's sharp command stopped him in his
tracks. 'No,' she repeated, grey eyes glacial. 'You're the
last person who has a right to be in that room—even if
you do own its occupant!' She turned to Brett. 'She's
having a dream, and, heaven knows, she has enough
horror in her past to dream of!' So saying, she pushed
aside Paul's broad frame as if it had no more weight than
a child's, and ran up the stairs.

Paul looked after her, dark eyes speculative. There were
obviously far deeper problems here than he had imagined.
In his mind's eye he saw again the girl on the 'vendue
table' as he had first seen her, and he re-lived that sudden
white-hot fireball that had smashed into his stomach,
churning his guts into a desire just as bestial as that of
the men about him. That was why he had delayed,
wanting to see those full, exquisitely formed curves
revealed. But then the frantic fingers of Beatrice Davenport had cut into his arm and brought reality, and he had
stepped forward . . . taking a pace out of the pit and

into civilisation.

Drawing a deep breath now, he said, 'At least they didn't take the brandy! Another, Cousin?'

In the spartan room above, Beatrice was hugging the trembling girl to her as Melody sobbed out the awful content of her dream. Her aunt's grey eyes were filled with pain as she listened in silence. There was nothing she could say; such horror went beyond platitudes, and only time, she knew, would end it.

Over the following days Melody slowly recovered, and aided by both Patrick's strength and Beatrice's caustic wit she was able to preserve a degree of sanity that enabled her to close Paul Savage out. The man himself appeared to encourage this, riding ahead whenever possible, and sitting apart, features brooding and satanic in the firelight when they halted for the night.

He and Patrick would occasionally converse in low tones, catching up on lost years, and more, and the latter seemed to lose some of the taut anger he had displayed at St Clare. But it was Brett who could not adjust, falling into moods of deep depression, finding oblivion in the hip-flask he carried, and only raising a smile at Melody's lightest touch.

'It's not entirely your fault,' she told him for the hundredth time. 'One might even say it would never have happened had not my father gone to visit an old friend in the wrong country at the wrong time and stayed to fall in love with entirely the wrong person. But it did happen, and no amount of apologies or regrets will change that. I've forgiven everything there is to forgive, so now you must forgive yourself.'

As they came down the Natchez Trace, the Mississippi, slow moving and wide at that point, and bearing the thick yellow mud of half America, gleamed golden in the sunlight. And then Natchez, where hundreds of flatboats, arks and broadhorns floated alongside steamboats and the gambling palaces of the great stern-wheelers that cruised from New Orleans north to Louisville and beyond.

Above them rose the great high bluff, its rich red-brown

earth cloaked in multi-coloured shrubs and crowned with giant oaks, and between them, the equally rich homes of the new aristocracy. But each member of that party knew it was not the ten-minute drive up the hill in a fringe-topped surrey that was their route. Their path lay far from such ostentatious splendour, the distance not in miles but in the social chasm that separated the Bluff from the sprawling slum of Natchez-Under-The-Hill.

'I suggest you walk close and wear your bonnets as far over your faces as possible,' Patrick advised, taking a position between the two women. 'There's only one kind of woman who walks this street, and I'd not have you embarrassed by unwanted attention, though it's only five minutes to our destination.'

'You managed moderately well before,' Beatrice reminded him with a smile. 'And you aren't alone this time, not by a long way!'

Melody had taken Brett's arm, and Paul moved to station himself on the blind man's other side. After one all-encompassing glance at the roistering rabble that made up the wharfside inhabitants, he had eschewed the riot-gun in favour of a loaded muleskinner whip. A half-way intelligent, though angry, crowd may entertain second thoughts when faced with the one blast riot-gun, but a drunken semi-literate mob would respect only the bloody mayhem that the steel-tipped, fourteen-foot whip could cause in the hands of an expert. With that curled negligently in one hand, and with the Walker Colt and knife he always wore, he presented the same impression of lethal power that he had brought to the auction.

'Do you really think you'll need that thing, Mr Savage?' Beatrice asked, and received a grim smile.

'No, but I might, were it not displayed so obviously. Even a lion watches out for jackals.'

An impassive Nanny walked behind her master, hawk-like eyes missing nothing. She had spoken only when forced to by necessity since leaving St Clare; not from any regret at leaving a house that held nothing but tragic memories, but from a total indifference to her fate. Her lovely Ereanora was dead, her wayward Celine sold into concubinage, her home gone, and her blind, gentle Brett too guilt-ridden over this Melody girl to need her, who had been his only family for two decades. It mattered little to Nanny, therefore, whether they took her to this sprawling, brawling city of sin or to some white-porticoed mansion on the Bluff. Her time would come. Tomorrow or the day after they would be gone, these strangers, and she and the young master would be alone again. A tiny smile curved her mouth—and at that moment the double swing doors of a tavern they were approaching burst open and a half-dozen ruffians erupted from it, stumbling and weaving, laughing and cursing in their drunkenness.

As one, they saw the newcomers and pulled up short, grins breaking out on their bearded, unwashed faces. 'Women, b'God!' exclaimed one.

'And a right pretty young lordling . . . He's for me!'

With a gasp Melody tightened her grip on Brett's arm, ready to urge him into some side alley or to defend him to the limits of her strength, all her instincts prepared to do battle, as a tigress for her helpless young, but already Paul had stepped in front of them, arms easy at his sides, and only the men facing him could have seen the strange gleam in his eyes.

A chuckle beside him brought him up short as Patrick murmured, 'Another time we'll have us some fun, boyo, but we've your cousin and the ladies to think of now. Allow *me* to make our apologies this time, since I'm somewhat more familiar with the type.' Without awaiting an answer, he stepped forward, feet apart, arms akimbo.

'The name's O'Shaughnessy,' he stated aloud. 'I was reared by a Texas rattler and suckled by a she-panther. I could take on any six men in this town afore breakfast and finish off the rest afore dinner, but right now I'm escortin' these ladies to my good friend, 'Gator McAlister. If'n you've a mind to detain us, you'd best answer to me now—and if'n there's anything of you's left, you'll answer to him and his boys after. Well? What'll it be?'

The transformation in the men's faces was unbelievable

as grins broke out. 'Hey! He's one of us for all his finery!'
one shouted, re-sheathing the knife he had pulled at Paul's
mute challenge.

Another nodded with a laugh. 'He even speaks our
lingo! If'n you be a friend of 'Gator's, there ain't a man
Under-The-Hill who'd be fool enough to block your way.'

'But we'll take up your offer another day,' grinned a
third. 'Come on, boys, let's go see what the Greasy
Spoon's got to offer in sport.' They turned, weaving an
uncertain path toward the appropriately-named tavern on
the far side of the street.

'They appeared to take a liking to you, Patrick,' Beatrice
remarked, putting a curb on her pounding heart, and
received an airy wave of the hand.

' 'Twas me modesty that won them over,' he grinned,
'but I suggest we move along afore they change their
minds. What say you, Paul?'

Paul gave him a skimming glance that held more than
a trace of disbelief. 'I say you've not changed at all,' he
stated laconically, then swung to search the taut features
of the girl behind him, finding both the courage and the
fear there, but said only, 'Are you ready to leave, or will
you stand like a lioness protecting my cousin all afternoon?'

Not deigning to answer, Melody turned again to take
Brett's arm and follow the others across to a side street
that led them away from the main thoroughfare. She
wanted to say, 'Yes, for as long as he needs me, with my
life if necessary', but she knew that this man of steel, who
had almost leaped toward danger, would never understand.

Within minutes they came to a rambling one-storey
wooden structure that no one could ever describe as a
house. It was probably old when Natchez was founded,
and its timbers solidified by time and storms to rock
hardness. Someone had attempted to add a porch at a
later date, but now only fallen spars strewed the ground,
covered by vines that crept over them and reached
tenacious tendrils into the cracks of the walls.

O'Shaughnessy gestured to the others to hold back, then, cupping his hands to his mouth, he called, 'Ho, the house! Is there a drunken razor-back boar in there, or am I wasting my time?'

Immediately an unbelievable figure erupted from the multi-roomed shack, as tall as Patrick and almost as broad, with such a shock of hair meeting the huge beard that only his much-broken nose and blazing eyes could be seen. 'Who dares insult 'Gator McAlister?' he bellowed, great arms bent before him, ready to seize his tormentor. 'Me mother was a she-bear an' me father was a bull alligator, an' I'll tear *any* man limb from limb.'

Incredibly, Patrick was chuckling as he stepped forward, bellowing in return, 'O'Shaughnessy's me name, and I eat bear-meat for breakfast and skin 'gators for boots.'

At that the man guffawed, closing the space between them. 'Well, if it isn't Irish Pat—the only man who could do it, too!' and he clasped Patrick to him in a bone-crushing hug, pounding him on the back.

Melody had taken an involuntary step backwards, over-awed in spite of herself, and felt a strong hand cupping her elbow. 'Not afraid of noise, are you?' the deep voice queried. 'For that's all it is: just two friends and a lot of noise. It's the way of things down here, and the language they use to prove kinship.'

Melody stiffened, resenting the amusement in his tone. '*You* may be used to such company, Mr Savage, but I'm not. One doesn't meet such creatures in Regent Street.'

'Perhaps in Regent's *Park*,' Beatrice laughed. 'At the Zoological Gardens there.'

'Are *you* not afraid of him, Lady Davenport?' Paul asked, and she threw him a twinkling glance.

'Whatever it is, Mr Savage, it's a male of the species, and it's been a very long time since I was afraid of one of those! Shall we go and meet our host?'

Before they could approach, however, a girl ran from the shack, a large wooden spoon in her hand, and to everyone's amazement, landed the big man a hefty blow on the arm. 'You behave, 'Gator! Can't you see these are proper folks, not the usual river-rats you keep company with?' She turned to Patrick first, forced to look up at him since she barely reached his chest. 'My apologies for my paw, sir. Though you did insult him first.' She was reed thin, with high, freckled cheekbones and light brown slanting eyes that still retained their previous anger. The corn-coloured hair was chopped raggedly about her head, undoubtedly by the sharp knife sheathed at her belt, and the boyish appearance was completed by the heavy miners' shirt she wore and the faded trousers of *serge de Nîmes*.

'My fault, missy,' O'Shaughnessy rumbled. 'Your paw and I go back a long way, and I know your two brothers, Seth and Jake, but I can't say I remember you . . . I'd never forget someone quite like you!'

The brown eyes raked his face, searching for sarcasm, and finding none, she grinned. 'I only came down here six years ago. I was ten. My maw died. She'd taken me away. Wanted me to be a lady. Some kinda dream, huh, me with a figure as skinny as a rattler and a temper to match?' She shrugged and moved forward to the others—then halted, eyes widening, before Brett. 'Jumping Jehoso-phat! You're prettier'n a speckled pup!' she breathed. 'Who *are* you, and just how long do I get to *keep* you here?'

Brett blushed to the roots of his hair, and beside him, Melody choked on a laugh, but it was left to Paul to make the necessary introductions, finishing, 'And you're 'Gator's daughter . . . '

'Mae Beth, but near everyone calls me Midget, 'cos o' my size, or just plain Midge.' There was a shout from inside the shack and Midge threw a glare over her shoulder. 'Come on in, folks, afore my brothers break up the place. I just cooked a passel o' catfish and corn bread, and it's about ready. You folks hungry?'

The honey-coloured eyes pleaded with them, and with a glance at her companions, Melody smiled. 'We'd love to accept your hospitality, but I'd not take your dinner,' and she warmed to the rich laugh.

'Lordy, Mrs . . . I'm sorry, I don't remember all of

your names . . . '

'Melody, then.'

'Great! That's near as beautiful as you are, 'cept nothing could be that beautiful . . . Back to the catfish . . . Well, we always got far more to eat in this here family than we can get down, since my brothers just live for huntin' and fishin', so you'd be doin' us a real favour.' With a totally natural gesture she took Melody's arm, then asked, 'Can I touch *him*, or will he vanish in a cloud of smoke?'

Brett gave a low chuckle, the first Melody had heard from him since that terrible day at St Clare, and for that alone she thanked this strange wild creature and whatever Fates had brought them to this place. 'I'll not vanish on you, Midge, but I may fade away with starvation.'

'That does it!' the girl said, taking his arm with her free hand. 'I'm gonna feed you until you're as content as a hog in a wallow!'

Inside the shack, Melody drew another breath of pleased surprise. The front door opened directly on to a large square dining-room and kitchen combined, a room that vaguely reminded her of the great kitchen at home with its central scrubbed pine table from which she had begged bowl scrapings and scraps of candy. Two more Neanderthals sat at the table, as heavily bearded as their father and almost as large. They rose awkwardly at the unexpected company, but once introductions were made, they soon recovered under Patrick's familiar badinage and Beatrice's easy warmth. Seated about the long table, the newcomers were plied with crisp-fried catfish, slabs of hot cornbread and corn-on-the-cob dripping with butter, and when they thought there was surely not an ounce more they could eat, they were presented with great portions of apple pie.

Only one small incident had momentarily marred the proceedings. Nanny had refused to eat with them, even though 'Gator had slammed his great fist on the table and stated, 'If'n you don't eat here and now, you don't eat! We ain't got no slaves. We can't afford them, nor see the use for them, since we kin do the work cheaper and better ourselves, so we don't have no separate quarters neither.'

'With respect, sir, it isn't right,' Nanny stated, looking him squarely in the eye. 'Mistah Brett wouldn't like it and the other white folks wouldn't like it. If there's a plate left, I'll eat later.' From that decision she would not be moved, only going to the table when the others had finished their meal and retired to the adjoining room.

'Now, 'Gator,' Patrick began, accepting a mug of almost lethal home-brewed corn liquor and settling into one of the deeply cushioned oak chairs. 'The reason for my visit . . . My friend Brett and I need a place to stay for a while.'

'You got it,' agreed the big man with such readiness that Brett was forced to protest.

'But you know nothing about me!'

'You're a friend of Irish Pat's and you're in some kinda trouble. What more should I know?'

'But we aren't talking about an overnight stay! I can't pay my way, nor even earn my keep.'

'We got food and we got rooms.' The thick beard parted to reveal the semblance of a smile. 'You talk like you belong on the Bluff, so you kin pay your way if'n you kin rub some of that lingo off on to Midget here, who could well use it.'

'Oh, yes,' the girl agreed eagerly. 'He can talk to me just as long as he likes! Mind you . . . ' and she threw a wicked, side-long glance toward Patrick, 'I'm almost a lost cause, so it could take weeks . . . months, even!'

Illogically Melody felt a wrench at her heart, but then probed that treacherous heart and knew it for what it was. She was jealous of this tow-headed wild thing who would care for Brett . . . her Brett. She read the adoration in the girl's honey-coloured eyes and knew that Brett, vulnerable as he was right now, would be quite unable to resist such innocent emotion. The thought hurt! 'Should we be leaving soon, then?' she asked quietly, and received a surprised look from her host and a searching one from Paul.

'You won't get a steamer now,' 'Gator said. 'There's a hotel in town, if'n you've a mind, but we got more rooms than people here . . . Not that they's as good as you're used to, ma'am, but they're clean . . . Midget keeps a fine clean house.'

'Oh, I didn't mean . . . ' Melody floundered, realising the offence her question had given. 'It's just that . . . '

'We didn't want to put you to any more trouble,' Paul interjected smoothly. 'But if you have the room, we should of course be most grateful for a night's lodging.'

'Then that's settled,' 'Gator stated. 'More corn likker?' Paul, whose palate ran to imported French brandy and was now quite certain his throat would never be the same again, held out his mug with a resigned smile, earning the accolade, 'You're a reall good ol' boy, you know, in spite of your duds. I knew'd it the minute I saw the way you wore that Colt slung low and business-like.' He sent Midget for more of the same, at which even Patrick's eyes became slightly glazed, and began recounting tales of the backwoods that had them all sitting on the edges of their chairs.

'But why the name 'Gator?' Melody had to ask later, feeling by then that already she had known these alien beings for a lifetime.

The man studied his big hands for a moment, and she feared that she had offended him again, but then his eldest son, Seth, broke in. 'Paw ain't proud o' the tellin', but we are. It was nigh on four year ago an' we had another brother, 'Skeeter. A big bull 'gator got him when he and Paw were hunting. Paw brought poor 'Skeeter back, but the boy died on the way. Well . . . ' He gave his father a proud glance. 'Paw, he went into them swamps in a mood like a hip-shot grizzly, and he killed eight o' them brutes with naught but his skinning-knife, then he comes back and gets as drunk as a skunk and tears apart two o' the worst dives Under-The-Hill. Put ten guys out of action for a week an' more afore they managed to hog-tie him and bring him on home.' The boy took a long draught, smacking his lips appreciatively. 'They called him 'Gator from then on in.'

'He was a good boy,' growled 'Gator—as if that explained everything.

Perhaps it did, but Melody's thoughts were elsewhere, and later, much later, she was able to catch the Irishman on his own for a few minutes outside, and without preamble asked, 'What will you do here, Patrick? Will you be able to find work?'

He covered the hand that rested on his sleeve and gave it a reassuring pat. 'Don't you fret, little one. I've a feel for rivers, whether it be the Hudson or the Mississippi. I can find honest work within hours of arriving at one, and not so honest, though far more lucrative, work within days.' Then, answering the question she was too proud to ask, he continued, 'That Midget is quite a cook and a durned fine housekeeper. She'll look after your man as if she was his little sister . . . which is all she'll be to him, Melody girl.'

Finally, then, she could say, 'You sound very sure. A year is a long time,' and received a knowing smile.

'We'll not leave you there a year, not with my knowledge of these riverboats. Apart from which, there are some women whom you can meet even the once, and they get so far into your blood that not only can you never forget them, but you'd travel to the ends of the earth to be by their side again . . . Which reminds me . . . I must rescue those backwoods babes from your aunt.'

Melody laughed. 'Are you sure it isn't the other way round?'

'Not on your life, little one! She has them eating from her hand already, but I'd not want them to become too attached. I'd hate to feel the need to take them apart— good friends that they are!'

He strode into the golden glow wrought by the home-made candles, and Melody was left on her own. 'And it will be that way for a very long time,' she murmured, the loneliness seeping through. 'I must let go of all that's precious to me and face a future I know nothing of. I'm black. I'm a slave.' She covered her face with her hands, fighting back the threatening tears. 'O Lord, help me to be strong!'

The following morning found Melody pale-faced and silent. She barely contributed to the breakfast conversation, and aware that she was watched by Paul, but indifferent, ate little of the thick slices of pork and the fried eggs put before them.

'We'll take the steamboat down to New Orleans,' he stated, 'and from there to Charleston, where we can link up with the clipper.'

'Shall we be staying in New Orleans for long?' asked Melody with a quick glance at her aunt.

'Why? Did you wish to go sightseeing?'

'No!' she stated, a little too sharply, amending, 'I—I just want to get under way . . . ' And for the benefit of her hosts, who so far had been told nothing of her situation, 'to—to get to New Zealand and start my new life . . . ' Even though it be a living death, her heart cried.

At their parting, she and Brett said nothing, but his hand came up to lie along her cheek, and her own held it there for a brief moment—both speaking volumes. And then it was over. She turned to meet Paul Savage's eyes, but was unable to read the carefully controlled expression there, so she went to thank her hosts before preceding the others towards the wharf.

'It won't be that long,' Patrick promised, as he and Beatrice stood, not quite touching.

'Yes, it will,' she answered, and smiled, belying the over-bright eyes. 'Mr Savage?' Paul turned from his contemplation of the isolated figure moving down the road. 'Do you have a hundred-dollar bill?' Puzzled, he handed her one, and watched her slip it into the Irishman's pocket . . . then walk away quickly after her niece.

CHAPTER ELEVEN

THE LONG VOYAGE to Wellington proved a hundred times more debilitating for Beatrice than the relatively short passage from London to New York, even though they had taken one of Donald Mackay's clippers, built for speed in Boston and undoubtedly the fastest ships afloat. The exceptionally broad beam helped her to stand up to the vast area of sail she carried, and even when others hit gales and were reduced to double-reefing their topsails, the Mackay ships could run with all sail set, testing the stout spars and rigging to their limit. And gales they met, when at 40 degrees South they reached the far edge of the iceberg zone and hit the Roaring Forties, where, with that peculiar roaring noise which the wind made over huge seas pounding at her senses, Melody found herself praying that she would live to reach dry land—any dry land!

'Those men are simply not mortal,' she remarked to her aunt, thinking of the sailors who brought the sleek ship through with scant attention to personal safety; but at that point Beatrice was far beyond coherent thought and merely answered with a low moan.

Melody had been aghast when she realised that they were not going to sail round Cape Horn and across the Pacific, but Paul shook his head, explaining, 'It's almost impossible, I'm afraid. Even before you reached the Horn, you'd hit the belt of westerly winds that blow right round the earth between about 40 and 50 degrees South. You'd be sailing against both wind and current your way, though of course you use the westerlies to come to America *from* New Zealand.'

She gave him a level look. 'I'll look forward to that!'

A slight frown touched his brow, but refusing to rise to

the bait, he merely said, 'It isn't an experience one antic-
ipates with pleasure, Mrs Van der Veer, unless one is
abysmally ignorant of the facts. There is, of course, the
odd storm or two whichever sea you're crossing, and
you'll meet some of the worst on your journey round the
Cape of Good Hope, though Cape Horn has its own kind
of hell. One of the books you should read is Richard
Dane's *Two Years Before The Mast.* I bought it before I
left, so knew a little of what to expect, but I soon found
that even the best author is a poor substitute for reality.'

'I'm not afraid of rough weather, Mr Savage. I'm a
good sailor, I've discovered.'

But the storm that they eventually encountered off the
Cape sent even the redoubtable Melody to her bunk, the
wind so strong that it tore the tops off the great waves,
piling the surging leviathans one upon the other, but even
then the captain ran it daringly and they logged over
three hundred miles that day. Incredibly, little damage
was suffered and they came out of it, still sailing high
seas, but making good time to just west of Amsterdam
Island, after which the sea settled and a good breeze
carried them on toward the coastline of Australia.

Unlike their previous voyage, Melody found herself
quite unable to enjoy the invigorating sensation of the
wind in her hair and the deep swell, for her confusion of
heart and mind overcame any pleasure that the journey
may have afforded. She tried in vain to overcome the fear
that paralysed her mind each time she imagined her future
in the alien land before them, but found herself becoming
more despairing as the days passed, not even able to
summon more than a smile at the antics of the dolphins
that followed the ship, cavorting and tumbling in the
waves.

There was, for the first time in her life, no one to turn
to, and as the grey seas turned to blue and they reached
the calmer waters of the Indian Ocean, she realised that
they were on the final stretch of their journey. 'Oh, Aunt
Bee!' she whispered to the sleeping woman on the opposite
bunk. 'What have I brought you to!' and tears came to

her eyes. 'Loyalty and Love personified—but surely better to have stayed in England than to have endured all that has happened since!'

Tired herself, yet unable to sleep, nauseous from the acrid odour of sickness that clung to the air in spite of the hanging pomanders, Melody wandered out on deck. To have come to this! Murderess—mulatto slave. What future? Deeply depressed, she leaned on the lee rail, unaware of the chill night breeze, gazing into the black waters below. What future for Aunt Bee? An alien in a strange land, torn from the gaiety she knew and loved, from friends and family. Would *she* ever return? 'Yes,' a small voice said. 'If she were alone!' Paul Savage would help her. He had indicated such on one or two occasions, which offers Beatrice had staunchly refused. He had sent fresh limes to the cabin, and a young boy with a daily supply of cool fresh water. Yes, *he* would see that her aunt received all the help she needed. It was not *her* debt to repay. Without Melody, she would be free. The water lapped soft as velvet against the side of the ship, murmuring seductive invitations it would be so easy to accept!

At that moment Paul came out on deck, and his heart leaped to his throat as he saw the girl leaning over the inky depths. He cursed himself for not having realised the depths of her misery and shame, for not having spoken or done something when he recognised the change of mood almost a month earlier, when that spirited anger had slowly deadened to a lethargic acceptance of her lot. He approached swiftly and silently with the cat-like tread of the hunter until he was within reach of her, then very carefully he said, 'Good evening, Mrs Van der Veer.'

Melody spun with a gasp, and in that instant, as her startled gaze met his, he read a depth of despair and defeat such as he had seen only in battle-torn infantry after a long and demoralising campaign.

'I wasn't expecting you.'

'Undoubtedly. The night's cool.'

'I hadn't noticed.'

'You should be wearing a wrap: I'll send one of the boys for it.'

'No . . . there's no need. I'll go below. My aunt will need my attention.'

'Your aunt will be sleeping, and your attention would best be served elsewhere.'

Melody could not deny his knowledge, or the fact that in her more lucid moments Beatrice had demanded to be 'left to die in peace', but the fear knotted her stomach and her throat went dry as she interpreted his words. He wouldn't! He couldn't! 'You—You want me to . . . to serve you . . . in some way?'

Paul looked down at her, seeing the suddenly wide eyes and the way her fingers had clenched over the rail. What in God's name did she expect him to do? Rape her on the spot? Steadying his anger with a deep breath, he said, 'Yes. I want you to stop being afraid of me, of my land, and of your future.'

Melody stared at him, the dark wall of despair crumbling beneath that mesmeric voice. 'I—I . . . ' But then, as despair gained hold once more, 'I can't! I'm your slave, nothing more, and for that I'll *always* hate and fear you. You bought me, took me from the auction block, gave me no choice but to accompany you on this nightmare voyage. I *have* to obey you, yet you're a stranger to me.'

She saw the scar whiten against the heightened colour of his face, but there was something in his face that she could not fathom. 'Very well. As a slave, you say you must obey. Kiss me, then.'

Melody felt her breath forced from her lungs as she searched the taut features in disbelief.

'Come, I command you!'

'You . . . mustn't!'

A gleam appeared in the dark eyes. 'That sounded remarkably like a challenge, Mrs Van der Veer.'

'No . . . It wouldn't be right. You agreed . . . '

'Then you're denying that you are my slave and that I can change my mind? Denying my power to command you?' And it was only much later that she remembered he had not used the word 'right'.

Her heart began to pound, and her voice emerged barely above a whisper as she was forced to admit, 'No.'

A faint curve came to that mobile mouth. 'Then I *do* command you, Mrs Van der Veer. I command my slave to put her arms about my neck and then kiss me.'

The trembling began deep inside, and it took a supreme effort of will to force her hands up that broad chest to clasp the back of his neck, feeling the springy black hair curling beneath her fingers, knowing suddenly that she would never be the same again. Beneath that strangely intent gaze she began to feel even more uneasy and looked away, running the tip of her tongue over her dry lips.

'Well?'

But the shame was too much to bear, and despairingly she threw back her head, eyes brilliant. 'I can't!' But in that instant his lips descended, and with a gasp she closed her eyes, fearful of what was to come, then caught her breath as the brutal ravaging kiss she had expected touched feather light against her mouth. His lips moved gently over hers, cool with the night air, slightly salty from the sea-spray, exploring, seeking, parting her lips to his tongue. The kiss deepened, became possessive, stirring her senses so that she felt her knees buckle, refusing to support her, and she clung to those iron-muscled shoulders as though she were drowning.

Paul's arms tightened about her, taking her weight, as a fire spread through him such as he had never thought to feel again, bringing with it a heady passion that almost rent his wire-taut control. Why not? Until they reached land, she belonged to him. He could do as he pleased: take her here and now on the planking or sweep her into his arms and carry her below. Other men had taken her: her husband, probably his cousin—considering his willingness to give his entire fortune for her—and undoubtedly others. No woman of such beauty could avoid taking lovers. There was a passion in her that he recognised, and yet . . . the lips beneath his seemed so innocent, so untutored . . .

A tiny whimper was torn from her and brought him the awareness of the crushing grip with which he held her captive, and at once he loosened his hold. Both were breathing heavily as he released her, gazes locked, molten fire beneath the strange kind of wonder, both shaken by the experience.

Angry with herself for the emotions that had rocked her very soul, Melody cried, 'Is this how you use *all* your slaves, Mr Savage?'

'I told you I had no slaves,' he said, mastering his breathing with an effort, yet rejoicing to see the fury that he had so missed in those incredible sapphire eyes. 'However . . . I'm quite willing to learn from the material at hand!'

'Not while I have breath to fight you!'

He gave an infuriating half-smile and a nod. 'It appears to take little effort to deprive you of that breath, but I knew I'd reach that fine temper of yours eventually. We lost it for a while back there.'

'Damn you!' Melody exploded, twisting away. 'Damn you, you . . . Savage!' running blindly back to her aunt's cabin, but . . .

'Be fair,' Beatrice had insisted after several searching questions on the following morning, though her expression had grown grim at Melody's first recounting. Then the girl's deep depression and despair had been revealed, and she re-evaluated the situation. Perhaps there was more to this man than even she had first suspected, having guessed already his strength and fortitude, his care—well hidden— for his cousin, the fairness and respect he accorded his people, and the undoubted love of his land. 'This situation, intolerable as it is for you, my dear, is not of his choosing either.'

'He could have freed me from the beginning . . . Bought me, then given me . . . what are they called . . . manumission papers?'

'And stood to lose eight thousand dollars. This way, he knows he'll be paid, either by your own efforts through work or by Patrick's . . . er . . . business acumen.'

She smiled gently, though she ached inside for the girl's pain. 'Face facts, sweeting. You are the only one all along who has insisted that you are nothing more than a slave. I'd give my life to change places with you, but there is a world of difference between a slave, and a hired servant who *can* pay off her debt. You must admit, too, that apart from last night's incident . . . '

'Incident!'

'Apart from that,' Beatrice continued, ignoring the explosion, 'he has treated us as no less than ladies since our first meeting.'

Melody shook her head violently, glaring down at the pale-faced woman on the bunk. 'How can you even be polite to him! He's arrogant and boorish, a monster without feeling. He barely spoke to poor Brett when we left. He had no concern about what would happen to him with those unbelievable people . . . ' She broke off chokingly, as the poignancy of that leavetaking caught at her throat.

. . . Brett had done everything possible to make their final time together memorable, yet there was an undercurrent of sadness that made every hour seem but a moment, and she knew that the same bitter-sweet melancholy had affected Patrick and Beatrice as much, even though their light raillery had continued as before, bringing the only laughter to the gathering.

Late the night before their departure there had been a light rapping at Melody's door, and, still wide awake, she had hurried to open it, thinking it was Aunt Bee, but . . .

'Brett!'

'I had to come,' he whispered. 'Don't be angry with me.' He wore a dressing-gown of bronze silk over his nightshirt, but his feet were bare and cold from the wooden floors.

'Oh, my poor dear!' She hurried him inside, lest the others hear. 'Come, sit on top of the bed. I'll tuck the coverlet over your feet and we can talk . . . '

'Stop it! Melody, you must listen to me, or I'll never get it said.'

The carved features betrayed a frighteningly deep emotion, and worriedly she took his arm, closing the door with her free hand before leading him toward the bed. 'Tell me, then. What is it?'

Suddenly his arms were about her, those sightless eyes burning into hers. 'Melody, I'd give anything in the world never to have met you . . . and my soul to have you belong to me completely. All these hours . . . it seems a lifetime of separate hours since first I heard your tread in the hall at St Clare . . . and now there are only a few more left to us . . . just tonight. The Lord only knows when, or if, I'll see you again. Fool to say that . . . But I *do* see you since our first touch.' His lips sought her temple, her eyes. 'My love, I need you so much! You're like a fire inside me. I can't think or act with any sense or reason. Give me a memory I can truly live for. Give me tonight, Melody!'

Heart racing, she felt one strong hand move over her back, the other slipping forward to cup her breast, before he kissed her, clumsily at first, missing her mouth, then fastening on to it as might a man dying of thirst take a draught of cool spring water. She tried to lose herself in that kiss, tried to feel pleasure in the pain his fingers brought as he clutched at her, communicating his desperate need . . . And she failed.

Gently but firmly she eased him away, and her voice was husky with feeling. 'I'm sorry, my dear, but . . . not like this . . . I can't be like this . . .'

'You don't love me!' There was disbelief in the words, as though nothing that had come between them in the past week could have changed her feelings for him.

Melody felt the tears pricking her eyes as she raised her hands to lock about his neck, drawing his head down. Very slowly she moved her mouth over his in sweet agony, knowing that the tears had overflowed and now coursed crystalline down her cheeks. 'I love you. Believe me,' she whispered. 'I just don't know how, or how much. Brett, I'll always love you, never doubt that, but you must leave me now . . . as I have to leave you tomorrow, though it breaks me in two. Leave me, please.'

'Melody, I need you.'

And she almost surrendered, but then, with a deep, shuddering breath, he straightened, turning away. 'Goodbye, Melody.' It sounded like a death-knell.

   . . . Thinking back on that moment, Melody wondered whether it would have mattered; whether she should have given them both a night to remember . . . and whether she would see that perfect, blind Apollo again. But then came the memory of that other kiss, burning her master's mark into her as surely as with a brand, searing her very soul, and she felt a traitor. 'I shan't go on deck again until we reach Wellington,' she vowed. 'I won't speak to him unless commanded to, and avoid him at all costs!' She knew that it would be almost impossible, but the shame she now felt for that one forbidden moment when she had allowed herself to melt against his heart hardened her resolve.

She had felt that heart pounding against hers as the steely arms had tightened about her, and in a flash had come the thought, 'It would be so easy!' She belonged to him; they both knew that. It was expected. But then the picture of Celine had swum before her, her half-sister, sold into concubinage. No! She was not like that! *She* was not a slave who'd surrender her soul to any man. But the lips plundering hers gave her heart the lie, and she knew that a small, hopeless sob had escaped her. In that instant she had been released and had covered her shattered emotions with anger.

'Oh, when will this hateful journey end?' she now cried. 'Anything would be better than being confined to this floating prison!' But it was almost three weeks later when a sailor called, 'Home ahead!' and pointed out a vague black smudge on the horizon. To him it may have been home, even though from first sighting of land came the difficult navigation through Bass Strait and up the coast to Sydney, but to Melody it never would be, she vowed. Even so, she was fascinated, as before, at the captain's skill as he tacked with over twenty square sails to command, each sail having ropes on all four corners and each one manhandled and trimmed, and brought them into peaceful waters beyond.

From there it was almost an anticlimax to board another clipper to Wellington. The ship was making the homeward journey, having spent a month and more in port loading up with wool and more passengers, and Melody felt her heart beat faster as thoughts of stowing away skittered through the corridors of her mind. But then, with a sigh, she thought of Aunt Bee, and gave up the impossible dream with a tiny, self-deprecatory smile.

It was several days later when Paul called Melody on deck shortly after the morning watch, the first time he had approached her directly since what Aunt Bee referred to as 'that incident'. 'I want you to see the end of your journey,' he said.

'It's barely dawn!'

'It is just dawn. That's why I think you should see what I have to show you. This is no command, Mrs Van der Veer, but I feel you will appreciate the view.'

Curiosity piqued, she rested her fingers as lightly as possible on the proffered arm and accompanied him on deck. The sky was clear, with the cloud-bank lying low on the water, and above, the brilliant golden orb was emerging from behind a colossus of a mountain, solitary and cone-shaped, its snow-covered peak gleaming crimson in the rising sun's rays.

'Oh, it's beautiful!' Melody exclaimed, clutching at his arm, her eyes wide in wonder.

'Mount Egmont . . . our answer to Japan's Fujiyama. Its real name is Taranaki, and it's one of the three great mountains that lived before the original canoes came.'

'Lived?' She turned to look up at him, but his gaze was fixed on the sleeping giant.

'Oh, yes,' he nodded. 'Everything lives . . . To a butterfly, a week is a lifetime, and we have our three score years and ten. The rocks and hills live at a far slower rate, that's all.' The deep-set eyes were unfathomable as he turned to look down at the fragile cameo of her face,

for once alive with curiosity and a touch of wonder. 'It is
said that, to find complete peace of mind, you have to
learn to watch the rocks grow.'

Melody was caught in that regard, and knew that he
was trying to tell her something, but fought the
overwhelming desire to whisper 'Teach me!' Tearing away
from that dangerous virility, she said, 'You mentioned
three mountains', and saw his lips lift as though he had
read her mind.

'Yes, their names were Taranaki, Tongariro and Tongariro's beautiful tree-topped wife Pihanga. Well, apparently,
they all lived quite amicably in the centre of the North
Island until Taranaki began to pay court to Pihanga, a
dangerous enterprise in any society! The two rivals
quarrelled quite violently, and as you can appreciate,
when two mountains quarrel it's quite a scene, with lava
and great fireballs being hurled back and forth. In the
end Taranaki had to admit defeat, and was banished. He
moved westward as far as he could go but still Tongariro
was not content, and even now, in an occasional fit of
jealous rage, he sends out great bursts of fire and smoke
from his crater, Ngauruhoe. It doesn't bother Taranaki,
though, for he knows he is still far more handsome, with
his cloak of soft green and the white hat trailing its
feathers . . . There . . . See them?'

She turned to see the snowy trails down the mountain's
craggy face, and Paul could watch the play of emotion
on the suddenly alive features. A deep ache began in his
chest, a gnawing hunger that threatened to suffocate him.
Damn her! Why did she have to be so incredibly beautiful,
so innocent in appearance—when he knew those appearances lied?

Looking over her shoulder to ask, 'Do you live near
the mountain?' Melody was shaken by the sudden inexplicable anger in the eyes that a moment before had gleamed
with the wry humour of the legend.

'No, much further to the south-east,' he answered
brusquely. 'We'll be coming to Cook's Strait soon. It's a
place most sailors avoid unless they are compelled to go

to Wellington, so I suggest you go below and prepare for some more rough weather.'

'Yes . . . Yes, of course.' She dropped her hand from his suddenly taut arm. 'Thank you for bringing me up here and—and telling me about the mountain.'

He swung to face her, made as if to speak, but then merely gave a nod and turned back to his contemplation of the scene, leaving her to find her own way back to her cabin.

'I hope he falls overboard!' she muttered vengefully. 'I hope a squall hits at this very moment and sweeps him into a watery Hades!'

The thought sustained her until the ship had passed through the dreaded Cook's Strait, which for once did not live up to its reputation as a place to fear. The vast mountain ranges of the North and South Islands forced the Roaring Forties into this channel, making Wellington one of the windiest cities in the world, and the narrow strait a veritable cyclone corridor. But this time the Fates were kind, and only a brisk force five blew the main skysail-yarder through to safe harbour.

As the ship off-loaded its cargo and took on more for the return journey, Paul summoned Melody to his cabin. She entered with a frown, then pulled up short as a second man rose from the single chair. Paul was standing in that arrogant pose that she hated, hands on hips, legs slightly spread to accommodate the roll of the ship, chin raised so that he appeared to look down on her even more than his height already allowed. He introduced the stranger as Martin Weldon, a lawyer from New Orleans, and the little bird-like man nodded an unsmiling greeting, his pale eyes assessing her in one swift glance, then widening a fraction in puzzlement, and she wondered what Paul had told him of her. On the table lay a sheaf of papers, and her heart leapt as her eyes swung to Paul's set features.

He gestured toward the pile. 'Your manumission papers, legally freeing you as a slave, even though the minute we step ashore you would be free anyway.'

'Then why . . . ?'

'The other is a contract,' he continued, as if she had not spoken, his voice suddenly hard. 'It is a document which acknowledges your indebtedness to me in the amount of eight thousand dollars and your willingness to work off this debt at Windhaven in any manner agreeable to both parties. Your wages will be no less than one hundred dollars and no more than three hundred dollars a year, depending on the work undertaken, and above this you will be provided with food, clothing and shelter.'

'Generous remuneration indeed!' the lawyer put in.

'And if I choose not to sign it?' Melody asked, knowing already that she would, for honour demanded that she attempt to pay off the debt. 'What is to prevent me, as a free woman, from seeking other employment in Wellington?'

The dark eyes glittered. 'I will,' he stated unequivocally. 'You may sign this contract only as a free woman. If you do not accept your freedom here and now and immediately afterwards place yourself in my service, you'll not set foot on free soil at all. You'll return to America as a slave . . . as you left it.' He saw her face drain of colour, and almost regretted his cruel words, but he knew that he wanted this woman bound to him at all costs. Without a word he held out the precious manumission papers.

Melody took them and flung them into the far corner, brushing past him to take up the pen, scrawling her name to that hated contract. 'I'm as much a slave as ever I was,' she stated, her voice low and taut with a barely perceptible tremor. 'And you'll still be a slave-owner, Mister Savage, until that detestable document is torn to shreds!' Spinning, eyes bright with tears she refused to shed, she ran from the cabin.

The lawyer accorded Paul a long look. 'You realise that an appeal to a British Court would shoot holes in that piece of paper?' At the bleak look and brief nod, he continued, 'Is she so important to you?'

Paul stiffened, drawing himself up to his full height, and the eyes that looked down upon, and through, the other man were clear and chilling. 'Thank you for your services, Mr Weldon. Your signature as witness, if you please, and then I'll trouble you no further.'

With a sigh, the man signed the document and received his more than generous fee. 'If you want my advice . . . ' he began.

'I shall call on you,' Paul finished, opening the door for him. 'Good day, sir.'

CHAPTER TWELVE

WELLINGTON WAS, as Beatrice remarked, 'A long shot from New York', but they were not unpleasantly surprised at the bustling busyness of the town, and realised that, although Auckland was the capital, people would come to trade in Wellington because of the constant ebb and flow of ships from foreign ports. Paul had advised them that already there were plans afoot to confer the honour of becoming the new capital on the city, delighting the populace who foresaw a positive explosion of trade and a soaring of prestige. City maps had been drawn up to change completely the area from Lambton Quay where the wooden façade of the town curved round the site of the old beach front, newly reclaimed, and beyond, where shops and offices, banks and hotels clustered in friendly disarray.

Beatrice had been reduced to a shadow of her former self on the journey, and remarked with a wan smile that she had quite regained the slender curves of her youth but had found nowhere to pack the leftover skin! That she was also still suffering from the ordeal was self-evident, and Melody heard with surprise the 'unfeeling monster' by their side declare that they would stay with friends in town until Lady Davenport was ready for the final leg of the journey northward.

'Not another ship,' Beatrice groaned. 'You may as well shoot me here and now and put me out of my misery.'

Paul looked regretful. 'A bare day's sailing to Wanganui, then a slow steamer up-river. From there only a short ride to the homestead, but you'll need your strength, for it's an arduous journey through barely cleared bushland. The Reids are English like yourselves, and came over twenty years ago with the first influx of immigrants, so they'll be glad of news from home.'

'Won't they object to giving lodging to complete strangers at a moment's notice?' Melody enquired in a worried voice, but Paul shook his head as he hailed a carriage.

'Not once I have explained who you are.'

Melody felt a chill slither down her spine. 'You mean they would turn away two solitary English ladies, but your coloured slave and her aunt would be quite acceptable?'

His features darkened, and a muscle tightened in his jaw. 'The Reids would condemn slavery as vehemently as any civilised person would, and I've no wish to give them cause for concern or embarrassment. I had anticipated introducing you as my house-guests enjoying an indefinite stay, but a bonded servant would probably be met with equal acceptance and possibly less speculation. As to your colour, they would give it no more thought than I, since their daughter-in-law is pure-blood Maori, but if you feel the need to mention it, do so by all means.' Deliberately then he turned his back on her and addressed Beatrice. 'Lady Davenport, I suggested you stay with close friends as opposed to a hotel only so that your health could be watched more closely. If you feel that it would give you any cause for distress, I shall be glad to book a room at a nearby hotel.'

Beatrice smiled, and Paul thought that for all her tiredness and the fever that coloured her cheeks, for all her past ordeals and present fears for her future that had etched deep lines about the cool grey eyes, she was still a very attractive woman. 'We'd be very glad of your friends' hospitality, Mr Savage, and I, for one, am most grateful for your kindness and consideration.'

He gave a short bow, and as his glance swept over Melody, she thought she detected a flicker of triumph there and inwardly seethed. He saw her high colour and the white teeth catch at her lower lip, and with an effort prevented a frown. She might have deceived his cousin with her low voice and soft touch, but there was tempered steel beneath it, of that he was certain. He had experienced flashes of her anger, sparked from a remarkably short fuse, and knew that her spirit would serve her well in the harsh life ahead, yet this continuing reference to and mental turmoil over her colour might be her undoing, limiting her friends and erecting a barrier that none could penetrate. He had experienced it on the sea voyage when she had deliberately cast herself in the role of slave, knowing how it annoyed him.

On several occasions during the last month of the voyage he had asked her to leave the bedside of her aunt and take a turn about the deck, but the quick spark of pleasure in those lovely eyes had been immediately extinguished and she had refused—'Unless you consider that an order . . . ' It rose between them now as a high wall, as Paul introduced them to plump Amy Reid and her equally corpulent husband. 'Amy, George, this is Mrs Van der Veer . . . '

'Mr Savage's bonded servant,' Melody interrupted, appalled instantly at her own rudeness.

Smoothly, Paul continued, 'And her aunt, Lady Davenport, both from England. We have come from my cousin Brett in North Carolina, and the journey has taken its toll. We were going to a hotel to rest for a few days before making our way to Windhaven . . . '

'But you decided to give us the pleasure of your company instead, and quite right too,' Amy Reid finished with a wide smile.

Melody noticed that her eyes had not betrayed the slightest shock at her introduction, and feeling gauche, irritated at her own lack of manners, attempted to make amends. 'It's most kind of you to take in two perfect strangers, Mrs Reid. We are truly grateful for your hospitality.'

Shrewd brown eyes took in the expensive watered silk and elegant coiffure that Melody had spent over an hour dressing that very morning, teasing out the side ringlets and arranging the low chignon just so. Amy Reid was no fool, and had met indentured servants before. They did not speak in such melodious tones and certainly did not possess a titled aunt, or wear with such an air of natural ease clothes that would cost her husband three months' wages. There was more here than met the eye, she surmised, and Amy Reid's curiosity was as large as her ample frame. Her smile betrayed nothing of speculation, however, as she took the girl's hand, noting the soft skin and delicate bones, and led her to a comfortable over-sprung chair. 'You can't possibly be strangers if you've come with Paul!' she declared, then turned to Beatrice, seeing the strength that kept the sick and weary frame upright, and made another of her snap judgments. Lady or not, *this* one was a woman of her own kind! 'And you, my dear, are going straight to bed with a hot toddy. No arguments, please!'

Beatrice, too, had gained an instantly favourable impression, and accorded her hostess one of those radiant smiles that had gained her entry to homes and hearts throughout Europe. 'I never argue with bribery, Mrs Reid, and the offer of a bed that doesn't move and a hot toddy definitely comes under the heading of bribery! I'll accept both with heartfelt thanks.'

Amy Reid beamed, and rang a tiny brass bell on the sideboard. 'I usually shout,' she confessed. 'But I'll restrain myself for company!'

Almost immediately the door opened and a lovely young Maori girl entered. At the sight of Paul, her liquid brown eyes lit up and she ran forward to take both his hands. 'Mita Paul! Mita Paul! You back! It been so very long!'

Melody stared in amazement at the transformation in the man's features as he looked down into the lovely laughing face of the servant-girl, his deep-set eyes sparkling and the slightly full lips lifting into a smile that showed even white teeth. *'Kia ora, kumara,'* he said, and the child, for she was little more, stamped her foot in mock anger.

'You *not* call!' she exploded, but Amy Reid was smiling

indulgently as she caught Melody's puzzled look.

'*Kia ora* is just an informal "Hallo". If you were meeting a stranger, you'd use the more formal *"tena koa"*. What Ani is objecting to is Paul calling her *"kumara"*, which is a kind of sweet potato, but she was only five when Paul found her, hiding in a *kumara* pit after a raid on her village by a band from a rival tribe had killed her family. He's called her *"kumara"* to this day. Now that she's a grown-up young lady of twelve, she objects.'

The other foreign words had drifted over Melody's head, but she smiled politely, as with a swift pat on her rump, Paul sent the girl further into the room.

'These ladies will be staying for a while,' Amy told her slowly and clearly. 'This is Lady Davenport. She is tired, and will go to bed now. This is Mrs Van der Veer, and she will wish to wash and change before dinner.'

The serious attention with which the child had listened, mentally translated, and understood, gave way to a wide smile. 'Good, Mihi Rid,' she agreed. 'You come up, Mihi Lady an' Mihi Van. I show room.'

'I'm afraid we have only one spare room,' Amy apologised. 'But it's quite large by Wellington standards and I think you'll be comfortable.'

'I'm sure it will be perfect,' Melody smiled. 'We appreciate your hospitality.'

Amy returned her smile, liking what she saw when that strangely aloof defensiveness broke down. 'The Maoris call it *"manuhiritanga"*—"gladly giving unlimited hospitality to a stranger". It's a pleasant and sometimes necessary habit to cultivate in a land as new as this. These are troubled times, Mrs Van der Veer, and we whites must cultivate close ties both with others of our own race, and also with the few friendly natives who have proved their loyalty. Now don't let me keep you. When Ani has shown you to your room, I'll send her back with your aunt's hot toddy and some water for you to wash in. She isn't much use as a hand-maid, but she's eager to please and a joy to teach.'

'*And* thoroughly spoilt,' put in Paul indulgently. 'I must

leave you for the moment, Amy, and find accommodation, but I'll be back for dinner and bring at least one small contribution to the meal.'

The so-far silent George put down the ancient pipe he'd been chewing on, not lighting it in respect of the ladies, and his round face lit up in anticipation. 'It couldn't be some of that quite illegal hootch you've smuggled in, could it?'

Paul dismissed Amy's expostulations with a smiling gesture, and gave a nod. 'But please don't insult a fine Armagnac by calling it hootch!'

'All brandy's the same to this heathen,' Amy said, aiming a table-napkin at her husband's head. 'You shouldn't indulge him.'

'A small price to pay for your cooking, Amy.' But then his smile was switched off as he turned to Melody, and his eyes were suddenly frosty. 'Mrs Van der Veer, would you accompany me to my carriage?' His tone was imperious, and after a swift glance at her aunt, Melody followed him outside. He stopped abruptly a few paces from the house and turned, taking her arm in iron-muscled fingers. 'The Reids are my friends,' he stated softly and without preliminary. 'They are simple people with neither delusions of grandeur nor appreciation of the theatre. Your little melodrama of a high-born lady acting as a lowly servant sits uneasily on their shoulders, and I should not wish to see a recurrence of it. Once we're at Windhaven, you may go barefoot, wear a cotton shift and your hair in braids for all I care, but if you do, you must carry the role of servant to its completion, lowering your head and according me instant obedience.' Vainly she tried to pull free, but his fingers tightened, and a sudden pain shot through her arm.

As the colour drained from her face, he knew the effect his calculatedly cruel hold was having, and the knowledge gave him a sick feeling. He had never deliberately hurt any woman in his life, yet with this one he felt an irrational desire to cause pain, to break her spirit and quench the challenge in those brilliant eyes, while aware that she would need just that spirit to survive the life to which he had brought her. Disgusted with himself, he dropped his hand and turned away. 'I'll be back for dinner. I shall expect you to have your script learned by that time, and if you've no pride in yourself, consider your aunt, who would, incidentally, in sackcloth and ashes be as undoubtedly a lady.' Angrily he flung himself into the waiting carriage and disappeared down the steep hill in a cloud of dust.

For a long moment Melody stood there, blinking back tears of rage and self-pity. 'I hope you overturn and break your neck!' she cursed aloud. A couple passing by hesitated, staring, but she glared at them so fiercely that they hurried on, whispering. 'I hate you and I hate your country,' she declared with a total lack of logic, considering she knew so little of the one and absolutely nothing of the other. The unfairness of the statement drained a little of her anger, and she brushed at her eyes with the back of her hand. 'But you won't beat me,' she vowed, and drawing a deep breath, she made her way back into the house.

The girl, Ani, was helping Amy Reid in the kitchen, and their laughing chatter was so different from that of the servants at St Clare or, for that matter, of even those in the house in London since the arrival of Luther Hogge, that she felt her throat ache with loneliness. Would she ever learn to laugh again? On first entering the Reids' living-room she had noticed the small, beautifully inlaid satinwood piano in one corner, and her heart had leapt— but then plummeted again as she realised that a servant would not be expected to know how to play. She crossed to it, and making sure that there was no one within earshot, raised the lid and ran her fingers over the keys. The tone was perfect. Dare she? The temptation was too great, and seating herself on the tapestry-covered stool, she began to touch the keys as softly as possible.

As before, when escaping the fear and revulsion of Luther's presence, she found peace in the music and the feel of the smooth ivory beneath her fingers. She progressed to a more intricate composition, a lilting mazurka, accentuating the triple time, and a tiny smile curved her lips as she remembered Hugh's patient teaching and his high praise when she had mastered that piece. Finishing it, she gave a deeply satisfied sigh.

'That's lovely, Mrs Van der Veer!'

She turned to meet Amy's smiling eyes and the delighted gaze of the child by her side. 'Oh, I'm sorry. I didn't mean to impose . . . '

'Please!' Amy laughed. 'I'm the one who intends to impose, by asking you to continue playing.' She came to stand at Melody's side and put a friendly hand on her shoulder. 'George bought me this from a work associate who was selling up and returning home after the death of his wife. I've always wanted to play, but I'm afraid a town even as civilised as Wellington is still rather short of music-teachers, and the only one we know had his books full of people far more affluent than we.'

'Why, *I'd* love to . . . ' She broke off in embarrassed confusion. 'Though I suppose where I'm going is much too far from here . . . '

Amy gave a regretful nod. 'I'm afraid so, my dear, though it was a lovely thought. However, I'd be most happy for you to play as much as you wish while you're here. Since you so obviously love it, it would give all of us a great deal of pleasure.'

Melody warmed to her even more. 'I'll play a piece, then, especially for Ani in her green cotton dress.' She turned, smiling, to the girl who had drawn as close as she dared, put out a hand, and drew her into the circle of her arm. 'There was once a king of England who fell in love with a beautiful young girl with hair of a rich dark brown like yours, and as long. Like you, she wore a green dress, and he composed a song for her. Would you like to hear it?'

Her eyes large in wonder, Ani nodded. 'Good, Mihi Van.'

Giving her a quick hug, Melody began to play 'Greensleeves' as Amy went to sit in a comfortable chair by the fireplace. Her own voice was lower than was fashionable, with a slightly husky quality that gave a richness and a totally unconscious sensuality to the words. Half a century later that same quality would be heard as the Blues were discovered, but in this time and place only the loneliness and longing came through, and it was this that Paul Savage heard as he entered.

He stood silently in the doorway taking in the scene, the child and woman smiling at each other with a warmth that went beyond creed or colour as they joined together slowly in the chorus, Ani picking up the words, putting the soft Maori pronunciation to them, and instinctively harmonising her clear soprano with Melody's lower tones.

'Greensleeves was my heart of gold, And who but my lady Greensleeves?'

The final note died away, and Paul moved into the room, seeing with regret the sudden stiffening as she became aware of his presence, and the polite mask that she turned toward him, rising immediately from the stool. The child ran to him as before, taking his hands. 'That was for me,' she told him. 'Doesn't Mihi Van play lovely music?'

'Lovely,' he said softly, allowing his eyes to rove over the averted profile and delicately flushed features. 'I shall regret not having a piano at Windhaven.'

Amy gave a chuckle, breaking the mood. 'You'd have some small problem getting one through that wilderness, though I'd never put anything past you!'

He crossed to stand before Melody, and for her ears only, said, 'Anything's possible with sufficient incentive.'

Confused as always when he was so near, she looked away from the collar of the midnight-blue dress coat to the pale grey watered silk waistcoat that lent a quiet elegance to his broad frame, to the drill trousers that fitted the muscular thighs as though they had been poured on, and down . . . then turned quickly. Her heart was hammering as she acknowledged the sheer animal magnetism of the man—and denied its effect with every-thing that was in her, murmuring, 'I can think of no incentive great enough, sir.'

With humour, he answered, 'A pity. It might have been an interesting thought.' He moved away, to allow her to go to her room to change.

'I shan't give in!' she muttered vehemently as she went to the cosily furnished bedroom, moving silently that she would not waken the sleeping woman. 'He may own my body, but he'll never own more!' With a grimace at her mirror-image, she pulled her hair into a tight, uncompromising chignon and dressed in a stiffly corseted, high-necked bombazine. '*Now* I can face him!' she muttered beneath her breath.

Dinner was less of an ordeal than she had at first imagined, even though her aunt was not there to smooth over the rough spots. 'Let her sleep,' Amy had insisted. 'She can eat later if she is hungry, but at the moment sleep is the best medicine she can have. Now you sit there, Paul, and you opposite, Mrs Van der Veer. Come, don't be formal, Paul! We are quite accustomed to seeing you eating in your shirtsleeves, and then poor George can do the same. You can pour the wine, too, and save time.'

With a smile, Paul removed his jacket to reveal a shirt of the finest white silk that stretched taut across his back beneath the waistcoat and encased his arms so that the muscles could be seen to ripple as he stretched toward the decanter. Their eyes met across the table, and Melody turned away quickly, studying the pattern on her glass, feeling her throat inexplicably dry, angry at the effect he always had on her. 'Pull yourself together, girl!' she admonished herself. 'Just because he's not like any man you've seen, he is no less a barbarian . . . cruel, arrogant and unfeeling, who takes what he wants and the devil take the hindmost.' But then her treacherous mind remembered the way his eyes had softened for the Maori child, his concerned attentiveness toward her aunt on that terrible voyage, and his willingness to mortgage his own home to help an adoptive cousin he barely knew. She caught those deep-set eyes on her, suddenly realising that they were of a deep dark brown, with golden flecks that caught the light from the candles on the table, and a quiver went through her, but deliberately she broke away and engaged her hostess in conversation.

The meal was a simple one, but the thick, flaky crust of the meat pie melted in the mouth and the green vegetables were crisp and fresh, the potatoes fluffy and creamy white. Melody commented on each course, laughingly admitting her own total inadequacy in the kitchen. Aunt Bee can make the best cornbread I've ever tasted! I never even knew she had the recipe, but when she stormed the kitchen at St Clare when my . . . when we were alone with Brett . . . ' She broke off awkwardly, wondering whether she had said too much and not knowing how to extricate herself, but Amy filled the gap as though quite unaware of any tension.

'Well, she can take over *my* kitchen any time she has a mind to, though as soon as she is well, you'll want to be moving on, won't you, Paul?'

He nodded. 'Much as I hate to leave,' he agreed. 'However, the ladies should have at least one day devoted to shopping. As you appreciate, neither one has a wardrobe suited to Windhaven, and I was hoping you'd be able to advise them. I'm no expert on female fashion, being more accustomed to homesteaders and those at Windhaven who are more familiar with fences than with furbelows.'

Amy patted his arm affectionately. 'Windhaven will be transformed by a lady's touch, so I'll not be sending them there in flax skirts or those shapeless wool smocks your Martha lives in.'

Melody felt a tiny inexplicable pang at the woman's words. Could it be that he was married? It would certainly explain his attitude towards her and his insistence that she be introduced as a mere servant, or at best a house-guest. What a fool she'd been, thinking he'd had some ulterior motive in bringing her out here! 'We'd be most grateful if you could spare the time,' she enthused, covering with a bright smile the strange emptiness she felt. 'I'm afraid my aunt and I outfitted ourselves in New York before travelling down to St Clare, and the thought of

staying on a farm in New Zealand was the furthest thing
from our minds at the time.' Again she felt that she might
have revealed too much, and a fleeting frown crossed her
brow. This was ridiculous! Why *shouldn't* these people
know what their precious Paul was really like, that he
had bought her as a slave and forced her to accompany
him against her will to an alien land on the far side of the
world to her home . . . Home? No, not any more.

. . . She thought of the crisp snow that would be
falling in England now, skating in the park, and fast-
paced rides in an open carriage, wrapped in blankets with
the fur-lined hood of her thick cloak drawn tight about
her face. All gone. Gone as irrevocably as her father, who
had loved and lost and, possibly, loved again; and the
fragile creature who had been a perfect mother in all but
blood, and poor, gentle Hugh, whose only crime was in
loving her . . .

'Oh, Mrs Van der Veer!'

With a start she came back to the present, meeting
shocked eyes and realising that the tears in her heart had
spilled over on to her cheeks. Embarrassed, she felt the
colour flood her face, and tried to cover it, stuttering, 'I—
I . . . please forgive me . . . Ridiculous . . . Do
apologise . . . ' Then a strong brown hand reached to
cover hers.

'Mrs Van der Veer, you have nothing to apologise for.'

Through the mist of her tears, she met those gold-
flecked eyes and saw a soft concern there that she thought
she must surely have imagined as, swiftly, she bent her
head. 'I've just realised that we are—are only a few days
from Christmas.' She drew a ragged breath and faced
Amy Reid's worried gaze. 'My father died just over a
year ago, and my mother at Easter. My husband was
killed early this year, and this will be my first Christmas
alone. It's something I have to get used to, of course, and
I can't rely on Aunt Bee to carry me through indefinitely,
but . . . I'm sorry, I didn't mean to burden you, or to
spoil your evening. Would you please excuse me? I think

I'd like to retire. It's been rather a long day.'

'Of course, my dear,' murmured Amy, dropping all formality before the pain she sensed in this lovely young woman's life, and resolving to discover the rest of the story. It hurt her to see such naked anguish in eyes that should sparkle and shine. It certainly explained the black gown she wore. She sensed a mystery, and Amy Reid, maternal defensiveness to the fore, decided to solve it and bring a little colour to those pale cheeks . . . whatever Paul Savage might think or say!

He was watching her, Amy observed, with the strangest expression, but the young woman seemed almost afraid of him, as, refusing to meet his eyes, she asked, 'Do I have your permission . . . sir?'

Again there was tension in the air, and Amy felt a warning prickle at the nape of her neck as Paul, the quiet, sometimes solitary, but never harsh man she knew and loved, said, 'Of course' in a tone that was as cold as ice.

Reiterating her thanks and apologies, Melody escaped to the bedroom, flinging herself across the bed and letting the tears flow, stuffing the sheet into her mouth lest the slightest noise waken her aunt, who, helped by natural exhaustion and the strong toddy, still slept deeply.

CHAPTER THIRTEEN

IT WAS ALMOST predictable, with Amy Reid's character and after Melody's confession, that her guests were cajoled and bullied into spending Christmas in Wellington.

'But won't you want to be at home with your family?' Melody ventured when she found herself momentarily alone with Paul in the drawing-room.

He looked out to where a corner of the wide, curved bay could be seen and the forested hills beyond. 'I always desire to return to Windhaven, whatever the time of year,' he stated softly, and there was something in his tone that wrenched at her heart. This . . . Martha the Reids had mentioned must be very beautiful, even if she did have a wardrobe full of shapeless smocks. She remembered him saying that Aunt Bee would be a lady even in sackcloth and ashes. Perhaps his wife had the same personality, where clothes were only a secondary adornment.

Probing, she asked, 'Will . . . Martha, is that her name? . . . Will she be able to cope over Christmas without you?'

His quick look held a flicker of surprise, but then he replied, 'She is accustomed to running the house, with or without me. In fact, I've often gained the impression that she'd prefer me to spend longer away and give her less work. Why do you ask?'

'Oh, I just wondered, with Christmas being . . . well . . . a family affair . . . '

'We aren't part of the Reids' family,' he pointed out, 'yet they were only too glad to have us join them.'

'And that reminds me,' Melody continued, diverted into less dangerous waters, 'whatever can I give them in the way of gifts? I have a little jewellery, though nothing of any real value, yet I would give a piece gladly if I thought it would suit Mrs Reid. I mean . . . She'd never have the chance to wear it here . . . '

He gave a brief, mirthless smile. 'What a barbaric country you must think I've brought you to! Believe it or not, there are almost civilised balls at the Governor's Residency, not that he comes down much, and even the formal luncheons there are a cause for the ladies to appear disguised as butterflies—or in some cases as *kakāriki*— our local parakeet—and the men to lace themselves into corsets and pretend they're still dazzling Don Juans. Only the militia look smart without effort, though the various regiments garrisoned here still bet quite heavily on the brightest button or shiniest boot and the effect it will have on the ladies of the town.'

'I didn't know there were several regiments here, though I saw a few soldiers on our way in. Why here? Surely there's no trouble in Wellington?'

He looked grim. 'There has been trouble on and off for the past ten years and more, when the whites started breaking the Waitangi Treaty of 1840, which gave each Maori chief the right of consent as to whether his land could be sold, and then only to the Crown. The old Governor, Charles Grey, was at least liberal-minded and fair, and although land was still purchased for the price of a few blankets, he stopped the shameful wholesale thievery that there had been. In '55, however, Gore-Brown was appointed. He has, frankly, used the Treaty to feed his own mendacity, and caring nothing for the Maori, has exploited them at every turn. His supporters among the populace may call him ill-advised, but the men about him are no more or less than he, and it's no wonder that unrest grows each year. There will be an explosion soon, the like of which we've not imagined. The Maori now want the *pakeha*, as they call us, out of New Zealand altogether, and will burn and pillage and torture and kill to gain that end, treating their own people who are friendly toward the whites even more harshly. I just hope to God they never find a leader!' He gave a shake of his head, clearing the dark thoughts and the leashed tension he constantly felt when away from home, and returned to the present. 'So that's why the militia are here. Now, as to the original subject . . . our Christmas with the Reids . . . you are quite right assuming that Amy would not wear your jewellery, simply because she is a home-loving soul who prefers her entertainment round a fire in the comfort of her own home or that of a neighbour. If you have a pretty scarf or something similar, I'm sure she would be most appreciative. Alternatively, I'd be glad to let you have enough for a few gifts . . . '

'No!' Her harsh rejection again raised that hateful barrier between them. 'I'm sorry,' she half apologised, though her tone was unrepentant, 'but I can't possibly accept any more of your money. I'll find something.'

'I'm sure you will, though with so much owing, a further few pounds would hardly go amiss,' he said with deceptive mildness.

'It would, if it meant one more day of working here.' Again she regretted her words as she saw the blaze in his eyes, but he was prevented from replying by the return of the others.

By Christmas morning all ill-feeling had been dispersed by the festive atmosphere and Amy's insistence that they all help to decorate. Despite the strange reversal of climate, this being the height of summer, Melody felt her customary excitement. She and Beatrice had scoured the town for gifts, her aunt quite happily selling a small diamond pendant for half its worth when she heard of Melody's refusal to accept Paul's money.

'The man owns me,' Melody had snapped. 'I'll not be beholden to him for anything, least of all putting myself further in debt financially. I loathe and detest the man, and everything about him!'

Beatrice entertained her own thoughts on that subject, having assessed the glances passed when neither thought the other was looking, and the immediate crackling in the air whenever they met. She therefore considered the sale of the pendant a small sacrifice and a pleasure, a token of her genuine gratitude and liking of the Reids, and of her increasing respect of Paul Savage. 'Wish I'd met him thirty years ago!' she told her mirror-image, tucking a tiny posy into the belt of her emerald-green satin crinoline. Then, putting her head to one side she amended with a smile, 'Even twenty years ago! There would have been a battle royal then, and he'd not have been the first unbroken stallion that ended by eating out of my hand.' She gave a throaty chuckle. 'You're a wicked woman, Beatrice Davenport, but still not too far over the hill to tell a real man from the majority!'

Melody, on the other hand, was wishing she had not set eyes on Paul Savage at all, or ever heard the Savage name. Going to the cosily decorated bedroom to change, her aunt having already stunned the family with her appearance, Melody stood before the long, wood-framed wall mirror in her petticoats, and gave a deep sigh. Slowly she slipped the lacy camisole from her shoulders and half embarrassedly studied her full curves in the mirror. The auctioneer had said, that one could always tell a nigra, by the blue line at the base of the nails, and the dark brown peaks of her breasts. Melody shook her head in anguish. Her nails, she knew, were delicate ovals of pale pink, her breasts ivory silk tipped with dusk rose. And yet that damning ledger had identified her as a negress! 'It can't be!' she agonised, but deep in her heart the sick knowledge remained.

'Melody! Don't take all morning, child!' Beatrice chided her from outside the door, and quickly she scrambled to dress.

Downstairs, two strangers had joined the assembly, a young man and woman, and Melody found that she could not take her eyes from the latter. She was introduced to 'Tarati Reid, our daughter-in-law, and our son Henry.'

'I am pleased to meet you,' the girl replied in careful English, and the full lips parted in a smile of devastating beauty, lighting long-lashed eyes that were a deep velvet brown.

Apart from the darker-skinned Ani, Melody had never

seen a true Maori at such close quarters, believing all natives either kinky-haired and black-skinned as in the negroid races, or possessing straight hair and brown skins as did the Indians and Chinese. This girl, however, had skin only a few shades darker than her own, and the glossy black hair fell in deep waves to her waist.

Unthinkingly, she exclaimed, 'But you're beautiful!' Then she blushed furiously in embarrassment, as did Tarati, and then both burst into laughter.

'Well *that* certainly broke the ice!' remarked the stocky youth at her side, a mirror-image of his father and with the same warm, lazy smile. 'It's nice to meet someone else who appreciates what a treasure I've found.'

'Henare, behave!' the girl said, laughing, using the Maori equivalent of his name. 'Mrs Van der Veer is already discomfited enough, though she should not be, for she is far more lovely than I.'

Now it was Melody's turn to colour, murmuring, 'May we please change the subject?'

The group broke up and the festivities started. Melody wondered at the efforts the Reids had made to ensure a 'real Christmas', with decorations appearing from ancient chests, and giant sprays cut from what they called their Christmas tree, the scarlet blossoms brilliant against dark evergreen leaves.

'It's a *Pōhutukaw* tree,' Paul explained. 'It grows only in the North Island, blooming at this time of the year, and it prefers the coastal cliffs where its root system reaches out like grappling-irons, anchoring in the most exposed places.'

'It's beautiful, almost exotic . . . a little like Tarati,' Melody smiled.

'And you,' he replied, not returning the smile, a slight frown touching his. 'You realise that eyes of such a brilliant blue are quite, quite wrong with that hair.' Then with an almost imperceptible shake of his head, as though trying to rid himself of troubling thoughts, Paul turned abruptly away, leaving Melody upset and confused. He was right, of course; a blue-eyed negress was almost

impossible to create, and as before, he refused to acknowledge the awful doubts that had assailed him all along—
that the ledger somehow had lied.

There had been other doubts, too, inexplicable and
darkly sinister that had caused him to hasten their departure when, in all humanity, he had been tempted to give
them the month that Lady Davenport had asked for her
to repay the debt by writing to England. It had been
revealed by accident from O'Shaughnessy that the two
women were being followed, but the Irishman would say
no more, so Paul had cast his own net. Even so, he had
found nothing to warrant his feeling of unease. There had
been rumours, of course, the kind circulated by men in
bars and back alleys with rough liquor clouding their
minds: rumours of a strange man turned beast, of murder,
and of thousands of dollars being spent in a manhunt.
Beyond that, the trail had faded into speculation and
legend, yet enough of it remained to determine Paul's
course of action.

As an extension of those disquieting thoughts he allowed
his brooding gaze to roam over the lovely features before
him, and reflected, 'One day I shall know, Melody Van
der Veer.'

Melody tried to avoid him after that, but when it came
time for the presents to be brought out, Amy hustled her
on to the long, deeply padded couch opposite the fireplace,
and invited, 'Come on, Paul, you sit here, and you, Lady
Davenport, on his other side if you don't mind. We don't
have much in the way of either furniture or room, so all
my guests must pretend a closer acquaintanceship than
they really share, otherwise we simply run out of space.'

With a quirk of one eyebrow Paul obligingly came to
sit between the two ladies, and Melody edged as far away
from him as possible. She could accept that the Reids'
tiny living-room was not entirely suited to the extra
company, and quite understood that two crinolines on
one couch precluded a third. She accepted Henry and his
wife going to sit, Tarati shockingly on her husband's lap,
in one of the large, over-stuffed armchairs, leaving the

other for George's bulk, but wished beyond hope that
Amy could have found a stool, preferably at some distance,
on which to seat Paul Savage!

The child, Ani, had been called in, her hair set in
ribbons for the occasion, to join the celebrations and
distribute the parcels that they had placed in a pile in one
corner. Excitedly she took each one to Amy, who read
out the name, and then she ran to hand them over, almost
tripping over herself in her eagerness. As soon as everyone
had received their small pile of presents, Ani looked
around, eyes brilliant, then cried, 'Go!' and began to tear
the wrappings from her own, raising a laugh from the
adults.

Melody held back from opening the mixed assortment
in her lap, guilty at having instigated this invitation to
spend Christmas with the warm and wonderful people
surrounding her, and embarrassed that they had seen fit
to bring her a gift from their obviously limited income. A
quick glance across the room found Amy's gentle eyes
and an understanding nod.

'Go ahead, Mrs Van der Veer. You won't see the
contents through the paper.'

Blushing, Melody said, 'Then I'll open yours first,
though you really shouldn't have. It was gift enough to
be allowed to join you for Christmas.' Her fingers revealed
a lovely comb for her hair, its ornate top decorated with
tiny shells, and her delighted exclamations brought a
pleased smile to Amy's face.

'It's not new,' she apologised. 'But it's never been worn.
Someone bought it for me shortly after we first came out
here—a foolish young man who was quite out of order.'

She exchanged smiles with her husband, who said, 'But
had impeccable taste in women!' and Melody felt a pang
at the complete empathy between them.

Amy, in turn, enthused over the cologne from Melody
and even more over the packet of needles and assorted
thread, a precious commodity, from Beatrice.

Melody lost track of who had given what to whom, but
knew that she did not want to open the small rectangular

parcel from Paul. He, too, seemed subdued since opening his gifts from herself and Beatrice, though the superb bone-handled hunting-knife from Beatrice had brought a gleam to his eyes, and warm thanks. He had been more restrained as he opened Melody's gift, a handsome morocco-bound case containing seven ivory-handled razors, one for each day of the week.

It had cost more than any of the other gifts, and Beatrice had warned her against buying it when they had seen it in the shop. 'It isn't suitable, sweeting, and you know it! Personally, I don't mind how you spend the money, but it's not the gift for a man you barely know.'

'Nor the sort of thing a servant would give her master,' Melody shot back, not knowing what had drawn her to the beautiful gift set out in the window, but knowing only that she wanted it for Paul the moment she saw it.

Beatrice gave a sigh. 'Stop fighting yourself, Melody. What are you trying to prove? That you're an independently wealthy young lady who just happens to be temporarily out of small change? We are poor, my dear, grindingly poor, in spite of all appearances. My few pieces of jewellery won't last for ever, and our better crinolines will probably end up being cut down to make two out of one. At least three of my skirts have over fifteen yards of material in them, and have you seen the skimpy hoops around town? The aristocracy don't *settle* a country, my dear, they take it over, once the wood has been cut. However, if you wish to buy Mr Savage such a handsome and undoubtedly useful gift, do so by all means.'

'Perhaps he'll cut his throat!' Melody muttered vengefully, but she bought the razors anyway. Now, seeing the slight tightening of his lips as the gift was revealed, she almost regretted her choice, but then counted it as just one more gesture in her battle to control her own actions in a situation that was, for her, intolerable.

A voice beside her said, 'It would appear ungracious if you don't open my gift, even though I can understand your desire not to do so.' She started from her reverie and gave a nod, not looking at him, slowly removing the

paper. Beneath the wrappings was a small box that
reflected all the brilliant blues and greens of a kingfisher,
shining with a strange translucence in the candlelight. 'It's
paua shell,' he explained. 'The natives use it also to
decorate their spears and their statues.'

Wonderingly, she opened it, and gave a small cry as
she gazed down at the exquisitely carved pendant in a
dark jade-green stone attached to a slender gold chain.

'They just call it greenstone,' he said quietly, his pleasure
at her reaction dimmed by the thoughts that still nagged
at him.

'It's very beautiful, and so is the box. I've never seen
anything like it. Thank you.' She gave him a quick, shy
smile. Why had he brought her such a lovely gift? What
would his wife, Martha, say? And why buy a thing of
such rare beauty for a mere servant?

The others were chattering and passing bon-bons and
drinks, with George opening the bottle of ten-year-old
bourbon that was his Christmas present from Paul, and
little Ani attempting to pass plates while clutching the
doll that Melody had bought her, and wearing over her
shoulders the length of rose silk that was her gift from
Beatrice.

'You make a dress from that, and no one will dare call
you little *Kumara*!' Beatrice had laughed, with a sidelong
glance at Paul.

With the noise and jollity diverting everyone's attention
from them, Paul said in a conversational tone, 'Mrs Van
der Veer, I think a breath of fresh air might be in order.'

About to refuse, Melody looked into those unsmiling
eyes and gave a nod, throat tight as she rose with him.
They went out to the back, where the Reids had cultivated
a tiny garden, planting exotic buttercup and *rata* trees
alongside fruit-trees bought from the early missionaries—
plum, apple, walnut, fig, orange and lemon—and, beneath
them, assorted vegetables, creating a haven for birds and
butterflies as well as a practical kitchen supply. But she
was given no chance to enjoy the peace and beauty of the
place, nor to appreciate with a musician's ear the

melodious murmur of birds and insects, as Paul said
brusquely, 'The presents you and your aunt gave, your
gift to me especially, cost far more than you had when
you arrived. I want to know where the money came from.'

Melody stared at him in amazement, feeling the slow
heat rising to her face with her anger. 'It was Aunt Bee's
money, and it's really none of your business when or how
she obtained it. How dare you ask such questions! You
may own *me*, Mr Savage, but not my *aunt!*' She made to
turn back to the house, but found her wrist caught in
fingers of steel.

'If your aunt has money, why is she throwing it away
on strangers, when she could have bought your freedom?'

'Because I did not have that amount.' An incisive voice
came from behind them, and Melody was released as
Beatrice stepped into the garden. Her eyes were cold as
the Atlantic when they met the man's frown, and her lips
tightened fractionally before she deigned to explain. 'The
only money we have is in the form of jewellery, some of
it a part of the old Davenport collection—family
heirlooms, if you like. I have very little left, but I would
gladly give it all if it would take my niece and myself
away from here, or if it could have prevented our arriving
at all! I sold a little to buy food for St Clare, though of
course I got only a fraction of its value, and more pieces
were used to grease grimy palms when I couldn't find you
at your hotel in Raleigh and had no time to wait for your
return.'

'But you would have got next to nothing from those
sharks!'

'It was obviously enough, and a necessity. There was
no time to bargain, and only children and fools put a
chunk of stone before a human life. This Christmas was
taken care of by an insignificant diamond pendant that
some insignificant Russian duke thought to buy me
with . . . a mere bagatelle in comparison with young
Ani's face at the sight of a length of rose silk, or the
Reids' hospitality. Are you now satisfied, Mr Savage?'

'And shamed,' Paul admitted with a wry smile. 'You

have my sincere apologies, Lady Davenport, and you, too, Mrs Van der Veer. We have loan-sharks in Wellington, too . . . Oh, yes, we *are* that . . . civilised! Having already offered you the money, Mrs Vvan der Veer, I was angered at the probability of your accepting their help rather than mine.'

Beatrice watched the play of emotions on the hawk-like features, and her eyes softened. 'I doubt that it was anger you felt, Mr Savage,' she said with a smile. 'But I trust you're answered now.' She turned away to the house before he could form a reply.

There was a long moment of silence following her departure, but then Melody, also, moved to leave. There was nothing of Christmas here, only recriminations and accusations, coldness and distrust.

'Mrs Van der Veer . . . ' The fingers on her arm were gentle this time, and the voice low, but she would not turn to face him. 'It was a handsome gift, and I do appreciate it.'

So he wanted to make amends now! His pride was satisfied and he was willing to accept the offering! She almost said, 'I hope you cut your throat with it!' but, putting down her anger, decided that discretion was the better part of valour. 'You're quite welcome, sir,' she said formally. 'And *your* gift was most generous.'

He moved to stand before her, blocking her path, forcing her to look up at him, reading behind those stormy eyes. 'But not what you would have had me give you?'

Melody averted her face. 'It was a very lovely piece of jewellery.'

'But?' A firm finger curved beneath her chin, raising her eyes to his.

'But shall I ever wear it, working on a farm in the wilderness?' she whispered, choking on the words. Then she told him more strongly, 'No, sir, it wasn't what I would have asked for.'

'What, then?' But she saw by his eyes that he knew already.

'You could have made me a present of my freedom . . . You could have let me go!'

He stared down at the lovely cameo of her face, the gold-flecked eyes burning like fire. 'No,' he said huskily. 'No, I can't . . . Not now.' But she couldn't question, and with a choking sob wrenched away from him and ran into the house.

. . . They left for Wanganui the following day.

Melody was in a subdued frame of mind as the frigate was carried on a crisp tail-wind to the tiny city overlooked by the two sandy hills with their twin fortresses, which Paul told her were called Rutland stockade and York stockade. She answered politely, but felt nothing when he offered other titbits of information, telling them that the town was named after the river, which in Maori means a large stretch of water. 'It rises on the slopes of Mount Tangariro, the still active and jealous volcano I told you about, and is over a hundred and forty miles long, so I've heard.'

They transferred to a steamship, which moved sedately up-river to the settlement of Pipiriki, past lush riverside meadows, towering rocky cliffs and bush-clad hillsides with tall ferns that crept down to the water's edge.

'You have no interest in botany?' Paul asked in an attempt to break through the barrier that the girl had erected since their departure from the Reids.

'Yes . . . Yes, of course . . . ' she answered abstractly, gazing out at the river, seeing little of the wild beauty about her.

There were small groups of natives gathered about the numerous bends in the river and an occasional glimpse of a fortified encampment that Paul called a '*pa*'. She had seen several 'civilised' Maoris in both Wellington and Wanganui who sported an odd assortment of European clothing and smiled a friendly greeting, but away from the towns the natives they saw appeared sullen and silent, and he told her that many resented the gradual take-over of their land by the farmers. 'It matters not to them,' he said, 'that the land they own is not put to useful purpose at present. They argue that it may serve their children and their children's children, who will at least have the choice of cultivating it or leaving it wild. The farmers in turn resent being cramped into the few acres that they are allotted while perfectly good land is, in their eyes, going to waste on their own borders.'

Melody privately agreed with the Maori viewpoint, but said nothing, refusing to agree with anything that Paul might support. She saw that the faces of the natives here were almost blue with the mass of tattooed whorls that covered them, some intricately beautiful in design. They were immodestly dressed in a type of flax apron, and Melody had averted her face in embarrassment several times until the exception became the rule and her adaptable mind accepted these fearsome, yet barbarically beautiful, people. Like Tarati, they were generally lighterhued than she had imagined, and some bore high cheekbones and aquiline noses that were almost Arabic in appearance.

It was this fierceness, in part, that bothered her, and at Paul's gently probing questions she finally said, 'The militia were in town to protect the people there from attack, but I've also seen some settlers along the river, living, I assume, as you do at Windhaven. Who protects the homesteaders?'

She had hoped to see that half-smile that Paul used when the question was not to be taken seriously, but instead his heavy brows drew together in a frown. 'We protect ourselves as you shall see, and no, Windhaven isn't as vulnerable as those farms we've passed. Wanganui had to be fortified and stockaded against attack in '46, but thanks to the diplomacy of George Grey and Donald McLean, the Native Minister—their beloved "Makarini"— the troubles died down a couple of years later. However, the outlying settlements like Windhaven rely on equally heavy fortifications (if they have any sense) and good neighbours, not to mention a close alliance with the "friendly" Maoris who have proved unbelievably loyal.' He read behind the carefully controlled features, and added, 'I'd lie if I said that Windhaven had never been attacked: we have been and we shall be again. That is why we are all well armed, but we are still there after a decade of unrest, and I envisage we shall be for another.'

'But do you not long for the safety and civilisation of the town?'

This time that familiar curve of the mouth did appear as he shook his head. 'No. I bought my land at five shillings an acre—a good price at the time—and went into debt for it rather than break the Treaty and give the Maoris some blankets, or bullets, but it's all to do with that alliance I mentioned. Now the land is almost paid for, and mine to do with as I please, fairly and legally. The neighbouring Maoris to the south are my friends, and their fighting *pa* is one of the most powerful on the river. I cleared the land and built my house. I paid no one, and made no promises I couldn't keep, yet at one time there were thirty men working on that place. Some of the young ones stayed. I'm independent and completely self-sufficient with fresh fruit and vegetables, and assorted meat on the hoof. I owe nothing to any man, and ask nothing of him. Of course I have monetary debts at the moment, but they are with honourable men and, even so, wouldn't ruin me if called in. No . . . I'd not change that for a grimy office desk and a tiny house such as the Reids own, cosy as it is.'

While speaking, his eyes roved over the full curves revealed by the tight bodice of the silk dress and there was a dryness in his throat. Would she ever adapt to this often harsh, yet infinitely rewarding, life? 'The dresses you bought in Wellington . . . ' he said as an extension of his thoughts. 'You'd best find a suitable one when we get to Pipiriki, if not before. Something you can ride in. The road from there to Windhaven is little more than a trail, long and mountainous, cutting back through the valley and over the hill. We'll use the mules and the horses I sent ahead for, but it's a fair distance.'

'Did I hear "horses"?' came Beatrice's voice, a hopeful ring to it.

'Yes, Lady Davenport. You do ride, I hope—even a little?'

Beatrice gave a snort. 'My dear young man, in my youth I was considered one of the best young horse-breakers in Rotten Row! The hacks I've seen so far are as easy as rocking-horses in comparison to the thorough-bred bay I once owned.'

Paul's eyebrows rose. 'A lady horsebreaker?' He earned a gurgle of laughter.

'Not the kind you mean, Mr Savage. The "pretty little horsebreakers", as we were called, were a certain breed of women who made it a habit to be seen in control of a spirited equine, thereby telling the world that she was wealthy enough to own one, strong enough to control one, and obviously unattached—since no husband would condone such ostentatious behaviour! Of course there were some who were distinctly below *ton*; certain ladies, and I use the word loosely, who lived in St John's Wood under lordly protection. I could mention a certain Catherine Walters, quite appropriately nicknamed "Skittles", who would cause absolute chaos in Hyde Park, careering about on that almost unmanageable grey of hers.' Beatrice gave a sniff, her twinkling eyes meeting those of Paul Savage and finding an answering spark there as he tried not to smile.

'I really don't think Mr Savage wishes to know such things,' Melody objected, only slightly ashamed of her aunt's somewhat colourful past, but he shook his head decisively.

'I am, on the contrary, deeply interested in your life in London,' he asserted. 'And I've often wondered what made you relinquish such a stimulating existence, going to stay with Brett, who, while a pleasant enough companion, can hardly compete with the sophisticates you must have been surrounded with.'

'Oh, look at that! A kingfisher,' Melody pointed. 'What is the Maori word for that, Mr Savage?' She met his quick, searching look as ingenuously as she could, heart pounding, until quietly he answered,

'It's called a *kotare*. There are many of them on this stretch of the river.' No, he thought, you don't intend me to know anything of London, not yet, but I swear one day I'll find out what you're running from. Accepting the diversion, he changed the subject as the boat slipped past the dense bush, laced with star clematis that came down to the river's edge.

It was not long before they reached Pipiriki and off-loaded their baggage—an incredible amount, it now appeared—on to a string of long-suffering mules. The Maoris here seemed far more hospitable, many wearing the strange assortment of European clothing that Melody had noticed in Wellington. There were white people of various races, English, German, French, who appeared eager for news. To Melody's disappointment, Paul declined an invitation to take dinner and spend the night, and releasing the tension that had built within her on the journey, she bristled, 'Don't refuse on *my* account, Mr Savage. I promise I shan't put you to the trouble of hunting down a runaway!'

His eyes had narrowed, but then he made a flat gesture of disgust and turned aside. 'Look around you, Mrs Van der Veer,' he threw over his shoulder. 'Beyond the settlement lies dense bush—what you would call forest—a fair amount of it yet uncharted by whites. There are both friendly and unfriendly Maoris out there, and the same goes for the wildlife. Quite apart from that, I am known and respected in Pipiriki and for a number of miles in each direction, so without sounding conceited, the likelihood of your being given sanctuary is pretty remote. I've refused the Connors' hospitality regretfully because I want to reach Windhaven before nightfall, because I want your precious New York finery to arrive in one piece, and because I don't want the provisions I've bought to be stolen in the night by these grinning heathens.'

He swung back then, reaching her in two strides and standing over her, hands on hips, legs braced. 'Mrs Van der Veer, you try my patience sorely, and there are times, increasing in number, when I wish to heaven I'd not listened to my infatuated cousin and had allowed you to be bought as a bed-wench by some sweat-stained planter!'

He regretted his harsh words the moment they were uttered, seeing the colour drain from her face as she re-lived that nightmare ordeal, seeing her previously flashing eyes widen endlessly, eclipsing her face. Swiftly he brought his hands up to catch her by the arms as she swayed; but at his touch she returned from that private hell with a start, biting her lip to stop the whimper that some tiny, hurt creature was making inside her. He made to speak, but with a choked denial she tore free from him, and eyes blurred with tears, ran off to where they were loading the mules, busying herself unnecessarily tightening a saddle-girth to control her shaking hands.

'Savage!' she spat. 'You won't break me, and your damned jungle won't break me, I swear it!'

CHAPTER FOURTEEN

THE JOURNEY PASSED all too quickly for Melody, whose only thought was that Windhaven meant the beginning of her life as a true slave, with all the degradation and humiliation that word evoked. She had seen the field hands at St Clare, and imagined all too clearly what it would be like to clear the land under even greater heat. Yet she knew that she could never willingly accept the alternative he had offered. How *could* he suggest that she become his mistress, living in the same house as his obviously hard-working, long-suffering, wife!

In spite of her inner turmoil, her senses still thrilled to the wild grandeur of the place, the small gorges and huge outcrops of rock cutting across the wide valleys, stands of *totara* and other trees, ferns and tree-ferns creating a paradise, a modern Eden.

Paul watched her face on which every emotion played, and the tiniest flicker of hope stirred in his breast. He realised Beatrice's stoic acceptance of the challenge that the place offered and her ability to overcome all odds for love of her niece. In Melody, however, he sensed a slow-growing wonder in the land, echoing his own, but then, as they topped a ridge and the forest thinned, he saw Windhaven below and all else was driven from his mind.

Beatrice noted his eager spurring forward, and her eyes met those of the girl. 'I should imagine that is what we are to call home for a while,' she remarked, seeing the prime farmland as a constant battle against the encroaching wilderness, and the heavy fortifications as a similar battle against the warring Maori tribes. But then she saw her niece's face, and turned again to the view with new eyes.

For Melody, all that existed at first was the house, and
her initial thought was that it was one in which a woman
could spend a lifetime of pleasure and wonder where the
years had gone. It was a sprawling, single-storey dwelling
of a burnished red wood, encircled by a wide porch, the
roof of which was supported by intricately carved pillars.
There appeared to be a central rectangular courtyard with
six rooms bordering it, each one irregular in shape as
though built by a man of many moods and varied abilities.
Melody had never seen such a novel design, yet as a
whole it blended perfectly with the surrounding land and
the giant *hoa* tree beside it.

'The courtyard contains a well in case the outside one
is cut off for any reason,' Paul told her, returning and
reining in alongside. 'As for the tree, well, I used that for
shelter when building my first cabin—that main room
beside it. I'd spread gum on the branches to trap the fat
pigeons that would come to watch me work, and smaller
branches provided me with wood for my fire.' He gave
an almost embarrassed shrug. 'Having been a source of
shelter, food and warmth, it would do me no harm, I felt,
to move my life over a little to accommodate it when
times changed.'

He indicated a larger stockade at a short distance from
the one surrounding the house. 'That houses the servants
and field hands with their families who work the livestock
and tend the crops. Those reed huts are called *whares*: the
Maoris always carve and paint the door-posts in that
way. The large building at the far end is a *hotonui*, a
meeting-house, and that's the head man's *whare* next to
it.'

'And which one do I sleep in?' Melody asked, the
twinge of fear bringing a huskiness to her voice and a
tightening of her knuckles on the reins as she thought of
her life among these tattooed savages.

The gold-flecked eyes flew wide, anger vying with
disbelief as he realised that her question had been perfectly
serious. 'You and Lady Davenport will obviously stay at
the house.' Then his incredulity exploded. 'Ye gods, girl!

Did you think I'd dump you and your aunt in some native hut?'

Melody recoiled, but her fear also brought out the spirit in her. 'I didn't know what to expect. I *still* don't know. I don't know why you forced me to come here in the first place, since I'm eminently unsuited to any role you have in mind.'

They had reached the stockade at this point, and eager hands opened the huge wooden doors. Bringing his annoyance under control for the benefit of those about them, Paul swung out of the saddle and came to help her down. 'For the moment,' he ordered softly, 'you will curb your tongue and work at removing that large chip from your shoulder. If you have any time or energy left, you might help Maata in the house.' His hands went about her waist and effortlessly he lifted her down, not releasing her directly, but meeting her smouldering look with something like exasperation. 'If you think you're hard done by now, I ask you to look back in time. I don't know what made you leave England, but I'm aware that whenever the subject is raised you contrive to change it faster than a card-sharp stacks a deck! You have limited finances, to say the least, and even in America—the land of opportunity, so they say—you would have considerable difficulty in making your way, excluding the quite obvious alternatives. I am offering you a new life without questions, a modicum of comfort and the chance to do an honest day's work—to earn your keep for once in your life.'

Melody lowered her head, not wanting him to see the threatening tears. 'But I'm still a slave!'

'You're a paid servant, able to earn your freedom,' he stated, a rough note in his voice that she put down to annoyance, not seeing the look in his eyes as he studied the gleaming sable hair gathered in too large a chignon for that slender neck. 'Don't fight my country, Mrs Van der Veer,' he added softly.

She wondered, at the strange intensity in his tone, whether it was his country to which he referred, but as she raised her head he released her, striding away to supervise the off-loading. Feeling lost and confused, she made her way toward the house, but as she reached the porch steps a tubby Maori woman waddled from the front door, her voluminous smock resembling a badly pegged tent, the high-piled hair heavily ornamented with combs and pins. She smiled broadly as she saw the girl, revealing strong, cream-coloured teeth. '*Tena koa, kui.* Mita Paul sent a man on from Wellington before Christmas, so we expect you any day. I am Maata.'

The shock rippled up from Melody's stomach, stopping her breath, as her mind screamed denial. She barely heard the woman's next words, and it was only when a plump golden hand patted her arm and the sympathetic brown eyes looked deep into hers that she managed to fight for, and gain, control. 'I—I'm Mrs Van der Veer.'

'Yes, of course,' agreed the careful, mission-educated tones that she remembered from Tarati. 'And the other is Lady Davenport. I have practised so that I get the names right. It is not easy for us. You must be tired after such a long journey. It is a very long ride. You could have come from the landing of the Operiki *pa*, but you would have had to come by canoe.'

'This conversation is not taking place!' Melody's confusion was absolute. 'I am not standing on a wooden porch in a jungle fort talking about canoe-rides with a grinning giantess who speaks perfect English!'

Suddenly she shied in panic as her elbow was taken from behind, and her wide eyes flew to Paul Savage's amused regard. 'You look as though you've seen a ghost,' he said, only half jokingly, wondering at her panic. 'No one could mistake Maata for a wraith, so I assume the long journey has taken your colour. Let's go inside. Here's Lady Davenport, too, and I'm sure she would agree that a glass of sherry would not go amiss.'

Melody allowed herself to be propelled forward as the Maori woman disappeared through a door to one side of the square hall, barely aware of her surroundings as she stared after her.

Paul gave a chuckle. 'Maata may not be the most exotic

of orchids, I agree, but I swear she's the best nurse, cook, social secretary and housekeeper in the North Island.'

Melody pulled up short. 'Housekeeper?'

He turned, puzzled. 'Of course! What else?'

Beatrice gave a choked laugh, having interpreted Melody's thoughts ever since their stay with the Reids. 'What else, indeed! I believe, Mr Savage, that I am more than ready for that sherry now, and then, perhaps, we may discuss our individual roles here.'

He gave a brief nod of acquiescence, leading them into a large drawing-room, yet not withdrawing his supportive hand from Melody's arm.

She could feel the warmth of his fingers burning through the riding-habit and fought the weakness that urged her to lean against him. Pulling free, she looked about her, wanting to find fault with what was surely her prison . . . but feeling only the same strange magnetism that had drawn her down the hill.

The room was dominated by a large bay window facing the front of the house, shaded by wooden louvred shutters that would keep out both summer heat and winter chill. A glass-panelled door opened on to a conservatory to one side, and out of curiosity Melody opened it, and immediately the moist heat assaulted the room, bringing strangely sweet scents from the hothouse plants. Quickly she closed it again with a murmured apology.

Paul urged her, however, 'Explore by all means; this is your home now. Maata knows more of that particular area than anyone else, and everything in there is entirely practical, I assure you. She cultivates herbs and other plants for both the table and as medicine, and I'm sure she'd be only too glad to explain them to you, should you wish it.'

Melody wondered at the gentle tones, feeling uncomfortable, but allowed her gaze to wander over the rest of the room, using it as an excuse to take a pace or two away from him. It was basically a male-oriented domain with large, solid furniture, some of it obviously made by hand, and carved, the couch and chairs heaped with cushions that almost beckoned in shades of green and brown; a warm and welcoming room, where the peace drifted across the senses.

'Sherry?'

'What? Oh, yes . . . Thank you.'

The dark eyes were amused. 'Mrs Van der Veer, you must stop leaping aside like a wild deer every time I speak to you! If we're to live together in any kind of harmony, you must try to curb your fight-or-flight tendencies.'

Melody bit her lower lip, accepting the glass of sherry, gaining time by taking a sip, but he had taken pity on her and moved away. 'Well, Lady Davenport, what will you have me say concerning your role here? You, of course, are my house-guest and Mrs Van der Veer's chaperon, until, I presume, you no longer see a need for that particular role.'

Beatrice tipped her head to one side, regarding him with the bright discernment of a robin. 'Mr Savage, I am not only Melody's chaperon, I'm also her aunt, and now her only family. I can't honestly foresee an end to that . . . role. Not in the near future, at least. Can you?'

His lips twitched. 'Put like that . . . no, Lady Davenport, I can't.'

'However, house-guest or not, I am quite unable to envisage a future of inactivity, and since this fortified village seems to be somewhat lacking in balls, soirées, opera or theatre, I should be most grateful if you could devise a means whereby I might make myself useful.'

'I shall certainly think on it . . . ' He halted as Maata entered, and digressed. 'If you'd like to see your rooms and take a rest before dinner, Maata will be glad to show you to them and give whatever assistance you need. There are one or two children belonging to the kitchen staff who would be pleased to help you to change and to act as your personal maids, though you'll find they speak only a few words of English. Like Ani, though, they are more than eager to learn, if you're patient with them.'

Melody was about to question whether they would not object to waiting on someone of the same social status as

themselves, but caught her aunt's eye and the slightest
shake of the head, so she followed in silence as the Maori
woman led them across the tiny courtyard to adjoining
rooms at the back of the house.

'We don't have many ladies here,' she apologised,
indicating the somewhat spartan furnishings and lack of
knick-knacks, 'but I put out little flowers to say welcome.'

She gestured to several bowls of wild clematis about
the room, and Melody drew in a deep breath, releasing
some of the tension within her. Whatever the future held,
the present had brought her to perfect surroundings, a
peaceful atmosphere and gentle, friendly people. She would
try to live for this moment, try to put the past behind her
and allow tomorrow to bring what it might. She must try!

She took in the beautifully carved four-poster with the
snowy muslin curtains and the cheerfully upholstered
chair and pouffe by the window. She appreciated the
gleaming patina on the ancient oak dresser, shipped from
far shores and tended by loving hands ever since, its shine
surpassed only by that on the wooden floor. How different
from the careless neglect of St Clare! 'Maata, this is
lovely . . . and the flowers too. So thoughtful of you.
How—How do I say "thank you" in your language?'

The wide mouth split into a beaming smile. 'Not many
pakeha—white people, especially their ladies—care enough
to speak our language, though they expect us to know
theirs. The words are *ka pai*.'

After Maata had repeated it slowly, Melody was able
to say confidently, '*Ka pai* then, Maata. *Ka pai* very
much!' They laughed at the mixture, a sound that seemed
strange to her, now that bitterness and tears were becoming
a way of life. 'I'd like to learn your language,' she said,
then, reflectively, 'I believe I'll have ample time!'

'You are staying with us a long time, Mihi Van der
Veer?'

So he hadn't told the others! What was she to do?
Cursing herself for her cowardice, she fenced, 'That will
be up to Mr Savage, Maata, but I think it will be quite a
while.'

'Good!' Maata beamed. 'Mita Paul he had no pretty lady around for a long time now.' For some inexplicable reason, her words brought a small lift to Melody's mood.

Taking off the riding-habit, she went to lie on the thick mattress, gazing up at the canopy, while Maata went to organise the evening meal. What does it all mean, she fretted; a slave being accorded the treatment and quarters of a lady? If Paul Savage is attempting to hide the fact that he's nothing but a slaver, maybe he needs a reminder. It was he who reprimanded me for putting on an act, a lady playing at being a slave. Well, maybe he, too, should face facts!

At that moment Aunt Bee rapped at the door and entered, fresh and smiling in a silk peignoir. 'Heavens, did I need that wash!' she remarked. 'Haven't you moved yet? You must have suffered more than I from that bony-backed excuse for a horse. Maata tells me that we have only an hour to dinner, so you really must think of moving, my dear. What shall you wear? I'll get something out for you. All my dresses look as if they've been thrown into the river and then left on the bank to dry, but one of the tweenies said she'd iron it for me, and Maata told me that she could be trusted. There's another on her way to you. What shall I put out for her?'

Melody rose and stretched. 'Something to annoy Mr Savage,' she decided, but her aunt clucked disapprovingly.

'How long will you keep up this running battle against odds you can't beat?'

'Until he tears up that contract! My manumission papers mean nothing, since they're exchanged for what amounts to a bill of sale—for one Melody Van der Veer—ex-mulatto slave, now mulatto servant, whose pay is only on paper, who'll see neither money nor freedom ever again. I'm no more free than I was before, and he's no different from any of those animals at the auction, in spite of this social whitewash he wears, pretending to be such an upright and beloved member of the community, when in fact he's just a slaver just as surely as those he condemns!'

With a despairing shake of her head, Beatrice left her to her toilette. There was a long road ahead, she realised, and whether it would be paved with dross or diamonds was still a matter of some conjecture.

Even she, however, was more than a little surprised, perhaps even shocked, at Melody's choice of dress, and felt, even before her quick glance confirmed it, Paul Savage's censure. Her niece had removed the lace fichu from the black ottoman silk with the midnight-blue markings. She had taken out all but the two base hoops from the petticoats, so that the skirt began to bell only as it reached thigh level, accentuating her slender hips. Above the deeply curved neckline the creamy swell of her breasts rose like the fruits of Tantalus. Her hair was set into loose ringlets with a love-lock caressing one shoulder, the whole effect bewitchingly beautiful, slightly wanton, reminding Beatrice of . . . whom?

The similarity eluded her, until Melody came to the table and with an over-bright smile, said, 'I'm afraid I don't know what a bondswoman wears for dinner . . . Mita Savage . . . but remembering my half-sister, Celine, this was the nearest I could come to it!'

'I suggest you go to change again, then,' Beatrice said quietly. This farce really had gone too far!

But Paul had raised a premonitary hand. 'No. Dinner is about to be served, and there is no time. I'll not have my kitchen staff kept waiting. Mrs Van der Veer, you'll be seated.' The chiselled features were carefully controlled as he turned then to Beatrice, biting back his anger and forcing a conversational tone. 'You may wish to rest tomorrow, Lady Davenport, or see more of the area. There are several horses in the barn; not of your standard, of course, but some improvement on the one they sent to meet you. If you ask Maata or myself, we'll speak to one of the men who will be more than glad to accompany you.' He talked on, the tension in his face belying the light tones, and completely excluded Melody throughout the meal.

Wretchedly she picked at the succulent roast pork, yams

and corn, and barely touched the rich whipped caramel pudding, fully aware that her gesture of defiance had succeeded only in angering her aunt as well, at least for that mealtime.

When the plates had been cleared, they adjourned to the drawing-room, where Paul went to pour himself a large glass of brandy, downing almost half of it in one draught, before flinging himself into a deep armchair. 'Tell me, Lady Davenport, do you think the Abolitionists in America will win if this question of slavery comes to a head, or do you believe, like my cousin, that the South has a God-given right to keep slaves—especially one as beautiful as mine?'

Beatrice pursed her lips. 'I assume your question is rhetorical, and only for the benefit of my niece.'

'Not at all,' he persisted, his smile as lethal as that of a friendly wolf. 'I think it a most interesting point. I mean, apart from the shipyards of New Orleans and Norfolk, Virginia, the South has virtually no one who could construct modern men-of-war, should it come to that. The South has, of course, a whole society of expert horsemen to lead the charge into the mouth of any amount of cannon, and they would obviously fight to the bitter end rather than have negroes making up any part of the State legislature, and with that as an incentive and their God on their side, how could they lose? No, I definitely think slavery is here to stay, so perhaps I am the one who should alter my views.'

'I'll just go to change while you're discussing the point,' Melody said, desperate to escape this strange and frightening mood he was in, but he stopped her with a gesture.

'There is little to be gained from doing so, do you not agree? No, I must adjust, as my cousin adjusted to having the lovely Celine around him at all times, though he, of course, had the distinct advantage of being accustomed to slaves. Here . . . ' He held out his empty goblet. 'You may pour me some more brandy. Is that an adequate beginning? You must forgive me if I appear new to this game.'

His sarcasm was more than Beatrice was prepared to take, and she rose with a shake of her head. 'I think you're learning exceedingly quickly, Mr Savage. I hope you take care not to forget that it *is* only a game—and, in my opinion, a somewhat distasteful and potentially dangerous one. I'll retire early, if you don't mind. Melody, I trust you'll not be long.'

'No . . . No, I'll be there shortly.'

Paul rose with Beatrice, making a short bow as she swept out, and when he turned back there was a trace of a smile about his lips. 'I like that woman. It's a pity it can't be reciprocated!' Then his eyes changed and the firm mouth tightened. Once again he held out his glass, daring her to refuse.

Melody felt her mouth go dry and a deep quaking start within her as she realised, for the first time, that she was actually afraid of this man. She had no way to refuse without confessing that she had acted in a fit of pique and begging him to forget the whole incident, so, biting her lower lip, she took the goblet to the sideboard and poured a generous measure.

He nodded his thanks as she handed it to him with a quick glance, and his eyes roved again over the dress, yet it seemed to annoy him rather than incite any other emotion, and his voice was clipped as he ordered, 'I don't wish you to wear that dress again—in *any* fashion.' Then, before she could answer, 'In fact, I see little point in your wearing black at all. I shall send to Wellington for some bolts of cloth—scarlet should be appropriate, and gold, jade, too, under the circumstances, and of course sapphire. You'll learn to make up dresses from those, for you are no longer in mourning, madam. You've made a mockery of the word!'

Melody felt his contempt as an almost physical blow and fell back, her features ashen. 'How dare you!' she said, but her voice was weak, and the shock came through.

With a violent gesture he tossed back the brandy, then strode across to slam the goblet down on the silver tray, and when he turned on her, his deep eyes flashed fire.

'You may have deceived Brett with that helpless pose—
the grieving widow, the helpless orphan, the high-class
lady in need of protection—but from where I'm standing,
I see no fragile flower—unless it's an orchid awaiting the
hunter. Is that why you altered the dress, Mrs Van der
Veer? Do you intend making *me* the slave, as Brett was
to Celine's undoubted charms?'

As before, her fear melted in the heat of her rising
anger and she spun towards the door, swirling the full
skirts aside as she crossed in front of him. 'I'll not listen
to this!'

But her shoulder was clamped in a vice-like grip as she
was dragged back. The gold flecks in his eyes glinted, and
there was a tang of brandy on his breath as his other
hand shot out and seized her other arm. Blue eyes met
brown, and lightning flashed. 'You'll listen to whatever I
have to say. You'll *do* whatever I say! You gave up your
options this evening when you chose the role of concu-
bine. But I'll not be as pliable as my cousin. I'll not
become emotionally involved with you in any way.
However . . . ' And without warning his grip changed,
one hand dropping to her waist, pulling her hard against
him, the other going to the back of her neck, thumb along
her jaw, hard as iron, raising her face to his. 'If you
intend becoming a bed-wench, you'd better start taking
lessons!'

His mouth descended hard on hers, punishing her for
her beauty and her softness—and the calculated avarice
he believed was in her heart. How *dared* she play Miss
Purity since St Clare, when she was only too glad to drop
the pose when the future as a housemaid lost its appeal!
He had planned to insult her, to humiliate her by his kiss,
then thrust her aside. But the lips beneath his were too
soft and warm, the body crushed to his too yielding. The
roughness and fury melted, and the kiss that had begun
so brutally became questioning, seeking. His arms shifted,
drawing her close against the length of him so that he
could feel the taut swell of her breasts through the thin
fabric of the dress, clouding his judgment.

Melody found her lips parting beneath the mouth that plundered hers, and she felt his tongue seeking the inner sweetness, searing hers as if by fire. Her mind reeled beneath the heady assault and the sensations that crashed in upon her, and a sob was torn from her throat. Then suddenly she was released, put away so violently that she almost fell. Regaining her balance, she attempted to cover her swollen lips with the back of her hand, staring at him over trembling fingers.

Breathing rapidly, Paul drew a mask of scorn over his own shaken emotions and gave a sneering smile. 'Very good, Mrs Van der Veer. You're an apt pupil. Your act of sweet innocence is quite stimulating!'

Shock turned to fury as Melody swung a palm with all her strength against the side of his jaw before turning to run to her room, lest he see the tears of anger and humiliation that washed her eyes and dulled her senses to the throbbing in her wrist. It was only when she had reached that sanctuary and poured cold water into the washbowl, splashing her face and neck, that she noticed the pain. 'Damn him!' she swore. 'Even slapping his barbaric face earns me a sprained wrist!'

Her anger made her impatient, and it was with a sense of helpless frustration that she rang for the little Maori girl to unlace her, addressing her sharply when she came. Her anger, too, caused her to snatch the dress from the child and hurl it violently into the corner, vowing never to wear it again. And it was . . . surely . . . anger alone that kept her awake for most of that night, re-living the shock of that kiss . . . a shock that had all too quickly turned to something else as a fire had spread through her, the like of which she had never known.

CHAPTER FIFTEEN

MORNING FOUND MELODY hollow-eyed and pale-faced, and no amount of pinching her cheeks could alleviate the ravages of a sleepless night. She slipped reluctantly from the cool sheets, and having washed, summoned the little Maori girl to help her to dress. The child entered hesitantly, liquid eyes fearful, and instantly contrite, Melody went to her and took hold of the rigid shoulders. 'I'm sorry,' she enunciated carefully. 'Sorry.' The eyes retained their wariness, and a little shiver went through the thin frame. At a loss how to explain, Melody finally took the slender brown hands and put her own in a gesture of prayer between them, then bent her head, touching her forehead to the child's trembling fingers. The trembling ceased, and Melody felt the fingers against her cheeks lifting her face to meet smiling eyes. The child nodded, accepting the supplication, and Melody reflected that in England it would not have occurred to her to apologise to a servant, yet here it had seemed right.

There was a simple dignity about the people of Windhaven that somehow put them above the category of servant, and it was with new insight that she watched the girl move gracefully about the room after helping her to dress, tidying and deftly making the bed. 'It could be so different,' her heart mourned. 'If only I could get to know these people and their land without this burden of servitude over me, and in so doing, find myself in some way and put the past behind me.'

Sadly she went to the dining-room, and as if in answer to her thoughts, Paul Savage appeared from the door, stopping to await her approach, features carefully neutral. 'Good morning.'

Murmuring a low 'Good morning', she unconsciously covered her swollen wrist, massaging it.

'You've hurt your wrist. I'm sorry.'

Instantly she dropped her hands to her sides, colouring, half in anger, half in embarrassment. 'Sorry for my hurt, or sorry for causing it?'

His lips tightened at once, and she regretted the friction between them that made her blurt out the first offensive thing that came to her tongue each time they met, as he said, 'I make no apology for my action last night, Mrs Van der Veer, since I didn't instigate the incident.'

'Then there's no more to be said.' She made to pass him.

'Wait!' Softly. 'I treated you as something even less than a slave, and you behaved as somewhat less than a lady. Can we not call a temporary truce?'

His words were so unexpected that Melody stared at him in silence, wanting to believe, yet afraid of ulterior motives, and a mirthless smile touched his mouth. 'I thought I'd visit a friend after breakfast. It's a fair ride through some interesting scenery, and I thought you might wish to see some of the land you've been abducted to and meet some of its people.'

Melody allowed herself a flicker of hope. Perhaps her actions of the previous evening had not, after all, spoiled her chances of making a life for herself that was not entirely devoted to serfdom. 'I'd like to see some of your land, Mr Savage,' she agreed, keeping her voice low.

'My land,' he mused. 'Yes, I suppose it *is* a savage land.' Another smile, this time with a trace of humour. 'I doubt that your aunt would have taken so long to tame it. She'd have had roses round the door a year after she arrived!'

Melody thought he was probably right. The Beatrice Davenports of the world took life in both hands and gave it a good shake before moulding it to their own designs. 'I'll be ready in half an hour,' she promised, and hurried into the dining-room to eat quickly a plate of fluffy

scrambled eggs and crisp golden bacon that she tasted
not at all.

It was less than the time promised when she appeared
on the porch, a little self-conscious in the high-necked,
tight-bodiced riding-habit that the shop assistant had
assured her was the very thing for 'a little backwoods
canter'. She knew now that the city people in Wellington
had as little knowledge of the real life beyond their
cosmopolitan confines as any in similar circumstances in
London or New York. It was therefore with a deep sigh
of relief that she saw his reassuring nod.

'You'll be comfortable enough for the distance we have
to travel, but I shouldn't advise any great journey.'

He was right, of course, and within the hour Melody
found herself surreptitiously unfastening the top two
buttons. They had skirted the nearby stockade and made
their way towards the river, its high banks covered in
veils of the wild star clematis that Maata had picked for
her room. He gave her the names of ferns and palms,
flowers and shrubs, as though conducting a lecture, and
once she daringly remarked, 'You should have warned
me to bring a notebook and pencil,' earning an apologetic
smile.

'There is someone I want you to meet. Someone that
personifies the real New Zealand.' He would explain no
further until they came to a flat-topped bluff high above
the river. On it she saw a heavily fortified *pa*, its inland
side protected by the Operiki stream which acted as a
moat. He reined in before the gates, suggesting, 'Hold
your judgment for a few moments after you see this friend
of mine. One other thing, the Maori greeting may cause
a little . . . surprise at first. I warn you in order to save
his embarrassment rather than yours: I wouldn't wish you
to slap *his* face! By the by, how is your wrist?'

Melody blushed, and lowered her gaze. 'I should not
wish to put any great strain on it, but it's well enough.'

Without warning, he reached over and took hold of it,
so firmly that she winced and pulled back. Immediately
he switched his hold to further up her arm, but he did

not release her, reining his horse in close so that their thighs were touching. Deliberately he raised her wrist to inspect it, gently touching the swollen flesh with soothing fingers. His eyes met hers, and there was an expression that she could not fathom, but all he said was, 'I'll bind it for you later.'

'You don't need to.'

'I need to.' Which was, she realised, the nearest thing she would receive to an apology.

They made their way into the stockade and were instantly surrounded by laughing, chattering children, calling, '*Kia ora*, Mita Savage.'

Melody wondered at the instant metamorphosis as Paul swung from the saddle and gathered bundles of warm, brown, near-naked bodies to him, smiling down at their upturned faces, conversing fluently in their own language, patting a head there, grasping a shoulder here, radiating a warmth and affection that she had seen only when he had met Ani at the Reids'. Believing herself forgotten, she went to dismount, but in that instant he was before her, swinging her effortlessly to the ground. His face gleamed with perspiration, and he smelled faintly of the fish-based oil with which the natives anointed their bodies, but it was his eyes that had changed. They had lost all wariness, and were clear and glowing with subdued laughter.

'My over-large and over-noisy family,' he smiled. 'Come, now, and meet the other half, not so noisy, but equally large.' He took her hand, as a path was cleared at the approach of the most awe-inspiring human being she had ever seen.

He was not as tall as the man beside her, but almost twice as wide, his massive shoulders accentuated by the floor-length cloak of tiny multi-coloured feathers. In one hand he carried a wooden spear with several long feathers tied to its head, similar to the eagle feathers he wore in his hair. Melody felt a quivering inside as he came to stand before her, barely hearing Paul's introduction.

'This is Te Whatitoaoraki, one of the greatest war chiefs of the people of Tukopiri. His name means the

Broken Warrior of The North, after one of his ancestors
who was betrayed by his brother and hunted down-river
until, crippled and scarred from his many battles, he was
taken in by the Tukopiri. Eventually he proved himself a
great warrior, in spite of his twisted limbs that had never
healed properly, and took himself a wife. They had three
children, the eldest son being given the nickname of his
father, as have each of the eldest sons born to the family.
A little confusing to the Western mind, but there's nothing
to be afraid of.' She knew that she had tightened her grip
on his fingers until her own ached, and was only a little
reassured by his easy laugh. 'I think they should have
named him "Taranaki" if they wanted to commemorate
a brother's betrayal. Taranaki, the great mountain of
legend, had to flee from *his* brother, Turi, and in so doing
forced a path up the coast. Because the mountain didn't
want to get his feet wet, he carved a deep and wide path
across the land—which is now the Wanganui River. Te
Whatitoa, because of his dynamic character and that
somewhat mountainous stature, has the same effect on all
who get in his way, too!' Uncurling her tight fingers from
his, Paul stepped forward with a smile, bringing the girl
with him. '*E hoa*, this is Mihi Van der Veer from England.'

The intricately designed tattooing on his handsome
features came closer, and closer still. '*Tena koe, kui*,' he
said, and smiled, then pressed his nose against that of the
girl, who had gone rigid at the first contact. He raised his
head, and his brown eyes were gleaming, taking in her
fight for control.

'How . . . do you do, sir,' she managed at last, and
heard Paul's choke of laughter.

The war chief put a huge hand on his friend's shoulder,
encompassing both Paul and Melody in his smile. 'It is
good to see you again, Paul, and good to see you with so
lovely a companion.'

Melody stared in amazement, wondering at the educated
tones emanating from this fierce colossus, until Paul chose
to enlighten her.

'I did suggest you withhold judgment! Te Whatitoaoraki

is one of the few chiefs who are friends of the *pakeha*. He learned English from the Catholic missionaries at Ranana as a child, was baptised Atami Katene—Adam Carter— and is considered a great diplomat during the present trouble.'

'How much trouble?' Melody asked, and saw the two men exchange looks.

Swiftly Paul broke in, 'Under the present circumstances, I don't think you need concern yourself with a few restless natives, Mrs Van der Veer.'

Decisively Melody shook her head. 'If you had brought me all the way out here on a purely social call, I shouldn't concern myself, but there is more to this visit, isn't there?'

There was a moment of awkward silence, then the warrior chief asked, 'Should we not talk at a distance, old friend? Even in the *pa* there are unfriendly ears, and since your lady is, for however long, a part of your household, she deserves reassurance.'

Paul nodded. 'But first—where is Rawiri? I didn't see him with the others when I arrived, and it's not like him not to be either leading them or somewhere in the middle of whatever trouble is afoot.'

The chief indicated with his chin toward a hut, slightly larger than the others, on the far side of the *pa*. 'My nephew is in disgrace.'

Paul's eyes sharpened. 'Now what? He is mischievous, but it doesn't usually get as far as this!'

'You can't beat the blood,' the warrior answered with a smile. 'He fought with the missionary's son because the boy called him a dirty *hāwhe kāehe*.'

Paul looked toward the hut for a long moment, and Melody's heart reached out at the inexplicable sadness in his expression. 'He was wrong . . . David is never dirty!' Then he smiled. 'Who won?'

'Rawiri, of course! The missionary's boy is only fourteen, and all white!'

Paul gave a nod and turned to Melody. 'I'll be back immediately.' He strode off toward the hut, leaving the girl feeling a little lost, but almost at once he reappeared with a young Maori boy clinging to his arm.

Melody frowned. 'Didn't you say the missionary's boy was fourteen? That child can be no more than eight or nine.'

Te Whatitoa nodded, and there was pride in his voice as he said, 'Rawiri is almost eight, but he's his father's son and doesn't know fear—cr defeat.'

When the pair reached them, Paul performed the introduction. 'Rawiri, this is Mrs Van der Veer. She is living at Windhaven now, so I shall expect your best behaviour.'

'Do you live there as well, then?' Melody asked, bending so that she was on the boy's level, and he nodded mutely, the large brown eyes serious, assessing her. 'Tell me,' she asked, attempting to break through that suspicious barrier. 'Is Rawiri the Maori word for David?' Another nod. 'You understand English very well, David. Did the missionaries teach you?'

The handsome features, finer and more chiselled than those of his uncle, darkened. 'They teach me plenty. I learn the *pakeha* words and about the *pakeha* god. I learn "love thy neighbour", but also about "a tooth for a tooth". Missionary's son, he don't believe in loving any Maori neighbour, and certainly don't love *hāwhe kāehe*.'

'What does that mean, David?'

He glared up at Paul, who so far had remained silent, but translated. 'It means a half-caste, Mrs Van der Veer.'

'Not Maori, not *pakeha*!' the boy muttered, tossing off the lean brown hand that had come to rest on his shoulder. 'So . . . ' He gave Melody a quick glance and a shrug. '*Hei aha*? Who cares? I learn the other lesson just as good, so took the first tooth, so he didn't take mine.' He gave his uncle a level look. 'And I'm still not sorry!'

Paul gave him a light cuff around the ear. 'Behave!' He turned to Te Whatitoa with a shake of his head. 'I shouldn't have been away for so long.'

'You needed to. Your cousin needed you.'

'Your people needed you, too,' Melody broke in. 'I'm sorry we kept you away for Christmas.'

'They were well taken care of.' The look that passed between the two men spoke volumes, and she wondered at such total empathy between coloured and white. 'But now we must talk of their future care, old warrior.'

'May I come?' the boy asked, but the men had already moved off and it was left to Melody to hold out her hand. For a heartbeat the brown eyes looked deep into hers, then some kind of decision was made and the boy linked his fingers into hers, work-calloused hardness against alabaster softness, as they made their way after the others.

To one side of the *pa*, the track wound down toward the river, and although the men were talking as though alone, Melody could not fail to throw the occasional glance at the two heavily-armed warriors who had followed their chief outside the fortress. Each carried a *patu*, that arm-length wooden short-sword, a hunter's knife, as well as an old Brown Bess musket. Since the last was still general issue for the British army stationed there, Melody could not help mentally questioning their presence. The maiming power of the enormous ball was legendary, and the girl felt glad that this fearsome bodyguard was friend and not foe.

A large pool was cut out of the rock at the foot of the cliff, where several women were washing linen. They smiled, and called a greeting to Paul, who excused himself for a moment to talk with them. He returned with a length of cold, damp cloth, and silently held out his hand to Melody. Flushing, surprised that he had remembered, she extended her still swollen wrist. 'An accident?' asked their host.

With an easy smile, Paul answered, 'Mrs Van der Veer was attempting to move an immovable object!' Firmly he bound her wrist, then took off his kerchief and made a short sling. 'We can't be too careful.'

Realising that he was laughing at her, Melody backed away. 'I don't need that!' Implacably he pursued her, catching hold of her arm.

'I shall tell you what you need,' he stated softly. 'What you *want* is a different matter entirely.' Deftly he slipped

the material over her head and settled her wrist into it.
She felt his fingers on her neck as he lifted her hair clear,
and a tremor went through her at his touch. 'You're
trembling.'

'No . . . The bandage was cool.'

'Only the bandage to blame?'

'What else?'

The gold-flecked eyes glittered as they searched her
innermost thoughts, disbelieving what he saw in her eyes,
mistaking innocence for intrigue. 'You're right. No experienced married woman would tremble at a man's lightest
touch.'

Irritated, Melody pulled away. 'Perhaps it was not so
much a tremble, sir, as a shudder. Now . . . I should
like to return to the house at your earliest convenience.'

'In a while,' he agreed, voice harder. 'I have a few
matters to discuss here, but it shouldn't take long. Stay
and listen if you will, or explore the area. You'll be
perfectly safe here, and there is a good view of the Operiki
waterfall from just up-stream. You may see a kingfisher
or two, or may wish to gather some wild flowers. Isn't
that the sort of thing a lady does?'

Melody did not deign to answer him, but went to settle
herself on a rock to one side of the smiling Maori war
chief. 'I should like to stay and listen, if I won't disturb
you,' she said to him, and he inclined his head, making a
surprisingly graceful bow from the waist.

'You will always be a disturbance to any man,' he
answered gallantly, proving that he had learned far more
than excellent English from the missionaries. 'Like a
candle in the night, your beauty will bring warmth and
light to our meeting.' He gestured to Paul to sit at his
other side. '*E hoa.* Let us talk.'

For the most part they spoke in English, but occasionally lapsed into Maori, when the girl was lost. Briefly Paul
had explained the Waitangi Treaty, signed on February
6th 1840 by most of the Maori chiefs. This ceded all
sovereignty to Queen Victoria, and, in the first article,
gave her possession of all their lands. The second article

gave each chief and his family the right to remain on that
land until they wished to sell it, the price of which would
then be agreed upon between all parties. The third article
was a simple, short paragraph extending to the 'Natives
of New Zealand Her Royal Protection, and imparts to
them all the Rights and Privileges of British subjects.'
Over five hundred chiefs signed the Treaty in good faith,
but that faith had been broken time and again by the
flood of immigrants since. Great tracts of land had been
compulsorily purchased for almost nothing and re-sold at
vast profits in spite of the efforts of the Governor, Sir
George Grey, to the contrary. Then the present Governor,
Gore-Brown, a man known to have anti-native tendencies,
had been appointed and the situation worsened.

Predictably, the natives had forcibly objected to the
betrayal of their faith, but had been put in their place by
even more stringent methods when the redcoats and the
navy arrived. 'Even I appreciate,' Te Whatitoa said bitterly,
'that wooden spears are of little use against guns and
trained troops, so it took little imagination to make the
decision to throw aside traditional weapons and fight the
pakeha on his own terms.' He shook his head, and there
was a great sadness as his eyes met those of the girl.
'People like Paul are like pearls in an oyster-bed, *kui*. The
others are both deaf and blind. I try to speak with them,
but, like you when we first met, they see only an illiterate
savage.' He brushed aside her embarrassed denial with a
smiling gesture. 'I'm a man who walks alone, *kui*. There
are those, even in my own *pa*, who would force all the
pakeha from New Zealand.'

He turned back to Paul, his velvet eyes sombre. 'It's
that time again, old friend; I can feel it in the wind. If
your lady is here for a holiday, I suggest most strongly
that she make it as brief as possible. This is no place for
an English lady—or any other—when the old religion
takes over from the new. It's the time when old hatreds
rise again and the young men smear their bodies with the
red fish-oil and dance round the *nui*.'

Paul gave a slight frown, staring down at his interlaced

fingers. 'Just feelings, *toa Koroheke*?' he queried softly, calling him 'old warrior'.

'That and news from runners,' he stated. 'You were away in June when the Somerset Regiment and the second Battalion of the Lancasters were defeated at the Battle of Puke-te-kaueri, near New Plymouth. The Ngati-Awa were helped by the Ngati-Maniapoto. The *pakeha* had been ordered to attack the twin *pas* of Puke-te-kaueri and Onuku-Kaitara. The *pakeha* major was caught by the swamp around the *pas*, since it was mid-winter. But of course the Ngati were like children with a loaded gun. They attacked New Plymouth itself, and many *pakeha* were evacuated in boats; but still, in the end, they were defeated, those fierce, foolish children.'

'But all this is too far off to bother us,' Paul insisted. 'I've heard that there are three regiments in New Plymouth now, as well as two companies of the Taranaki Rifles and a variety of other volunteers. Our own Wanganui can hold its own against attack, and if the Maori come down-river, the settlers will go south and lodge there. It's happened before. Are you saying that we should strengthen Windhaven as we've done previously? Operiki *pa* has never fallen, neither has Windhaven.'

Melody stared at him, at the sudden squaring of his shoulders, the gleam of battle in the deep-set eyes. He was actually welcoming the thought of a battle, she realised, remembering O'Shaughnessy's stories of him and the way he had stepped forward almost eagerly when they were confronted by those ruffians in Natchez. But then she studied his features afresh, the scar, livid with the tightening of the skin beneath, the jaw taut. No, not *welcoming*, she re-assessed, but *ready*; firm, proud in his possession of his land, and ready to fight to the death for what was his.

'There's more,' Te Whatitoa said, and she knew that this, too, was part of Paul's land, one friend not sparing the other the pain of knowledge, as she and Aunt Bee had spared each other so often.

'Go on,' Melody urged.

No fear there, the Maori estimated, drawing a deep breath and giving her a sympathetic smile. This was not her war, he thought, yet there was a steady regard in those incredibly blue eyes and an inner strength about her that he had discovered in so few white women. They were those who accepted the land, while some fought it in vain, and others gave in and were broken by it. And then there was that rare person, like Paul, who loved it with a fierce passion and a pride that would never let go.

Te Whatitoa realised that even the woman herself was unaware of her feelings and that there was a battle of some kind raging within her, for some private cause. Yet still there was a fearlessness of this particular battle that enabled him to say, 'It will become worse. The runners have brought news of some half-crazed seer, one Te Ua Horopapera Haumena. He is having dreams and visions of the Maori people receiving divine help in driving the *pakeha* from the land. He's from a village called Tatarai-maka, south of New Plymouth.'

Paul made a sharp chopping gesture. 'No threat. The *tohungas*—the priests—have always called on the old gods for divine intervention in battle.'

'Te Ua uses *your* god, *kui*, and his communication is direct from Anahera Kaperiere.'

'The angel Gabriel,' Paul murmured, and for the first time looked uncomfortable. 'If he uses the old religion and corrupts the new, he could be a powerful force to reckon with.'

His penetrating gaze met that of his friend. 'Will it come?'

'Yes, without doubt.'

'Has it come?'

'Not yet, but if they combine old and new they will make it a religious war.' The velvet eyes turned to Melody. 'I have read some of your history, Mihi Van der Veer. You have known wars of religion in your country. I support the Kuini Wikitoria, but your country has done much evil in the name of religion, and our own ancestors, too, were expelled from their land by such persecution.

both know the strength of a people who believe that God is on their side.'

Melody blenched. 'You're saying that this will come to New Zealand?' His silence gave consent, and she felt a tightening within her as if a great hand had clutched at her heart. 'Is there no way of stopping it?'

'Young men will be young men, and the *tohunga*—the priest—is a persuasive speaker. He fans the flames of nationalism with chanting and strong liquor.' He gave a fatalistic shrug. 'It's the same all over the world, I believe.' Turning back to Paul, he put a strong hand on his shoulder. 'But we are not there yet. Go and prepare your people as last time and the time before, as I shall. I have family, my daughter who married into the Ngati-Tuwharetoa from the Taupo area, and there are also her son and daughter. I must send men to guard them. A woman's place is with her man, but I would be far more at ease if she were at Operiki.'

'Yes, it is safer here.' Paul turned to the boy, who, until this time, had sat in silence, absorbing every word. 'Rawiri, you'll stay here.'

'No!' It was a cry from the heart, and Melody saw the two men again exchange looks.

Te Whatitoa gave a nod. 'He should stay. They'll not attack the Operiki *pa*: our reputation spreads throughout the river people. He will be safe here.' But the boy had leapt to his feet and stood defiantly, hands on hips, reminding Melody of Paul. How these people must love him, she reflected with a wrench of the heart. Even the children ape his mannerisms.

'I'll run away,' the boy challenged, head defiantly high.

'You'll do as you're told!' Paul snapped, but then relented, recognising that he should not communicate his own strain to the boy. Bending, he took hold of the mutinously rigid shoulders, speaking to him in soft Maori, the musical words flowing over him until the defiant head lowered. He gave the child a quick hug, and rose with a nod at Te Whatitoa. 'He'll be safe here,' he said. The two men clasped hands, and Paul turned to take Melody's arm, lifting her from her seat. 'There's work to do: the stockade to strengthen and arms to be distributed.' His mouth was tight as he swung her into the saddle, jarring her wrist, but this time he was unaware of her indrawn breath.

Melody said nothing, putting down the thin blade of fear that trickled down her spine as they pushed the horses hard back to Windhaven. Her heart pounded, and her throat felt dry, there was more than rebellion here— there was evil, a sense of something dark and alien. She had felt it stalking her for weeks—yet why should she think of Luther Hogge when she thought of this fanatical medicine-man?

Paul left her immediately on their arrival, striding over to a group of Maoris outside the gates, and Melody hurried into the house, calling, 'Aunt Bee!'

She appeared from the drawing-room, where she had been poring happily over some of the books that Paul had brought back from St Clare. She began to chatter, but broke off at Melody's expression. 'What is it, girl? You're as white as a sheet!'

As succinctly as possible, Melody told her all that had transpired, and the grey eyes sharpened. 'This chief, this friend of Mr Savage, said that there *was* going to be trouble, or that there *might* be?'

'Well, he seemed to think that the time was right, and speaking from past experience, he was going to warn his daughter in the north and send guards to her. Mr Savage certainly seemed to take him seriously. He's talking to the men now, and he mentioned strengthening the stockade.' The blue eyes betrayed her fear, though her tone was resolute. 'Aunt Bee, there *is* going to be fighting, an attack, here at Windhaven. We must do something!'

Beatrice squeezed her shoulder reassuringly. 'It's happened before and it will undoubtedly happen again, but if anyone can protect what's his, this Paul Savage can.' She gave a crooked smile. 'I'm just as afraid as you, my dear, but I've absolutely no intention of being killed off in my prime by some religious fanatic! Look around you. This place has stood firm for the past decade—built to withstand anything but an act of God—and God's on *our* side!'

Melody raised a weak smile. 'Are you sure?' She received a look of mock amazement.

'Of course! We're British! That's better . . . a smile! Now, let's see where we're needed.'

During the days that followed, Windhaven became a hive of activity. The stockade was strengthened, each foot examined for weakness, the arms were checked and double-checked and the livestock brought inside. Paul moved among his people with quiet confidence, issuing orders and giving encouragement, and it seemed to Melody, who found herself constantly watching that broad frame, that each man and woman grew an inch at his passing.

Beatrice and Maata had formed a strong, though to Melody inexplicable, bond, and were in the kitchen exchanging recipes—which left Melody feeling both useless and isolated. Wandering from room to room brought no peace, in fact the chatter of the others served only to accentuate her mood. If only there was something I could *do* . . . someone who needed me . . . No, mustn't think of that . . . 'Oh, when shall I be free?' she murmured, sinking on to one of the cushioned chairs and resting her head in her hands.

'Whenever I allow it.' A soft voice sounded behind her, and she jerked upright as Paul Savage came into the room. His close-fitting buckskins were dusty, and the linen shirt clung to him, both emphasising his superbly muscled physique, and Melody felt the familiar tremor inside her that his presence always inspired.

'You can't keep me a prisoner here for ever,' she declared.

His voice remained soft, yet she sensed the ruthlessness and implacability behind his words. 'You'll stay until I allow you to leave.'

A sense of unreality swept over her. It could not be happening, not to Melody Van der Veer, English lady!

Her throat felt dry as she realised that the fantasy was all too real and the nightmare unending. The lean, dark face was turned in profile as he stared beyond her and out of the window, and she studied its chiselled outline, her emotions in a turmoil. How could this man terrify her, yet at the same time exert such a mesmeric fascination? Her senses were stirred unbelievably and she fought emotions she did not understand.

He turned at that moment, seeing the wide eyes and slightly parted lips, seeing the fear there, and something else too—an unawakened desire of which she was totally unconscious, and his eyes darkened. 'Is your prison so intolerable?' he asked almost gently, and saw her bite her lower lip and avert her gaze. When she did not answer, he came to stand behind her, looking down at the shining hair piled high in carefully arranged curls, leaving her neck bare. It seemed such a vulnerable neck!

Melody went tense as she felt his hand, warm and strong, on the back of her neck, his fingers massaging the taut muscles. She wanted to draw away, but the gentle yet firm manipulation held no threat, no passion, and in spite of herself she moved her head, the better to accommodate those soothing fingers.

'And is your jailer so much a savage?' he added, and there was a knowledge in his voice that brought the heat to her face.

Twisting aside, she sprang to her feet, her voice low with anger. 'Yes . . . Yes to both your questions! I tolerate my prison because, as you reminded me earlier, it would be almost certain death to leave, and I bear your touch on my flesh because you own it. But you own nothing more, Mr Savage, nor ever shall!'

With a toss of her head, she stalked past him, nearly colliding with Beatrice coming in. 'I am sorry! Have I interrupted something?'

'Not at all, Lady Davenport,' Paul assured her, his light tone belying the rigid features.

Knowing that there had been yet another contretemps between the two, Beatrice gave a sigh and turned to the matter in hand. 'There's a young Maori boy asking for you, Mr Savage. He's with Maata. He says his name's David.'

Paul's jaw tightened, and the gold flecks in his eyes shot fire. 'Dammit, I *ordered* him to stay at the *pa*! I'll skin him alive when I get hold of him!'

Melody explained to her aunt, 'He's Te Whatitoa's nephew. We met him there and he wanted to accompany us back, but Mr Savage made him stay, for safety's sake.'

'So the son of Satan comes up-river alone,' Paul muttered, a stress in his tone that went far deeper than his condemnatory words.

Melody felt a twinge of anger. 'The child has disobeyed your orders, it's true, but he's shown remarkable bravery in reaching us, considering his age. You must see him; and he deserves praise, not punishment.'

A little drily, Beatrice said, 'He probably regards you as some kind of god. Everyone else here seems to!'

Paul's lips curved, annoying Melody even more. 'Except you, of course, Lady Davenport.'

'Well, *I* certainly don't!' Melody broke in, hating him for his superior expression. 'And neither would they, had they seen the other side of you.' They both stared at her, a little surprised that she had taken the jest so seriously. She faced them, eyes stormy. 'Of course the child loves you: I saw the way you treated the children at the *pa*, as though each one was your own. The people here see you as some benevolent dictator—strong, protective, dispensing wisdom and justice, tending to their needs before they're even aware of them. Maata tells me they call you "kaiārahi nui"—big leader. But don't forget I've seen your dark side, and I know that you are benevolent only as long as you are obeyed without question. Oh, yes, New Zealand suits you fine, *Mister* Savage! You're surrounded by a wilderness you can tame, savages you can fight, simple natives you can rule. That's your whole *raison d'être*: conquering adversaries and winning wars. There's no love in you, only passion; no warmth, only fire.' She spun away then, aware of the desolation and self-pity that ran beneath her words and afraid lest they, too, discover it. 'I'll send David to you. Perhaps you'll give him time to tell you how he loves you enough to risk his life coming here, before beating him for doing so!' With a choke she ran from the room, leaving behind a stunned silence.

Beatrice eventually gave a small cough. 'I don't often apologise for someone else . . . '

'Nor should you now.' There was a tautness in him, and his eyes were bleak as he stared at the door.

Attempting to ease that tension, she ventured, 'Her anger isn't directed at you personally, Mr Savage. Not really. She has so much pain inside that if she didn't lash out occasionally it would engulf her and break her spirit entirely. Her whole life has been turned upside-down, but more than that is this irrefutable fact of her colour.'

'She knows my feelings on that.'

'As does everyone. However, it's one thing to believe that all men are equal—even though some are undeniably more equal than others—but quite another to find yourself tumbled from the pedestal to the pit. Not only is Melody coloured, but also, in her eyes, a slave, and that combination is a cross that is almost impossible for her, a once free, white member of the aristocracy, to bear.' She looked round as the door opened. 'And talking of the aristocracy, I believe you are just about to be visited by a member of that élite.'

The boy stood in the doorway, uncertain of his welcome, changing his weight nervously from one foot to the other. 'Don't beat him too hard,' she smiled, knowing by the man's expression the absolute impossibility of any punishment at all being meted out. But already she was forgotten.

Paul's voice was husky as he said, 'Will you *never* obey me?' holding out his arms, and Beatrice left them alone, as with a breathless laugh the boy hurtled across the room to that broad chest.

In her own room Melody fumed, pacing the floor, muttering imprecations against the man, his country, the natives and the whole intolerable situation. 'I need to get away,' she exploded softly, taking another turn about the room with the gait of a caged tigress. 'A short walk can't hurt: just outside the walls. Why, that child came all the way up-river alone. I'd be in view, and at least I wouldn't have to watch that strutting savage! He may gull the others, but not me! Why, he's even got Aunt Bee smiling and chattering as though he's some genial host, instead of our jailer.'

Changing into a light blouse and skirt, pulling on narrow hoops and eschewing the whalebone girdle completely—tired of *all* man-made restrictions—she went out to the stockade. Paul was not in sight, and heaving a sigh of relief, knowing that he would stop even this small excursion, she approached the gate. There was a small door within the large double gates which could accommodate a single rider, for the gates were opened only for wagons or if a group of riders needed entry. Two men were stationed just outside as lookouts, and they turned with friendly smiles as Melody reached them. 'I need some fresh flowers for the house, and saw several growing near the trees. Do you think I could go out to pick some? I'll only be a few minutes.'

The elder man looked doubtful, but Melody gave him her sweetest smile and put a soft hand on his arm. 'I'll stay within sight, I promise, and it's only a hundred yards or so.'

The man coughed embarrassedly. 'I suppose so, but don't be long.' Then he returned her smile. 'This is no place for a lady like you, but it is good having you around.'

'Brightens the place up,' his companion added, and Melody laughed wryly.

'In my black dresses?'

'It doesn't matter what you're wearing,' the elder stated sincerely. 'Someone as pretty as you makes a man feel good just to see you, so you take care. The boss'd shoot us if we let anything happen to you.'

'Nothing will happen,' Melody assured him, and with lifted heart crossed the clearing to the trees.

Keeping her word, she stopped at the perimeter, turning

to wave at the watching men before bending to gather some of the flowers that grew there. Straightening, she looked about her, breathing deeply as the mingled woody scents teased her nostrils. Flowers and ferns grew in profusion, vines curled loving tendrils round tree-trunks, and insects hummed lazily amid the greenery. The quiet pervaded her whole being, bringing a calm that not even Chopin could have achieved.

A clump of tiny blue flowers peeped shyly from beneath a flat-leafed bush and Melody moved to pick a few for her bouquet. The men were still in sight, but in the black blouse and skirt she blended too well with the dark shadows behind her, and the guards grew concerned. A tiny smile touching her mouth, she followed a brilliantly-hued butterfly, almost able to touch its quivering wings as it settled, then it fluttered off at her approach, settled and rose again, almost beckoning her to play. She found herself experiencing a deep peace for the first time in many weeks . . . until she heard a rustling in the undergrowth far behind her. There was something out there. Something stalking her, she knew. Another crunch of fallen leaves and twigs. Mouth dry, she looked round, seeing nothing, then her heart leaped as a heavy crack indicated a broken branch, and only a large animal—or human—could break a piece of wood large enough to cause so loud a noise. With a choked cry she panicked, only then realising that the butterfly had drawn her out of sight of the stockade and deep into the trees. Stumbling over clinging vines and heavy undergrowth, she ran in what she thought to be the direction of the stockade. There was a shout, and the undergrowth crashed beneath her pursuer's weight. A branch caught at her hair, tearing out the combs, and another ripped the thin material of her blouse, but all she could think of was the tattooed horror pounding after her. Another shout made her glance back, and she screamed as her foot caught in a trailing vine, and she fell.

She sprawled, face down, sobbing in terror, rolling sideways as the footsteps reached her, instinctively ready to fight until killed—and saw Paul Savage, his eyes black with anger, standing over her. Her first sob of relief died in her throat before a new, colder fear, for there was something in his stance that reminded her of a beast of prey—legs slightly apart, lean fingers on leaner hips, eyes narrowed as he looked down at her, more deadly than any hostile savage.

'I should beat you to within an inch of your life!' he thundered.

An irrational terror took hold of her as she realised that he was quite capable of such an action. 'Please . . . ' she whispered. 'Please leave me. I'll go back. Just tell me the way. I'll go.' Throwing her head back to look up at him, she was totally unaware of the picture she made, hair wild and tumbling down her back, eyes wide in fear, lips parted as she caught her breath. The white column of her throat and up-thrust breasts, partially exposed by the rents in her blouse, tantalised and beckoned—and she saw his expression change. A quick glance downward, and she gave a gasp, bringing her hands up to cover herself, then her eyes flew to his. 'No!'

He bent down, and Melody gave a small choked cry, closing her eyes. She was lifted in arms of steel, and for that instant, as she was swept up and held against him, she was aware of every muscle in his body, aware as she was crushed against the length of him, that he desired her. He bent and found her lips, teasing them apart with his, moving slowly over her mouth in sensual persuasion, setting her blood pounding in her veins. He curved her to his hard body and she bent helplessly into him, feeling his urgent desire, powerless to resist. She could neither see nor hear, nor think of anything but the sensations within her and the muscular frame without, as his hands moved over her in practised sensuality. His kiss deepened endlessly, and she could not help responding, but the moment she did so, that steely embrace loosened and she felt a warm hand along her cheek.

'Did you expect me to rape you?' he said unsmiling, as her eyes flew open.

Melody felt confused and trapped by her own emotions, but fought the inner turmoil with bitterness as she pulled free. 'Why not? Isn't that the usual fate of a coloured house-wench?' She saw the warning spark in his eyes, but her anger, and the hysterical relief that her pursuer had not been one of the terrible savages that she had heard of, drove her on recklessly. 'Well? Don't tell me you haven't taken a woman against her will, that you fought only Mexican *men* in that war! Don't say you haven't acquired a taste for dark women, especially a white nigra you've bought and paid highly for!'

'That's enough!' His voice cracked out like a whip, and cruel fingers bit into her shoulders as he gave her a hard shake. 'I've never raped any woman . . . Not yet. So don't drive me, girl!'

As she felt the burning pain of his grip, anger mingled with blind fear and she lashed out, fighting him with fists and feet. 'Savage!'

The next moment he had dragged her hard against him, wrists pinioned behind her back as though in a vice. She was about to scream when his mouth slammed down on hers, hard and brutal, punishing her, thrusting his tongue in. She kicked at him, raising a muttered curse, and he bent her back until her knees buckled and she was forced to the ground, his body moulding itself to hers, his hard thighs trapping her legs. She thrashed beneath him, feeling sick and dizzy with the terror deep inside her. This could not be happening! Oh, dear God, not like this! She could not fight him; he would only hurt her more. Tears sprang to her eyes and pushed her between tightly closed lids as she surrendered to the inevitable, and with a tiny sob, allowed her body to go limp.

At once he raised his head. 'Will you surrender to me, then?' There was a questioning in his voice that went beyond his words, and the tears flowed faster as mutely she shook her head in denial. 'Yet I have you helpless. There is no way you can escape.'

She did not believe the gentle probing in his tone, only her own despair. 'I hate you, Paul Savage!'

Incredibly he laughed, a dry chuckle that made her eyes fly open. 'I believe I could change your mind about that,' he stated, 'but not at this time. However, a lesson must be taught to those who provoke their betters.'

Before she could protest, his mouth captured hers again, not with the brutality of his previous kiss, but with a searching, searing, sensual passion that drove the breath from her body. At the same time, expert fingers curved over her exposed breast, teasing until she writhed beneath him. Then without warning she was released, and in one fluid movement he rose to his feet, leaving her panting, fighting the fire that raged within her. Eyes narrowed, feral, he looked down at her, hands on hips, legs apart— the master, and certain of it. 'Next time, hold your temper, woman, or I'll not guarantee mercy! The next time, obey orders without question and don't leave the stockade, or I'll not even guarantee you your life!'

Melody felt degraded, humiliated and very afraid of him, yet the memory of that superb body crushing hers and the fingers that had brought her to writhing helplessness flooded her cheeks with colour. She could not face him, bending her head as she attempted to gather together the tatters of her blouse.

His voice came again, but curiously soft. 'Get up.'

She flinched at his touch on her shoulder. 'Don't touch me! Oh, please don't . . . '

There was a moment of silence, then gently he ordered. 'Take my hand, then. Just reach up and take my hand.' Trembling as if with ague she did so, and was raised, averting her face. With a quiet movement he put his shirt round her shoulders. 'Come, put this on properly. You wouldn't wish to be seen like that, would you? I've no intention of sharing such perfection.'

Numbly she allowed him to put the garment on her, then to take her by the hand and lead her back to the house. She stared at the ground, at her skirt, at the tumbled curls that fell over her shoulders in disarray almost to her waist—at anything but the man beside her. She heard him reassure several people who approached them, telling them that a deer had frightened her, but she would not raise her eyes even to them, wishing that she could die, or at least disappear for ever.

He escorted her through the house to her room, at the door turning her to face him, his warm fingers curling over her shoulders. 'Woman, what shall I do with you?' Then, more quietly so that, afterwards, she was sure she had imagined it, 'And what should I do without you?' Then, opening the door, he pushed her gently inside, closing it behind her.

Melody stared sightlessly at the floor, but as the full horror of what might have been flooded in on her, she sank to her knees, burying her face in her hands. It could have been a band of marauding savages. She could have been beaten, raped and murdered in slow degrees by a dozen or more, and the men in the stockade would have been helpless to prevent it. That she had been assaulted by Paul Savage had been, in part, her own fault, and she wondered at the iron self-discipline that had stopped him from taking her, driven on by her taunts, as brutally as the natives would have done. The tears came then, a scalding cascade that cleansed the pain and the shame and the fear, leaving her as weak as a kitten—a kitten that in the future would think twice before exhibiting the claws of a cat.

Slowly she rose, discarded the torn and dirty clothing and washed all over, shivering a little in the cold water. It took almost an hour to brush the tangles from her hair, dress in a high-necked, long-sleeved black silk, and re-set her hair in a severe chignon. She would have to face him over dinner and undoubtedly have to withstand knowing looks as well as *doubles entendres*, but she would show no outward sign of the trembling that assailed her each time the memory of their encounter seared her mind.

Pale, but finally composed, she made her way to the dining-room. Beatrice had heard a much-edited version of her escapade from Paul, who had warned her in no uncertain terms that she, too, should not leave the stockade under any circumstances until the danger had passed. She had acquiesced graciously, but now, looking at her niece's rigid frame and colourless features, she wondered at the truth behind his vehement insistence that she obey him.

Now, however, their host showed none of the fury born of sick fear that had sent him racing unarmed into the jungle. He conversed quietly and apparently naturally, addressing some of his remarks to Melody, who concentrated on moving her food about her plate, but mostly drawing Beatrice into talking of her mis-spent youth, his eyes gleaming at her outrageous stories. By the time the mouth-watering apple, raisin and honey pie was served, Melody had begun to relax, and even to raise her eyes from her plate on occasion to glance at the smooth, golden features opposite when she knew that he was absorbed with her aunt.

She was disoriented and unhappy. She *wanted* to hate him. God, how she wanted to hate him! Without warning, those gold-flecked eyes swung to her face. She tried to tear away from that searching regard, but found that time had frozen. He seemed to find something disquieting in her frightened face, and a barely perceptible frown touched his forehead. 'Nothing would have happened out there,' he said for her ears only. 'Nothing to harm you.'

Breaking free, she looked down at the fingers tightly laced in her lap, wanting to believe him, yet unable to lose the memory of the arrogant stance of the conqueror. There was the breath of a sigh, surely imagined, as he turned again to Beatrice, allowing her to compose herself, gathering that composure about her as a cloak that protected her through the rest of that long evening.

That night, almost predictably, yet another of her nightmares returned to haunt her. The auction block again, not in North Carolina but here, for she had escaped as that monstrous shrouded form reached for her, run into the trees, running, running, heart pounding and it was as if the very trees were alive, reaching out dark, creeper-covered arms to seize her. Falling. Endlessly falling. Then that shape, hooded, cloaked. A skull this time. No face. Reaching out thick, bloated, beringed fingers. Luther

Hogge's fingers. That soft voice. 'I'm alive, Melody. Alive'
. . . And she awoke sweating and shaking uncontroll-
ably, knowing it was just a dream. And yet . . . 'Dear
God, will it never end?'

CHAPTER SIXTEEN

AT THE END of that week a group of mercenaries rode in; lean, hard men, war-wise veterans with nothing to lose but their lives. At first Melody would not approach them, but her aunt had no such qualms. 'A man is only another breed of animal, sweeting,' she chuckled. 'And I've yet to meet one who couldn't be tamed by a touch of discipline and a surfeit of kindness.' So she moved among them with the genuine charm that had captured the hearts of barons and barrow-boys alike. The men were totally captivated. In their harsh lives there were only two kinds of women—ladies and whores—and no one—not even the privileged few who had been allowed into her bed would ever have called Beatrice Davenport anything but a lady. She possessed that rare quality later to be praised by Rudyard Kipling of being able to 'talk with crowds and keep (her) virtue and walk with kings nor lose the common touch'.

'Wherever did you find such a cut-throat crew?' she asked Paul over dinner, and his lips lifted in that familiar half-smile.

'I sent two of Maata's brothers down-river to Wanganui. There are jetsam in every town willing to sell their souls. Three I've used before, and it was those I contacted first. Matiu and Tamati are large enough to withstand a fair degree of bother, but they're still Maoris, and there are places where they would not be allowed. Personally, I'd not trust those that rode in this morning further than the money I pay them, but you appear to have wrapped them round your little finger quite successfully, Lady Davenport.'

Beatrice's eyes looked inward. 'I've met a fair variety

in my life,' she admitted, and, as so often before, Melody
wondered whether she would ever know all that this
remarkable woman had endured to arrive at her present
position.

They talked on, but behind their calm conversation she
knew that both felt the strain of the battle preparations
as she did. She could not forget a chance remark made
by one of the mercenaries, overheard and quickly
suppressed when they became aware of her presence. 'Will
they take heads?'

'Hell, no!' the other answered. 'That's a European
refinement.'

She remembered reading somewhere among Brett's
books that before the white man came to America the
Indians never knew the meaning of scalping: they merely
decapitated their enemy. Then, during the colonial conflicts
when the French and English were doing battle, the
distinguished British officers put a price on the French
heads . . . and the roving bands of Indians brought
them in by the basketful. Having found the repulsive pile
rising to more than bearable proportions—it being
midsummer, too—the British decided it would be far less
cumbersome, not to mention sanitary, to accept just the
hair. Far tidier in the long run!

'Will they take heads?' The words reverberated round
the room as her mind sought tiny nooks and crannies to
escape the dreadful picture the words brought to mind.
'Please, Lord,' she prayed, 'if it has to be, then let it be
quick and clean.' And, fitfully, she dropped into a whirlpool of sleep.

. . . Melody gave a mew of protest as an insistent
hand on her shoulder shook her awake. 'Come, Mihi
Merody. You come now.'

'Yes, Maata, yes. What is it?' Then, as reality flooded
in, 'Is it time? Have they come?'

'Mita Paul say you get dressed as quickly as possible.
Any time now, and we got trouble. Smoke up-river mean
Mita Randolph house gone. If he lucky, he will come
with family and be here soon, but if not, I think we will

not see him again.'

'I'll come at once,' Melody assured her, noting the
heavy knife strapped to the woman's ample hips and
wondering whether this gentle giantess could ever use it,
sinking it into the flesh of another human being. Worriedly
she asked, 'Maata . . . the knife?'

She gave her a long, level look, then said, 'Don't you
worry, Mihi Van der Veer. You just get dressed like Mita
Paul say.'

Melody was unnerved by the resolute expression on the
normally placid features, and felt a chill raise the hairs on
the back of her neck. 'Maata, I want to know.'

The other gave a sigh. 'No, I won't be fighting, Mihi
Merody. But if the Maori break through, there are seven
children here, some just babies. I have spoken to Mita
Paul and he has spoken to Te Whatitoa. If the old ways
come again, I must make certain, in the heat of battle
when there are no guns to spare—or at the end when all
bullets gone and battle lost—that the children of
Windhaven are not used for a victory feast.'

Melody felt sickened. 'That's not possible!'

The Maori veiled her eyes. 'Of course not. It will not
happen. I told you not to worry.' Refusing to say more,
she left.

Praying to all the gods she had ever heard of, Melody
dressed hastily, then took a long look in her mirror. The
wide hoops and deeply flounced skirt were the height of
fashion in New York. 'But this isn't New York,' she
muttered. 'It's a battlefield in a wilderness.' She gave a
passing thought to the narrow hoops she had worn for
her sortie outside the stockade, but then determinedly
removed all but one of the petticoats and threw the hoops
aside. The hem of the dress trailed on the floor, falling in
puddles about her feet. Her lips tightened in decision, and
going to her sewing-case, she took out the long scissors.
'I'll probably hate myself tomorrow,' she muttered, 'but
there may be no tomorrow to worry about.' She bent to
cut the complete bottom flounce off the full skirt, doing
the same with the petticoat beneath. Taking another long

look, she felt herself blushing at the rounded curves of her hips revealed by the skirt now falling in a straight line to her ankles. 'Perhaps no one will notice,' she murmured hopefully as she hurried to join an already seething household.

As expected, she discovered with a rueful smile, Aunt Bee was already in the thick of it, helping with the tearing of bandages and the making of thick, hot soup as though she had been up for hours. 'Take some bread for breakfast and put something on it,' she instructed her with a grin that registered nothing but excitement—until she took in Melody's attire. 'Good grief, child! What have you done? . . . No, I can *see* the devastation!' Then her grey eyes narrowed in speculation as the first shock gave way to her inveterate practicality. 'Do you think you can do the same for me?'

'Aunt Bee! You can't!'

'And why not, pray? If you can make a spectacle of yourself for a good cause, I'm sure I can do the same. Apart from which, it looks deucedly comfortable!'

Melody gave an embarrassed smile. 'Well, I must confess that it is. I wonder if it will ever become the fashion?'

Her aunt chuckled in answer. 'For young ladies to reveal their figures—not to mention a good deal of ankle, since you cut too much off? Not in a hundred years! Young men are quite without scruple, as it is. They need no encouragement!' Her eyes were bright with laughter, and Melody wondered at the total insanity of the situation—two English ladies facing a pending Maori attack and discussing fashion. 'It's unreal,' she whispered, and Beatrice gave her shoulder a reassuring squeeze.

'Of course it is. If you think it's other than a dream, you'll find time to be afraid, and that would never do. Now . . . why don't you see if you can help Mr Savage? He's out with the men reinforcing the defences yet again, but I'm sure he'd appreciate some of that almost solid coffee the girls are making with a good teaspoonful of honey in it.'

Melody went to the kitchen, wondering at her aunt's

character. The woman was as many-faceted as a diamond, equally at home in a London gambling-hall or on a fox hunt, organising the servants for a garden party or for a Maori attack. 'I'll never know her,' she realised with a shake of the head. 'Not in a million years!' As instructed, she took a thick slice of fresh bread, and covering it with some of the honey, washed it down quickly with a mug of coffee which was, to use an old phrase of her aunt's, 'Black as hate, sweet as love, and hot as Hades'. She cut a dozen chunks more, took part of the honey, a knife and several mugs, filled a jug with coffee, and went outside.

There were men moving purposefully to and fro with wood and arms, there were shouts and curses and the occasional burst of laughter, but there seemed a certain order to it, and then she saw Paul Savage, his back to her, directing the whole with short, chopping gestures and clipped orders. Hurrying over, she called his name, and he turned with a frown.

'What are you doing here?'

No welcome there. 'Aunt Bee thought you'd appreciate some coffee. I thought some bread and honey, too, for you and any of the others who've apparently been up since dawn.'

He nodded, too preoccupied to smile, not even noticing her dress, and she heaved a sigh of relief. He took a mug and the jug from her, filled it, then helped himself to a chunk of bread from the basket. 'No honey, thanks. That group over there haven't had breakfast. Go to them.'

Short, terse sentences. Orders. But she understood and obeyed, not feeling at all hurt under the circumstances. It was a different story with the group of Maoris: tough, golden-skinned veterans of many a raid, whose eyes lit up at her approach. 'Mr Savage thought you might like some coffee and some of this bread and honey.'

'Good, Mihi Merody. You good lady.' And with effusive thanks they finished both coffee and the food. 'My son Matiu up same time as me. Same hungry,' one of the men grinned, gesturing to another group stacking and loading a pile of rifles. Melody smilingly took the hint and went to refill her jug and basket, finding that, too, eagerly emptied by the famished men. Before long, however, there were no more mouths to feed, no more assistance she could give. The others also felt it as the day wore on. She knew then that the waiting was the worst part. Every minute seemed like an hour. Where were they? Each leaf that trembled in the breeze made a watcher draw in his breath, each crack of a falling branch caused the heart to pound. The defenders stood at the ready, rifles carried with deceptive negligence, yet ready to aim at the instant. Melody felt her nerves stretched to near breaking-point, the strain making her want to scream.

Suddenly a high-pitched cry rent the air. She whirled, shocked. It had come from outside the palisade, within the darkness of the trees, and for an instant it froze everyone within, and then Paul Savage shouted something in Maori and the men stiffened in readiness. Those who had not taken up guns went to the piles that were stacked at intervals around the perimeter.

Melody was aware of Beatrice at her side, and reached to find her hand taken in a firm grip. 'Has it begun?'

'I think so, child. Come, let's see what Mr Savage will have us do.'

Silence had fallen again, but Melody's heart was still pounding as she ran with her aunt to where Paul stood, grim faced. Beatrice cut through his frowning objection before he could speak. 'We can either load or we can join the others at the house, but I think I should tell you that I'm a fair shot.'

His gaze swept over them in instant assessment. 'Get a gun then, Lady Davenport, and thank you. Mrs Van der Veer, you stay and load for us. Think you can manage that?' There was an edge to his words that had not been there when he addressed Beatrice, and she bristled.

'With difficulty, but I'll manage.' Already he had turned his back to her and she stood there frustrated until another cry rent the air, an almost inhuman sound that seemed torn from a body suffering all the tortures of hell. 'Oh, God! What's happening?'

He turned back to her then, and momentarily his eyes cleared as he put a firm hand on her shoulder. 'Sorry. It's always bad the first time. It's just beginning. They want us to hear. They want us to know what will happen when they over-run us. They have victims brought from other battles up-river. Before attacking a stockade or a *pa* as well defended as this, they'll torture some of the poor devils to upset the defenders.' There was another anguished cry—a high, gurgling shriek that rose, growing more shrill, and Melody covered her ears, yet still the sound seemed to echo in her head.

Then from the shadows came a new sound, a strange chanting, and Paul echoed it, his eyes hard. *'Riria! Riria! Patua! Patua!* Fight on! Fight on! Kill! Kill! Don't let it get to you. They have to gain more courage. This isn't the first time Windhaven has stood in their way, and they have dead fathers and sons and brothers to prove it.' He bent to look through a gun-slot in the stockade wall, and nodded as the chanting suddenly ceased. 'Soon, now.'

Melody felt her mouth go dry, and found Beatrice beside her. 'Just like a grouse shoot,' her aunt said, and Melody turned to her, incredulous—and then saw the mingled fear and courage in the cool grey eyes.

'These grouse shoot back,' she said, attempting an answering smile.

'More sporting,' Beatrice agreed, then raised a soft hand to Melody's cheek in a brief caress. 'Don't fret, sweeting. Your Mr Savage will see us through.'

Melody was about to reply, when another cry came from the trees, a shrill, *'Hape! Hape! Hau!'*

'To protect them against the *pakeha* bullets,' Paul interpreted, then stiffened and raised his rifle.

The attack, when it came, was shocking in its suddenness. The shadows moving from deeper shadows suddenly erupted from the trees, became brown-skinned killers, screaming fiends of hell. 'Fire!' cried Paul, and the fusillade that broke out on his command deafened Melody.

She was pushed roughly to the ground at his feet, and then there was no time for coherent thought, no time for fear even, or to wonder what would happen if the attackers broke through that barrier. Her first fumbling efforts became automatic as she reloaded the rifle that was tossed to her, and handed the other into clutching hands. On and on it went; the screams of the savages, occasionally the cry of a badly-wounded man from inside the barrier, a cacophony of sound that beat at her eardrums. Maori women came from the house to fight alongside their men, rolling them aside when they fell, not keening or wailing, but taking up the rifle and firing on with tight lips and dry eyes. Later they would mourn; now they must survive.

Melody loaded and re-loaded, shutting out the banshee howling, the screams of anger and cries of pain. Each man reacted in his own way. Some shouted defiance as they fired, threw their empty rifle down to be re-loaded and seized a fresh one; some were stoical, expressions masked as they killed with an almost cool detachment. 'It can't last much longer!' she thought, even as her hands worked mechanically, picking up a rifle, loading it, handing it up and finding another beside her. They grew hot, and her hands blistered on the burning metal, but there was no feeling there, either.

Then, as suddenly as if had begun, it ceased, and the attackers melted back into the shadows. 'Oh, thank God! It's over!' she cried.

Paul shook his head grimly. 'No, just regrouping.' She stared at him, unable to comprehend, and he bent to take hold of her shoulders, lifting her to her feet. 'Te Whatitoa is on his way. We know that, and so do they. It's just a matter of time. They must finish us off before they make good their escape, or it will be a crushing blow to the *tohunga*. Te Whatitoa's warriors are known throughout the region for their fierceness. No other tribe will face them. Be brave. We're not beaten yet.' He reached out to touch Beatrice's arm, drawing a tired smile from her. 'It would do me no good at all if I advised you to return to the house, would it?'

'None at all, Mr Savage.'

'This next attack will be fiercer than the first, and my

men are tired, my forces depleted.'

The grey eyes, though red-rimmed, were very calm. 'I know what you're trying to say, but I'm sure I speak for my niece, too, when I refuse your kind suggestion.'

Melody felt the warmth of the searching gaze that turned upon her. His eyes moved to her hands, and reaching out, he raised them, palms upward. 'These are in no condition to fight with. I should order you to the house to cover them with liniment and bandages—but in truth I need you here. Can you stay?'

Melody felt a strange tightness in her throat as she met that level regard. 'As long as you need me.' She wondered whether she was speaking of the battle, or whether her heart had answered for her, and her hands trembled within that firm, yet gentle, hold.

Something in her eyes found an echo in his, and in a different tone he softly warned, 'It will bring you more pain.'

'I accept that.'

There was a stillness, a moment when the hubbub faded and the battleground disappeared. Only the touch of their hands was real, and the searching in their eyes. He made to speak—would have spoken—but his words were cut off by another shrieked order from the *tohunga* and the air was again rent with that demoniacal unified chant of 'Kill! Kill!' Again the nightmare cacophony of sound. Again the frantic loading and re-loading and cutting off of all thought. Again the acrid stench of gunpowder, and sweat, and blood as men fell on both sides.

As the defenders weakened, the attackers gained the palisade, and some were thrown up to clutch at the top. A head appeared, heavily tattooed, face split in a grimace of hate—and a musket cracked beside her. A crimson fountain gushed from his forehead and he was thrown back, crashing to the ground like a broken doll.

Screaming his hatred, another warrior gained the top and leaped down to land a bare ten feet from them, his knife aimed at a young Maori's throat, but the cry had warned the boy and desperately he twisted aside. Diverted,

the knife slashed deep into his arm, but Paul had already
spun and emptied his rifle into the attacker's chest, swiftly
moving to go to the boy. Beatrice, however, had already
flung down her rifle and was beside him. 'Each to his
own, Commander!' she snapped, already picking up the
fallen knife and shredding the bottom layer from her
petticoat. With an expertise that caused Paul to raise an
enquiring eyebrow, she bared the arm and applied a thick
pad and tourniquet within seconds.

The boy smiled his gratitude, the pain beading his
forehead, and gestured toward his rifle. 'No, my brave
lad. Try this,' Beatrice instructed, lifting Paul's revolver
from its holster. The boy took it after receiving a brief
nod from his leader, and continued his defence. 'Loyalty
and courage. You have good men, Mr Savage.'

He turned, his smile encompassing both women, and
Melody felt that familiar tremor in the region of her
heart.

'My women are also fair fighters, Lady Davenport!'

More brown-skinned fanatics gained the inside of the
barricade, and the battle became more desperate as men
fought hand to hand. Two savages leapt down, screeching
their death-defying prayers, but this time their god had
turned away. Melody saw one hate-filled face dissolve
into gore as he hit the ground, blown apart by Beatrice's
rifle. The other charged at Paul, knife held high, his blue-
whorled features contorted, the stench of the fish-oil that
anointed his body reaching Melody even before he brushed
her aside in his rush towards the one man he aimed to
kill. There would be death or glory for the man who
found *kaiārahi nui*. Paul raised his rifle, then at the last
minute realised that it was empty and threw it aside. He
appeared unbelievably cool, awaiting that mad rush, arms
held loosely, a little in front of him, and only at the last
minute did he move. In a blur of speed he seized that
knife arm, twisted, and using the arm as a fulcrum and
the man's own impetus against him, threw the killer over
his shoulder to slam him into the ground. Smoothly he
followed him down, in the same movement drawing his

own knife from his boot and plunging it into the man's heart. Blood spurted like a fountain, but Paul, rising without a second glance, wiped the knife on his already filthy trousers.

'Rifle!' Still shocked, Melody mutely handed him the loaded gun. The carnage about her was unbelievable as savage after savage gained the top of the barricade. Most never made it further, dropping bonelessly, blood-spattered, to the reddening earth. She threw yet another rifle to Paul. He raised it . . . fired . . . nothing! It was the empty one he had just tossed to her! Panic! Blind terror! But then his eyes, the gold flecks gleaming, suddenly creased in a smile. 'Easy, girl!' he said . . . and the world ceased its crazy gyrations. Melody choked down the sob in her throat, and for a heartbeat let the cool confidence of the man wash over her. Quickly she handed him the loaded rifle. No apology necessary. It went on.

Suddenly she cried out as a painted body reared up over Paul's head. There was a crash of gunfire and a choked-off scream as the man disappeared. She spun to Paul, then gave a sob of disbelief at the sight of the short spear, flung in dying vengeance, protruding from his side. Cries of hatred filled the air, bringing her attention to where other savages had gained success. The rifle! Not daring to tend the fallen man, she snatched up the gun and loaded it, aimed at a blue-painted face . . . and found that it had turned into Luther Hogge! 'No! No!' Again she aimed, but found the nausea and horror in her memory impossible to control. Her hands shook, sticky with sweat on the butt. Her heart pounded and she was unable to breathe. 'I can't! Oh, God help me! I can't!'

Paul gave a deep moan and made to rise, one hand pressed to his side, not daring to pull out the spear, the other reaching for the gun in her hands. No condemnation in the deep-set eyes. But then, with a despairing curse, he fell back, slipping into unconsciousness.

Melody screamed out his name, shattering the wall of terror that had paralysed her, lifted the rifle, and fired. There was a roar, a sharp pain as the recoil slammed

against her shoulder. Again she fired. Not at humans—
she could think of them as that—but at Paul's would-be
murderers.

From a long way off she became aware of another
sound, a chanting that held a deadly, fearless quality;
deep throated and reverberating above the noise of battle—
the war chant of Te Whatitoa's warriors. The *tohunga*
heard it, and his voice rose in frustrated fury to call his
men away, but they, too, had heard the sound which
drove terror into their hearts and were already
withdrawing, running for the trees and melting into the
shadows.

From the south, erupting into the clearing like avenging
angels of death, rode Te Whatitoa's fierce warriors, red-
oiled bodies gleaming, the blue whorls on their faces
standing out, but not frightening Melody now, only filling
her with a wild joy. The defenders on the palisade gave a
cheer and the gates were opened wide, allowing the heavily
armed reinforcements to ride in. With a sweeping glance,
their leader rode directly to Paul's side, sliding from his
horse while still in motion and dropping to his knees
beside his friend. Beatrice and Melody had both knelt,
but neither dared to move the badly wounded man, even
though Paul had slipped in and out of consciousness
throughout.

'Into the house,' the Maori ordered, calling to three of
his men, who eased Paul on to a blanket from one of the
horses and carried him carefully across the yard, the spear
held firmly in place by Te Whatitoa himself, who showed
no concern at all at the sight of it.

Running alongside, Melody asked, 'He will be all right,
won't he? Please say he'll be all right?'

The man's eyes flickered to her face, and he gave a
sympathetic nod. 'Paul is a hard man. It's a bad wound,
but he'll live.'

They set their burden down on a long, scrubbed table
in the kitchen, the blood stains on the floor about it
telling Melody that Paul was not the first casualty to have
been brought here during the lapses in battle. Maata

bustled up, and at a word from the Maori chief, helped him to cut away her master's shirt. Melody felt helpless as they worked, not even being as enterprising as Beatrice, who had left them the moment Te Whatitoa arrived and now appeared with bandages and clean linen, followed by one of the girls who carried the bowl of hot water. A young warrior brought his knife, whose long blade had been thrust into the embers of the kitchen fire.

Te Whatitoa took it, and poured some spirit on the blade, then gave Melody a level look. 'You don't have to stay.'

'I'm staying.' But she almost wished she hadn't, as, with a deft double cut he opened the wound even more, then eased out the spear, whose barb would not now tear the flesh. Paul cried out as the knife bit, but the men held him, and he lapsed once more into semi-consciousness. Melody held tight to her own senses as the wound was revealed, a deep chasm that went through his side, barely missing the lower ribs, and tearing through nerve and muscle almost to the spine. There was blood everywhere; his torn shirt, trousers and the table were soaked in it.

Te Whatitoa shot out an order, and a man appeared at his side, handing him a second knife still glowing red. Melody gasped, holding back her nausea, as the warriors sprang to hold Paul, and Te Whatitoa applied the knife-blade to the wound. There was a hissing sound, then a sickly-sweet scent—and Paul screamed—just once—before falling back again. One of the women came forward with a bowl of herbs and honey, and gently scooped the aromatic mixture on to the terrible wound, covering it thickly. A pad of linen went over that, then a handful of mosses and a thick wad of cotton, before the men raised the unconscious man and Te Whatitoa swiftly bandaged his whole torso from waist to armpits. Only then did he look up and encounter Melody's shock-filled eyes.

'I'll send one of my men for the *pakeha* doctor, but this will stop most of the bleeding until he arrives. It may take two or three days before he can get here—the raiding tribes have been busy all up-river.'

'Two . . . or three . . . *days*?'

'He'll not die, our *kaiārahi nui*. He has the strength of ten men, but the dressing will need to be changed daily and someone should be with him all the time.'

Paul moaned, twisting against the pain, subconsciously fighting the burning agony within him, his forehead beaded with sweat, the muscles in his arms straining against the men that held him. His agony was too much to bear, and Melody bent to hold his head, her blistered hands firm on each side of his face. 'Oh, please don't fight it,' she implored. 'You'll only hurt yourself more. Be still, Paul. Be still. Easy, now. Easy,' she crooned. 'There. Be still. Gently, now. Ease back. Believe in me. Soft, now.' Over and over the mesmeric voice washed over him, seeking the far recesses of his mind. Suddenly a shudder went through that tortured frame, and the writhing ceased. Her whole being concentrated on the man lying there. She did not hear the murmur that went round the watchers, and Beatrice allowed a smile to touch her lips as she caught the puzzled look of the Maori chief.

'I've seen her do it with her father's sick stallion when no one else could get near him,' she explained drily. 'I suppose one stallion is much like another!'

Te Whatitoa gave an answering smile, tinged with relief. 'Will she stay with him?'

Melody, who had straightened a little, heard his question, her fingers still smoothing back the sweat-soaked hair. Her eyes never left Paul's face, but she answered, 'I'll stay. Can he be moved yet?'

'We'll take him to his room,' Maata said, coming forward, 'and move some of your things to the room next to Mita Paul.'

Melody kept her peace, but when the men had eased Paul on to his bed and turned to go, she asked Te Whatitoa, 'There's a large armchair in the drawing-room. Would it be too much for your men to bring it in here?'

The man's eyes questioned for an instant, then understood, and he nodded. 'They'll bring it.'

'But you must still use your bed occasionally,' Beatrice

stated. The three exchanged looks of understanding, and
there was some inexplicable bond formed at that moment
that went even beyond their already firm friendship.

The chair was brought, and the Maori chief put a
supporting hand on Melody's shoulder. 'We need more
pakeha women like you in this new country!'

For a moment she was about to tell him the truth, but
looking into the gentle eyes, could not bring herself to
denounce his friend as a slave-owner who had forced his
coloured slave to accompany him against her will, in her
eyes a slave still, who worked only until the day of her
freedom. 'They will come, one day.' She smiled. 'Now
you must return to your people. For all of us, I can only
give you our totally inadequate thanks. We owe you our
lives.'

He gave a cheerful shrug. 'If I gain a friend, I become
a greater person. If I lose that friend, I am even less than
I was before I met him. Paul is my brother, my friend,
my family, and more. It's only right that I care for all
that is his—as he would for me and mine. Now I leave
him in your care. I have watched you, and I am content
to leave.'

Melody blushed, feeling the warmth deep inside. 'You're
a good friend: I only hope I can be worthy of you.'

He left silently, taking the others with him, and she was
alone with the injured man. His words on the battlefield
returned to her. 'I need you here. Can you stay?' The
erratic beat of her heart warned her that some indefinable
change had been wrought at that moment and nothing
would be quite the same again, yet she accepted the slow
thunder, and reiterated her own words. 'As long as you
need me, Paul . . . Just as long as you need me.'

CHAPTER SEVENTEEN

IT WAS ALMOST MIDNIGHT, and Melody had been dozing fitfully in the large armchair. She had made Paul as comfortable as possible, after Maata and Beatrice had returned and shooed her out of the room to strip the tatters of his shirt, bloodstained trousers and boots from him, changed the bed-linen and only then allow her back to start her long vigil.

'Did you think I'd faint at the sight of a naked man?' Melody had asked mutinously.

Beatrice had given one of her chuckles. 'Not if you'd seen as many as I, my dear! But when you had to face him later you might well have blushed—which would have been far worse!'

Now, the slightest sound brought Melody into instant wakefulness, and she rose to cross to the bedside. Paul was twitching spasmodically, as he had been over the past hours, tossed between life and death. His forehead was bathed in perspiration, the craggy features contorted in the pain that filtered into his unconsciousness. She turned up the lamp and went to soak a cloth in cool water, tiredly brushing a curl back from her forehead, wringing out the cloth, and no longer worried that a few drops splashed on her dress. Gently she bathed the man's forehead and throat, bringing instant relief, as she had done several times before.

There was a stain on the bandage about his torso, and fear caught at her throat. The Maori chief had told her that there would be seepage from the wound, that the strange glutinous mixture that covered it would prevent infection, and that she must change the dressings daily. She wondered whether she should call Beatrice to help her to change them now, or wait until morning. Paul, however, had quieted under her ministrations and fallen into a light sleep, and reluctant to disturb him, she again went to settle into her chair.

It was dawn when she awoke to Maata's gentle hand on her shoulder. 'You go eat now. I sit with him.'

Melody smiled, but shook her head with a glance toward the still sleeping man. 'I'm not really hungry. Perhaps you could ask one of the girls to bring bread and honey, and some hot coffee. I'll wash and change in my own room, if you could arrange for some water to be brought.'

The Maori woman nodded. 'You want to put clean bandage on Mita Paul?'

'Yes, after I've changed and eaten. Will you ask Lady Davenport to help?'

'I go to mix medicine.'

'What exactly was in that bowl of stuff spread on Mr Savage's wound?'

Maata gave a wide smile, spreading her hands in an expressive gesture. 'Lotta things. Plants used by my people long before *pakeha* come. Bind together with honey, because honey clean. No dirt from bees. Like spider-web, but too many webs needed for this job. I shall teach you some day. My mother teach me. Didn't your *pakeha* mother teach you?'

'No, I never seemed to take the time to learn about simples when my mother was alive, though the women of the village where father kept his horses knew about them. I come from a town, and we buy our medicines from shops; the large jars of pills and potions are mixed at the back of the shop, so the customer never really knows what mixture he's getting, or even how hygenic it is. I'd like to learn, if you have the time. I've a feeling I'm going to need it in a country as harsh as this.' Then, seeing the other's slight frown, she apologised, 'Oh, I'm not saying it isn't a beautiful country, it is. But there is this constant war with hostile elements that seems to have gone on for years. There's the lack of roads, so that it takes a doctor

days to get here. There's the bush to be kept at bay, wild
pigs and disease that attack the crops on what little land
you *can* clear.' She was near to tears, all her fears and
unhappiness and exhaustion flowing out in a spate of
nonsensical complaints, none of which related to the one
sick fear that had enveloped her from the moment she
had turned to see the spear protruding from Paul's side.
'Oh, Maata,' she finally whispered. 'Say he won't die!'
And she sobbed on to the voluminous bosom to which
she had been gathered.

'Hush, Mihi Merody. Mita Paul be all right! You see.
You just bit scared and lot tired.'

With difficulty, and thoroughly ashamed of her outburst,
Melody straightened. 'I'm sorry. I'm all right now. Of
course he'll be well. The doctor will be here tomorrow or
the next day, and in the meantime your old ways will
hold the infection at bay and we'll keep the wound clean.
He'll be up and about in no time.' She smiled with an
optimism that she was far from feeling, but later, when
with Maata and Beatrice's help she uncovered the wound
to change the dressings, her hopes plummeted.

The terrible burn created by the Maori's cauterisation
of the wound had pulled the skin into a dark red scab,
wrinkled and cracked where the blood still seeped. The
olive skin around the wound, however, showed no tell-
tale redness of infection, and was only warm to the touch.
'Good!' Beatrice nodded, echoing Maata's satisfied grunt.

'But it's still bleeding,' Melody objected, still fighting
her nausea at the sight of the wound. 'Shouldn't it have
stopped by now?'

'Be all right,' Maata insisted, smearing on more of the
thick herbal and honey mixture. 'You hold him up now.'

They had cut the first lengths of bandage from the
wound without disturbing the semi-conscious man, easing
them out from under him and throwing them in a bucket
to be burned. Now, with Beatrice on the opposite side,
they had to raise him so that Maata could pass the
bandages round him. 'Put his arm over your shoulder to
keep it clear, but whatever you do, don't pull him up by

it or you'll tear open all our good work,' Beatrice instructed, but even so, Paul gave a low groan as they eased him up.

Ignoring him, Maata swiftly passed the bandage round, again from waist to beneath the arms. Until that moment, Melody had been too preoccupied to think of anything but the awful scar, but now that it was covered, she became suddenly aware of her arms tight about the muscular body, her cheek pressed to that broad golden chest, and the weight of the arm over her shoulders. She shuddered, and Beatrice, supporting his back, misunderstood and said, 'Not long now, sweeting, and you can let this great ox down.'

Melody drew in a deep breath, catching the musky tang of him mingled with the sweet scent of the herbs, and for one wild moment she fought the impulse to flick out her tongue and taste the salty sheen on his skin—but then Maata pronounced the bandaging complete, and Beatrice was moving carefully aside to enable Melody to lower him to the bed.

'I'd not want that as a regular job,' Beatrice stated, brushing back her disarrayed hair. 'My admiration for Miss Nightingale grows with every hour, but at present I think I need a breath of air. Pity it won't hold the aroma of a good Havana and the click of a roulette wheel, with the sound of a waltz wafting up from the ballroom below . . . ' She rose crisply. 'But I'll accept that the breeze outside will undoubtedly be more healthy, so I'll suffer through it. You need a break too, child. Will you join me?'

'No, thank you, Aunt Bee. I'm quite content here for now.'

Beatrice gave a long, considering look at the sunbronzed figure, relaxed now against cool sheets, and nodded sagely. 'Yes . . . Yes, at your age and given your position, probably I should have been, too! Come on, Maata. I don't think we're needed any more.'

Within minutes of her departure, however, she was back, her normally cool eyes worried. 'Melody, it's young

David. He's disappeared!'

Melody came from her chair with a rush. 'Are you sure? Have they looked everywhere? You know what children are. Perhaps he's hiding, just playing a joke.'

'No, I don't know what children are like, thank heavens, but Maata says they've been searching for an hour or more. No one has seen him since the battle, but with all the turmoil—cleaning up the compound, burying the dead, Mr Savage's wound and others . . . well, the absence of one small boy wasn't thought to be important until now. Maata says the mercenaries are willing to comb the area, but they're not on their own territory and could fall to some Maori ambush.'

Melody felt sick fear, desperately trying to remember when she had last seen David. 'I must get to Te Whatitoa. His people will help,' she decided. 'David's their kin, and they know every inch of this wilderness.'

Beatrice nodded in relief. 'One of Maata's brothers will go and take some of the men with him.'

'No, we can't leave the place unguarded. Paul said that the *tohunga* would lose much face if he had to retreat, so there is every possibility, with Te Whatitoa away . . . ' She swallowed hard, controlling her rising panic. 'We need every man we have.' Before she had finished speaking, Beatrice had read her mind and begun to object, but Melody reiterated, 'No. I'll not have any arguments. I'm going. I'll take one of the men and go by canoe. Paul once said it was the fastest route to anywhere on the river.' She hadn't noticed her instinctive use of his Christian name in her concern over the safety of his people, nor that she had used it since he had fallen in battle. She dared not think of the possibilities or reasons surrounding the boy's disappearance, or of her own safety. She knew only that it was the only choice to ensure the safety of Windhaven.

'You've never been in a canoe in your life!' argued her aunt.

'And I hope I never have to again.' Already she was hurrying to the kitchen.

'What can *I* do?' called Beatrice, for the first time in her life at a loss, and earned a quick smile.

'Don't leave Paul for a second, and then . . . call on all the gods you can think of.'

As expected, Maata's reaction was much the same as Beatrice's, but Melody cut into those objections as cleanly, ordering two horses to take them to the jetty.

'Take Henare, then. He's the eldest, and strong like an ox.' Maata's liquid brown eyes were deeply concerned. 'You are a good woman, but a very stubborn one. You do this for just a little *hāwhe kāehe* boy? Why?'

'It makes no difference whether he's half-caste, white or Maori, as far as I'm concerned. He's a lost child, and very dear to Mr Savage. That's enough for me. Now, where's Henare? I'll not waste any more time.'

'Very well,' nodded Maata. '*Kia tupato i koe . . . Kia ora koe*. Go carefully, and I wish you luck.'

Within minutes, Melody was mounted on one of the rangy work horses, and with the hugely muscled Henare leading the way, rode her mount hard to the river. Once there, however, her heart almost failed her, for the canoe, one of three hidden beneath dense bush, seemed too fragile to bear her own weight, even without that of the giant Maori. He grinned at her trepidation and with no hesitation lifted her bodily and dumped her in the craft, following her with an agility that belied his great frame. Taking up the paddle, he pushed out into the river, and Melody closed her eyes, clinging tightly, not daring to open them until the fast-rushing waters had brought them to the familiar rocky outcrop of Operiki.

News of their coming had been carried to Te Whatitoa by repeated blasts on Henare's conch-shell horn, and he met them at the water's edge—Rawiri at his side.

'David! Thank heaven you're safe!' Melody burst out, flinging herself from the boat, running to the boy and hugging and shaking him in turn. 'You've had us worried sick! I came to organise a search-party. Don't you dare do such a thing again! First you come *up*-river alone, and then you disappear while the enemy are still in the area.

What were we to think?' Still gripping him by the arm, she turned to his uncle, eyes bright with strain. 'I'm sorry. I was so afraid for him, and then that awful canoe-ride . . .'

A frown touched the aristocratic features. 'You are right, and it is I who must apologise. One of my own men brought Rawiri back here, not knowing that Paul was hurt, but thinking it would be safer for the boy here.'

'Hurt?' the boy cried. 'You didn't tell me he was hurt.'

'He's going to be all right, David,' Melody soothed, regaining her scattered emotions. 'But he still needs constant attention, so I must get back at once. There's a doctor on the way, so everything will go well. You'll be better off with your uncle, and I'm quite happy for you to stay here now that I know you're all right.'

'No! No, I must go back!' The Maori chief shook his head, but the boy pulled free, expression mutinous, arms rigid by his sides, fists clenched. 'You'll have to tie me up to stop me, and then I'll find a way to get free!'

Torn with indecision, Melody realised that in all proba-bility the child spoke the truth. He was quite unlike any child of his age that she knew, and in the Victorian society in which she had been brought up would have earned the belt for his defiance. But this was a wild and alien land that seemed to breed people to match. 'Let him come,' she decided. 'At least if he promises to stay in the compound, I'll not worry about him.'

There was no denying the relief in Te Whatitoa's eyes as he nodded agreement. 'But you must allow me to give you an escort back. I do not think that the raiders are still in the area, but it does no harm to take precautions.'

'No, I'm sure you're right. We'll be safe enough. It's very kind of you, but I'm sure the pace will be a little more sedate now that the panic is over.'

'You must make all haste back to Windhaven, even though there is little chance of danger. The slightest chance is too great.' He raised an arm, and several of his warriors came down to join him. 'These are my best. You are a remarkable woman, Mrs Van der Veer, and deserve only the best for your bravery.'

Melody basked in the warmth of his approval and allowed her long lashes to veil her eyes, hiding her pleased embarrassment. The men pulled out a longer version of Henare's canoe, undecorated, as were most of those used routinely on the river, and helped Melody into it.

'Henare will follow you,' Te Whatitoa said. 'He is a good man, Maata's *toa nui*—great warrior.'

'I'm surrounded by great warriors!' Melody told him. 'I feel like a queen with her bodyguard.'

The war chief returned her smile. 'A queen with the heart of a warrior herself. *Haere ra*.'

'Goodbye,' she echoed, raising her hand as the warriors dipped their paddles and the canoe shot away, skimming the water with the speed and grace of a dolphin. She was surprised to find that this time she felt none of the fear of the rocking craft that had terrified her on the way down, and could even thrill to the exhilarating race over the wide river. 'A little like racing over the Downs on a high-spirited thoroughbred,' she told David, encircling his slender shoulders with her arm, but the boy could not be diverted from his worry. As soon as they arrived at the stockade, he ran to Paul's room without even thanking their escort, or exchanging words with the worried Maata.

Melody saw to that task, but Beatrice saw the fine lines that the strain had etched about her niece's mouth and the pallor of the ivory skin. 'Go to bed, child. Mr Savage is resting as he should be, and it would do you no harm to follow his example.'

'Not yet. Not until I know for certain that he's going to be well. What if he turns sharply in his sleep and the wound re-opens? You and Maata have enough on your hands with the other wounded. No, this is something I must do. I'll wash and change—I got quite splashed during my little escapade—and then I'll go back to him.'

'I'll get that little hellion out of there, too,' Beatrice stated firmly. 'The boy's caused enough trouble for a whole barrel-load of monkeys. I'll not have him disturbing the patient.'

Wearily Melody nodded, going to splash cold water over her face and neck before washing thoroughly and changing out of the spray-soaked dress. Her neck ached with the tension of her ordeal, but she refused to acknow-ledge it as she returned once more to the dimly-lit room. They were alone. Paul lay peacefully, heavy lashes masking the gold-flecked eyes that had been filled with agony yet still shone with the determination to fight it, lips slightly parted, a sweet, unfamiliar odour coming from them, so that Melody knew that Maata had administered some sleeping-draught. 'Live, Paul!' she commanded softly. 'Live, damn you!' The tears of exhaustion flooded her eyes, but she brushed them away angrily, knowing that there was a long way to go before it was ended.

Another night passed and another day before the doctor arrived, a bone-weary, over-worked little man who had been too long in New Zealand either to condemn or condone, and treated *pakeha* and Maori alike. He examined the wounded man and talked at great length with Maata, finally accepting that there was little more he could do. 'I wish all my patients had as wise a friend and as devoted a nurse,' he said. 'The mixture you've been putting on the wound is, in my considerable experience, far better than any modern medicine I could prescribe; though, of course, not one of my learned colleagues would agree with me! But then *they* treat burns with grease, which simply fries the already burned flesh. They won't listen to me when I tell them of the sailors with burns, and those natives who live on the coast and use salt water, who rarely if ever blister. I've used saline solutions most successfully for some years now. One must adapt to one's environment, not fight it, especially in a land like this.' He rose with a gentle smile. 'I'll leave him a draught which will make him sleep more deeply, and *my* one is better than yours this time, Maata! The longer he sleeps, the faster the wound will heal. I'd advise you to do the same, Mrs Van der Veer, or I'll be treating you instead of the real patient!'

'Oh, I'm perfectly all right,' Melody answered, not

having bothered with a mirror lately, and so missing the pale, drawn features and dull, red-rimmed eyes that concerned the doctor.

'She'll do as she's told for once!' interrupted Beatrice. 'I never had half this problem with her when another young man needed nursing: in fact she was only too glad to escape the sick-room! This time, we can't pry her loose! But enough's enough. Mr Savage will sleep deeply, with the good doctor's help, and there's absolutely no reason why you shouldn't do the same—and not in that armchair you've not moved from for the past two nights.'

'Yes, Aunt Bee.' But Melody had absolutely no intention of leaving Paul's side until he was fully recovered and able to sit up. Her aunt's allusion to Brett's accident and his time in bed had quickened her heartbeat for an instant, but with a glance toward Paul, she knew that there was absolutely no similarity. Brett had not been badly hurt, she argued with herself, but the fact remained to torment her that she *had* been glad to be relieved of her nursing, while here she fought it with all her fading strength. How could it be? How could she feel irritation and even boredom nursing the one, while sacrificing both appearances and health to be with the other? 'Can you stay?' she remembered, and, 'For as long as you need me,' the answer.

However, she had reckoned without the understanding of the old doctor, well versed in the easy acquiescence from women such as she. Having said his farewells, he went to the Maori woman and gave her the small bottle. 'Maata, I want you to see that Mrs Van der Veer takes a half-spoonful of this in her drink tonight, and twice that for Mr Savage. She'll not take it if she knows, but it has neither smell nor taste, so I'll leave it with you. Do you understand?'

Maata nodded, her relief apparent. The *pakeha* doctor was known to be a good man, and if *he* was concerned over Mihi Merody, then she, Maata, would make sure that stubborn lady slept tonight! The other *pakeha* lady, too. She and Maata were the same, Maata reflected, both old and tough and with much living behind them. Both had loved well, and neither had children to show for it. She considered that a sadness, and one of the puzzles of life that she was unable to bear children. But the Lady Bee, as Maata called her, did not seem to mind at all, and gave all her love now to Mihi Merody. Maata had heard her moving in her room at night, just as the shadow of Mihi Merody had crossed and re-crossed her door since she had been brought here by the master. It was as if both the *pakeha* women had great burdens to bear, yet each shared it with no one, not even each other, and paced their rooms alone. She had heard the way Mihi Merody sometimes talked to the master, yet had seen her eyes tell a different story. Could it be that she was not as wise as the youngest Maori girl, who knew that she wanted a warrior the minute she saw him? It was all very perplexing, but she was not one to be concerned overlong with problems beyond her understanding. The *pakeha* doctor had decreed that the people in Maata's charge needed sleep, so sleep they would have!

That night Beatrice retired early, feeling unusually drowsy after the delicious hot chocolate that Maata had prepared, and Melody, too, found her eyelids heavy after her untasted chocolate had been replaced with a concoction of fresh squeezed lemon and honey and, Maata said, a touch of whisky—'just a spoonful'. Paul obligingly swallowed the tiny cooling sips that they had trickled down his throat since the attack and, for once, the house was absolutely silent. Maata entered the master's bedroom and smiled as she saw the girl sprawled bonelessly across the chair, head back across one arm, breathing deeply and regularly. She crossed to her and very gently pinched one earlobe. Melody did not stir. A slightly harder pinch caused no reaction either, and she gave a satisfied smile. She had doubled the dose that the doctor had prescribed, but was confident now that her charges would sleep through this night and a fair amount of the following day as well.

As gently as possible Maata slipped the crumpled dress

from the sleeping girl, the shoes and stockings, leaving her in the lacy camisole and single petticoat. Carefully she eased her out of the chair, and, stumbling only once, carried her to the bed—where she allowed her charge to slide down on top of the bed beside the master. Panting a little, she nodded. 'Bed too big for one,' she muttered, wondering why someone as beautiful as Mihi Merody and a man like the master had not shared the bed long before. 'No sense, these *pakeha*! Pretty lady. Handsome man. Not make love, make happy, make babies. No sense.' Pulling a thick blanket over them both, she left, her mind at ease.

The sun was high when Melody awoke to birdsong. There was a dryness in her mouth, and it felt as though a lead weight was pressing down on her ribs, but the birds persisted, and she opened her eyes with the greatest reluctance. It took several more seconds for reality to creep in and gently re-arrange the room to the correct angle, assuring her that she was not facing the bed or a wall and was therefore not seated in the armchair. It took a second more to give her all the facts, and as her eyes swept downward, a gasp escaped her and her body went rigid. Her shoulders were bare, and the blanket had slipped off during her sleep, revealing the cobweb-thin camisole—and the smooth golden arm across her waist!

Turning her head, dreading what she might see, she gave a slow exhalation of relief. Paul Savage was still fast asleep, the thickly-lashed eyes closed, only inches away from her own, his regular breathing fanning her cheek. He was sleeping on his side, his wounded side beneath him, yet he showed no sign of pain, and his features were relaxed. She lay still, realising that it must have been Maata who had undressed her and made her comfortable, knowing that her sleep had been drugged, yet feeling only gratitude for the consideration and concern that the woman had shown.

'But now I must get up and dressed before anyone comes in—or before Paul wakes!' For she knew also that the time elapsed had been long enough for the man's crisis to have passed. His forehead was dry, his position relaxed. The fever had broken, and at any time now he would regain consciousness. Breathing a prayer of thanks, she eased herself upwards—and with a low groan Paul moved in protest, his arm rising defensively, his hand closing over her shoulder. Muttering imprecations against the devils within him, he fought her weakly, his nightmare casting her as a vengeful, tattooed assailant. 'Your wound! Oh, please be still!' she whispered, then, casting inhibitions aside, she gathered the sleeping man close, holding him fast against her, murmuring soothing words over and over again until she felt him slump, and the tense muscles moulded themselves against her as slowly he settled down.

Immediately she went to withdraw her arms, but he turned his head, and his mouth was against the curve of her breast. Just a moment more and he would be fully awake, yet for that moment she could hold him like that, and no one—no one—would ever know! The heat of his lips seared her flesh like fire, spreading down to her stomach, and lower, where a dull ache spread throughout her whole being. It was against all her upbringing, all her moral teachings, yet for a moment out of time Melody allowed her body to succumb to the warmth that suffused it, closing her eyes and arching very slightly against the possession of that firm mouth. 'Oh, Paul!' Then, 'If only I were white!' The tears pricked her eyes, and with a sigh she slid sideways off the bed, moving swiftly and silently to prepare for the day.

Having dressed in her own rooms, she went downstairs to ask Maata for something to eat, feeling hungry for the first time in days. She would take a cool drink for Paul when he awoke, and with a small smile, vowed to watch each ingredient that went on to her own plate!

Maata looked up as Melody entered the kitchen, her eyes wary. 'Mihi Merody sleep well?'

'Yes, thanks to you and the good doctor. I am, however, quite capable of undressing myself in future.' Maata looked so downcast that Melody could not help laughing, and at once the brown eyes flew to hers in relief. 'Yes, I should be angry with you. It isn't at all proper for any young lady in any society to waken in the circumstances I found myself in! Thank heavens Mr Savage was still asleep!'

The other woman beamed. 'You sleep better in bed. Mita Paul sleep better. Why you don't sleep together all the time?'

Melody felt herself blushing. 'It's not . . . not . . . '

Taking pity on her, Maata continued, 'You eat now. Too skinny anyway. Not enough woman.'

Melody eyed her ample lines, and shook her head, laughing. 'I could never be as much of a woman as you, Maata, so a little fruit and some toast with that delicious preserve you make will be most welcome. I'll take some lemonade up to Mr Savage afterwards. Is Lady Davenport awake yet?'

Maata looked suitably embarrassed. 'I gave Lady Bee more'n even you and Mita Paul! That lady, she scare me when she mad, and when she know what I do, she gonna be one hella mad lady!'

'Don't worry. I'll intercede for you.'

After a light meal and several cups of hot black coffee to clear her head, Melody took a jug of fresh lemonade and returned to Paul's room. Setting down the jug, she went to pull the curtains, allowing the warm sunlight to flood the room. Would he waken, or dare she wake him? She approached the bed, then gave a gasp, her hand covering her mouth to cut back the cry. Paul had turned on to his stomach, face toward her, one arm outflung, the other beneath his cheek. And the scars, a dozen or more criss-crossing the sun-bronzed back—old scars, and faded, but their origin obvious. Paul Savage had been brutally flogged. Brett's words came back to her, driving the breath from her body. No wonder this man had changed, had forgotten how to laugh!

Almost against her will, she allowed her fingers to trace one of the deeper lines. 'Oh, Paul! Who in God's name could have done such a thing?' she murmured brokenly.

'Southern gentlemen every one,' came the husky voice,

and she sprang back to see the dark eyes looking deep into hers. Painfully he turned on his back, and she moved instinctively to help. 'It's a long story and not a particularly pleasant one,' he continued, 'so I shan't upset you with it.'

'Upset me? How do you think I feel *now*?'

He gave a crooked smile, flexing his stomach muscles experimentally and wincing only a little. 'Like a nurse whose patient has just refused medication, I suspect, but these are old wounds, Melody, and I doubt you have the cure for them.'

Neither realised that he had used her given name, but in a small voice she asked, 'Won't you let me try?' She did not have the answers, only knowing that there must be some way in which she could assuage the hurt that went far deeper than healed scars.

His expression changed subtly, and although the smile still hovered about his mouth, there was a feral quality to it. 'Very well. Kiss me!'

'No!' She sprang back like a frightened doe, then halted, feeling the tremor that those deep-set eyes always produced within her, whispering, 'Your wound . . . '

Restlessly he turned his head away from her. 'Leave me, then.'

But she could no more do that than the other, and hesitantly went to sit on the bed beside him, repeating, 'Your wound,' but without conviction, so that he turned again, and their gazes locked.

Slowly, very slowly, his hand came up, settled on her shoulder, then moved up to remove the first pin from her hair. He held it out to her. 'If I keep my arm raised like this, it will ache.'

Melody could hardly believe her ears, and incredibly a smile was tugging at her mouth, stilling the trembling. Lifting her arms, unaware of the sensuousness of the age-old movement that pulled back her head, presenting him with the alabaster curve of her throat, and arching her back so that the full breasts were thrust out, uptilted, Melody took out the remaining pins and allowed the raven curls to tumble about her shoulders. 'There. That didn't make your arms ache at all, did it?'

Paul Savage looked at her, and something deep inside him twisted like a knife. 'No,' he answered, and there was a huskiness in his voice. 'Not my arm.' Lean fingers drifted upward to touch a curl of hair, gathering it in his hand and drawing her slowly down. Melody felt a tingle along her spine, but then he kissed her, the touch of his lips so light that it was more the sensation of a warm breeze moving over cheeks and temples and chin and again on her parted lips. And he kissed her again like that, over and over, until the quivering ceased.

A gentle knocking propelled Melody upright, and she was frantically attempting to gather her tumbled hair into a rough knot at the nape of her neck when Beatrice entered. With a quick glance at her, and then another, more searching, which brought the colour to the girl's cheeks, she crossed to look down at the wounded man. 'I see you have finally decided to return to the land of the living, Mr Savage. How are you feeling?'

'Better than I've a right to be. I'll be up and about within a day or two, but just now I need answers to some questions.'

'It was thanks to your Maori friend that any of us are here at all!' She recounted, with many digressions in answer to the occasional sharp question, all that had transpired, finishing, 'So here you are.'

A flicker of a smile touched his mobile lips as he asked, 'I do hope, Lady Davenport, that it was Maata who got me into this situation, not yourself or your niece?'

Melody felt the colour flood her face, but Beatrice showed no such embarrassment as she helped herself to a glass of lemonade from the bedside table. 'Oh, we spared Melody's blushes,' she replied with a twinkle, 'but I don't think you need to concern yourself with mine. You aren't the first man I've put to bed who was incapable of doing the job himself, and, with luck, you won't be the last.' Now it was Paul's turn to look embarrassed, but she went on, 'I really came to see whether you are well enough to see young David. He has been haunting the house like a restless wraith when inside, and making a thorough nuisance of himself when forced outside.'

'You'd best allow him in, then.' And, as she left, 'The boy needs more discipline.'

'The boy *loves* you!' Melody objected. 'Though heaven only knows why! And you? Have you no feelings for him? You should. He's as wild and stubborn as you, with as little respect for authority and an equal determination to have his own way.'

His eyes narrowed. 'Would you have us both weak? Would you have me in the same mould as Brett, soft and tender at all times and relying only on you? Would you have David a subservient missionary-trained child, fearing his own shadow, doing as bid without question? Would you then wish to rule as a mother to the one and wife to the other? Is that your design? You're certainly vixenish enough!'

'Not in a million years!' she cried—gone the softness of a moment before. 'If I had any design at all, it would only be one to escape you, but if I *were* your wife, I'd make you acknowledge that you had a heart. I'd force you to respect me, and admit you loved the boy!'

'But you're not my wife,' he flashed back. 'You are not, nor ever will be with that explosive temper, for if you were, I'd . . . '

'Yes? What would you do?' The tears of frustrated anger and deeply hidden, unacknowledged love cascaded unheeded down her cheeks as she raged at him. 'Would you beat me? Turn me out? I wouldn't feel it, and I wouldn't go. I'd stay here and . . . ' She stopped, aghast at her almost finished 'I'd stay and love you.'

But his own anger had flared, inflamed by hers, as anger or passion invariably was when this spark flashed between them. 'Do? I'd tame you, you little witch! I'd beat your temper out of you, or I'd . . . ' Suddenly he seized her, pulling her down on the bed beside him, and those steely fingers rose to capture her face. His thumbs found her mouth, wet with tears, parted with her stormy breathing . . . and time stood still. They froze for an instant, then, his voice slightly husky, he said, 'Or . . . I would change your mind . . . ' And his mouth came down on hers, moving with achingly tender exploration over hers, caressing, parting her lips further, tasting the inner sweetness, until . . .

'No!' She broke away, breathless. 'No, you wouldn't.' Her voice was barely above a whisper. 'For I'd not be your wife. Not ever. I want love, not just passion; understanding, not domination.' She took a deep breath and rose, trembling. 'If I were free, it might, conceivably, be different between us. If I were white . . . but not a coloured slave . . . There could be no love there. You may love the boy because he's your best friend's nephew, even though he *is* coloured, but having him—or me—as part of your blood, that's something else again.' She stopped at the look of incredulity on his face.

'Did you not know? Didn't Maata tell you? David *is* my blood. He's my son!' Melody felt as if a great fist had been punched into the region of her heart, and she sat down abruptly at the foot of the bed, staring at him. 'My wife was Te Whatitoa's sister, a full-blooded Maori, and to me at that time the most beautiful creature on God's earth. She was killed in the last tribal attack here three years ago.' He saw the turmoil and the shame in her eyes, and reached out, but before he could speak, David came running into the room, pulling up short at the sight of Melody.

Gazing at him with new eyes, she wondered how she could ever have missed it; the same arrogant stance and untamed character, the same patrician features and golden skin, no darker than his father's, and the eyes holding the tiniest golden flecks that had previously gone unnoticed. '*Kia ora*, Rawiri. Won't you come in?'

'I'm David when I'm here and Rawiri when with my uncle,' the boy corrected her with a tentative smile. 'Are you still angry with me, Mihi Van der Veer?'

'Angry?' Paul asked. 'What have you done now?'

'Nothing,' Melody broke in quickly. 'It's all past now, anyway, and no, David, I'm not angry with you.'

'Maata told me it was because you were worried,' he said, crossing to face her, searching her eyes for reassurance. 'You've been crying. Are you still worried? You shouldn't be. I'm quite safe.'

'No, I'm not still worried. I—I had a speck of dirt in my eye and it has made them water, that's all.'

He gave a relieved smile. 'But you were very brave . . . for a white lady.'

'I think you'd better explain,' Paul interjected grimly, and missing the tone, David turned to his father, eyes shining.

'It was after the battle. I didn't know you were hurt, or I'd never have left. Maata kept me with the other children.' His tone conveyed in no uncertain terms what he felt about being regarded as a child. 'Some of the warriors wanted to get back to the *pa* and tell the others of the great victory. I went with them . . . ' His head dropped then, and he stared at the floor. 'And I forgot to tell anyone.' His voice dropped to a little above a whisper, and Paul had to strain to hear him. 'Mihi Van der Veer and the others . . . they didn't know where I was. They—They thought the enemy might have taken me.' Paul's explosion of sound brought the child's head up, and he blenched at the fury in his father's eyes. 'I'm sorry! I know I was wrong. Mihi Van der Veer, she wouldn't let any of the men go out to search in case the raiders came back. She said Windhaven had to be protected at all costs, but she thought uncle could send some men to look for me.'

Paul's disbelieving gaze swung to Melody's face. 'Go on.'

Glad that he was no longer the focal point of that piercing look, David finished, 'Mihi Van der Veer and Henare came down-river in a canoe and Mihi Van der Veer was very angry with me . . . At least . . . I *think* she was angry, because she couldn't make up her mind whether she was hugging me or near shaking my head off!' He broke off with a quick glance at her, but she was studying her skirt, so he added with a rush, 'Then we came back in uncle's big canoe, and Mihi Van der Veer came straight up to see you, but I saw you first because she had to change her dress because it was all wet from the river, and you were asleep, and then Maata made me stay with her until you were really well, and she said Mihi Van der Veer would chase anyone who came in, and she would know, because she had been sleeping in that big chair since you got hurt, so—so I didn't come until now.'

Melody could not look at Paul, but softly he said, 'So you went to Operiki by canoe, even knowing that those devils incarnate might still be out there.' His voice was charged with emotion, and he coughed to clear the horror of his imagination that threatened to choke. 'And you accuse *us* of stubbornness and a determination to have our own way! Tell me, had you ever been in a canoe in your life?'

'Not even in a row-boat,' Melody confessed. 'I—I can't swim!'

'Oh, ye gods!' Paul groaned. 'What am I to do with you!'

She gauged his anger, sensed the incredulity there, and felt a deep warmth at the worry and frustration she knew to be at the core of it. Slowly she raised her sapphire eyes to his, smiling tremulously. 'It seemed the only thing to do at the time, even before I knew that David was your son. Now, it makes my decision even more right. However . . . I think I need to get my life back on a relatively even keel, if you'll pardon the phrase. I'll leave you to come to terms with each other, for I'm afraid it's quite beyond my ability!'

'Melody . . . '

They both acknowledged the change. 'Yes . . . Paul?'

'Thank you.' She nodded acceptance, turning at the door, stopping with one hand on the knob as he spoke her name again.

'You belong to New Zealand. Give it a chance if you can.'

She wondered whether it was the land, this barbarically beautiful land, that he meant—or himself. 'I don't know,' she said, answering both trains of thought. 'I don't know whether I'm ready, or even whether I have the strength for that.'

'I never doubted your strength.'

Closing the door behind her, she returned to her room, deep in thought. 'I *don't* belong to this land,' she argued against her heart. 'And I certainly don't belong to Paul Savage—other than as a slave. Oh, I wish I knew! Sometimes he treats me as a recalcitrant child, at others as an honoured guest. He assaults me . . . and then shows tenderness such as I've experienced only with Brett . . . ' A tiny frown, as her conscience reminded her that she had not thought of him for weeks. 'Poor Brett. I wonder how he is faring? He'd be well taken care of, I know. Has he changed?' Then, with a rueful smile, 'He'd hardly recognise the girl he knew. Shall we ever meet again, I wonder? O'Shaughnessy did promise. A year at the most. Can I last here for a year?' She regarded her image in the cheval mirror with a grimace of disgust. Not Melody van der Veer, English lady. Melody the slave. Melody the peasant homesteader. *They* might survive.

She went to the dozen or so dresses and skirts bought from the best couturiers in New York, and the three reluctantly purchased in Wellington. The difference was jarringly obvious. 'This is most certainly not New York,' she stated unnecessarily. 'And I'm not the pampered aristocrat who fled there. I must face facts, but, more, I must take some action to help me to look the part!'

An hour later, Beatrice found Melody surrounded by piles of material, attacking the remaining two dresses with vengeful scissors, cutting off the hems and slicing deep gores in the massive skirts. 'Dare I ask what you're doing?'

'I'm tired of acting the lady, so I may as well dispense with the fine features. You yourself said it would come to this: two dresses being made from one. I've thrown out those hoops, and have kept just one set of the skimpiest—those I bought in Wellington. As for the rest, I shall wear the dresses without hoops. He won't notice either way, and at least Maata will stop treating me as a house-guest. Why, she accepts your help more readily than mine, and you are the house-guest!'

'Maata and I do well enough together,' Beatrice agreed. 'But you don't have to make such gestures to be accepted for what you are. These are simple people who have a civilisation far older than ours, and a wisdom and an honesty deeper than we'll ever know, with all our political chicanery and social mendacity. I simply allow myself to be their friend, that's all. Friends share their lives; they teach, and are taught. If you'd allow the tiniest of cracks in that barrier you've built about yourself, it would achieve far more than the destruction of Monsieur Worth's designs.' Her grey eyes softened. 'On the other hand, you will be far more comfortable without the hoops, and look even more alluring than you do now.'

'I don't want to look alluring, and if I achieve anything by demolishing poor Monsieur Worth's best efforts, it will be the reminder that I don't fit them any more, socially or economically.'

With a sigh Beatrice changed the subject, upset by the chameleon-like changes in her niece's moods, but for the first time unable to reach her. At times it seemed as if the girl might adapt to the life at Windhaven—at times even as if she loved this strange land and its even stranger people—something Beatrice knew that she could never achieve herself, though she was prepared to make the best possible job of it until she and Melody were free. Then one ill-chosen word from Paul Savage would inflame that quick temper of hers, and all the hurt and resentment inside would break loose in an eruption of bitter diatribe that nothing seemed to soothe.

Melody's inability to adjust to her situation worsened over the next two weeks as Paul grew stronger, at first controlling the running of Windhaven from his bed, then moving slowly outside. His wound had healed well and he constantly exercised the muscles around it, fighting the pain and concentrating on recovery with a single-mindedness that completely excluded the rest of the household. Melody watched him as he rode out with the three of Te Whatitoa's warriors who had chosen to stay even after the mercenaries had left and the danger passed. She saw him deliberately choose the largest mount, the heaviest gun, giving his wound no quarter; when they returned from the hunt, it was he who carried the antelope or pig.

He had made no comment on Melody's appearance, though she often found his gaze on her as she wandered about the stockade, and her anger at his apparent indifference mounted. How dared he ignore her after his previous behaviour! To kiss her like that . . . not that she had wanted him to . . . and then to act as though she was a veritable stranger! In her efforts to find other interests, she formed what was at first a casual friendship with David, tutoring him and improving his English. But as the days wore on and his quick intelligence and avid interest grew, she found herself looking forward to their all too short periods together, and a deep affection was formed between them. Yet still it was not enough. She felt alienated and of little use in a household that constantly seethed with activity and laughter, and eventually went to confront Paul, catching him on his way out. As usual, the boy was with him and he smiled brilliantly at her approach, but this time without effect. 'Paul, I must talk with you. It won't take a second.'

A visible hesitation—impatient to be away—but then, 'Of course. David, you go ahead and get the horses tacked up. Now. Shall we go into the drawing-room?'

'No! I'm tired of the drawing-room, since I virtually live there. Paul, I must do something of use here.'

'I heard you were improving David's English.'

'We've spent some time together—when you aren't teaching him to shoot or snare game. He's good company, and a more than willing pupil, but those times are few and far between.'

'He has a very real affection for you. I'd not want his

lessons to stop. Maata says that you have embroidered some cushion-covers for your room, and if you need to expand that occupation I know that some material arrived for you the day before yesterday—and hasn't even been opened.'

Melody lowered her eyes, remembering only too vividly the scene that had instigated his sending for the material. 'I—I don't want to wear those colours yet. I'm not ready.'

His voice held an edge of irritation, though he spoke gently enough. 'I believe you *are* ready to come out of mourning. I have no objection to your gowns being practical—in fact the style you have adopted since the battle makes you appear even more feminine than before, while yet being eminently suitable for homestead life— but I am tired of this endless black, knowing it to be false. If you are bored, ask Maata to send a seamstress to help you to make up some new dresses from the material I ordered—something befitting your position here.'

She clutched that as a drowning man a straw. 'And what *is* my position here? I was bought as a slave— brought here to work off that debt as a bondswoman, but since I've been here, I've done nothing. No one gives me work, or apparently expects any of me. Maata, the other servants, the people outside, none of them knows how to treat me or what my position here is. How can they, when even I don't know?'

'You do realise,' he said, brows drawn down, eyes glittering, 'that I could use—or not use—a slave, since that rôle you insist on playing, in any way I see fit? And the others are not confused or in any doubt, only you.'

Melody's eyes widened as he crossed to stand over her, fingers curling over her shoulders, the dark eyes mesmeric. 'Tell me you understand,' he ordered. 'Say "Yes, Paul." '

Melody's voice came out a husky whisper, 'Yes . . . Paul', and she realised that she never would lose her fear of him, but then, without warning, his eyes changed. The glitter turned to a gleam, as, very slowly, he bent forward and kissed her—on the nose!

He released her then. 'You're dismissed . . . slave . . . On the other hand, if Mrs Van der Veer wishes to stay and enjoy what company I have to offer . . . or anything else I have to offer . . . '

Emotions in a turmoil, she retreated into anger. 'I want nothing of your company, nor your warped sense of humour! I came here to work, *Mister* Savage. Good, hard work. Remember?'

His lips tightened and he turned away, frustrated. 'Very well. You want to work, then work you shall. I'll respect the choice you made at St Clare. Some of the women are weeding a patch of land cleared last year out at the ridge to the south ready for the spring planting. It's a bare half-mile away. Tell Maata to send a girl out with you. You'll find tools on site.'

That was not quite what Melody had in mind, but already he was striding outside, his heels making an angry drumbeat on the wooden floor. Wishing she had never approached him, she went to seek out the housekeeper, first changing into what she thought would be appropriate for the job in hand.

Maata heard her out, then shook her head with a frown. 'It's not right, Mihi Van der Veer. It's not right at all. *Pakeha* women don't go workabout in the fields. Not never.'

Melody drew a deep breath. 'Maata, I—I'm not a white woman—at least, not according to American law.'

The velvet brown eyes stared endlessly. 'You *look* white!'

'I know . . . I know.' Feeling the tears pricking her eyes, Melody told Maata all that had transpired from her arrival at St Clare onward, finishing, 'So Mr Savage bought me as he would any slave, and I must work as one.'

'Mita Savage never bought no slaves in his life!' Maata told her emphatically, still unable to believe that this lovely young girl with the ivory skin and brilliant sapphire eyes was of mixed blood. 'We're all free here,' she stated.

'Mita Savage don't have no slaves never. This isn't Amereeki.'

Melody's lips curled into a smile in which there was more than a trace of bitterness. 'Well, as far as I'm concerned, it might as well be. You and the others are free to come and go as you please, but if you're in any doubts as to whether I am, you might ask him yourself. I'm bought and paid for just as any slave in the South, so let me get to those fields, and I'll show him how an English slave can work!'

But it was far worse than she had dreamed possible. With the sun blazing down, even the coarsely woven kerchief that Maata had insisted she tie turban-like over the midnight hair did not fully protect her. All her gowns were too constricting, even though she had left off the torturing stays, and she could not fail to envy the light cotton skirts and loose blouses of the Maori girls as they wielded their hoes with ease. Never having handled a hoe in her life, she found the long handle unbelievably cumbersome, the blade jarring at every stroke. She could not join in the laughter, the quick jokes in the alien tongue that convulsed the others, many, she suspected, directed at the strangely attired *pakeha* woman who had appeared in their midst. They had smiled and greeted her in a friendly fashion when she first arrived, accompanied by one of Maata's girls, but when the girl explained what was required they had at first stared in disbelief, but then burst into laughter. There was no doubt in their minds that all *pakeha* women were strange, but this one was surely the strangest of all!

As the sun climbed higher, Melody found herself counting the strokes and breathing in counterpoint to stay on her feet, too exhausted to think of poetry or popular songs. The roots of the weeds seemed to grow deeper and cling more tenaciously as the day wore on. She drank the lukewarm water from the water-barrel at the end of the field as though it were the finest champagne, and tipped the last of every gourdful over her face and neck, returning to her row without complaint. 'You got yourself into this situation, Miss High-and-Mighty,' she muttered, 'so you put up with it.' She swayed as the field appeared to tilt sideways, and one of the young girls who had been watching her moved forward, but with a forced smile and a shake of the head, she gestured her away. Her vision cleared and she bent to pick up the fallen hoe—but it receded before her and with a sigh she crumpled down across it.

The earth was soft and warm and comforting, and her pain and exhaustion drained into it like water in a desert. From a distance she heard the thunder of hooves, a harsh male voice and the young Maori girl answering, but nothing mattered so long as she could rest.

'Come on! Get up!' A rough voice ordered, and she vaguely identified the angry tones of Paul Savage.

'Tea-break,' she objected, slurring her words, her tongue cleaving to the roof of her mouth, but she opened leaden lids and struggled to rise all the same. He would *not* get the better of her! She was able to get to her feet, and he did not help her.

He watched her as she turned to face him, eyes brilliant with unshed tears of exhaustion, face reddened by the sun and blackened by the earth, yet still incredibly beautiful, and his throat tightened. 'You haven't finished your row,' he said, and saw that indomitable spirit blaze within her.

'Damn the row!' Her voice came as a harsh whisper from her parched throat. 'And damn *you*! I'm not a field hand, or a work horse. I'm a human being, and I'm tired. I'm almost too tired to hate you—but I'm making the effort! I'll finish your row, but at present I need a rest. Leave me. Just leave me alone!' Turning her back on him, she finally broke down and sobbed into her hands. She felt a movement, then an arm encircled her, another went beneath her knees, and she was swung up against that muscular chest. 'No!'

She stiffened, attempting to pull free, but with a curt, 'Be still, woman!' he tightened his grip, subduing her effortlessly as he carried her to the waiting horse. In spite of her protestations, she was swung into the saddle and

he sprang up behind her, moving her up so that she was
on his lap. Every muscle seemed to scream in protest as
he turned the big roan towards the stockade and kicked
it into a canter.

Melody tried to adjust to the heavy high-pommelled
saddle, but could barely keep her balance, and earned a
harsh reproof as she almost slipped sideways, causing the
arm about her waist to tighten like a band of iron. 'Stop
fighting! The horse isn't accustomed to your stubbornness,
even if I am!' Roughly he pulled her hard against him, as
with his free hand he guided the restive stallion.

Melody wanted to rant at him, to beat at him for his
unfeeling behaviour, but the bone-deep weariness in her
overcame all else and she allowed herself a moment of
surrender.

Paul felt the mutinous muscles relax, and a smile
touched his mouth as the once rigid frame curved, albeit
reluctantly, against him. Her turban had fallen off in the
initial struggle as he had swung her into his arms, and
now her ebony curls tumbled about her shoulders, soft
wisps blowing into his face, tantalising his nostrils with
the scent of the flowers she had crushed into the rinsing-
water after washing her hair that morning. For him, it
was all too soon that they reached the house, and he
lowered her to the ground before slipping down beside
her. 'Inside!' he ordered brusquely.

Too exhausted to fight any more, Melody preceded him
through the front door, throwing him a questioning glance
as he took her firmly by the arm and led her across the
hall. The tight lips gave no indication of his thoughts,
and only when Maata put a tentative head round the
kitchen door did he speak. 'Water, and something for her
hands,' he ordered, then continued dragging her across
the courtyard to her room, where he kicked open the
door and thrust her inside. 'Now . . . ' spinning her to
face him, iron-hard fingers biting into her arm. 'I'm sick
to death of this Greek tragedy you've written for yourself!
I have had all the mulishness I'm going to take, and from
now on you'll behave as an intelligent young woman of

breeding, and not a combination of a martyred Joan of
Arc and a warring Boadicea.'

Melody was stunned by the anger and frustration in his
voice, but at that moment Maata appeared with a jug of
cool water and a tiny bowl of sweet-smelling cream, both
of which she set down on the washstand.

'Ask Lady Davenport to come here, Maata.' Then,
turning back to the still speechless Melody, 'Now! Your
hands!' Quickly she put her hands behind her back, but
was propelled toward the washbasin, which Paul quickly
filled. Transferring his grip, he pulled both wrists apart
and forward, raising her hands, but instinctively Melody
clenched her fists. 'It's not so bad!' She knew that it was.

'Melody . . . Melody!' Softly, huskily. Their eyes met,
and suddenly the previous anger, his treatment of her in
the field, all melted away before the look in his eyes . . .
and her fingers opened. She watched his face as he saw
her blistered and bleeding palms. She saw the muscle that
leapt in his jaw, but he said nothing. Slowly he lowered
her hands into the water, and she gasped as the pain bit.
A shudder went through her, but she allowed him to
clean the dirt and blood from her burning skin. Gently
he patted the hands dry, barely touching them, then
applied the soothing cream, his fingers light as swans-
down.

A muted explosion at the door heralded the approach
of Beatrice Davenport, but only Paul noticed. Melody's
eyes were still on that pagan yet strangely sensitive face,
searching it for something that still eluded her. He looked
up, and again their gazes locked, causing the earth to
move beneath her feet. He raised one hand, and one finger
trailed a fiery path across her cheek. 'Sunburn, too,' he
said, a catch in his voice, but then he turned aside. 'Lady
Davenport, would you please get your niece bathed and
put to bed? I doubt that she can do it alone, and I want
her to be awake and presentable for dinner.'

Holding back the horror at Melody's appearance, having
seen that magnetism, that fire that had flashed between
them and unwilling to criticise something she did not

understand, Beatrice gave a nod, moving forward as Paul released the girl's hands, reluctantly it seemed, into hers, and left.

'When will you learn?' she scolded, unfastening the dusty black dress and throwing it aside. 'When will you stop fighting yourself and him?'

'Don't . . . please don't lecture, Aunt Bee!' choked Melody, finally allowing the tears of pain and exhaustion to overflow and course down her reddened cheeks. 'At the moment, I'm not fighting anyone! All I want is a quiet word and a gentle touch, not the brutal grip of that . . . savage! I can't talk to him, or reason with him.' Unbidden came a picture of a warm fireside, 'At least I could *talk* to Brett. At least he was a Savage only by name, and not by nature!'

'That's right,' Beatrice agreed, untangling the raven hair. 'He'd never have survived out here, let alone carved a home out of a wilderness and earned the respect, even the love, of its people.'

Melody shook her head, knowing that her aunt would never understand the emptiness within her and the loneliness that could be dissipated only by a man she knew she could no longer hate, but who regarded her as nothing more than an item of passion or profit.

CHAPTER EIGHTEEN

THE FOLLOWING MORNING, almost against her will, Melody went to open the parcels of material that had arrived from Wellington. She had no curiosity about them, remembering all too well the scene that had instigated their purchase, sure of the type of material that, in his contempt and anger, Paul would have ordered. Her hands were still sore from the work of the previous day, but it was her mind that felt the exhaustion more. Each time she tried to fight Paul Savage it resulted in humiliating defeat, with even her own mixed feelings working against her, and now she needed one day—one day at least—to recover.

Listlessly she knelt to cut the string of the first of the four large packages, throwing aside the wrapping—then froze, drawing in a sharp breath at the sight of the deep blue velvet, the colour of the sky moments before it is covered by the black night clouds. A gift for a princess, rather than a servant. With trembling fingers, she lifted it clear of its tissue paper, holding it for a moment against her cheek, closing her eyes for a moment, absorbing its feel against her sun-roughened skin. Beneath lay watered silk in jade-green and several yards of lace to edge a matching shawl, and in her mind's eye already she could see the design, a day dress with the bodice and skirt cut in one, the bodice with a deep vee neckline revealing a white chemisette beneath, the sleeves bell shaped and very full to reveal the chemisette sleeves, frilled at the wrist and edged with a length of the lace.

The next parcel held a practical merino for the cool days ahead, and a poplin. The third held glacé linen and *de laine*, muted shades that would mingle with the cool bush about them that she loved. A sense of wonder gently invaded her being. Paul Savage had been angry, scornful, contemptuous—surely—when he sent for this material, yet he had not given a thought to the pastel silks of a young girl, or the sombre hues of a matron. He had not ordered the gaudy scarlet and golds that Celine would have delighted in, or the rich emeralds and copper-browns that Beatrice wore so well. Why? How could he have known her so well? Why should he care? She opened the final parcel, lighter than the others, and at the sight of its contents a tiny cry broke from her as she lifted out yard upon yard of chiffon. It was of an oyster hue, yet with a barely perceptible pink of the magnolia blossom—almost flesh-coloured if held in a single layer against her skin; tantalisingly translucent even when in several folds. It would make a breath-taking ball-dress fit for London or Paris, but what place did it have on a homestead? It was surely the essence of dreams, no more. Did he mean to torment her? 'It must have cost a fortune!'

'Not quite,' came his voice from the doorway, and so deeply was he embedded in her thoughts that she did not even turn. He came into the room and picked his way across the piles of material to sink bonelessly on the bed, half-reclining, supporting himself on one elbow, watching her.

'It's too much!'

'No.' He gave a twisted smile. 'One can hardly call next year's stud bull a fortune.'

'But you *needed* that bull! Oh, why, Paul?'

His eyes roved over her kneeling form clouded in the subtly changing shades of the chiffon, and that half-smile touched the fine mouth. 'You might say that if I want something, I don't haggle over the price.'

Bitterly came the memory, 'Ten thousand should satisfy your client,' and Melody stared up at him, feeling the colour drain from her face. 'Can . . . a slave . . . be worth so much?'

A muscle leaped in his jaw. 'Yes,' he stated shortly, then gestured toward the chiffon. 'I'd like you to begin with that. We're going to Wellington at the end of the month. I've some business there with the Governor.'

'But I thought you . . . '

'I can't stand the man,' Paul answered with a grim smile. 'But there are more ways to crack a nut than with a cudgel. In fact, we'll be attending the Governor's ball, as will a number of prominent and influential people, one or two being friends of mine—at least enough to guarantee me an invitation. The Maori people must have representation, but of course not a single Maori, however friendly or high born, will attend. Invitations will be mislaid or sent astray with all due apologies, but the results will be the same.'

'So that leaves you.'

'And others like me who were sorry to see Sir George Grey leave the post, and have worked tirelessly ever since to have him brought back. He was fair and just; no one could ask more in these times. There are only a few of us, but we're a vocal minority, and some have enough social standing to engineer interviews, however reluctantly they're given. We shall arrive late and probably be invited to leave early, but between the two events much can be accomplished.'

'But why would you want *me* there? I know little of the people and even less of your politics. The few words of Maori I speak I've picked up from Maata and David, and there's so much more I'd need to know of their history and customs, their beliefs and their place in New Zealand's future, for they must have a place. They won't remain ignorant savages for ever, and men like Te Whatitoa should have a say in the governing of his people; he, who is so eminently suited for it. I would have so much to learn . . . ' She had risen, putting aside the billows of oyster chiffon, and was pacing the floor worriedly, only stopping when confronted by him standing in her path.

'You've three weeks to learn, if you've a desire to do so. You could be a quite irresistible emissary. I've no need to tell you how to make a man say far more than he intends or to ask loaded questions that are almost impossible to sidestep.' His hands came up to rest lightly on her shoulders, and he studied her as if memorising every line of that lovely face. 'I want you to do this one thing for me and for my people, for they *are* my people, through blood as well as friendship.'

Melody felt the passion in him, not for her this time, but for the land he loved and for a people he demanded should be treated as equals. How could she have thought of him as a conqueror! 'I—I'll do what I can,' she promised, suddenly shy beneath that warm regard. 'Will Aunt Bee come, too?'

His eyes crinkled at the corners. 'I've a feeling she will be more formidable than the two of us combined! Your aunt doesn't have a colour prejudice, I've discovered, only a people prejudice. Some people she likes, some she doesn't. I'm banking my future on her not liking that pompous racialist Gore-Browne and his fawning friends.'

'Why don't they vote him out? Did they not think Governor Grey a better man?'

'In my estimation, there was none better, but many of his ideas were unpopular. They'll bring him back—they have to—but this whole situation will erupt in their faces before they see it.' He gave another crooked smile. 'Don't start me talking politics: I reserve that for politicians! What I need from you is a dress they'll not forget, a dress that will fill their minds and dull their natural wariness, draw them as moths to a flame.'

Her mouth felt dry. 'You mean I'm to be the bait.' A small flame started within her as his fingers stiffened. 'No, don't answer that: I don't think I'd like what you have to say. Is there nothing you'd stop at to win another battle? The cause may be an honourable one, Paul Savage, but the methods certainly aren't. Are you *selling* me down-river, Mr Savage, or just renting me out?'

'Melody!' he warned, his voice low, vibrating with suppressed anger.

'Let me go!' She felt the knife twist within her, destroying her pleasure of a moment before. 'You didn't have to go all through that beautiful emissary nonsense! Aunt Bee says that one should always coat blarney with a light—a very light—coating of cream, but you have drowned it in the stuff!' She wrenched free, turning away. 'Next time, Mr Savage, remember that a servant is expected to obey. You could merely have given me a direct order. It's easy. Your slightest wish is my command. See?' She picked up a length of the chiffon, holding it towards him. 'This one, Massa Savage, suh? Anythin' you say, suh. I'd be real pleasured to show mahself off to yo' frens, suh.'

Paul drew a deep breath, wanting to shake her, kiss her . . . *shoot* her, even! 'You have three weeks,' he said, leaving that disturbingly beautiful and totally infuriating presence and finding his way to the nearest glass of brandy.

'I'll give him a dress!' Melody raged at Aunt Bee later that day, having fumed and fretted and twice thrown the material across the room. 'He wants bait, he'll get bait! Of all the unfeeling, uncaring, selfish . . . Aunt Bee . . . you're not listening to me!'

Beatrice looked up from a length of the midnight velvet, her eyes for once sombre. 'I'm listening, sweeting, but I'm not hearing. I'm listening to a lot of empty anger, but that's not what I'm hearing.' She gave a sigh and rose from her knees. 'Melody, love, it's about time you made some decisions about this place . . . *and* Paul Savage, but I'm not the one to help you, not this time. This business of the dress, however—that's an easy one. Paul may have used the wrong words, I don't know, but if he's taking you to the Residency, to accompany him into the lion's den, then he doesn't want . . . bait, as you call it; he wants help.'

'Help? Paul Savage?'

'Yes, help,' Beatrice snapped. 'You see only the man you want to see, the man you're trying in vain to hate. And why? Because he saved you from being sold in the only way possible and then refused to treat you as a slave? Because he brought you to this wilderness and dared to protect you from it? Introduced you to his friends and made them yours? He's more of a man than any you've ever known, and it's too much for you. You'd prefer the Bretts and the Hughs of the world, but let *this* man show one degree of weakness, one instant where he needs you by his side and doesn't know how to ask, and you reject him. Perhaps, when you use the words unfeeling and uncaring, you are looking the wrong way . . . You should try the mirror there!'

Melody stared at her aunt, aghast. She had never heard one word of condemnation, of real anger, directed at her from this woman in all the time she had known her, and could only shake her head in blind rejection. 'He's using me!'

'He needs you!' Beatrice gathered up the velvet, holding it in a shimmering cascade over one arm. 'These aren't the materials he'd buy for a field hand, or some high-tone bed-wench, and he's surely not going to take such a creature to the Governor's ball.'

Melody dropped on the bed, burying her head in her hands. 'Aunt Bee, I'm so confused!'

Instantly she felt familiar arms hugging her close. 'Of course you are, pet, but this is surely something we can work out together. We've already been through so much, fighting everything from bullies to bullets, so we're not going to let this beat us. Now, however, we have a ball-gown to make . . . for someone that John Brown would be proud to escort to the Palace. Do you agree?'

Melody straightened, drawing a shaky breath. 'Aunt Bee, I'm a fool . . . but a fool that loves you dearly! All right. Let's take a look at this dress.'

After that, the days flew. Melody spent hours on end with the diminutive seamstress that Maata had sent, and the length of formless material began to evolve into a creation of breathtaking beauty, classic in its simplicity, the material alone providing ornamentation, artfully tucked and cross-cut to billow in ever-changing hues. Paul had gone into Wanganui on business, and there were ten days in which Melody was spared the tension of his presence.

'But I'm afraid all isn't a bed of roses,' Beatrice informed her half-way through the tenth day, holding out a letter. 'This came from Patrick yesterday, and it's taken me until now to decide to give it to you.'

Her expression was so grave that Melody's heart gave a leap of fear. 'Is it Brett? Has something happened to him? Tell me quickly!'

'No, not Brett,' Beatrice hastened to reassure her. 'He is well, though obviously missing you dreadfully. Here, you'd best read it for yourself.'

Melody took the sheets, scanning them fearfully. 'So they're still in Natchez . . . Patrick has a job on the riverboats and doing well, he says.

> Brett is developing incredible senses of scent and sound since the boys have taken him over, and they've even taught him to load a gun and fire at any target that makes a noise . . . He even hits one or two on occasion. He is still moody, though, and says very little—unless Melody's name is mentioned, and then he'll talk for an hour and more . . .

'So he still cares! I did wonder . . . Again, she felt guilty that the warm affection she felt each time she thought of him was nothing more. Suddenly she stopped reading, then read and re-read the next few lines.

'You've got there, I see,' said Beatrice quietly, and met the girl's wide eyes.

With an effort, Melody read:

> The two men I saw in town when we were at St Clare were not entirely the fools I took them for, and somehow they traced you here to Natchez. I imagine 'Gator's boys couldn't help but boast of entertaining a real English lady and her niece, and the Pinkertons came to the house when I was up-river. Of course Brett knew nothing of their purpose, and had no cause to disbelieve when they said that there was some money you had inherited from a deceased relative in England. Knowing the fix you were in, the boy gladly gave them Paul's address

and began to worry only when they asked whether Melody was still travelling with you, but of course by that time they had all they needed. They said their client would be contacting you, so watch your back, my dear, and take care of the little one. They can't bring you back, so you're safe as long as you stay where you are. I'll get a couple of thousand to you, in case you need to move before I can get the rest over. I've made arrangements with a bank in Wellington, since Paul had mentioned that as your nearest large town.

Melody gave a low moan. 'I knew! I just knew there was something hanging over us. I've felt it all along—something dark and awful. There must be something we can do . . . Patrick is right, of course: they can't touch us here.' She shook her head, not wanting to believe. 'I never knew the Hog had such powerful friends . . . such a terrible influence. I wonder why they're hunting us like animals? Do they think we stole something from him that they were owed? To go to such lengths . . . '

Beatrice attempted a reassuring smile. 'Well, they've spent time and money in vain, whoever they are.' But the smile did not quite reach her worried eyes, and Melody felt again the icy chill of fear touch her spine.

If Luther Hogge had owed people money—a great deal of money—and they thought she had it . . . She bit her lip, reflecting, but then gave a determined shake of her head. 'No, I refuse to think about it. We've been warned, and although these people—whoever they are—may well spend money trying to find us from New York, though heaven only knows how they got from there to St Clare, I can't envisage them wasting money to employ detectives, or whatever they are, over here. They would know that they couldn't do anything . . . ' Then, with a shudder, 'Even if they were vindictive enough to hire some thug . . . well, we've dealt with worse. That man at the auction must also have been something to do with all this. Could he have been one of Luther's friends? He

certainly looked evil enough and he knew my name. No,
we shall take as much care as possible, but we are well
protected here and shall be equally well escorted in
Wellington. I've a dress to finish, and David will be
coming in an hour. He's teaching me Maori in exchange
for English. It's a lovely soft language, Aunt Bee, and far
easier than I imagined. For instance, they have only fifteen
letters in their alphabet . . . ' She went on, resolutely
changing the subject.

When finally the dress was finished, even Beatrice was
impressed. 'And we still have a few days to go.'

During that time, too, Melody deepened the loving ties
that bound her to the boy. He had taken to waiting for
her each morning after breakfast and asking her approval
of something he had made or some small goal he had
achieved. He would disappear moments later, almost as if
embarrassed by their friendship, but return again in the
afternoon with some item of idle gossip, or some new
vocabulary for her. One day she had suggested a game of
spinning tops and they had taken tops and whips into the
courtyard, racing round the well and collapsing with
laughter as Melody's top spun out of control and went
careering against the house wall. They played games of
pretend, where she was a Maori princess and he an
English lord, and she had to speak only in Maori and he
in perfect English. Coming to love him, she found learning
his language and the history and legends of his mother's
people remarkably easy. Their life had fallen into a
pleasurable pattern without the unsettling presence of
Paul, yet still there was a waiting, an emptiness that only
he could fill. He was due to return on the Saturday, and
it was Wednesday when Melody and David were once
again deep into a game of pretend, a game she feared
might be their last, when once more she would have to
watch her every move and put her love for David aside.

Paul rode into the compound, glad as always to be
home, passing a word with Beatrice, who was teaching
one of the Maori girls embroidery, moving among his
men and bringing a new surge of life to the place. He

went into the house, greeting Maata, commenting appreciatively on the aroma of roasting wild pork. The chops would be served with an accompaniment of baked potatoes and the tender *puha*, or wild sow thistle, that grew as a weed about the place, but was a favourite dish of the Maori. Savoury corn, dripping with butter, and baked *kotero*—potato cakes—would also be on the table, as well as crowns of the *kouka*, or cabbage tree, which did taste a little like cabbage and were relished by Maori and *pakeha* alike.

'Are you trying to fatten me for next Christmas?' Paul asked.

Maata shook her head, laughing. 'If we eat people for next feast, I would feed the whole of Windhaven, so don't *you* worry, Mita Savage.'

He made a comment in Maori that no *pakeha* should know and the woman doubled up with a bellow of laughter. 'Mita Savage, you are one awful man for a Maori, but you impossible for a *pakeha*!'

'Is David here?'

'Yes, sir, Mita Savage. He and Mihi Melody in the yard by the well.'

Paul gave a nod and made his way through the house, but pulled up short at a burst of laughter from the courtyard. A slight frown of puzzlement clouded his brow as he carefully opened the door, then that bare smile curved his lips at the sight before him.

David, that dignified, stubborn little warrior, was leaping round and round the well, giggling and capering and whooping with an abandon that Paul never knew existed in him. At the centre of his attentions was a captive Melody, laughing as infectiously and helplessly as the boy, while trying in vain to free her hands which had been tied behind her to one of the well posts. 'All right!' she laughed breathlessly. 'I surrender, O Great Chief!' The boy leaped in once more, fingers curling into her ribs, bringing another soft shriek. 'No more! I give in!' Her head swooped, and she snatched a kiss from his ear as he ducked away, then turned and . . .

'Papa! You're early. We weren't expecting you for ages!' He ran to hug him.

'Apparently not,' Paul commented, his eyes taking in the girl's flushed features and brilliant eyes in which the laughter still shone. Her chignon had slipped, and several midnight strands had escaped down her back and over one shoulder, but she had gone tense at his appearance, her tongue flicking over her lips.

'Untie me, David. Game's over,' she ordered quietly, but Paul put a restraining hand on his son's shoulder.

'You need a wash! I'll see to Mrs Van der Veer.'

'Auntie Melody,' David corrected him. 'She said I could call her Auntie Melody. I was the wicked chief Rawiri and Auntie Melody was my prisoner. We've had the greatest fun!'

Paul gave the boy's ear a light cuff. 'Go, brat!' but he was smiling, and with a grin the boy ran for the door, vanishing into the house where he could be heard calling to Maata. Paul turned to the lovely captive who, he noticed, had been fighting her bonds while she thought his attention was on the boy. 'If you struggle,' he advised softly, 'the knots will tighten and I'll need to cut you free. Hold still, and I'm sure even David's complex knot system will give way to persuasion.'

'You could send Maata with a kitchen knife. It would be faster,' Melody said, though with no expectancy at all that he would comply.

'I could indeed. Be still, now.' He came close, sitting on the wall of the well, his muscular thigh pressed against her as he worked at her bonds.

Fighting the waves of heat that rose from the pit of her stomach and caused her heart to pound, Melody sought a safe subject. 'I hope you don't mind David calling me "Aunt Melody" . . . I know I'm not a real aunt, but we've become such good friends that "Mrs Van der Veer" seemed wrong.'

'I don't mind at all.' He was close, too close. She could see every fleck in the darkly lashed eyes, notice the way his eyebrows winged upwards and how his skin had darkened in the summer sun. Her gaze slipped to his mouth . . . and breathlessly she murmured, 'After all . . . he called Maata and the other servants by their Christian names . . . ' Her words trailed off, as, aware that in her efforts to constrain the heat within her and subsequent panic, she knew she had made an error.

The fingers at her wrist froze momentarily, but then he affirmed coolly, 'I said I had no objection. There . . . You're free . . . from this game, at least!'

She was forced to look at him. 'Thank you. I'll make sure I don't trouble you again.'

Again that smile. 'You'd have to work hard to achieve that.' There was a glint of humour in the eyes that looked deep into hers and only added to her confusion as she felt the colour flood her cheeks.

'I . . . must change for dinner.' Her voice emerged more huskily than she intended, and she found the hands he had released trembling. He stood in her path a moment longer, then wordlessly moved aside, and Melody found it difficult to walk, not run, toward the refuge of her room, still feeling the searing contact of his thigh against hers, trying with all her being not to think of it. She concentrated on her love for David, that laughing, serious, brave, shy little warrior. But then the words 'Sweet Savage Love' came unbidden to mind—and she knew that she would have to avoid them both for the rest of that day, since one so reminded her of the other, and in loving David . . . 'No!' she murmured softly. 'Impossible! I refuse!'

Determinedly she allowed Beatrice to monopolise the conversation over dinner and retired early to bed, but the following day she again found herself in his path. It was typical of the man that if a tree was to be felled or a stump removed he would immediately strip off his shirt, take up the long-handled axe or iron bar and join the work party until the job was done. Melody came across one such event the day after his return, and stood frozen for a moment, drawn as if by a magnet to that olive-skinned frame, the muscles rippling as he pulled at the iron bar that would lever out ancient roots. The stump came up with a rush, and the Maoris cheered involuntarily, but at that moment he turned and saw her, the joke dying on his lips, turning to a frown as he crossed swiftly to her side. Half-shyly, she averted her gaze from the expanse of deeply bronzed chest.

'Should I spare your blushes?' he asked. 'A married woman who blushes at the sight of a man's torso? Did your husband never remove his clothing while the lights were lit? What a polite little pair you must have been!'

'Don't sneer at things you don't understand,' Melody retorted, her embarrassment vanishing. 'It doesn't signify that because a woman has been married she is accustomed to seeing *other* men in a state of undress!'

'Forgive me! I shall in the future always try to be correctly attired when you pass my way.'

'A gentleman would,' she shot back, then realised the stupidity of her remark, but before she could retract it, his eyes had darkened.

'A gentleman? Like your husband . . . or my precious cousin, Brett?'

'Hugh was a gentleman, yes, and so is Brett. I've heard that all Southerners are, by reputation at least.'

'Southerners?' He flung himself away from her. 'Gentlemen? Oh, yes! Gentlemen all! Do you want to hear about your Southern gentlemen—excluding, I presume, those gentlemen that were calling for a certain slave on the vendue table to be stripped? A Southern gentlemen joins a war for glory and the fight for freedom, but there's nothing glorious and damned little freedom in war . . . unless one counts the glorious bombardment of Vera Cruz for days on end, and the glorious charge up that sandy beach with bayonets fixed in case one small pocket of resistance might remain—and finding all Mexico spread before you—with not an enemy in sight! Does one count the glorious battles against the desert, the fleas, the rotting food and the dysentery . . . and women and children?' His eyes were tortured as with sudden anger he presented her with his back and the cruel lattice of scars there.

'Especially the battles hard fought against women and children!' He turned again, capturing her eyes, holding them, as softly he said, 'It was a tiny, unimportant village, and she was a tiny, unimportant Mexican girl. The enemy. Yet I was too new to the game of war to realise that the enemy can expect no quarter. The Southern gentleman already knows this, of course—especially when the enemy is coloured! She was no more than fourteen, her brother a little younger. They tried to hide in the barn when the glorious army came through, but those Southern gentlemen found them. I was foolish enough to attempt to prevent rape, and torture, and murder, and for that I had to be punished. I was lashed to a beam, and all six of them took it in turns to use a length of rope on me . . . carefully frayed and knotted at the end . . . And *then* they raped both boy and girl, and finished them off with bayonets; tiny cuts so that they bled to death, whimpering. One mustn't waste bullets, of course!' His glittering eyes returned to the present and focused on her face—saw the tears streaming unchecked down her cheeks, the sapphire eyes wounded, as hurt and sick as he had been. 'Melody . . . I'm sorry . . . I didn't mean you to know.'

Without thought, she came into his arms and he held her, stroking her hair, all speech pointless, but it was she who drew away. 'Paul, I'm glad you told me.' She forced a shaky smile. 'Aunt Bee would say that the hurt is decreased each time you share it.'

'Not this one.' And again she thought of how he had forgotten how to laugh. With such nightmare memories to haunt him, it was no wonder! But he had put the incident behind him, returning it to the deepest recesses of his mind, saying, 'But why were *you* out as far as that? The Maoris who attacked us are far more than an unpleasant episode, the danger far from over. You must be accompanied at all times if you leave the safety of the stockade.'

'I—I'm afraid I didn't notice how far I'd come. I've formed a habit of picking fresh flowers and ferns for the house. It keeps me occupied to arrange them, and they make the rooms much more . . . ' She was about to say 'like home', but caught herself in time, amending, 'comfortable'.

'I've noticed, and I appreciate it,' he said carefully—as aware as she that there were some emotions that dared not be acknowledged—not yet. 'However, I think you should return now. It's nearly dusk, and the night falls very quickly. I've finished here. I'll see you safely back.'

'You don't need to.'

He stopped, giving her a direct look. There was an instant when she thought he was about to snap at her again, but then apparently he changed his mind. 'I'll escort you back, anyway.' He went to retrieve his shirt, pulling it on, and when he rejoined her she caught the tangy scent of him, mingling with the wood-smoke where the crew had burned other logs.

He helped her up over a ridge that she had jumped down on her way out, taking her hand and pulling her up beside him—and forgetting to let her hand go—and it stayed quite naturally enfolded in his until they reached the house.

'We've finished the dress for the ball,' she said at the door. 'Do you wish to give it your approval?'

'I'm sure it will be all I expect of you. I'll wait until I see it on. I can curb my curiosity for a few more days.'

'Thank you for seeing me . . . back.' There it was again. That word 'home' pushing insidiously into sentences, trying to trap her.

'You're more than welcome,' he answered formally, then took the hand he was holding, and before she could snatch it free, brought it to his lips.

. . . It was dark, but Melody still tossed and turned on the wide, canopied bed. Icy waves of fear swept over her as she assessed her emotions. Surely she could not be falling in love with this arrogant tyrant, this man who was her master in more than just name? When he was near, her whole being became aware of him, whatever she was doing, however involved. She breathed as he breathed, watched for his frown, her heart quickening at his slightest irritation, and beating with a slow drum-roll at his most casual glance. It was almost as if she had become a part of him. She felt that she was losing her identity—and fought that with every fibre of her being. If she once allowed herself to love him, she would wish only to serve and please him, and then he would have total power over her. No longer would they be master and servant in name only, but she would become a willing subject with no desire but his. She would indeed be a possession. 'No!' she rejected the thought aloud. 'I am Melody van der Veer. I am myself!' She thought of Beatrice, still attractive to all men, still loved and wanted and courted—and respected for her spirit and envied for her freedom and independence of mind. *She* would never be crippled by love, handicapped by her emotions! 'And neither shall I,' Melody vowed. 'I shall go to this ball of the Governor's and enjoy myself, not suffer the oglings of some ancient politicians. I shall dance, even flirt a little if it pleases me. If someone asks my views, they'll get my own opinion, not some patriotic speech that I'm sure Paul Savage has prepared for me.' Yet she could not forget the fire in those dark eyes as he talked of his people, and knew that the same fire was in her, that his views were an echo of her own, his love of his land compelling her to respond.

CHAPTER NINETEEN

TIRED FROM THE long journey, Melody and Beatrice were
thankful to arrive at the Reids', where they were greeted
as old friends, with Amy asking a hundred questions
without waiting for answers, and even the reticent George
giving Melody an unexpected hug. There was an additional
member of the family this time, a ceaselessly wriggling
scrap of canine mischief appropriately christened Aitua
Iti—'Little Trouble'—bought for Ani, but adopted by the
whole family. The moment Melody sank on the couch, it
launched itself at her and tried in vain to scramble on her
lap.

'Aitua!' Amy scolded, but already Melody had gathered
up the ecstatic puppy and held it to her, vainly attempting
to prevent the pink tongue from re-washing her.

'He's perfect!' she laughed, then, addressing the furry
bundle, 'You, sir, are absolutely adorable!' causing the
creature's whole body to convulse in frantic wriggles.
Laughing with the others at the pup's gyrations, she
looked up at Paul, eyes alight, cheeks flushed . . . and
looked quickly away at the glow on his face.

'I haven't heard you laugh like that since David held
you captive at the well. You should do it more often.'

Handing her burden over to his giggling mistress, she
murmured, 'I have had little reason to.' She quickly
engaged Amy in conversation, not wanting the moment
to be spoiled.

Later that evening, with the Reids insisting on them all
staying to dinner, Melody went to walk in the tiny garden.
The chatter and bursts of laughter from the house warmed
her, so that she did not notice the cool breeze, only the
scent of night flowers and the rustle of leaves. The peace

of her surroundings seeped into her, causing a feeling of love for this land and its people such as she had never known for any other; for both Maori, like Maata, and *pakeha*, like Amy Reid, but even more for the unfortunate, often victimised, half-castes like David, whose only crime was that his parents had succeeded all too well in bridging the chasm between white and coloured. She had seen the wild beauty of the wilderness and the lush meadows, she had experienced the stormy seas and the tranquil lakes, the power of the Wanganui River, and the rippling laughter of its tributaries. 'I never want to leave this land!' she suddenly recognised. 'I never want to go home, for I *am* home now!' The tears started in her eyes as she realised the impossibility of her dream, and her mood changed.

Needing the warm comfort of her friends, she turned, finding that she had wandered to the far end of the garden where low-branched trees hid her from the house. Hurrying blindly along the narrow path, barely discernible in the fading light, she gave a stifled exclamation as a branch caught at her hair and another at her sleeve of her dress. 'Drat!' she muttered, pulling up sharply, the pain bringing her back to reality. Carefully she explored the sharp branch that had caught at her high-piled coiffure, and grimaced. 'Now I'll have to re-pin the whole thing!' With a wry smile at the expense paid for her dreaming, she carefully freed her dress, but in her twisting succeeded only in entangling her hair even more. Vainly she tried to free it, then cursed again beneath her breath as she heard Paul Savage calling her name—but acknowledging the uselessness of trying to hide—'Here I am!'

He stopped before her, head slightly tilted to one side, trying not to smile at her half-angry, half-embarrassed expression. 'You seem to make a habit of wandering off the well-beaten track,' he observed, and she flushed at the memory, glad that her colour was hidden by the shadows.

'Will you please release me?' she had to ask. 'I seem to tangle it more with each effort.'

He slipped into his pocket the folded sheet of paper he

had been carrying, and moved forward. 'I cannot manage to preserve that hairstyle! Lord knows why you women bother to contrive such elaborate concoctions when there's nothing more alluring than free-falling tresses that a man can lose his fingers in!'

'We dress for other women far more than for men,' she smiled.

'Then I suggest a fast release, and a retreat into Amy's bedroom to re-design it!' He began taking out the pins.

'Oh, but . . . '

'Would you rather spend the rest of the evening here until you consider it time to take down your hair for bed? Bear in mind, though, that we're staying at a hotel this time, and surely far better to re-do your hair in some simple style in Amy's room than to walk through the hotel lobby looking as you do.' Without further ado, he began extracting pins and unwinding curls from sharp twigs, standing behind her at first and then, as that sable cascade fell about her shoulders, moving to face her, brushing out broken twigs and leaves with his fingers. For longer than strictly necessary, his lean fingers moved through the silkiness of her hair, his eyes roaming over it, his features unsmiling.

Melody felt the leashed emotion in him, and at first was afraid to speak, but then, as those mesmeric fingers caressed the nape of her neck, creating fiery tongues of sensation up and down her spine, she ventured. 'I'm free now.'

'Yes.' And his eyes, almost black in the shadows, moved down to that half-wondering, half-fearful gaze. 'Yes,' he repeated, his voice husky. 'But I came to release far more than a lock of hair.' His eyes never leaving her face, he took the sheet of paper from his pocket and handed it to her. 'This document sets you free, Melody Vjan der Veer. You're no longer the servant of any man.'

For a long moment she did not understand, holding it in frozen fingers.

His features tightened, but his voice was under remark-able control as he continued, 'It's now your choice whether you go or stay. I think you could be of great help to me at the ball, though you have almost a week to think on it. The task that needs doing could never have been carried out by a servant under orders, only by a freed woman who felt the same needs as I for the future of these people.'

'Is—is that why you freed me?' She grasped the minutiae while her mind rejected the whole, and saw that twitch of a smile.

'In part. The rest need not concern you. You are free. Isn't that all you've wanted from the start?'

'Yes . . . Yes, of course . . . ' Still her voice lacked conviction, and he asked, 'It *was* the only thing keeping you here?' The question probed far more deeply than she was prepared to acknowledge.

'It's too sudden! I—I can't think straight.' She glanced at the paper clutched in her hand. 'Is it real?'

There was a deep sigh. 'It's quite legal, Melody. You are completely free of me.' She searched his face, but then abruptly he turned aside.

'Do you wish me to escort you back to the house, or would you rather be alone for a while?'

'Do they . . . Does Aunt Bee know?'

'Not yet. I'll let you tell her in your own time, in your own way.' He extended his arm, and after a moment's hesitation, Melody slipped her hand under it.

'The ball . . . '

'It is still your choice. I have a few days with business acquaintances in town, so you'll be alone to consider.'

She allowed him to lead her almost to the house before she could take in the full implications of what he had said, and she stopped dead, bringing him to a halt. 'I'm Melody van der Veer again!'

'You always were.'

'No!' The eyes that sought his were brilliant with emotion. 'No . . . I'm really me again. I can go where I will; within reason, do as I please.'

'Yes.'

'Then . . . ' She drew a deep breath, recapturing that

previous exhilaration, that thought of the land and the people she loved. 'Then I'll go to your ball . . . But not for your sake, Paul, and under no restrictions but my own. I'm doing it for Maata and David and all those like them who must have a voice in the running of their country. Your own country fought against British domination before, and as an Englishwoman I was against you in that war, but now I know what it means to be totally subject to another's will, and, yes, I can argue against it with more conviction than you could ever imagine.' Bathed in the light from the window, she took his breath away with her loveliness, eyes glistening with suppressed tears, lips parted with her quickened breathing. 'Thank you, Paul. I won't ask the reasons you had for freeing me, but you've given me my life again.'

'Was it so bad before?'

'Yes . . . No . . . Not really, but to me, freedom was the most important thing in my life. I could have had a golden cage in England, and I . . . ' She stopped, appalled, realising that she had almost confessed. 'I killed to escape that one.' Shaking her head, she left him wondering, and hurried inside, joining the family's chatter, watching him come in a few minutes later, seeing him with new eyes. Why had he done it? she wondered. What was his motive? What did he hope to gain? More than just her services at the ball; that was too short term, and he stood to lose her completely the day after.

With Amy's chatter and Aunt Bee's outrageous anecdotes ricocheting off her, she found it impossible to concentrate, so allowed her emotions to rest. However, each time she glanced at him, the gold-flecked eyes were burning into her, and she even felt their intensity when she attempted to converse with the others. An early night was in order, so, acquiring a sudden headache, she asked to be escorted to the hotel. 'No, please stay here, Paul,' she said, as he rose. 'If you could just call a carriage . . . I don't want you to cut your evening short.'

'It is no trouble.'

'Please.'

He nodded, and within minutes, a carriage pulled up outside. 'I'll come with you,' insisted Beatrice. 'I need my beauty sleep after that journey.' Her eyes searched Melody's for gratitude, and was disappointed when she simply agreed. 'Well?' she asked, the moment they were in the carriage and clip-clopping down the steep hill toward the harbour front hotel.

Melody shook her head, unable to share her thoughts—not even with Aunt Bee, confidante, advisor, the only relative she had, the truest friend. 'Please . . . I'll talk about it all in the morning, but now I really need to get to bed.'

'Was it something Savage said? Did you two have another of your squabbles in the garden this evening?'

'No . . . Nothing like that, truly. We'll talk tomorrow, if that will be all right?'

Beatrice patted her cheek. 'Of course, sweeting.' There was a strange light in her niece's eyes, a high-sprung tension about her that was somehow tearing her apart, but she also knew that she should certainly not force a confession. All she could offer was, 'You know I'll be here.'

Melody smiled, and gave her a quick hug. 'I know, and I love you for it. Tomorrow.'

A morning of activity and shopping gave Melody no chance to tell her of her new freedom, but it seemed to the girl that a great weight had been lifted from her shoulders. Another, however, had taken its place, and when over a late luncheon she finally confided her news, Beatrice immediately realised the same dilemma. After hugging her niece, sharing tears of joy, she returned to her practical self. 'So now that the world is our oyster, so to speak, we must think of our future, and plan ahead. In all truth I never saw myself spending the rest of my life in some homestead, however comfortable, surrounded by jungle and marauding savages. However, this is a growing town, and if more settlers come from England, it may be almost civilised one day.'

'Do you not think of returning to England?'

'You can't, so therefore I won't. No, I don't miss London so very much. It's people who count, not places— so long as there's the occasional opera, ball, soirée, horse race . . . '

'Oh, Aunt Bee, you're impossible! We'll go wherever you wish. I can become a piano-teacher or a governess, and you can do . . . whatever you did before to become such a celebrated and loved person by half the London aristocracy! We can go to Paris, or even New York. I'm told New York is quite the place to be . . . '

'I see a "but" in your eyes, and I know you far too well.' She gave her a searching look, then a gentle smile. 'You love Windhaven, don't you? It's more than just New Zealand, more than just its people . . . ' She sighed at the girl's too slowly averted profile. 'It's more even than Windhaven,' she finished softly. 'Well . . . We'll think about that when the time comes. We have to plan our campaign, and the Governor is no fool: a pompous bigot who seems all too eager to accept bad advice, but no fool. We've a day or two for preparation, but also to see what Wellington has to offer for a future.'

Nothing in their elaborate plans, however, could have prepared Melody for her first view of the ball that night, the line of carriages spilling their brilliantly-hued cargo at the steps of the porticoed white mansion. Had she ever thought of Wellington as a new colony, populated by poor emigrant workers in drab costume, she was to revise her ideas completely within the space of the next few minutes, as the green, scarlet and gold dress uniforms of the three British regiments on duty in town seemed to vie for attention with the multi-hued silks and satins of their companions, and even the stark black and white evening suits of the other gentlemen stood out in rich contrast.

Paul was greeted with wary politeness by some and warm enthusiasm by others, but Melody was immediately the centre of attention. Not one of the fulsome compliments showered upon her by the men, or the barbed glances shot by the women, however, counted for anything in comparison with the one burning look given by Paul

Savage on first sight of her in that dress.

She had slipped into the cloud of oyster chiffon an hour
before his arrival, dressed her midnight hair in the simplest
of styles . . . 'there's nothing more alluring than free-
falling tresses,' she remembered . . . allowing it to fall
in a gleaming cloud about her shoulders, tiny, curling
tendrils framing her face, and, as a last thought, rejected
all jewellery. Her shoulders, rose creamy-gold above the
froth of chiffon that barely skimmed them and the full
curve of her breasts was a tantalising torment; almost, yet
not quite visible through the translucent folds. Drawing
the eye downward was a single spray of star clematis
pinned at the lowest point of that deceptively modest
neckline, to match those scattered in her hair.

She came gliding down the hotel stairs to where he
waited in the lobby, her head high with her new-found
freedom, sapphire eyes sparkling, not needing the added
shine of olive oil behind the long lashes. The dress curved
outward like the most delicate of magnolia blossoms, its
purity and simplicity like the note of a bugle—its subtle
hint of wantonness demanding that the blossom be
plucked! And this personified the woman he had freed,
allowed to escape him for ever! This, the spirit he had
attempted to tame—and in turn been tamed. This, the
beauty he had tried to possess—and had found himself
possessed. It cut into his heart like a knife, and before his
self-control veiled his eyes, they had met hers.

Melody froze before the shock of that white-hot gaze,
feeling the heat of it burning into her very soul, and
something atavistic within her rose to meet it, her
innocently parted lips over which the nervous tongue
flicked belying the look in her eyes as every fibre of the
Eve within every woman begged him to act out the hunger
she saw in his.

He took a pace forward . . . but then halted with a
deep, shuddering breath. She was *not* his! Not his to
sweep into arms of steel and carry back up that staircase.
Not his to tear that misty mirage from and discover the
substance beneath, to mould, caress, explore, to cause to

cry out in sweet torment. Clenching his hands to stop their trembling, he gave a short bow. 'It is, indeed, an unforgettable dress, Melody. Every man attending this evening will fall instantly at your feet.'

Melody lowered her eyes, matching his light tone while putting down that shocking, forbidden hunger that had risen within her. 'How uncomfortable for them! I do hope enough recover to dance a turn or two!' Aunt Bee, you'd be proud of that! she told herself, as that very person appeared behind her at the top of the stairs, magnificent in bronze satin.

'Did someone mention dancing?'

Paul turned with a warm smile, bending over her extended hand as she reached the bottom steps. 'I wonder that I dare take you, Lady Davenport, for I shall undoubtedly spend my entire evening fighting off would-be seducers.'

The grey eyes twinkled, and dimples appeared at her mouth. 'I beg you, don't try too hard, Mr Savage; I'm expecting an eventful evening!'

The evening was indeed eventful, though not in Melody's wildest dreams could she have imagined the outcome, and only afterwards found it possible to blame the wine and the rich food. They had begun the evening well, dancing every dance and using the lightly flirtatious conversation to promote their cause.

'Each in his own way,' Beatrice had advised. 'Men don't appreciate women who think, my dear, and abhor those with strong views, so with apparently guileless questioning and wide-eyed ingenuous glances we must force them all to reconsider their whole philosophy.'

Melody, however, found the whole charade rather tiring; having her feet trampled on and pretending to be a hen-witted ninny. She felt obliged to dance only with those who might influence the Powers That Be, and envied the girls in the arms of young officers, swept effortlessly around the room. Paul had disappeared into an anteroom shortly after their arrival, and Melody caught enough comment from the men who came and went through the heavily panelled door to realise that the opposing factions were becoming as heated as she. Begging a lime cordial from her partner, she gladly allowed him to lead her to the edge of the dance floor, where she joined a small group of men and women from the upper echelons of the community, to some of whom she had been introduced earlier. It was an unfortunate choice, as a shift in the group confronted her with an overbearing matron whom she had privately christened the Pompous Porpoise.

'Why, Mrs Van der Veer, how good of you to join us. We were just admiring that pretty little dress . . . So . . . simple as to be outstanding.'

Melody smiled through gritted teeth. 'Yes, I do tend to follow the classics, Mrs Cavendish, and I hear that Monsieur Worth is quite revolutionising the Paris collections with similar lines, but I've no doubt they will take simply ages to reach Wellington.' The lovely eyes darkened then into violet flame as she took in the woman's crimson satin crinoline with its large spray of white silk roses at the breast, and she was unable to resist a small, theatrical sigh. 'I would love to wear such a brilliant and ornately decorated costume such as your own, but I fear I simply don't possess your Junoesque proportions to counteract its effect.'

Since Mrs Cavendish's intelligence was in direct opposition to her size, she was somewhat uncertain as to whether she was being complimented or insulted, and like many of her type, chose the former. 'I suppose I do have a certain . . . *je ne sais quoi*.' The accent was atrocious, but the fact that she spoke even a few words of any other language caused her retinue to twitter approval, and her husband gave her an affectionate pat on the arm.

'My Amelia has always had a flair for languages,' he beamed. 'Why, she's even picked up a word or two of Maori. It does so help with the servants, don't you think, Mrs Van der Veer?'

Melody caught sight of Aunt Bee edging towards them through the throng, and gave a quiet sigh of relief before turning to the man with a forced smile. 'I'm afraid there

are no servants at Windhaven, Mr Cavendish. Of course
there are people who work there, but I shouldn't call
them servants.'

'But there are Maoris, aren't there?' the man pursued.

'Perhaps Mrs Van der Veer doesn't regard her workers
as servants,' suggested a young man with gentle brown
eyes. 'There is, after all, little distinction in this new land
of ours between the paid servant and any other employee.'

Melody returned his smile, but before she could speak,
a friend of the Cavendishes, a plump lawyer with heavily
ringed fingers testifying to his exorbitant fees, expostulated, 'All the difference in the world, sir! Why, a servant
is nothing more than a menial, doing dirty work for low
income and long hours. My office clerks certainly don't
come into that category!'

Melody gave a choke of involuntary laughter. 'No, but
I'd wager that most of the settlers around here do, and
the people, if any, who work for them, Maori or *pakeha*!'

'Bravo, Melody!' laughed Beatrice, who had finally
reached them. 'If you go on this way, however, you'll
have Mr and Mrs Cavendish believing that all that deter-
mines a servant is the colour of the skin and the lack of
education.'

The lawyer gave a vehement nod. 'Certainly a combination of the two, as far as this country's concerned. They
are all witless heathens, every one!'

'The servants, you mean?' Melody enquired with wide-
eyed gravity. 'You can't mean the hundreds of mission-
educated Maoris who read and write far better than most
of our brave white soldiers who are fighting them in the
north; or those chiefs who have learned to negotiate for
peace in our language, since they realise that we shall not
bother to learn theirs.'

'But they are heathens, are they not, Mrs Van der Veer?
You must agree to that,' insisted a well-fed Baptist, who
had fought long and hard to instil the fear of God into
his congregation.

Melody faced him squarely. 'No, I would not agree to
that, sir. The Maori have as strong a belief in their religion

as you have in yours. Most of their confusion comes after what you call conversion, not before. One of my dearest friends is a Maori chieftain, a Christian, yes, but he lived and practised Christianity long before he was baptised.'

'Impossible!' expostulated Mrs Cavendish. 'That you should even confess to befriending heathens . . . '

Melody ignored her, pursuing her argument with only a derisory glance. 'Would you not agree that many of the finest ideals of Christianity are based on the Ten Commandments?' she asked, and continued without awaiting his reply, 'Then you must also admit that there are all too few Christians in high places at present, for the Commandments said nothing, to my knowledge, about its being commendable to kill a man's family; steal his lands and possessions; covet, and take, his wife or daughter; simply because his skin was of a slightly darker hue or his faith not one's own. Convert them by all means, but not with broken promises and false hopes: use will-power, not fire-power. And forgive their confusion if you send Catholics, Presbyterians, Baptists and Protestants to teach them all at the same time . . . and Buddists and Muslims, for all I know! Forgive them, too, if they find their confusion overwhelming, and return to the old ways, to the gods who are at least consistent. Surely a man is as Christian as he acts out in his life, and if I live my life to the best of my ability, helping whomsoever I'm able to, harming no man, and taking each new dawn as a miracle of re-birth, then surely that is being one of God's people—whichever name I call him by? If I need to talk with my god when I'm in the middle of a field on Wednesday, why should I wait to be crammed into some stuffy, over-populated, man-made structure on Sunday? If I wish to talk with him in a Catholic church, a mosque or a temple because it is the nearest place, why should I be turned away because I'm not wearing a hat, or can't understand the language of the prayer book?'

She drew a deep breath, cheeks flushed, eyes blazing, unaware that several other people had drifted closer at the low, yet clearly enunciated and carrying, tones of the dramatically beautiful girl in the fairytale dress. 'And if I choose to worship *my* god in *my* home on *my* land, which I've fought for, conquered, tamed, cultivated and lived off and for . . . then tell me, if you can, why some pompous ass who isn't of my colour and doesn't even deign to speak my language should demand that I cease . . . and give him my land to boot!'

There was a crashing silence . . . a sudden exhalation of breath . . . then an explosion of sound . . . 'bravo', applause, snorts, boos . . . and the very quiet rustle of Mrs Cavendish fainting clean away.

'Judge not that ye be not judged!' Beatrice grinned at the poor Baptist who had started it all, and firmly taking Melody's arm, propelled her on to the terrace. 'I'll get Paul,' she declared. 'Don't move, and for heaven's sake don't open your mouth . . . I heard a rumour that they keep hungry wolves below!'

'Oh, what have I done!' Melody whispered, gazing appalled at the soft lights from the display of Chinese lanterns that bathed the trees and lawns.

Paul came from the ballroom and saw her standing there alone, apart from the chaos she had wrought, and his throat constricted. Her stark isolation was almost too much, and his hand went out . . . then dropped to his side. She was no longer his to touch. And she turned, too late to see the pent-up longing and unutterable sadness on his face. She saw instead a carefully controlled neutrality that she misinterpreted as censure.

'I am so sorry, Paul! I don't know what I was thinking of. I've ruined everything for you!' She came to him, eyes deep violet in the moonlight, lifted to search his. 'I'll apologise to everyone, of course . . . '

'You'll do no such thing.' His jaw tightened as he resisted the urge to sweep her into his arms. 'You've created an explosion that has divided the whole gathering—something my diplomacy could never have achieved; something that only you would have dared.'

'You don't hate me!'

With studied care he put her cloak about her shoulders,

hiding that creamy skin and the full curves that were
almost revealed by that unbelievable dress. 'Hate you?'
She felt the leashed power in his grip as he took her hand,
and at his touch a trembling siezed her, a mingled fear
and inexplicable longing. Slowly he brought it to his lips,
moving his mouth lightly over her fingers, his eyes never
leaving hers. 'Melody Van der Veer, I was more proud of
you tonight than I have ever been of anyone.'

For that moment she thought her heart would burst
with happiness, but grasping at sanity, she whispered,
'I'm . . . I'm glad I could . . . do something to
promote the cause,' and saw his smile.

'You were, as predicted, an irresistible emissary. I
should have realised that you would give no quarter, to
either Maori attackers or whites. Perhaps you'd like to
stay on in Wellington and run them *all* into the sea?' His
gentle humour had an underlying questioning, but it was
lost on her as she shook her head, suddenly weary.

'All I want to do now is to go home as quickly as
possible . . . to Windhaven, I mean,' she amended
hastily, and saw his puzzlement and the tiny spark of
hope—swiftly quenched.

'Yes, of course. You'll be wanting to pack and say your
farewells, now that you're free to leave.'

She nodded, feeling suddenly cold within, unable to
speak, and wondered at the slight huskiness in his voice
as he continued, more slowly, 'Your freedom also gives
you the choice to stay, you know. There will be arrangements to make, plans for your future. You may not wish
to make them from a wilderness homestead that has
brought you so much unhappiness, but should you have
no immediate alternative in mind . . . ' He stopped at
the flash of joy in the brilliant eyes turned up to his.

'I've no plans . . . ' Then she said, more carefully,
'None for a few days, at least . . . '

'Then it's settled. You'll stay at Windhaven until you
wish to leave.'

Melody hesitated. 'I'll find it strange being a guest
rather than a servant. Will you find the same difficulty in

not being my master?'

'I was never your master, Melody. No man ever could be.' Briefly the warm tips of his fingers touched her cheek. 'Let's find your aunt. One more night at the hotel and then . . . home.'

Melody thought, later that night, that it must have been her preoccupation with her future—and how it was so governed by her past—that made her eyes deceive her so cruelly on the carriage-ride back to the hotel, but the shock of it remained with her for several days. The carriage had turned from the drive of the Residency and on into the main thoroughfare. There was a brilliant full moon, and the night was almost as light as day. They passed a number of run-down wooden shacks, some with women for rent. A man stepped from one of them, the light from the door behind him. He hesitated; then, apparently having forgotten something, turned immediately back inside. The carriage was moving at a good pace, and the man's features could not be seen, but something about him, his build, the set of his head, caused Melody to cry out and grip Beatrice's arm. But then she gave a shaky laugh and apologised. 'Sorry, Aunt Bee, I'm seeing ghosts. What were you saying about the dashing Major Oglethorpe?'

She tried to listen, tried to concentrate, while the colour slowly returned to her ashen features and her heart resumed its normal beat. Yet, for that instant of dreaming, she had been quite sure that she had looked upon the resurrected form of Luther Hogge!

CHAPTER TWENTY

IT WAS IMPOSSIBLE! It was a nightmare, but at dawn one awakens. Yet this remained, and the shock of her hallucination kept her subdued during the whole return journey, yet it took only the sight of Windhaven to drive it from her mind, and she spurred forward eagerly.

Paul's quizzical frown was caught by Beatrice as they exchanged glances, but she held her counsel, hoping that these two proud, stubborn people would come to their senses before the week was out—at which time Melody had told them quite firmly that she would be ready to leave for America. But only Beatrice had seen the dark-ringed eyes after the night of tears and heartbreaking decisions. 'Why not stay in Wellington?' she had suggested, but Melody had shaken her raven hair out violently, pulling the brush through it as if punishing it for her own pain.

'Too close,' she had stated, and would say no more, though privately Beatrice thought that it would take far more than distance to take Windhaven and its arrogant master from her mind.

Maata was there to greet them, and David, who hurtled down the porch steps and into Melody's arms—then realised that he should be a young man now and said formally, 'Welcome home, Aunt Melody', but he was lost as she laughed and pulled him into a hug. Then her laughter died as she caught Paul's searching look over the boy's head. There was such a bleakness there and a tightness in the chiselled features that she felt, inexplicably, that she had betrayed him by her loving action—when they both knew how short her stay would be.

Gently she put the boy away. 'What news?'

'Great news!' he exploded, hopping from one foot to the other in excitement. 'Uncle Brett is here from America, and he has brought a friend. They arrived two days ago.'

'Brett? Here?' All else forgotten, Melody almost ran for the house, closely followed by the others. 'Brett!'

He turned from the fireplace as she burst into the room, and the perfect features registered a brief flash of utter joy—but then the smile died as he spoke her name, his voice unsteady. She ran into his arms, drinking in his beauty, holding him close as she gazed up at him. 'You came! You came!'

'We surely did!' boomed a dearly familiar voice, and Patrick O'Shaughnessy strode in, crossing the room with the single-mindedness of a charging bull and swinging the stunned Beatrice up into his arms, kissing her soundly. 'Begad, but I've missed you, woman! Why didn't you write? Even a god-forsaken place like this must have some form of pony express!' He set her back on her feet; then his face, too, became serious. 'We must all do some talking, Beatrice . . . especially young Brett here.'

Paul had regained his composure after the blow of seeing Melody fly into his cousin's arms, and after suggesting to David that he leave the adults to talk for a while, came forward with a bleak smile. 'I thought you safely ensconced in Natchez, Brett.'

'Natchez and safety don't walk hand in hand any more,' Patrick broke in. 'Neither, for that matter, does anywhere in the South, which is why we're here in person. Those blithering idiots have finally started their war!' They stared at him aghast, and even Melody turned from Brett eyes wide in disbelief. 'In December,' he continued, 'shortly after you left, the whole slavery matter came to a head, and on the twentieth a State convention in South Carolina dissolved "the Union now subsisting". Of course most of the other Southern States followed suit, with even Texas joining them, and by the beginning of February they'd formed their own Confederate States of America. A month later a new president, an Abe Lincoln, was elected—more because of the division and wrangling of his enemies than by any overwhelming majority vote, but he decided that the secession was void. Well, one little incident that resulted from all this ballyhoo was that he sent a boatload of troops—the *Star of the West* it was—to relieve the men at Fort Sumter—apparently the forces there were pretty short of supplies. This little fort was on a sandbar in the mouth of Charleston harbour, and you wouldn't think anyone would have cared one way or the other *what* happened to it, but on April 12th the Confederate forces opened fire. 'Course it may have had something to do with the fact that it was 4.30 in the morning—a totally uncivilised hour to be shot at, and enough to make any man go to war! Anyway, the following afternoon, the fort surrendered and all hell broke loose all over the States. Before that, of course, in February, New Orleans was smothered with pretty boys in prettier uniforms, and it was all a grand bit o' fun, with parties and dances and military music everywhere, and no one took any of it too seriously. Once I read of the start of it, though, I arranged for us to leave on the first boat out. Brett here was in no fit state to carry a gun, and I certainly had no intention of doing so for such an ijit cause.'

Beatrice had recovered from the shock predictably faster than the others, and now raised a quizzical eyebrow. 'Did you feel no inclination to fight a whole half continent, then, Patrick?'

He turned that brilliant gaze on her, and gave a broad grin. 'Why, bless you, milady, I always have an inclination to fight—but never for lost causes!'

'Do you feel no loyalty for either North or South, then?'

'I've lived in both, and my loyalty is for me and mine, since I've managed to survive in spite of the so-called ideologies of other men, rather than because of them. But that is the reason we left Natchez. We could have gone west; so far, California is safe territory, I believe. No, we came here for a far more important reason than a mere war. Perhaps Brett should tell you.'

'He's undoubtedly rehearsed his speech all the way

over,' Paul put in drily, but Melody would not allow him to spoil the moment.

She took Brett's arm, drawing him close, and confessed, half laughing, 'If it takes a war to bring us all together again, I'm glad it happened. I've thought about you so often, and now you're here.'

He stiffened at her words, then gently loosed her grip. 'And I've thought of you, Melody. In fact I've thought of little else since you left. I found myself unable to sleep, barely able to eat. I thought of you as a slave in this wilderness, working in the fields . . . or worse. Has he treated you well?'

'Paul? Yes, indeed.' His fists slowly unclenched, and she whispered, 'You really were worried. You . . . love me still!'

But he turned away with a violent movement, and a harsh incoherent sound broke from his lips. 'Yes . . . And may the Lord forgive me for that sin!' He clenched his fists, and all the torment of hell was in those ravaged features, his mind unaware of the company who were riveted by the drama being enacted.

Fingers of ice touched Melody's spine. 'What is it, Brett? What's wrong?' As she touched him, a hand was flung out in denial, but she seized it, bringing it to her cheek. 'It's all right, my dear. It doesn't matter, whatever it is. I'll help you, we all will. We can overcome anything together. Are you thinking of your blindness? Oh, Brett, I can take care of you, now that you're here. I love you, too, you see. Of course I do.' And she did. She loved his gentleness, his tenderness and the easy warmth that had once enfolded them . . . and for that moment believed herself capable of taking on any adversary, Paul, or the whole of New Zealand, to retain that.

That Greek god's face registered only unutterable sadness at her confusion as he sought and found control. 'Of course you do, my dear. It would be quite, quite natural for you to love . . . your brother.'

Melody stared at him, her mind refusing to acknowledge the words. 'What . . . did you . . . say?'

There were tears then in the sightless eyes. 'Melody . . . I am your brother.'

'I don't understand.' She was deaf to the exclamations of Beatrice and the sharply indrawn breath of Paul, each as incredulous as she. Holding her suddenly icy hands tightly, Brett drew her down beside him on the couch. Still she was unable to tear her eyes from his face, as uncomprehendingly she shook her head. 'It can't be! I don't believe you!'

'Oh, my dear, I'd give the world for it to be otherwise. When Patrick was determined that we should escape the war, Nanny told me the secret she had held for all these years, fearing what would happen between us if we met again over here. I tried, like you, to pretend it wasn't so. I even beat her to make her say she'd lied, God forgive me.'

'Tell me,' Melody begged, her voice barely audible, features ashen.

With many halts, once too tormented for several seconds to go on, he gave her the whole story, finishing, 'You see, Nanny loved our mother as much as she hated Father. She feared for your life, and reasoned it was better to be a slave, than dead in the revolt. And then, when Alex appeared, it was like the answer to a prayer. She would be revenged on our father by telling him his daughter and wife were dead, and have you brought up safely. She never thought to see or hear of you again, but, of course, you had to be registered in the slave-log as Ereanora's daughter.' With a groan, he dropped his head forward into his hands. 'Oh, Melody, why did you ever leave England!'

She had sat in numb shock throughout his story, a story too fantastic to believe, but now she felt drained, mentally exhausted. 'It hardly seems to matter now,' she murmured dazedly. 'Nothing is as it was. I'm not who I thought I was, and twice now that has been told to me. I don't know what or who to believe any more. Only a few months ago I was the daughter of Alexander and Charity Davenport, a cosseted English aristocrat. Then I became

the illegitimate coloured child of Alex Davenport and
some slave called Ereanora. Now . . . I don't even know
this Arabella and Luke Savage, both dead within hours
of my birth, who were supposedly my parents.'

Beatrice went over and pulled her into her familiar
arms, the one centre of reality that never changed. 'Melody,
love, I think we must believe this. It's too fantastic to be
a lie. It gives so many answers; your blue eyes, for one.
Oh, sweeting, you've been through so much . . . ' She
gave a thought to the blond Adonis by Melody's side.
'You both have!' She put a comforting hand on his arm.
'Poor Brett! It must have been terrible for you, too.'

'I'd more or less come to terms with it on the voyage,
but then having Melody here . . . touching her . . . '
A deep shudder went through him.

Each of them had forgotten Paul, who was fighting his
own battles, silent, alone, and within himself as always.
Melody's first confession of her love for his cousin had
cut through him like a knife. He knew then that he had
achieved nothing in freeing her except the probability of
losing her for ever. Then, hearing Brett's story, he had a
moment of hope, but that first confession still told him
that she would always be drawn to the weak, the soft, the
gentle—the opposite to him in every way—and he felt a
blaze of anger. That such a free spirit, such strength and
raw courage should be wasted on men such as Brett and
this Hugh Van der Veer! Striding to the bell-pull, he
summoned an already hovering Maata. 'I think we could
all do with a drink,' he stated with unwarranted harsh-
ness. 'The place is awash with sentiment and tears, so a
little more liquid won't go amiss. Mr O'Shaughnessy . . . Patrick.'

The Irishman gave a nod, reaching behind the words.
'Sure, don't mind if I do.'

Maata had reappeared with a full tray of assorted
bottles and glasses which she set down on a side-table,
and Paul poured two generous goblets of brandy. 'Lady
Davenport?'

'Beatrice . . . I'll have the same, if you don't mind.

One feels the need of a restorative.'

'Melody? Brett?'

She seemed to see Paul for the first time, and gave a shaky smile. 'I'm inclined to echo Aunt Bee, even though I don't usually drink. This time it's purely medicinal, and much needed. Brett?'

But Brett had risen with a shake of his head. 'No, nothing, thank you. Maata?'

'Yes, Mr Savage?'

'I want to go to my room.' Melody put down her surprise at his tone, having forgotten the way he normally addressed servants, but then he had turned and given her a smile that wrenched at her heart. 'I beg you all to forgive me. I'll be more company tomorrow, and you, too, will probably be better apart from me for awhile.' Without awaiting any response, he allowed Maata to lead him from the room.

At his departure there was a momentary vacuum, then Patrick said, 'Why don't you take me for a walk, Beatrice? You can tell me what mischief you've been making without my sobering influence, and I can tell you of the war no one can win.'

Quickly she glanced at Melody, who nodded. 'Go ahead. I'm all right.'

'No, sweeting, you're far from that, but I don't think anything I could say or do just now would help, and I do have some questions for Patrick that need answers.'

Melody turned to Paul, but he was staring broodingly into his glass, which already he had emptied and refilled, so with a sigh she agreed, 'Yes, please go. We'll all feel better by dinner.' But her words rang hollowly even to herself, and as soon as they had left, she murmured, 'I think I'll go and see how David has fared in our absence.' When he did not answer, she pursued, 'Paul . . . Will they be staying here . . . Brett and Patrick?' and winced before the glare he gave her.

'Where else?' He emptied his second glass . . . at which point she retreated, not to the boisterously happy David, but to her room. There was no way in which she could school her mind to believe this fantasy, yet, as Aunt Bee had said, it did explain much. 'Oh, Brett!' she whispered, taking the pins from her hair to relieve the sudden headache. 'Oh, my poor love!' In that moment, realising what she had said, she understood the depth . . . and manner . . . of her love for him, the love she had always felt for him, the warm, totally passionless love of a sister for her brother.

Over dinner, the emotion of the moment had abated, but the tension was equally as high, with Paul obviously drunk and frostily polite to everyone.

'And why not?' Beatrice exclaimed sympathetically later that evening. 'He's given up a coloured slave and gained a white adoptive cousin all in one foul swoop. You aren't the only one for whom life has turned upside-down, my dear, though to each of us it seems that our own problems are far worse than any around us.'

'Oh, I do understand, Aunt Bee, but I just can't feel sympathy for someone who not only refuses to ask for it, but surely denies the need of it with every breath. Brett, now . . . ' She shook her head. 'And yet he seems changed, somehow. Oh, not the obvious results of good food and exercise, but something more, a confidence in the way he moves and speaks. He—He doesn't seem to need me any more, either!'

Beatrice gave her a long look and for once held her peace. During the next few days, however, her patience was sorely tried. Paul found his own escape, riding to all points of the compass on any excuse at all, but the others had been asked to stay within the confines of the stockade since there had been further Maori attacks up-river.

It seemed to trouble Patrick not at all, for he, like Beatrice, had a totally instinctive penchant for making friends of all types, and the two could always be found together, drawn as if by a magnet, yet always in the company of others, as though fearful of their own emotions. It soon became apparent to Melody that their separation had served only to cement the strange relationship that they had previously formed. The raillery was still there and the badinage, but they now exchanged looks that totally belied his calling her a 'muleheaded female' and her constantly referring to him as a 'fool' and an 'overgrown leprechaun'. She told him of her mis-spent youth, and he spoke of his grindingly poor childhood in the peat-bogs of Ireland. 'But, o' course, you being a lady an' all, you wouldn't know too much of that sort o' thing.'

Beatrice smiled, but for once without humour. 'Perhaps you're right, but possessing a title doesn't necessarily mean that doors always open of their own accord, nor does money buy love, or even honest affection, though it can command a fair degree of envy.'

'But you never went hungry or walked barefoot.'

'No,' she admitted, 'though I could have, for all it would have been noticed. My father demanded sons, and plenty of them—to inherit the draughty, crumbling edifice he called the family seat—to inherit, and to marry well enough to support it. When mother produced a daughter that nearly killed her, the doctor warned her never to have another. My father never spoke to either of us again, apart from the social politenesses like "pass the salt", and moved to the top of the house.'

'But your brother, Melody's father . . . supposed father?'

'The rainbow after the storm. The intolerable situation had endured for well over five years. Divorce was inconceivable at that social level, and for me at least, knowing no other life, it was not too unendurable. He was never cruel or deliberately unkind and I wanted for nothing material, but for my mother, the woman who had loved him, it was a living hell to be banished so, and one night she attempted suicide. But despair broke through the barrier he had erected, and it was probably on that night that Alex was conceived. From *his* birth, carried out with such physical agony that it left my mother bedridden for the rest of her life, he received every particle of my father's love. His treatment of me was that of a stranger, and I went through a succession of nurses and nannies and tutors entirely alone. I turned to my books for companionship and the exploits of women who held men's hearts in the palms of their hands, as I wished I could my father's. I studied their strengths and weaknesses, and gathered every morsel of gossip I could. I studied politics and would listen to my father's friends, sitting in my chair so silently that they quite forgot I was there and revealed far more than they should.' She gave a rueful smile. 'I was only fifteen when I forgot my self-imposed vow of silence and gave one particular socialist such a tongue-thrashing for his views on the poor that my father banished me to relatives in London, to be taught the correct manners of a young lady!'

'They would have had their hands full!' Patrick laughed.

'I must admit that I was a constant cause for concern, and two years later I left them also, expressing my pent-up desire for love and attention by joining a somewhat over-theatrical theatrical company. What one might call using a musket to kill a fly on the wall. What I lacked in talent I made up for in enthusiasm! But, needless to say, that didn't last very long, either.'

Patrick gave a sympathetic chuckle. 'It must have filled the house for a while, though, to see the Lady Davenport treading the boards.'

She sent him a glare of mock reproof. 'I may have cordially disliked my father, but I never would have brought the family name into disgrace . . . not at that time, anyway!' But then she gave a gurgle of laughter. 'Apart from which, I was only seventeen, and the name Beatrice Davenport was far too dull. I gave myself the name of Boadicea Devine!'

Melody, who had heard the story a dozen times before, stifled an appreciative giggle, but Patrick's explosion of laughter shook the candelabra. He surged up from his chair and swept Beatrice off her feet. 'Woman, you're worth all the gold at the end of the rainbow, and I love ye for it!' Their sparkling eyes and laughing lips were only inches apart, and Melody drew an involuntary breath. Beatrice looked suddenly shaken and Patrick even more so, but it was his self-control that overcame the explosion of feeling that had ripped through him. Firmly he set her down again, and his voice bore only the slightest tremor as he finished, 'But enough o' that! I'd better be seeing to some fences, or the boss man will be demanding money for my keep.' At the door, however, he turned, blue eyes gleaming. 'You surely chose well, though, my divine warrior queen!' With another chuckle, he left.

'Fool!' Beatrice smiled, no condemnation in her voice. 'Overgrown, blarney-kissing leprechaun!'

'But you'd not change him one iota!' Melody stated. 'You like him. You like him a great deal!'

A flicker of something deeper appeared in her aunt's eyes before she snorted, 'Rubbish!' belying the expression in the gaze that followed his giant form through the window as he crossed the compound.

At the end of that week, Paul announced his intention of travelling into Wanganui for supplies, and immediately Patrick suggested that, if he had no objection, he and Beatrice should accompany him. 'I saw precious little of the town on the way in, and Beatrice could do with some more fripperies.'

'I've already experienced that riverboat once too often, and the horse-ride betwixt and between.'

'But not with Patrick Aloysius O'Shaughnessy,' he stated, and the matter was settled.

'I've friends there,' Paul offered. 'A missionary couple who believe that teaching Christianity to the pagans is like lighting a campfire at night on the African plains, where they once served. It can cast a warmth on all about it, and a glow that can be seen for miles. Misused, it can also become a forest fire that destroys hundreds of miles and millions of tiny lives. We can't give them the warmth without teaching them to use it wisely.' He frowned, lost for the moment within himself. 'We teach them to take revenge and then tell them to turn the other cheek. They hear of a god of love, and then see the way he mowed down thousands of innocents in the plagues. We confront them with all the variations—Catholics, Baptists and the rest—that you mentioned at the ball, Melody, and then are genuinely puzzled when they turn away from such a patchwork of beliefs.' He smiled. 'Generally, I've no use for the missionary set, as you'll have realised, but these are good and genuine people who will be glad to offer you their hospitality for a few days if you'd like to explore the area!' The deep-set eyes flickered over the girl, who was concentrating a fraction too hard on the Shakespeare sonnets that they had brought from America. 'You could accompany us if you wished, Melody. I'm sure Maata could take care of Brett quite adequately.'

Since nothing in the carefully neutral tone conveyed more than polite interest, she shook her head decisively. 'I'd rather stay here, thank you. I promised Maata I'd help her to put up some preserves in exchange for cookery lessons . . . I'll need them when I get . . . back. And there are some sketches I'd like to make: portraits of Maata and David that I can keep . . . ' She hesitated, not wanting to say 'when I leave here' when everything in her cried out against such a move. To leave this perfect setting and the warm friendship of its people would be bad—but to part from David . . . at least David . . . would break her heart! Beyond that, she could not allow herself to think.

Early the following morning the trio set out, accompanied by several Maoris who would act as bodyguard against the still marauding hostile bands. They could visit relatives and friends in town, and knew that Paul would be generous with his money for this extra service, though each one of the men would gladly have laid down his life for this strange *pakeha* who was like a brother to them.

Immediately they had gone, Melody went to find her sketch-book: the staple of every Victorian miss on a country visit! Already half-filled with detailed drawings of flowers, birds, landscapes and the rapidly changing skies, it showed all too clearly the artist's growing love of the land, from the first tentative strokes to the uncaring adoration of Maori children playing in the dirt, and David in a hundred poses. There were sketches of old people gazing into the future with quiet dignity, and Maata kneading dough, smiling, singing, head to one side or thrown back in a laugh. Every view of the house had been preserved, and the carved door-posts copied with an eye to the minutest detail, as she found a talent she had not known she possessed. But now it was time for a work of even greater care, and her eyes softened as she studied her subject.

Brett sat half reclining on the porch, leaning back against one of the wooden supports, face turned up towards the sun, quite unaware of her presence. His skin had tanned, and Patrick said that much of it had been the work of the roisterous family in Natchez who had seen his disability only as a minor inconvenience and had insisted on his accompanying them on canoe trips. He had, she knew, developed even keener senses of sound and scent because of it, and could unerringly detect the position of a person at first sound. He could load and unload a rifle with confidence, confessing a little ruefully that he had even shot a 'gator once . . . then had been knocked off his feet by that lethally-lashing tail and had had to be rescued by Seth. More and more he moved about the house without his cane, almost as though he could sense objects before him, and once or twice she had seen Paul watching him with narrowed eyes as though he, too, was reassessing his once helpless cousin.

There was still a certain tension between her and Brett when they were alone, but as Beatrice had said, 'The knowledge of the head makes little difference to the feelings of the heart!' and she knew that Brett was still in love with her. She mourned the circumstances that prevented her from touching him as she once had, of making him laugh, yet she knew that in time his feelings would change, and, surely, there would be a closeness between them again. In the meantime she tried to ensure that they were alone as little as possible, to assuage her loneliness and to quell her desire to confide in him as she never could in Paul.

Watching him stretch now, unself-consciously, sure that

he was alone, Melody gave a satisfied smile and settled to draw him, laying her materials down on one of the large logs that awaited splitting for the fire. She sat down beside them, at a distance, so that he would not be aware of her searching regard, wanting only to capture the pose, knowing that each line of his face could be filled in later, since she knew them so well. An hour passed, though she was quite oblivious of both time and her surroundings, straining to catch a likeness, a turn of the hand, a ripple in the hair, wishing with all her heart that she had taken her art lessons more seriously, unaware of just how accurate she was in assessing the shadow, how lovingly she had recorded the substance.

The compound was empty for a change, the men either working outside or patrolling the area, riding out in pairs, quartering the surrounding wilderness, hunting both game and danger. The sun was high, and it grew warm. Setting aside the sketch-book Melody loosened the tight chignon, then, with a quick glance around, took out the pins and allowed her hair to cascade over her shoulders. 'Better by far,' she murmured, pulling her dress a little off the shoulders and allowing the light breeze to caress her skin.

The dress was the one from which she had removed the lace fichu on that disastrous evening when, in anger, Paul had kissed her so brutally. She had, as bid, never worn it since, but it was one of her lightest, and, having replaced the fichu and altered it to fall without hoops, she found it less stifling than many of her others in the warmth of the day. Memories of that encounter—and others since— left the sketch-book forgotten, and she closed her eyes, leaning back on her hands, face upturned to the warmth of the sun. For a moment, her wild imaginings had his footsteps approaching her over the hard-packed earth, his broad frame blotting out the light . . . 'Lovely, my dear. Quite lovely.'

Her shock-filled eyes flew open to see the horribly scarred features of Luther Hogge.

Hogge! Alive! Not even in her worst nightmares had Melody believed anything like this. Never believed that

the bloody features she had last seen on her father's office
floor would ever confront her again, the scar-tissue drawing
one side of his face into a grotesque snarl. She wanted to
scream denial of his presence, but no sound would emerge
from her parted lips. The blood drained from her face,
yet the blessed release of unconsciousness was not allowed
to her, and she could only stare at him, her whole being
turned to ice.

'Yes, Melody, I'm alive,' he stated softly, that familiar,
hated voice unchanged. 'For a time, I thought otherwise—
a time when the surgeons worked on my face when I
wished it otherwise, *begged* them to finish the job you'd
bungled. At first I wanted revenge—I think that was
probably the only thing that kept me alive—and I spent
a fortune in trying in vain to trace you.'

Mutely she shook her head, attempting to gather her
shattered emotions, finally managing, 'How . . . ?'

'Pure luck. Your aunt wrote a letter to someone she
called John Brown. He was away on a diplomatic mission
in India. His butler recognised the name on the return
address and brought it to me, assuming I knew all about
it. Most enlightening. From there, it was easy. The
Pinkerton Agency in New York, their contacts in North
Carolina and New Orleans . . . and here I am.' He took
a pace forward, and sickened as she was by that awful
visage, she was unable to move. 'Your face was in my
mind every minute of the day. At first I hated you. Then,
slowly, over months of torment, that hatred died and the
old thoughts of you seeped in.' His mouth drew up into
a ghastly semblance of a smile. 'I knew that I must have
you, Melody. Even when I discovered that you were
coloured—sold as a slave to some dirt-farmer—I knew
that you still belonged to me.' Another pace forward, and
he was standing over her, eyes devouring the curve of her
ivory shoulders and the swell of her breasts accentuated
by the low décolletage. 'I know you're no virgin, know
you've been used as a slave, felt peasant hands on your
flesh, but I don't have to marry an innocent young girl
now . . . I can simply buy an unbelievably still beautiful

and experienced woman. You'll appreciate the scent of cologne over the stench of sweat, and hands that aren't calloused by the ploughshare.'

'No!' But her voice was still choked, and a shudder went through her as his hands—those thick fingers with their sprinkling of black hair as repulsive as she remembered them—closed over her arms, raising her to her feet.

'A down payment, my dear, for all the months of waiting.' But before that deformed mouth came down on hers, the scream that had welled up inside her burst out in a despairing, horror-filled cry.

Brett sprang from his half-dreaming state and stumbled to his feet. 'Melody? Melody!'

Wrenching free of that hateful embrace, she cried out, 'No, Brett! Stay there!'

Such anguish was in her tone that the blind man ran forward, wielding his stick, knowing that she was in some danger, cursing his affliction. 'Get behind me. Where are you?'

She ran to protect him, but the man was there first, stretching forward to tear the stick from Brett's hand. 'No!' Melody screamed. 'You can see he's blind.' But brutally Hogge clubbed Brett to the ground, the heavy butt of the walking-stick slamming into the temple, and, as the man went down, again on the back of his head.

Then, from the house, drawn by her scream, ran David, pulling up short, eyes widening at the scene. 'Run, David!' Melody sobbed. 'Get help!' She was struggling against the man's brutal grasp of her arm.

But with a shout the boy launched himself forward, bravely kicking and pummelling his enemy, shouting, 'You let her go!'

And Hogge did, turning almost casually, eyes glittering, and brought his hand up in a smashing blow to the side of the boy's face. Melody screamed at him, lunging forward to tear at his face, but he had the boy by the arm, holding the half-conscious child upright while his free hand cruelly pulled back his head. 'You love this nigra?' he hissed, breathing hard. 'You got a taste for dark meat since you discovered your own blood?'

'Let him go,' Melody begged. 'He's only a child! I'll do anything. Please let him go.'

That deformed mouth moved upward again in the grimace that served as a smile. 'Yes, I believe you would. Very well. We are going to leave here quietly. My horse is at the gate. I told the guards I was a relative of yours, and that's the way we'll leave.'

David began to struggle. 'I'm not going anywhere with you!' Then he gasped as the man wrenched his arm behind his back.

'I beg you, Luther!' The tears spilled over as Melody's whole life fell in tiny shards about her feet.

On the packed earth, Brett gave a low moan, but as she moved instinctively towards him, the silky voice warned, 'No, my dear.'

'He's badly hurt!'

'So was I, and I shall relive that hurt each time I look into a mirror. Can you imagine what my life has been like? Can you guess at the number of drawing-rooms I was barred from, the clubs that would empty as I walked in, so that eventually I went out only at night? And that was something else. You have never met, never even seen, I'm sure, the only kind of woman I could have. But that brings us back to my presence here, doesn't it? And now . . . ' his voice sharpened, 'it's time to go. The child will come with us, just to the coast, to ensure your compliance.'

Melody looked at him through the mist of tears and felt a strange hollowness build within her, as if every feeling, every emotion, had drained away, and it was with a voice not her own that she stated softly, 'I'll come with you, Luther, and you have my word that I'll do as bid, but if you harm David, I swear I really shall kill you.'

The man's tiny eyes looked into hers, and for that moment their entire attention was on each other. 'She has changed,' he realised. 'There is something in her . . . ' Then came sudden shouts and the thunder of hooves . . .

A shot rang out, kicking up the dust at their feet, and

an icy voice stated, 'That first shot introduced us, Mr Hogge. My second will certainly sever any future acquaintanceship we may have.'

Melody swayed, not daring to turn, not daring to believe, her eyes still fixed on that hated face, seeing the colour leave it and the basilisk eyes glitter malevolently. But then he stepped aside, releasing the boy, and David, with a cry of 'Papa!' ran to fling himself into Paul Savage's arms.

As though in slow motion, Melody saw Beatrice run to her side, and felt warm arms tight about her, saw Patrick bend over the fallen Brett.

'You're making a mistake, sir,' Hogge said, those silky tones conveying nothing of the white-hot fury within. 'Melody and I go back a long way—a *very* long way. She was once to be my wife.'

Paul's lips tightened, and in horror Melody cried, 'No! Paul . . .'

But his whole attention was fixed on the man beside her, and his voice held only one conviction. 'No man lays a hand on my son, or assaults my guests, and you, Mr Hogge, have done both. What is between you and Mrs Van der Veer will be resolved later, but you are now on my land, and I'm asking you to leave it.'

'Melody is coming with me. I have the money to buy her from you, and she has agreed to it.'

'This is preposterous!' snapped Beatrice, pulling her close.

'Only for David's sake!' Melody cried, but those gold-flecked eyes did not even flicker towards her.

'No, Mr Hogge, not just now, and should you be unwise enough to contest the issue . . . ' He moved the deadly Walker Colt a fraction higher, 'You'll lose the other half of your face.'

Melody heard the man's sharp hiss of indrawn breath, but then he turned to her with a short bow. 'You have my apologies, Melody. Buying you from your dirt-farmer will be more . . . expensive . . . than I imagined.' He turned to Paul, his emotions now under complete control.

'I, myself, never make empty threats, sir, and I judge you to be a man of similiar principles, so I'll leave quietly. However, I'm quite *au fait* with Melody's status here, as well as her blood-line, and shall return to talk business when you are more open to reason. You'll not lose on the deal, I assure you, but I'm determined to have her.'

Paul's face went white and his muscles tensed, but at that moment Brett gave a deep groan and attempted to rise, deflecting Paul's attention for a moment, and when he turned again, Hogge was already striding across the compound to the gate. With a curse, Paul allowed him to leave. He would settle with Luther Hogge at a later date. Swiftly he crossed to the fallen man, but Melody had reached him first, having pulled free of Beatrice at that agonised sound, and ran to fling her arms about him.

'Brett! Oh, Brett, you're all right!' Desperately, fearfully, she searched his face, with trembling fingers touching the deep bruise at his temple and finding the rapidly swelling lump at the back of his head.

'Melody? What . . . ? Where . . . ?' He shook his head, a frown marring the too perfect features.

'No, don't speak. It's safe. Paul's here, and Luther has left.' Then she found a sudden shortness of breath as the long-lashed eyes moved to her face.

'Light! . . . There's . . . light!' Slowly he brought up his hand to cover his eyes, while the sudden silence crashed about them with an almost physical force. His hand came down . . . and up . . . and down again. He raised his head, fighting his own fight—then turned unerringly toward the sun. 'It was always blackness, but now there's some—some degree of light.'

'Come now, Brett, me boy,' Patrick said gently, a catch in his throat. 'You've had a nasty blow on the head and we must get you to your room. You'll be resting for a few days, I'll be bound. We'll get the doc to you, just to check things over.' A quick glance at Paul received an affirmative nod, and without further ado the Irishman bent and lifted the fallen man into his giant arms, carrying him inside.

'Don't be a fool!' Brett protested vainly. 'You don't understand what I'm saying . . . and *I can walk!*'

'And collapse in a series of untidy heaps all the way to your room, no doubt! Now hold your tongue, and pretend you're dead drunk in Natchez . . . that shouldn't strain your imagination over much!'

Melody began to shudder helplessly as she watched them go, still arguing, and allowed herself to be led into the drawing-room, accepting the measure of brandy put into her hand, but not touching it until Beatrice's soft voice commanded, 'Drink!' She took a sip, coughed, and then with something like a sob she drank the fiery liquid down. Slowly she looked about her—Beatrice beside her on the couch, Paul standing by the fire, dark eyes intent on her face, one arm still about David's shoulders. 'How . . . ? Why did you come back?'

'You can thank your aunt for that,' Paul said, a thread of anger running through his words that she could not understand.

'We reached the jetty for the down-river steamer,' Beatrice explained. 'The captain knows Paul well, of course, and asked him about his visitor, the one that had disembarked from the up-stream boat and stayed the night at the Pipiriki Lodge, asking whether he could rent a horse there.'

Patrick entered the room at that point with assurances that Brett was in bed, well attended by Maata. 'The lad still says that he can see lighter patches in his darkness, but I'll not allow him to raise his hopes. A blow on the head can do funny things, and it could be all in his imagination. He's probably still seeing stars!'

'Poor Brett,' Melody exclaimed. 'I'm so glad that he is not badly hurt. He must have been out of his mind to attempt to save me, but it was a wonderfully brave thing to do. I'd never have forgiven myself if . . . if . . . ' But she could not think, would not think, beyond that.

'The man's in love with you,' Paul stated drily. 'It can affect the mind strangely at times!'

Beatrice flashed him a sharp look, continuing quickly,

'Well, it soon became clear, from what the captain told us, who this visitor was. Even *I* couldn't believe it at first, but then the captain described the Hog and that awful scar, and I knew that it had to be him, in spite of all belief.'

'She ranted at us like a madwoman!' Patrick continued the story, a sympathetic hand covering Beatrice's shoulder. 'Said it was a matter of life and death and we had to return here, even if we killed the horses in the process.'

'I'm afraid I didn't explain very well,' Beatrice apologised. 'I just told Paul that Luther was the reason we had left England, that you thought you had killed him, and he was undoubtedly here to exact revenge. Thank God we arrived in time!'

Melody gave a sob. 'It was only thanks to Brett's intervention and then young David's that you did.'

'David's?' said Paul sharply.

Quickly Melody set the scene, finishing, 'So David flew at Hogge like a young panther, to defend me,' then, turning to the boy, 'Oh, but David, don't ever tackle a grown man again—for any reason! It was the bravest, most wonderful gesture, but I beg you not to think you can fell Goliaths with sling-shots! That works only in stories.'

He left his father at that, and ran to hug her. 'But I *love* you!'

For a heartbeat, she held him tightly to her, closing her eyes, savouring the moment. 'And I love you, too, my brave warrior.' But then she opened them again to meet those darker gold-flecked eyes, and her heart plummeted. She read anger there and frustration, and a hunger that reached out to her like a tongue of flame—but also something indefinable—something deeper than hunger— and gently she put the boy away, ruffling the dark hair. 'I should beat you for your foolishness,' she smiled shakily.

He gave an answering grin. 'But you wouldn't! You never, ever would!' Then, with the resilience of youth, 'May I go to Maata for a cake? . . . I do deserve it!'

'Go!' she smiled, the love plain in her eyes. 'Have a

dozen . . . But don't make yourself sick!' She watched
him race off, then turned back to the others. 'Aunt Bee,
what would I do without you? And Patrick, too.' Then
blue eyes met brown. 'Paul . . . I haven't even thanked
you for saving my life.'

Again that careful mask. 'Not quite as dramatic as that,
surely.'

'Had I gone with Luther, it would have amounted to
the same thing.'

'Would it? I wonder.'

'Paul!'

'The man obviously knew you well—how well I don't
wish to know. However, he was on my property and
obviously intended harm to both yourself and David.
Brett's condition was self-evident. I take exception to men
who do violence to blind men, women and children. There
is nothing more that need be said.'

'You must let me explain. The man's dangerous. He
has already spent a fortune to track me down. He'll not
give up now.'

Something flickered in the deep-set eyes that belied his
cool tone as he advised, 'Then I suggest you resolve your
lovers' quarrel in some suitably public place under appropriate chaperonage. Now, however, another knight that
fights under your colours is awaiting your ministrations—
and I have a farm to run!'

Interpreting Beatrice's frantic glance, Patrick asked,
'You'll not object to another pair of hands?'

Paul gave him a searching look, but then nodded and
turned wordlessly for the door, leaving the other man to
follow.

When they had gone, Beatrice took her niece's hands
reassuringly. 'Patrick will talk to him, and later, when the
time's right, we'll tell him the whole story. At the moment,
though, our Mr Savage is suffering from the after-effects
of a large dose of fear, anger, and jealousy—all in about
that order, and a pretty lethal combination it is. There's
no cure but time, so I suggest you take up his last
suggestion. Young Brett showed remarkable courage in

attacking someone he couldn't see, though a high degree of stupidity, also. Go to him, child, and give him the praise due. This new brother-sister relationship is something that has to be borne in mind, and will take a great deal of thought from both of you, but it wasn't a brother that attacked that man Hogge today!'

Melody nodded, biting her lip. 'I must talk to him, Aunt Bee. I know I must talk to him. But I don't know what to say! When Hogge attacked him so brutally— knowing that he was blind—I wanted to throw myself between them, to protect him . . . as I'd protect David . . . but not Paul. The—The feelings would be different. Even if Brett weren't blind, he's different . . . so gentle, so tender and loving . . . I'd always want to protect him.'

'And when Paul is gentle—and don't tell me that there haven't been times?' Beatrice enquired softly, and caught the tiniest lift of the mouth.

'Oh, with someone like Paul, one feels comforted by his gentleness, protected by his strength. One fights along-side him, even kills for him, as in the Maori attack. And if he falls, as then, one feels fury, not fear.' She broke off then, aware that she had revealed too much. 'But men like Paul don't need women as soul-mates, only as bed-wenches!' The bitterness came through. 'I'll go to see Brett. At least I'm needed there!'

And needed she was, for in the days that followed, only she knew that slowly—so slowly it was like a knife twisting in both their hearts—Brett was regaining his sight. It began that first afternoon when she had gone to him and seen him lying so still, eyes closed, on top of the narrow bed. He had turned as the door opened, and smiled. 'Melody?'

She had run to him, flinging herself on his chest and murmuring his name, scolding, 'Oh, you fool, Brett! You sweet fool! You should never have attacked Hogge—or anyone else for that matter! But I love you for it, I really do. Your selflessness and your bravery . . . '

He had put her away gently, the lean fingers firm on

her arms. 'And I love you too, Melody mine . . . but not as a brother . . . And that is my affliction!'

'Brett . . . '

'No. Listen to me. When I'm fit to travel, I'll be returning home. Not to Carolina: there's nothing left for me there except a war I'm not fit for: not even to Natchez, for it represents a past I can no longer live with. It taught me that slavery has a quite different meaning from that which I knew. Patrick knows someone in San Francisco, he tells me—a friend who disappeared into the goldfields with others of '49. Maybe I'll go there . . . I just don't know. I know only that I have to get away from here.'

Melody studied that handsome face, the finely chiselled cheekbones, the slightly flared nostrils and full, mobile mouth, and her heart twisted painfully. 'Shall I ever . . . see you again?'

'Perhaps . . . one day.' He smiled, a little crookedly, but it was a smile nevertheless. 'I've seen the light in more ways than one today, my love. Many men take a lifetime; some never achieve it.'

'Do you still see a lessening of the blackness, even now that you've rested?'

He turned towards the window. 'There. Yes, but I'm still blind, and a blind man is no use to you at all. Even were we not related, I'd not stay, though there was a time—a lifetime ago it seems now—when I thought differently.' He swallowed hard. 'Go now and join the others. I'd like to be alone for a while.'

It was the following day when he turned at her entrance, smiling, and saying her name, and then, 'You are in a pale dress! You're out of mourning.' She had sobbed aloud, clinging to him, feeling his tears mingling with hers as she called to the others. They had crowded in, even Paul, his voice harsh with emotion, questioning, probing, holding up objects. 'Still just shapes, but I can see you . . . a shape . . . grey . . . a light shirt . . . holding something!'

Another day and night, Maata and Melody taking it in turns to sit with him. Then that final evening, over a week after Luther Hogge had viciously clubbed him to the ground, Brett had turned from the window as Melody came in and his eyes had roved over her from head to toe while she held her breath. But then he had spun away, and she had gone to him in fear, seeing the tears on his cheeks, and terror closed over her heart. 'Brett? Oh no! Don't tell me it's gone! Don't tell me you can't see my dress! It's an oyster chiffon, a ball-dress. I wore it especially to show you.'

He turned again, the ice-blue eyes moving over every sweet curve of her face, and this time he did not attempt to hide the anguish in their depths. 'Melody . . . sweet . . . sister!' His trembling fingers came up unerringly to touch her cheek. 'Had I known you would be so unutterably lovely, I'd have left long before this! You see . . . I never thought it possible that I could love you more than I did! Sapphire eyes, and hair blacker than a raven's wing, skin soft as a breath of summer wind with the bloom of the first musk rose.' He took a deep, ragged breath. 'This is something that I must live with, sister mine . . . But not here . . . not now. I'm simply not strong enough.'

Melody felt her heart must surely break. There was a desolation such as she thought she could never feel again since her father's death as she put her arms about him. 'Brett . . . Shall I always love you?'

'Always,' he said shakily. 'As I shall love you . . . or work at loving you . . . as a brother should. It may well take the rest of my life!' His mouth moving over hers—for the last time, they both knew—held no incest, only the bitter-sweet longing for what—surely—should have been.

CHAPTER TWENTY-ONE

'WHAT THE HELL!' came the furious voice from the doorway. 'Or would you like it put in more explicit terms?' Paul Savage stood there, the scar blazing, an angry gash across the grey features, the leashed tension in him a physical thing as he stepped into the room to confront them.

With a curse, the agony of separation still cutting deep, Brett pushed Melody aside, spun, and slammed his fist into his cousin's jaw. As a stunned Paul stumbled across the room, Brett stated, 'The first time I wanted to do that, I was eight years old!'

'You really *can* see!'

'Enough to make my own way out of here. I'll be leaving tomorrow.'

'Brett! So soon?'

He smiled down at her, and there was a wealth of meaning on his face as he said, 'The sooner the better, don't you think?'

Melody studied her hands, clasped before her, hiding her confusion, but Paul had already caught the crackle in the air, and his tone was surprisingly gentle. 'You don't have to go, Brett, but I think it would be for the best, under the circumstances. I'll get one of the men to take you to Wanganui.'

'That won't be necessary. Patrick and Beatrice said that they would accompany me when I was ready, and bring back the supplies you needed a week ago.'

On impulse, knowing that it had to be done even though it would break her heart, Melody said, 'That will make things easier for you, Brett, and while they're in town, they can book a passage for me on the next boat back to England.'

The silence thundered round her, and unable to meet those dark, gold-flecked eyes boring into her soul, she continued, 'I'm no longer wanted as a murderess over there. I should have returned long ago.'

'And what of Luther Hogge?' Brett asked, concernedly.

'The law will protect me, and Aunt Bee has a friend in high places.'

No sound of dissent came from Paul, and at last she forced herself to look at him, but encountered only that inscrutable mask. 'You must do as you please. You're free now, and there's nothing here to hold you. If I remember correctly, the only reason you came back from Wellington was to say goodbye. I'll talk to Patrick about it, for they'll obviously wish to accompany you.'

'No . . . Don't tell them yet. I'll tell Aunt Bee after dinner. They may have other plans.'

Again that searching look, but all he said was, 'As you wish. I came only to ask Brett if he'd like to go north with me next week, to Rotorua where the hot springs are, but that's out of the question now, so I'll leave you to your . . . discussion.' He did so, closing the door unnecessarily firmly behind him.

'Damn him!' Brett muttered, then said, 'Melody, are you doing the right thing?' Unable to take the soul-searching that his question demanded, she nodded firmly, hoping beyond hope that he would believe her.

'I'd be a fool to stay where I'm neither wanted nor needed. I'll have a good life in England,' she improvised wildly. 'Catch up with old friends, parties, soirées every week, the opera—Lord, how I've missed it all! You *do* understand, don't you? I'm a Londoner. Nowhere is the same in the whole world.'

'I once believed you could have cared for St Clare.'

'No, Brett, only for the master of St Clare, and for him I would have lived in that mausoleum and called it home, but the Fates have a way of not only tipping the scales but turning the whole thing upside-down, don't they?' She gave an over-bright smile. 'So the wheel has turned full circle. I shall return to London. Hogge is alive and well, and will soon find other lives than mine to ruin, since I shall be well protected by John Brown, who has far more power than Luther ever could, and would be able to ruin him completely if he wished. It will be almost as if this year never happened, but for the fact that I now have a brother to write to.'

'Don't!'

Before his pain, her pretence dropped and she went to him, putting her arms about him and hugging him tightly for a moment. 'I'm sorry. I'm only trying to make the best of this awful business. In time, both of us will come to terms with it, I'm sure.' She held him away, looking up at the too handsome features, realising how incredibly blue his eyes were, even more, it seemed, now that they had vision. 'I must change for dinner.'

'The dress is lovely. Thank you for allowing me to see it. I'll hold it as a memory—with all the others I have of you.'

Melody felt a tightness in her throat, knowing that there could be different kinds of love, each as strong as the other: her love for Brett as real and as strong as her love for David, for her father, and the separation would be equally as heart-breaking, with only time and space bringing a cure. 'Until dinner, then.'

'Yes, but until then I need to be alone. I've something that needs careful thought.'

When Brett appeared in the dining-room, the change in him was apparent to everyone, and Melody knew that whatever had been troubling him that afternoon had been resolved. He had dressed carefully in black jacket and trousers which tapered fashionably to the ankle, accentuating his slimness, with the white figured silk waistcoat and matching fine linen shirt making a striking contrast. He approached the table with confident tread and there was a new tautness in his jaw and a strange light in the brilliant eyes as he took his place.

David had taken to joining the family for dinner instead of eating earlier with the Maori children in the kitchen,

and he looked from one to the other, sensing an atmosphere that he didn't understand, yet knowing that he
dared not speak until spoken to.

Waiting until the wild mushroom and herb soup had
been replaced by a rich saddle of venison, Brett ventured,
'Patrick . . . You mentioned earlier that this war in
America was one that no one could win, but surely the
South will finish it quickly simply because they are fighting
to retain what they believe is a God-given right, and
therefore they would fight twice as fiercely for it.'

The Irishman grinned. 'No amount of outdated *beliefs*
in the right of the aristocracy—and a self-made aristocracy at that—to rule working people will provide the
wherewithal to enforce that right. The North can put four
men in the field to every one of the South. They have
foundries and raw materials aplenty to feed them with, to
manufacture gunpowder and cannon. What will the South
use? Will they pelt the Yankees with cotton-bales? Beat
them to death with tobacco-leaves? How about roads, or
even a good waterway system? I'll not even mention
railroads for troops and supplies . . . ' He shook his
head. 'They're fools, every one.'

Very quietly Paul asked, 'What's this leading up to,
Brett?'

Brett studied his plate, then looked up directly at
Melody, saying, 'I've decided to join the Confederate
army.' It was, at that moment, as though they were quite
alone, and the exclamations of the others were far outside
the fragile bubble in which they floated. Melody felt
everything within her cry out, wanting to cling to him,
shake him, order him not to go to what was surely his
death because of her. And he, looking into those lovely
tortured eyes said, 'Only a war is big enough.'

She understood then, and felt a deep aching, felt the
scalding tears that would not come, and nodded. And,
with acceptance, the bubble burst, the noise broke about
them.

'You're a fool!' Patrick was saying.

Beatrice expostulated, 'But you don't even believe in

slavery now . . . surely!'

Only Paul remained silent. Only he had seen and understood that agony of spirit that had passed from one to the other.

Brett gave a wry smile. 'Oh, I'm not fighting for any belief in slavery—I've seen at first hand the misery it can cause, and simply can't believe now that any one man should own another, even though the Bible itself commands, "servants obey your master". And yet I *am* a Southerner, born and raised as one of that élite, useless aristocracy who are invariably surprised if a dog they've beaten bites them, or a horse they've lashed throws them. If there must be a socially acceptable reason, say that I'm fighting for a lost cause—a dream of a yesterday that will never come again.'

'But you know nothing of war,' Patrick insisted. 'It's not a romantic duel on a green sunlit field. It's not a stirring march to the sound of fife and drum. It's spilled blood and guts, and screams and cries, and the stench of sweat and dirt and fear, and of corpses that no one has had the time to bury. It's loneliness and heartbreak and boredom, and the feeling that everyone knows what they're doing except you. In *this* damned stupid war, it's the chance of looking down the sights of your gun and seeing your brother at the other end . . . looking down his sights at you!'

'I've been protected since the age of seven,' Brett said with forced patience. 'I've been told what to do, what to wear, what to eat and even what to say to the right people at the right time. I think it's about time that ceased, don't you? I appreciate your concern, my friend—for friend and more you've proved yourself over the past months—but I think it's time I allowed you to resume your old itinerant ways.'

'You can't sidetrack me, boyo,' Patrick objected stubbornly. 'Why, you have not even the vaguest notion of warfare, of survival, and even if you can load a gun and scare hell out of the odd possum or two, you have no experience at all of killing.'

'No more than your average banker or lawyer, but I doubt that it takes much intelligence to learn.'

'None at all,' put in Paul drily. 'The only intelligence required is in knowing whether to maim or to kill your man—and if the latter, which man to kill—the innocent country boy facing you whose only crime was in being born a dozen miles too far north, or the maniac general who is ordering you to make a suicidal charge down the mouth of the enemy cannon for his own glorification. But that's all somewhat irrelevant, isn't it? You've been talking a fair amount for the past few minutes—but you've not *said* anything that counts.' Brett's smile died, and he glanced instinctively toward the girl at his side. Paul's eyes darkened. 'I suppose there isn't much to be said, after all. You're determined to find yourself a war—any war—aren't you?'

'Yes.'

Their gazes locked in an understanding that made Paul nod. 'I hope you find what you're seeking, then.'

David could contain himself no longer, not understanding all that had been said, only knowing that somehow this war they spoke of was to do with men who liked negroes and men who didn't, and with bitter memories of his arch-enemy the missionary's son, asked, 'You're not going away because of me, are you? You're not going because you know I'm a half-caste?'

'David!' Brett exclaimed, reaching across Melody to take the boy's hand clenched on the table. 'What a thing to say! No, I don't see a half-caste when I look at you. I see a young warrior who put his life in danger to save Melody and me. I see a handsome young man bred from a leader of men, born of a princess among women. No, David, I see only a friend I'm truly proud of, whatever his blood.'

David smiled, shy of the compliments, but unable to hide his pleasure. 'Well . . . I suppose if you must fight you must, but I shall miss you.' Then with the adaptability of youth. 'At least I'll have Auntie Melody to keep me company when you're gone and Papa's away.'

There was an awkward silence in the room, and Brett looked askance at Melody. It was the moment she had been dreading. She had planned to tell each of them in turn, treating them individually, but now it was too late. 'David . . . ' she began hesitatingly. 'David, love, I shall be leaving, too. Not tomorrow or the next day, but very soon.'

The boy froze, disbelief in the dark eyes, gold-flecked like his father's, but without the buffers of life that enabled the man to hide his deepest emotion. 'You can't!'

She swallowed the lump in her throat. 'David, I must. It's time for me . . . and the others . . . to go back home . . . to allow you and your father to get on with your normal life . . . the real life you had before . . . before . . . '

'But I thought you came to be my new mother!'

'Oh, David!' The tears were there as she reached for him.

He flung off the arm that would have drawn him close and pushed his chair back, rising violently. 'I don't need a new mother anyway. I don't need anyone, especially you!' With a harsh sob, he ran from the room.

'David!'

'Leave him!' ordered Paul, the anger like steel in his voice. 'You've said all there is to say.'

'I must go to him . . . explain . . . '

'No, sweeting,' Beatrice said gently. 'I'll talk to him: I'm a more accomplished liar than you!'

Patrick looked uncomfortable. 'I think I'll take some air.'

'You, too, think I did wrong!' said Melody, stormily. 'You think it was ill timed. Well, of course it was, but I could not continue the deceit and lies any longer. The boy had to know sooner or later. Go out and take a breath of air. You can! You can all back away from this intolerable situation. Even Brett can find a war to join in!'

Paul said her name quietly, attempting to break in on her tirade, but turning on him, she blazed, 'It's all your fault, so don't utter platitudes! You forced these circumstances on me. You dragged me here in the first place. I never wanted to come. I never wanted to love your damned country or your son, or . . . ' She broke off, breathing hard, fighting back the tears, magnificent in her fury, eyes bright with pain, colour high. 'I'm glad I'm leaving! Do you understand, Paul Savage? Glad!' With a sob, she sprang to her feet, sending her chair crashing backwards, and ran from the room.

In the ensuing silence, Maata came in to clear the table for the next course, took a sweeping glance round, and retreated hurriedly.

Patrick gave a cough, and received a glare from Beatrice.

'I'm inclined to appreciate her point,' she said to no one in particular. 'But I think she's making a mistake.' Not bothering to explain her last remark, she rose calmly and went to right the fallen chair. 'I'll have a word with her, and leave you men to talk of your personal wars.' She found Melody sobbing into her pillow, and went immediately to gather the girl close. 'Hush, sweeting. Hush. No one is worth your tears.'

'But Brett's going away to get himself killed because he loves me. David is breaking his tiny, brave, wonderful heart because he loves me—and Luther Hogge has turned into some kind of monster because he loves me! What kind of person am I, Aunt Bee? I'm not strong enough to stop it all happening!'

Beatrice gave a small sigh, smoothing back the tumbled hair. 'Brett will fight his war and will find whatever oblivion—or acceptance—he needs while doing it, and he'll survive because Nature has a strange affection for fools. David has the resilience of youth and will recover in time. As for Luther Hogge . . . there is nothing on God's earth you could have done to prevent that chain of events. What he feels is a world away from love. He saw a beautiful, priceless, and to all intents and purposes unobtainable, *objet d'art*, and has developed an unswerving desire for it.'

'I wish I had been born a man!' Melody spluttered

mutinously, then said with a tremulous smile, 'But then I might have been a Brett or a David or a Luther . . . ' Drawing a deep breath, she gently released herself. 'I'm a fool to take on so! I should be thinking of young David, not of myself. Would you go and find him, Aunt Bee, and try to explain? He must feel as if we are all deserting him. I'd give anything . . . ' Then she shook her head. 'No, not anything. I'll not endure Paul Savage's overbearing arrogance and pride a moment longer than I have to. How dare he be angry with *me*, when it's all his fault!'

Wisely, Beatrice remained silent, contenting herself with a quick, comforting squeeze of the girl's shoulders before leaving.

Melody took her time in unlooping the many buttons down the front of her bodice and slipping out of the tiered petticoat and other undergarments, the anger and despair still in her, but also a confusion of other emotions such as she had never known. Splashing the cool water from the washbasin over her face, she unpinned and brushed out her hair, pulling on a filmy, lace-collared black silk peignoir she had purchased in New York. 'I won't allow him to hurt me!' she vowed. 'I shall make my own way. I can even take care of Aunt Bee, if I have to . . . ' She smiled as O'Shaughnessy's craggy features crossed her mind. 'Though I've a feeling I won't need to! I'll be alone then . . . Still, better alone than dictated to by that . . . Savage!'

As though echoing her thoughts, there came a sharp double knock—not Aunt Bee, for she would have entered without knocking, always sure of a loving welcome—and certainly not Patrick or Brett. 'Go away, Paul!' But he entered anyway, and she turned on him, reiterating, 'Go away! There's no more to be said.'

'There's much to be said.'

'No! I'm leaving. Not tomorrow, though heaven knows it's tempting enough, but on the next boat to England. Now . . . I've no wish to talk with you . . . and you're in a lady's room when she is in a state of undress.

Please leave.'

'Why *not* leave tomorrow?' He ignored her statement. 'You could follow your precious Brett to the front line. You could play nurse, and he could play with his fantasies!'

'Stop it! Brett has more heart than you'll ever have; more compassion, more love, and,. what is more, he is a gentleman through and through. His love for me has a purity you'll never know.'

'Purity!' Paul snapped. 'That isn't my impression. And you revel in this touch-me-not attitude, don't you, Mrs Van der Veer? You enjoy carrying your banner of scalps aloft, but heaven help anyone who dares to call your bluff! When your boorish friend came too close, you actually put a bullet into him. God, your husband must have lived in terror of you!'

'Don't!' Melody cried, covering her ears, terrified of the anger that ran like cold steel through his words, yet feeling the pain of the knife that he twisted within himself as well as her.

'Maybe it's as well, after all, that you are leaving, for who knows how many more of your past conquests are likely to appear? Perhaps even the supposedly dead Van der Veer will rise from the grave and come to claim you! I've heard of ladies—and I use the term loosely—who prefer to call themselves widowed rather than deserted.'

'No! Hugh is dead, and Luther . . . ' She turned away, shutting out the hideous memory, 'was dead . . . '

But that merciless voice cut in, 'An excellent performance, but I've seen better. You're no trembling virgin. You're a married woman who, after her husband's death, assuming he is dead, went to live for, what . . . six months or more? with a man of Luther Hogge's character. And then New York . . . too brief a halt there even for a grieving widow as obviously in need of comfort as yourself! The long journey south? I know the country, girl. I know what can happen to two women travelling alone . . . Or was your aunt's chaperonage as lax as it has been here? Then . . . my dear helpless cousin Brett

arouses all your finer feelings. How long with him while
not knowing his true identity? A month? Two? An experienced married woman would have to move fast to supplant
the delectable Celine.'

Melody spun, sapphire eyes blazing. 'That's enough!
You can believe what filthy lies you like of me, but not
Brett!'

His eyes narrowed. 'So it was Brett! Do you add incest
to your list? You were cool enough on the auction block,
God knows! Did you think he'd raise an army to free
you—or had his attentions palled by then and you were
on the hunt for bigger game?'

Melody's fist came up, but was caught in fingers of
steel and twisted behind her back, dragging her hard
against him. 'No, you don't! Not a second time! I've been
a fool over you. For a time I almost believed in your
disdain, but now I know it for what it was, an act. How
many more do you have in your repertoire? What an
actress you are! Your aunt once intimated that for a short
time she trod the boards. Did you join her as juvenile
bait? I've heard of it happening. Did even the poor
besotted Van der Veer marry used goods—even at that
tender age?'

This last was too much, his accusations cutting too
deep for anger, shocking her to her very core so that the
fight went out of her. A deep shudder ran through her
frame and her head dropped on to his chest. 'Yes,' she
whispered brokenly. 'If you believe that, you'll believe
anything.' The eyes that she raised to his eclipsed her
ashen face, naked with the agony that was equal to his
own as they tore at each other. 'Yes, of course I've lain
with other men . . . I've lost count of how many! Is
that what you want to hear? Does that satisfy you? I'm
leaving soon. Won't you let me go now?'

'No!' The word came out as a harsh groan expressing
his deep pain. 'No!' Almost against his will his mouth
descended on hers, strangely gentle, yet with an aching
longing that went beyond bearing. 'No!' he echoed. 'I've
waited too long.'

She cried out his name, wrenching her mouth away, fighting the memory of those sensual lips and lean hands. 'Please don't! It's not true, none of it! I beg you! There's been no one . . . no one!'

'Not today. Not this week . . . this month . . . this year? Liar!' His voice was almost a sob. 'Liar!'

He would never, ever believe the truth now, and Melody felt the anger and desire in him as she struggled against his restraining grip. 'Oh, Paul!' she murmured against his mouth. 'You're wrong! You're so . . . wrong.' But again that mouth was stopping all coherent thought as his arms crushed her to him and he kissed her with a passion, mingled with his anger, such as she had never experienced. She caught at his hair, tugging, fighting both him and the fire that raged within her, but it was futile, for in truth the battle had been lost in that instant of surrender before he had swept her into his arms. She was spinning in a whirlpool of sensation and felt her body mould itself to the whole demanding length of him. Treacherous body!

His arms tightened even more, so that she cried out— and as her lips parted, she felt his tongue ravaging the inner recesses of her mouth. Paul felt the tears, and at their taste immediately lifted his head, searching her eyes.

'Please . . . Please don't.' But her eyes betrayed her, and, instead, he kissed her again, her lids, her cheeks, temples, chin and throat, then returned to her mouth, moving over it softly now, murmuring soft words in an alien tongue.

'I've waited for you,' he said against her lips. 'Too long now. Far too long.' And when he swept her into his arms it seemed that too long was all of her life, and that this moment was the culmination of all those half fearful dreams. Sure fingers removed the peignoir, yet she was aware of it only when a warm hand cupped her breast. Again she murmured a protest, which turned into a moan as those fingers began their own tender torment. His teeth moved to her earlobe, nipping gently and the tiny pain was transmitted down to her breast, its peak tortured with sensual expertise. The sensations blazed inside her, creating an ache, a throbbing, as she felt herself lifted and laid down on the bed, that steel-in-velvet form never leaving her.

Pinioned beneath him, Melody resisted one more time, crying out his name, but it emerged not as a protest but as a litany.

'Too long,' he repeated, and she felt his hands moving over her and into her. 'Did they teach you this?' he asked huskily. 'And this? And this?' She cried out at the agonising worship, and as she felt his need of her she was lost, her limbs yielding as they had always wanted to.

He moved and her body opened to him. He said her name, lashing himself with his need of her, and the sick thought of all the others who had sunk into that velvet pool. Almost angrily he thrust—and his own shock echoed her soft cry of pain. He froze, but the fire within had already consumed all remorse, and he moved again, but gently now, kissing the tears from her closed lids, tasting the salt on her mouth, saying her name over and over. When it was done, he moved aside slowly, yet still retained that touch of flesh to flesh along the length of them. He went to speak. 'Melody, why . . . ?' He received his second shock as he met those deep sapphire eyes and saw the pain mingled with dying passion—and a despair such as he had never imagined possible.

'Leave me,' she said. 'I never want you to touch me again.'

'Melody . . . '

'You were my first, Paul Savage, and you took me in anger and lust and believing in your own jealous fantasies. I had dreamed . . . all these months . . . perhaps for years, how that first time would be.' She rolled away, denying the passion and the soaring pleasure that he had brought her. 'Go! Get out of here!'

With a sick heart, he rose and dressed. He turned once at the door, searching for some small surrender in that tightly curled frame, speaking her name again softly.

'Go!' she reiterated, the hurt and anger coming through.

When Beatrice came in, without knocking as usual, to

say goodnight her eyes first went to the peignoir crumpled on the floor and then, in horror, to the girl's naked form curled defensively on the bed. 'Oh, love!' she choked, running to her side and gathering her close.

Melody stopped her by straightening with a tremulous smile. 'It's all right, Aunt Bee. It's really all right. But you're going to have to tell him. Find him and tell him everything . . . Please.'

'I'll tell him!' Beatrice vowed. 'I'll tell him that and more! When I've finished with Paul Savage, he'll consider that last Maori attack a picnic!'

'No . . . I told you, Aunt Bee . . . I'm all right. He didn't hurt me.' Then, with a shaky laugh, 'Well . . . not much! Oh, Aunt Bee, is it always going to be like this? Is it always like this between a man and a woman?'

Misunderstanding, Beatrice assured, 'No, my poor love, it won't hurt like that again.'

But Melody shook her head violently. 'No . . . No, that's nothing. That lasted but a moment, and he was so gentle afterwards, when he realised . . . No, I mean the loving and hating all at the same time. Oh, Aunt Bee, what am I going to do? I love him so much!' There! It was out! It was the first time she had admitted it aloud, that which she knew had been in her heart for so long.

Gently Beatrice smoothed back the raven hair. Words were unnecessary. No answer was possible. She rocked the girl gently, then felt a shuddering breath, only then saying, 'You must stay, you know.'

'No!' Melody cried vehemently, pulling away. 'We must go! I don't want to feel like this for anyone, not ever again. I want it to be safe and gentle and calm. I want a lake, not a sea. You must, please, make arrangements for us when you go to Wanganui with Brett. You must get me a passage on the next boat home.'

'*Is* it home?' Beatrice asked. Then, without waiting for a reply, she said, 'I'll talk to Paul. Don't worry about anything.'

She found him in the study . . . and hesitated in the doorway—shocked by the dejection and utter misery apparent in the man before her, bowed over the desk, his head in his arms. She spoke his name softly, and as he lifted his head, for once that polite mask did not come down over those ruggedly handsome features.

'You know.'

She nodded. 'We must speak frankly, Paul Savage.'

'I'll marry her, of course,' he interrupted.

Her lips quirked upwards. 'She may not want you . . . But before we discuss the question of love versus duty, there's a story I think you ought to hear . . . '

It was late, very late, when he came again to her room. Melody had washed, changed the sheet that showed undeniable proof of her lost virginity and put on a high-necked cambric nightgown. She had brushed out the tangled hair and crawled into bed, her whole body aching from his lovemaking, yet concealing a far deeper ache in her heart. 'Go away!' she said, turning her head from him.

'Melody . . . We must talk.'

At that she sat up, leaning against the bed-head, legs tucked sideways as he came to sit on the side of the bed. 'I don't think there's any more to be said. Aunt Bee obviously found you and filled in some . . . I thought necessary . . . background information. I have nothing to add.'

'I don't want you to leave Windhaven.'

'Oh, you don't!' She felt the slow anger rising within her again. 'I see! Now that I'm not the coldly calculating man-hunter you took me for, I'm good enough to grace your home. On the other hand, I'm also . . . used goods . . . by society's standards, a fallen woman, so that makes me available I suppose to be used as your . . . your doxy!' His hand came out. 'No! Don't touch me! I've had enough of your overbearingness. I won't listen to you!' Hating him and loving him all at the same time. 'I've fought alongside you in a Maori attack and nursed you for days afterwards. I've cleaned your house and even hoed your damned fields! I've been a loving companion to your son, I've listened to your dreams, entertained your friends and played spy to your enemies. I've seen you drunk and stone-cold sober, angry and laughing, sick and well. Paul, I've done everything that any man could ask of a wife—and more—but I will not be your whore!'

'But would you be my wife?'

'You can't ask it of me,' she ranted on. 'I'd sooner leave all this that I love; I've already taken that step by telling Aunt Bee . . . What did you say?' Her incredulous eyes lifted to his and saw something in those dark depths that she had never dreamed of.

He was unsmiling as he caught hold of her shoulders. 'Melody . . . I'm asking you to marry me.'

'But . . . '

'I love you,' he said simply. 'Nothing else seems to matter beyond that.'

But still she could not believe the sincerity she heard in his words and shook her head. 'It matters to me. It matters that you raped me, and then, just because of some belated feeling of honour—or a lecture from Aunt Bee on duty before devotion—decided to offer me respectability.'

'I've said I love you. Isn't that enough?'

'Once—but not now. A few weeks ago I'd have rejoiced to hear those words because you might possibly have meant them, but not now. Now, I know that my standards are far higher than yours. You're simply making your ex-slave a legalised bed-wench. I want—no—I demand more than that. Loyalty and trust, companionship, and the equality that comes from sharing hopes and fears and decision-making, the good times and the bad. I'm sorry, Paul.' There were tears in her eyes as she surrendered her last hope of happiness. 'I simply don't want the kind of love you're offering. It's not enough.'

'Is that your last word on it?' There was a deep sadness in the soft question, a confusion that she never thought to hear from this arrogantly confident leader of men—and so she did not believe it. Mutely she nodded, unable to fight her own pain, holding tightly on to her self-control. 'I'll bid you goodnight, then.' She nodded again, averting her face, and heard the door close softly.

'Oh, you fool!' her heart cried. 'You proud, stubborn fool!'

In the morning, however, there were other things to think about: the preparations for Brett's journey . . . and the absence of David.

'I tried to talk to him yesterday,' Beatrice said worriedly, 'but he wouldn't listen. It's not like reasoning with a young adult. Being so independent, such a fighter, one forgets he's only seven years old.'

'He'll be back,' Paul reassured her—a subdued Paul this morning, with more on his mind than a missing son who made a habit of wandering off. 'He'll be taking some thinking time. There's an old disused hut where the stream meets the Wanganui, and he often goes there when he wants to be alone. I'm sorry, Brett, he should have come to say goodbye, but possibly you may pass him on your way to the jetty.'

Brett nodded absently. 'Yes . . . of course . . . ' But his eyes were only for Melody. She was pale-faced and there were dark rings beneath the lovely eyes that bespoke a sleepless night, and his heart went out to her. Would they ever meet again? he wondered. Would he ever learn to love her without feeling that wrench deep inside?

Beatrice, too, seemed quiet this morning, and when it was time to go, she gave Melody a close hug. 'We'll be back in a few days, and then you and I can have a long talk about our future. The world is your oyster, sweeting.'

'And you're my pearl,' responded Melody. 'More precious than diamonds, more constant that the sea.'

'Enough gush!' laughed her aunt, always embarrassed by emotion. 'Coming, Patrick? Brett?'

The Irishman put a huge hand on Melody's shoulder. 'A few days,' he promised. 'And when you have that talk I want a say in it, you hear? I don't trust either of you to roam your own back-yard alone, let alone the world. Even if it's only a chaperon you'll be using me for.'

'I've a feeling you're far more than that, Patrick
O'Shaughnessy,' she stated, then turned to Brett, her smile
dying. There was nothing—nothing at all—that could be
said. She could not even speak his name, but went quietly
into his open arms.

Briefly he clasped her tight, crushing her to him as if
he would fuse them, while his free hand caressed her hair.
Then they stepped apart. 'Walk away,' he said. 'Don't
look back.'

One last hungry gaze, then she turned and walked back
into the house, back rigid, eyes burning.

Within minutes Paul joined her, and she knew that the
others had gone, but she could not face him, or speak of
Brett leaving. 'I'm worried about David,' she admitted
instead.

'He'll be all right. He's just seeking attention. He'll do
anything to keep you here. Once you're gone, he'll get
over it. Children do, though of course it will take time.
Things will be the same as before—at least as far as
David's concerned.'

She hesitated, but could not bring herself to confess her
own feelings, or the emptiness that she felt whenever she
thought of separation. 'You're probably right. However,
Aunt Bee and Patrick won't be back for a few days, and
David will surely return for dinner at the latest. I'll talk
to him then.'

'As you wish. In the meantime, there are still fields to
patrol, fences to mend. I'll call in at the hut later this
evening. Melody . . . '

'I'll read a little. There's plenty to keep me busy if I
become bored,' she said, forestalling any further conversation, deliberately avoiding his eyes. 'I'll find something
of Shakespeare—he seemed to prefer fantasy to reality.'

'Perhaps that will suit you . . . But there's only reality
here, Melody: cold, harsh reality. The land. The Maoris—
Christian and otherwise. The constant battle with man
and Nature alike.'

'I'm not evading reality, Paul, I'm taking a well-earned
rest from it, or did nothing of what Aunt Bee told you

leave any impression at all? I'm not a simpering débutante
fresh from her coming-out party; I'm the one who shot a
man, not one but many, defending first my honour and
then my life and yours. I'm the one who had to stand on
the auction block, stripped by a hundred eyes, bought
and sold like a piece of meat. How much more reality do
you want? Oh, leave me alone! Just give me some peace.
There was a time when I could find it at the piano. It
helped me over the death of my parents, made even
Hogge's presence almost bearable, and comforted me
briefly when a prisoner in this alien land. Please, Paul.
You've surely no need to bait me now, and will have no
opportunity later. Can't you just allow me the last few
days without this onslaught?'

He moved forward, about to speak, but then changed
his mind. 'I'll be out at the bluff to the north,' he stated,
'then I'll circle down to the river and back that way. If
you need me, you can send one of Maata's brothers; he
knows the route. I'll probably bring young David back
with me. You can tell him of your reality, though I can't
guarantee that a seven-year-old will understand all your
reasons for deserting him.'

'That's unfair!' But he was gone, the front door
slamming behind him.

Almost an hour passed, with Melody trying in vain to
concentrate on the Bard, while the word 'desertion' washed
back and forth within her head. 'I'm not! It's not like
that at all!' But the deep knowledge that it was precisely
what she was doing tore her apart, and she was glad of
the respite of the sudden commotion outside. As she came
out on the porch, Te Whatitoa and six of his men reined
in before her.

The war chief's features were grim, and without preli-
minaries he ordered, 'You must come with us, Mihi Van
der Veer.' He followed his words with a sweeping gesture
of his hand. One of the men pulled forward a horse he
had been leading, and, tied across the saddle, a white
man.

'Te Whatitoa! What's the meaning of this? Let him down!'

'Gladly,' the man agreed. 'He contaminates a good horse!' With a slash of his knife he cut the man loose, allowing him to fall to the ground.

The prisoner had been roughly handled, but appeared to bear no permanent injury, and quickly Melody went to help him to his feet. The stench of unwashed flesh and filthy clothing only served to accentuate the man's physical appearance. Lank-haired, ferret-eyed and snaggle-toothed, the creature was a typical denizen of the lower orders who frequent wharves and slums the world over.

'He was caught at Te Tuhi Landing by some of my cousins from the Mangatoa *pa*. He'd been drinking, and gave one of the young girls cause to seek help,' the chief explained, tight-lipped. 'He had a message for you, Mihi Van der Veer, and this . . . ' From his belt he pulled out a piece of material, and handed it to her.

'Why, it's . . . it's . . . ' Ashen-faced, Melody stared up at him, not wanting to believe the evidence before her. It's the sleeve of David's shirt!'

The warrior nodded. 'And the message, *kuri*?' he growled at the man.

The derelict sniffed, wiping his nose on his sleeve. 'You ain't got no reason to call me a dog, you painted savage! I'm a white man, and I got rich friends, I have.'

'The message,' Melody demanded, barely able to keep from tearing the news from that ugly mouth.

'My rich friend, the one with the boy, he said to tell you he'd meet the next boat, and the next, but after that the boy would vanish. "Off the face of the earth" he said. I'n you met him all alone, the kid wouldn't get hurt, but you bring just one person and you'll not see the brat again. So you gotta meet him alone, and you gotta be there in time. He seems to think this half-caste brat is pretty important to you.'

Melody closed her eyes for an instant, and gently Te Whatitoa told her, 'It will be well. We shall send a man

for Paul, and then my men and I will go with you to meet
this man.'

'No, I must go alone,' Melody argued. 'He means what
he says. Luther Hogge is a vicious animal in human guise,
and he'd kill David with neither a second thought nor a
care.'

'Rawiri is my blood,' the Maori replied evenly.

'But he's my . . . I love him as a son!' Then, with a
flash of inspiration, she said, 'Patrick and Aunt Bee will
be in Wanganui shortly. If I got there before Luther was
expecting me, I might be able to find them. I don't know
how they could help, but . . . Oh, my friend, can you
get me to town before the steamer he's expecting?'

He glanced down at the tight-bodiced morning dress
with its many layers of petticoats. 'There is a war canoe
at my *pa*. Can you take a hard ride and then the canoe
down-river? My men are the best on the river.'

'Ten minutes,' she stated, turning to run into the house.
Selecting one of her lightest blouses and least restricting
newly-cut-down skirts that revealed several inches of ankle
wearing neither stays nor petticoats, she hurried back to
join them, finding a horse already saddled for her. One of
the few Maori bands to use horses, they were formidable
on their restive half-wild mounts, and she was glad that
she could call on such allies. She immediately noticed the
absence of the pariah who had given her the news of
David's abduction, and at her query, Te Whatitoa gave a
shrug.

'He was only a messenger, and not worth soiling our
hands by killing, so we turned him loose. He has no horse
and can attempt to walk back to Wanganui.'

'But that's impossible! He'll never survive without a
canoe, or arms, or any form of protection.'

'It is not for us to say who the gods will favour. Would
you have him come with us and report like a fawning dog
back to his master on arrival?'

Melody drew a deep breath, accepting his judgment.
'Let's ride.'

The man nodded approval, noting the girl's figure

revealing yet entirely practical outfit. His friend, Paul, was lucky indeed to have found another woman as beautiful and courageous as the first; one who would fight alongside him in battle and, as now, put her own life in jeopardy for his child—a child she had almost, he knew, referred to as *her* son. 'One of my men will go with Maata's brother to find Paul and tell him the story, but we must waste no more time ourselves.'

Melody swung easily up to the back of the prancing horse, and with a gesture the war chief wheeled his mount and set off at a gallop, leaving the others to stream out behind him.

They pushed their animals to the limit to reach the fortressed village, and moments later Melody saw the beautiful *waka taua*, the war canoe. Even in the stress of the moment, she could wonder at the exquisite craftsmanship that had gone into this work of art, with its tall carved stern and defiant prow. This canoe was of *kauri* wood, made in three sections, and over thirty feet long. Needing no command, Te Whatitoa's men took their places, took up the six-foot-long paddles, and when Melody was settled in the hollow centre section, moved out into the river.

The moment the canoe was into the current, the war chief gave a sharp command, and, as one, the men bent their golden torsos and the paddles bit into the water, shooting the great craft ahead with the speed of a dolphin. If her first canoe-ride with Maata's brother had unnerved her, this suicidal race against time set her heart leaping to her throat. Clinging tightly to the sides, she closed her eyes and prayed as the green mansions of the forest flew by. The journey seemed unending, and she wondered whether she would ever regain her equilibrium again. The men paddled unceasingly, and showed the strain that their screaming muscles had been put under only when their leader finally announced, 'Wanganui!' and the last bend in the river revealed their destination.

Before they rounded that bend, however, they pulled into the bank, and at Melody's enquiring glance, Te

392 A SAVAGE PRIDE

Whatitoa gave a thin smile. 'If you wish to announce your arrival to the whole town, we can certainly take a war canoe and a full crew of armed warriors right up to the jetty. I think, though, that it would be best if we *all* faded into the background. I have a cousin who owns a trading schooner, and who will provide us with clothing and information. *You* must not be seen until you are expected, *kui*, unless your friend and aunt can find the Hog-man first. You are not the kind of woman who could pass without notice, but in European clothes my men and I become just another group of "friendlies" in town.'

Melody put her hand on the smooth brown arm. 'We will find him, won't we? We will save David.'

He smiled down at her, yet the smile never quite reached his eyes. '*Iti noa ana, he pito mata*. It means literally "It is only a morsel, but at least it has not been cooked." You would say, "Where there is life there is hope." We shall do our utmost best to find Rawiri, and when we do, this man Hog will wish he had never come to New Zealand.'

'But now I must find Aunt Bee and Patrick. If we can't find Hogge first, I'll have to go one stop up-river to catch the steamboat and arrive as expected. Patrick can be in hiding when I meet Hogge and follow us.'

'As we shall, in every doorway and behind every shadow along his way. Now I shall go to my cousin's schooner and you to your aunt. Stay there with her. You have three hours before the boat arrives; two and a half if you are to board it at the first landing up-river. *Kia tupato te haere*—Go carefully.'

'You too, my friend. I feel safer knowing that you are in the shadows.'

With a nod he gestured to his men, and leaving two to guard the canoe and disguise it with branches and ferns, he melted into the bush, leaving Melody to make her way into town. It would raise comment for a white woman to appear escorted by a Maori male—any Maori, let alone a man like Te Whatitoa!

Feeling very alone and suddenly vulnerable, she walked

the half-mile into town, her shadow going before her, giving her the stature she wished she possessed. 'I will find you, David, love,' she murmured. 'And when I do, I'll promise anything, anything, to ensure your safety.' Her throat felt dry. 'Yes, even to leaving you and everything else I love, and accompanying that animal back to England. Oh, David, will you ever understand?' Miserably, she thought, 'If your father can't, how can I expect *you* to? I love you both so much, yet neither of you will ever know it now.' Drawing a deep breath, she lengthened her stride. It was no good dwelling on the past, or even on the unknown future. She had to make all haste to find Patrick and Aunt Bee. 'Dear God, let me be in time,' she prayed aloud, and then, in a smaller voice, offered up a similar prayer to Rangi-nui-e-tu-nei, the Sky Father, the primal father of the seventy gods of the Maori pantheon, admitting, 'After all, I need all the help I can get!'

CHAPTER TWENTY-TWO

THE GODS HAD decided to favour the loving and beloved that day. Beatrice was at the second hotel that Melody entered, and after hearing the news, immediately sent a young Maori boy in search of Patrick, who arrived a bare twenty minutes later. The Irishman's brow was like thunder as he listened to her story, pacing the floor as she spoke, and slamming his giant fist into the palm of his hand. 'We'll find the lad, I promise you.' Echoing the Maori chief's sentiments, he swore, 'When I get my hands on that man, he'll need more than a surgeon to put his face back together again! Stay here, and I'll get back as soon as I can.'

After an hour and more combing back alleys and bars in vain, Patrick saw Luther Hogge disembarking from one of the dozens of trading schooners moored along the waterfront. He had already picked out some of Te Whatitoa's men, for even in the ill-assorted European garb worn by most of the 'friendlies' about town, they could not hide their true identity—though it often took one warrior to recognise another. It was with confidence, therefore, that Patrick approached the Maori leaning too casually against the wall of a tavern. 'Te Whatitoa's man?' The other stared at him, nothing in the rugged features showing that he had understood, yet he had noted the slight dilation of the pupils and the fractional tightening of the jaw. 'M'name's O'Shaughnessy. Do you know Lady Davenport? Mrs Van der Veer?' Then, in frustration, 'Dammit, man, your chief's nephew, Rawiri as you call him, is in mortal danger from that fat man over there, and you stand there playing Wooden Indian! Where the hell's Te Whatitoa?'

The man straightened. 'Te Whatitoa near. You want me follow Hog-man?'

'The saints be praised! Yes, you and one of your equally talkative mates, and wherever the Hog stops, you stick with him and send your mate to me. I'm at the Queen Victoria Hotel. You know the place?'

'Kuini Wikitoria good woman . . . Rotten hotel . . . I know the place.'

Patrick raised his eyes to heaven. 'If you people ever decide to take over and stand for government, our diplomats will have to re-think their whole approach. You sure don't waste words, do you?'

For the first time the young Maori smiled. '*Matua whakapai i tou marae, ka whakapai ai i te marae o te tongata.*' He chuckled, quite aware that Patrick was a *pakeha* with absolutely no knowledge of his language.

'All right, you painted, grinning heathen, what did *that* mean?'

'It mean: You clean your own house before you clean another man's!' With another wide smile, the incongruousness of his garb belied by the pantherish stride, the man turned and walked away in the direction Luther Hogge had taken.

Patrick stood staring after him. He saw him make a small gesture, and another 'scarecrow' detached itself from a dice game on the pavement and strolled over to join him. Patrick shook his head in disbelief. If these prime fighting men could enter a town in force—a town swarming with Her Majesty's militia—and pass unnoticed, what chance would the town stand against a calculated assault? 'I'm surely glad they're on my side!' he breathed, and went to re-join Melody and Beatrice fretting within the confines of their room.

'Maybe we should call in the military,' Beatrice was suggesting as Patrick entered, but already Melody had made up her mind.

'They'd think nothing of a half-caste Maori boy. Luther Hogge can buy off far more influential people than a few army men. No, I have to do this myself. I must meet the

Hog and accede to any demands he makes.' Then, with a flash of spirit. 'I'll do anything, anything to ensure David's safety, but once he's free, it's just between Hogge and myself. Were you able to get that passage to England, Aunt Bee?'

Beatrice looked a little uncomfortable. 'Well . . . we were going to make the arrangements tomorrow, before we returned to Windhaven.'

For the first time in days, Melody smiled. 'You're a fraud, Aunt Bee! You'd no intention of getting me on that boat!' Without awaiting a reply, she continued, 'Where is that animal Hogge?'

Patrick came forward quickly. 'Melody, I really think you must hand this situation over to Te Whatitoa's men and myself now.'

The sapphire eyes swung to his, blazing with fear and anger. 'You've wasted time! You should have told me you'd found him. Where? Take me to him!'

Patrick had never seen this side of her—the tigress defending her young—and in some surprise he answered, 'I've two of the chief's men trailing him at the moment. When he settles, one of them will come here.'

'Where did you see him? We must start now!'

'Wait, love!' Beatrice insisted, seeing the girl's high colour and flashing eyes with the same surprise that Patrick had experienced. She knew that Melody and the boy had formed a deep and affectionate rapport, but never knew the depths of her niece's feelings. 'We'll find him and the boy, never fear. No harm will come to the child.'

'He's not "the child", he's David, and—and he's mine!' Melody blurted out, and to her chagrin, burst into tears. She heard their platitudes and words of comfort, felt Beatrice's arms about her, but none of it seemed to matter, and when the soft knock came at the door she thrust them aside and ran to open it.

The golden-skinned warrior met her eyes with instant understanding. 'Not far. Come now.' Without a backward glance, Melody followed him into the brilliant sunlight.

'Stay here. I'll go with her,' ordered Patrick brusquely.

'Certainly not!' countered Beatrice, throwing a shawl across her shoulders before preceding him through the door in the wake of her niece.

They followed their guide to a small flax-barn on the outskirts of town, part of a disused mill with several outhouses surrounding it, but when Melody would have run forward, the Maori caught at her arm, his dark eyes troubled. 'Wait. Hemi not here. Maybe Hog-man gone another place.'

'We're wasting time.' Melody stated. 'If Hogge's here with David, I must go to him. You're here, and so is Patrick. If I can't reason with him, you are two against one. He'll not harm David with the odds against him and if I agree to go with him. It's me he wants. If he isn't in the barn, we must begin our search again. Your friend will be following him.' Then, seeing that still he hesitated, she cried, 'Oh, do as you please!' Throwing off the gently restraining fingers, she ran out into the street again and hurried up the track toward the barn.

'Let her go,' Patrick urged as the Maori moved to follow her. 'If Hogge thinks she's alone and helpless, she'll stand a fair chance of talking to him. In the meantime, you circle that way and come in from the rear. I'll take that track to the right and come in from behind those sheds. We can't await your friend, though I've a feeling we're storming an empty citadel.' The other man had been watching Patrick's sweeping gesture rather than attempting to understand his words, and now he nodded and moved off on silent feet. 'You stay put, Beatrice, for I've no wish to worry about you if, as I suspect, Hogge has a gun . . . No . . . No argument! Melody will be there by now. Yes. There she is at the door.' But as he began his approach, he heard her cry out his name, and putting all caution aside, he bounded up the last few yards to the open front door, slamming it wide to see Melody on her knees in the far corner.

'Hurry!' she cried. 'For heaven's sake, hurry!' She was on the crumpled body of the Maori, Hemi, trying in vain to staunch the terrible knife-wound in his chest. 'It was Hogge, damn his black soul to hell! I know it was him.'

Within seconds the other Maori had appeared, closely followed by Beatrice, but already Patrick had stripped the wounded man's shirt from him to pad the wound, and his own to bind it. 'We need a doctor fast. Here, man, you put your hand there and push down like so. I'll get a doctor here within minutes, even if I have to carry him.' Spinning, he ran back the way they had come, and Melody bent to reassure the young Maori.

'Your friend will be all right. Look, he's regaining consciousness.' To the wounded man she said, 'Don't try to speak. You're safe. The doctor will be here soon.'

But he cut her off with a feeble gesture. A harsh, painful whisper. 'Wikitoria . . .   Hog-man . . . Wikitoria . . . Made tell . . . '

'The hotel? He's gone to the hotel.' Melody sprang to her feet. 'He's found us . . . Left a message . . . I must go.' Eyes brilliant with mingled fear and fury, she seized Beatrice's sleeve. 'Tell Patrick where I am. If there's a message, I'll leave it there for you and follow whatever instructions he has given.'

'No!' Beatrice cut her off. 'This boy can tell Patrick where *we* are. I'll not allow you into the lion's den for a second time. You'll not find Hogge at the hotel. He may be the son of Satan, but he's no fool! He's fighting this war as much against the mind as the body, and now that he knows you're here, he'll make you suffer before he renders the *coup de grâce*.' But already Melody was hurrying out, and she could do nothing but follow.

At the hotel, they saw no sign of a note at the desk, but the clerk came forward quickly. 'Mrs Van der Veer, a man was asking for you. He asked to go to your room. I—I'm sorry, but he—he wasn't the kind of man one argues with.'

Running to the room, hearts pounding. The key sticking in the lock. Finally . . . and on the bed . . . 'Sweet Jesus!' whispered Beatrice at the sight of David's tattered shirt, blood soaked, a rent as if made by a knife in the

back. She turned, eyes brimming, but Melody was shaking
her head violently.

'No! He's *not* dead! I'd know if he were dead!'

'The blood . . . '

'I don't know . . . A cruel, terrible warning . . .
The Maori was bleeding badly. Yes . . . That's it!' The
sapphire eyes were hard as flint. 'You said yourself that
he was making war as much on the mind as on the body.
He *wants* me to despair. Wants me to suffer as he has
suffered. He won't kill David. It's the only pawn he has.
Think! I must think!' She sank on the bed beside that
terrible evidence of Hogge's cruelty and buried her face
in her hands, mind reeling.

There was a knock and Patrick entered, features set.
'The boy will live; but another hour, and your Mr Hogge
would have had another murder to account for.' Taking
in the blood-soaked shirt and Melody's bent head, he
whispered, 'No! It can't be!'

'David's alive,' Melody stated with conviction. 'I *know*
he is. I just don't know where.'

Patrick ran frantic fingers through his hair, a frown
drawing down the heavy brows. Suddenly he slammed his
palm against the door. 'The schooner! I saw him coming
off one of those schooners at the docks. It's a perfect
place to keep the boy, and if he got you on board, they
could sail on the next tide with no one the wiser. You'd
just vanish off the face of the earth.' He held up a hand
as Melody surged to her feet. 'But we must prepare, this
time.' A crooked grin. 'I'd gladly take on the entire crew
singlehanded, Melody girl, but I've a feeling it wouldn't
do David much good. No, I'll find Te Whatitoa and his
men, and we'll go in force.'

Melody nodded, accepting that they had lost the element
of surprise and knowing that Hogge was playing with
them as a cat with a mouse. 'Hurry!' Only when he had
gone did she allow herself to sink back on the bed, noting
with a spark of gratitude that her aunt had removed
David's shirt and consigned it to the far corner.

'We'll find him, never fear,' Beatrice comforted her.

'With your warrior friends on our side, there isn't a bolt-
hole in the town he can hide in.'

Melody stretched to squeeze her soft hand, grateful for
the ever-reassuring presence, but with her mind concentrating only on one small frightened boy who had only
come to this horrendous situation because she had betrayed
his trust and love.

It seemed an eternity, though it could have been no
more than an hour, before one of Te Whatitoa's men
appeared to take them to the waterfront. He could speak
no English, so that the moment they came in sight of the
Irishman, Melody ran forward anxiously. 'Which ship is
it? Have they seen Hogge? Do they know whether David's
aboard?'

'Whoa, lass! There's the schooner yonder, and no,
there's been no sign of either Hogge or the boy. There's
a fair amount of activity aboard though, and an outgoing
tide in less than two hours. They may be below decks,
but there's only one way to find out.' Boldly he led
Melody up the gangplank, closely followed by Beatrice
and the Maori chief, together with six of his best men, to
the untrained eye a rag-tag assortment of seamen and
itinerant 'friendlies'. The crew of the schooner, however,
had no such illusions and drew their weapons as their
captain approached Patrick.

'We've no room for passengers, matey,' he growled, his
accent betraying London dockland and a variety of ports
between there and Wanganui. 'As you see, we've also
little time for the niceties of small talk, so say what you've
come to say and off with you.'

'Friendly type, isn't he?' Patrick grinned at Melody, the
blue eyes alight with the anticipation of battle, then said
to the glowering man, 'I'm of a similar mind, sir, so I'll
come right to the point. We both know that a certain
Luther Hogge has been aboard here and we know he has
a lad with him. Now, I've a mind to separate the two of
them, so I'd be obliged if you'd have the kindness to tell
me where they are.'

'They ain't here. Now get off my ship.'

Patrick's smile widened. 'Well, now, that may be so, and you'd therefore have no objection to my friends looking around before we leave.'

'You heard me! Off my ship, or I'll set my dogs on you.' He indicated the shifting dozen or so men who had gathered behind him, wielding an evil assortment of weapons, from ancient cutlasses to marlinspikes.

Te Whatitoa stepped forward, gently setting Melody aside, his vast bulk a lethal complement to that of the Irishman. 'Captain,' he said softly and with precision, 'if you do not at once allow my men below, you will have neither dogs nor kennel. The . . . "friendlies" you see on the dock are not as friendly as they appear and would take much pleasure in burning your boat where she lies.' Then, as if in explanation, 'The boy with Luther Hogge is my nephew.'

The captain looked from one to the other and ran a tongue over his lips, knowing he was beaten. He had done all he had been paid to do and now admitted it, seeing death in their eyes. He gestured to his crew, and growling, reluctant, they moved back. 'Like I said, they ain't here. See for yourself. Mr Hogge paid me well to give him and the lad the use of my cabin for a while, and told me to keep you here for as long as I could. He knew you'd come eventually. We're going out with the tide. I'm to leave a man behind with a row-boat, and you are to come out with him as soon as we're clear, miss. Then he'll let the boy go, he says.'

'Where is he now? You must know,' Patrick demanded, having seen Te Whatitoa's men return from all corners of the ship with grim features and tight lips that bore testimony to the failure of their search.

'I swear I don't.' Then, as a knife appeared in the Maori chieftain's hand, 'I swear it! Before God, I swear it! He said I was to signal when you was aboard, miss, and then he'd meet the ship after she'd sailed. He said he'd be in the last place you'd look, so you may as well give up.'

'Never!' stated Melody. 'Patrick, we *can't*!'

'No, of course not, m'dear. We'll find them. So the hunted becomes the hunter.' For once the blue eyes held no conviction as he followed her back on to dry land.

Melody saw the same hopelessness reflected in the faces all about her, even in that of Beatrice, coming to put a comforting arm about her. 'Of course we'll find him.' She lacked her usual optimism, and Melody felt suddenly terribly alone.

'Oh, Paul,' she whispered, 'if only you were here!' Then, louder, 'We must think. The last place we'd think of looking?'

A young Maori approached his chief and spoke urgently to him as the others milled about uncertainly. Te Whatitoa nodded, and with a smile of relief and gratitude the boy hurried off. 'Forgive him,' the warrior said. 'He will be back, but the wounded man, Hemi, is his brother and he was anxious to see that all was still well with him.'

'I'm grateful that he has stayed with us for so long.' Melody smiled, then the smile died as a fragment of an idea kept nagging at her. 'No,' she thought aloud. 'It's impossible! He wouldn't!' Then as the idea glowed with the brilliance of a star-burst, she spun round to Patrick. 'The last place we'd look? The last place we'd dream he'd return to? The flax-barn. It must be!'

And Beatrice, eyes flashing, said, 'He's doubled back! Like a fox before the hounds . . . Like the wild boar he is!'

Already the word had been passed, and as one the band turned for the mills, and once there, Te Whatitoa dispersed his men to the shadows of the outhouses, out of sight of the barn but near enough to bring their considerable fire-power to bear if given half a chance. Melody put down the churning of her stomach and went to step into the sunlight, but the chief put a firm hand on her shoulder. 'We'll all go.'

'I must talk to him alone. If there is any chance of his harming David, I can't risk it.'

The chief was adamant. 'We shall go together.'

Having no choice, and secretly glad of their support,

Melody agreed. With the Maori on one side and Patrick and Beatrice on the other, she went forward, heart pounding, praying to all the gods, especially the Blessed Virgin, and Papa-tu-a-nuku, the primal Maori Earth Mother, since they, above all, should know the hopes and the joys and the pain and the fear that motherhood can bring. One, she reasoned, would protect David, the other Rawiri—two cultures in one small frame.

Before they reached the barn, there was a glint of metal at the window and a shot rang out, then Hogge's voice calling, 'That's far enough! You've been clever in finding me, Melody, but it was very stupid to bring your friends along. You were warned!'

'Luther . . . I beg you . . . Let David go. I'll do anything you ask. Please, Luther.'

'Tell your nigger army to back off, or this half-caste brat will suffer for it.'

'No!' stated the chief before Melody could answer. 'Free the child and live, or harm him and die. The choice is yours.'

'I'll free him, but I want safe conduct to a schooner that's waiting for the next tide. I'm taking the woman back to England with me.'

'I'll go with you, Luther. Just free David.'

'You can't!' cried Beatrice.

'Over my dead body!' stated Patrick.

'I have to. Don't you see?'

'Hogge!' called Patrick. 'How do we know you have the boy safe and so far unhurt in there?'

There was a moment of silence, then slowly the door opened and Hogge appeared, holding David before him. Immediately the hidden men brought up their muskets, but then reluctantly lowered them again. They weren't marksmen, and the guns were not accurate enough to guarantee they would not hit the boy. Melody gave a sob at the sight of the child, and there was an angry murmur from the others. David had obviously put up a struggle at some time, for there was a large blue-black bruise on his cheek. He appeared tired, and at that moment, simply a very frightened, very small boy. He began to struggle when he saw his rescuers, calling 'Auntie Melody!' But then Hogge twisted the arm he held, pulling it higher up the child's back, and David cried out in pain.

'As you see, he's alive and still in need of discipline!' He dragged the boy back inside and slammed the door shut, before demanding, 'I want your word that I'll have safe escort. I want Melody in here, and I'll release the brat as soon as we're under way. I shall have protection enough there.'

'I must go!' Melody cried. 'Oh, did you see him? I must go!' she ran forward before they could prevent her.

'Come back!' Beatrice cried. 'Oh, you little fool!' But it was too late. The door opened, and Melody was seized and dragged inside.

In the light from the oil-lamp on the table, she saw David on the floor lying against a bundle of flax, where he had been thrown. He was knuckling his eyes, refusing to allow the tears to flow, but when he saw Melody he sprang up, running into her arms, and she hugged him tightly, rocking him, kissing him and murmuring inconsequential love-words and reassurances.

'Very pretty,' came that hated voice. 'I never knew you were so maternal, my dear, but I'm delighted that you are. It serves my purpose admirably.'

Melody raised glittering, tear-washed eyes to his. 'I'll never forgive you for this, Luther! I'll accompany you to England and live with you under any terms you choose. I'll be nothing but a slave, obeying your every whim, but I'll hate you to my dying day.'

His features had tightened and the eyes were ugly, but his tone remained as silky as ever. 'No doubt, my dear. No doubt. That is why I shall be taking the boy with us—to ensure your compliance.'

'You can't!' The horror was too much to bear. The thought of this perfect, loving, barely-tamed creature of the bush being submitted to cruel slavery in that dark house, beaten and abused for any real or imagined fault of hers, brought the bile to her throat. Stars flashed behind her eyes. 'You won't!' she screamed at him, and sprang, tigress claws curled to tear at that deformed, hated face.

He caught her wrists, staggering back, shocked by the suddenness of the assault. For an instant they struggled, knocking aside the table, sending the oil-lamp crashing to the flax-strewn floor, but then he crashed a fist into her stomach and she doubled up, choking and writhing on the floor. David leapt at him then, but was knocked aside with a contemptuous back-hand. 'I'll deal with you later!'

Melody heard the crackling first and turned in horror, seeing the flames licking at the tinder-dry flax. 'Luther!' she croaked, her voice barely audible, but already he had whipped round, taking off his jacket. He beat at the flames, stamping on them and kicking aside the small bales, but the dry flax caught in seconds.

Just as instinctively Melody had stumbled to her feet, grabbed David and made a desperate bid for freedom. As she reached the door, she heard Hogge's curse. There was a deafening crash, and a bullet thudded into the wood beside David's head, but already she was tearing the door open, falling through it, and feeling strong arms around her.

Patrick swung her up as Te Whatitoa grasped David, running with them to where the others waited.

'The fire!' Melody cried, still in pain from Hogge's cruel blow. 'The lamp went over. You must help him.'

'He would have killed you!' Patrick growled.

'You can't let him burn! Not even Luther.'

The door was ablaze now, and the inside of the small barn an inferno. There was a scream, an inhuman cry more of rage than pain. 'Help him! For pity's sake!'

'It's too late,' Te Whatitoa stated softly. 'No one could get into that . . . or get out.'

Then their blood turned to ice as a long drawn-out cry of 'Melodeee . . . ' was followed by a final shot.

Melody collapsed against Patrick's broad chest. 'It's over, little one,' he soothed. 'It's all over.' But she knew that she would remember that terrible cry calling her name for as long as she lived.

'Can we go home now?' asked a small voice, bringing
her back to reality.

'Yes . . . Oh, yes, my love! We'll get you home just
as quickly as possible.' She turned to Te Whatitoa, but
already he had read her thoughts.

'The *waka taua* is waiting.'

'Aunt Bee, you and Patrick will be coming straight
back now, won't you?'

'Yes, but in a more civilised fashion: we'll take the
steamer up-river.'

'I'll have the horses waiting at the landing. I must get
David back quickly. Paul must be out of his mind with
worry.'

The Maori touched her arm. 'We are wasting time.
Paul has been told to meet us at the *pa*, and he's not a
patient man.'

Beatrice raised a smile. 'Your art of understatement
beats even that of us English! Go ahead, Melody, child.
I'll get back to the hotel and change. I'm becoming
accustomed to the metamorphosis from London Lady to
Farmer's Daughter at the drop of a hat—or hoop, as the
case may be.'

Patrick took her arm as the group turned to make their
way back. 'Don't change too drastically,' he ordered.
'That bronze taffeta will do nicely.'

Grey eyes opened wide. 'But that's one of my better
dresses!'

'You can change for riding when we reach the landing,
but I've a mind to see you in your bronze taffeta on the
boat. I've a thing or two to say, and the saying will come
easier if you're looking like an angel out of heaven.'

Not for the first time since the Irishman had entered
their lives, Melody saw her aunt blush. 'Angel, indeed!'
Beatrice scoffed. 'If I am, I'm a rather overweight, middle-
aged and definitely tarnished one!'

Patrick grinned. 'I'd have you no other way.'

'You'll have me not at all, Patrick O'Shaughnessy!'

But that incorrigible grin remained. 'I've a mind to be

discussing that very point in me own way in me own good time! Melody, m'dear, you must go your way, too, for there's that overgrown dinghy of yours waiting. Good luck. We'll see you tonight.'

Impulsively, she gave him a hug. 'Goodbye for the present, Patrick. We'll have a celebration dinner! We've much to celebrate already, and, who knows, we may have more by the time you arrive.'

Beatrice gave a snort, turning away to hide her sparkling eyes, but Patrick gave Melody a broad wink before joining her.

'All right, Te Whatitoa, let's go home,' Melody said, but in her heart there was a small sadness, for she knew that Windhaven would never be *her* home while Paul Savage saw her only as a freed slave whom he had wronged. It was with mixed feelings, then, that she boarded the sleek war canoe and heard the beginning of the chant that would regulate the long strokes, as Te Whatitoa stood upon the thwarts, proud and as handsome as some pagan god, using that deep voice and wild gestures to urge his men on. The men, too, joined in the song, a familiar action song, *'Uia moi, toia mai, te waka'*—'Behold the canoe'—their paddles sending the giant craft skimming through the water until the foam rose on either side. Paul had told her that after the signing of the Treaty of Waitangi, a flotilla of sixty-nine such craft had left on a single day for Hawke Bay carrying members of one tribe back to their homes.

Part of Melody, therefore, revelled in the exhilaration of the ride now that her previous fear and tension were dispersed, and she felt a deep pride in being a part of this magnificent team; yet another part of her experienced the familiar desolation that came with the knowledge that soon she would be torn from them and forced to return to England.

'England!' She said it aloud—waiting for the swell of homesickness that she had felt upon leaving it—a lifetime ago. It never came. 'Home,' she said, but the word no longer conjured up images of green rolling hills or soft rain drifting onto shining pavements. She saw, instead, a high bluff breaking out of the lush bush vegetation and, below, a house, oddly angled, shaded by a giant hoa tree.

'Don't cry, Auntie Melody,' David comforted her. 'It's all over now. We'll soon be home. Papa is waiting, and everything will be all right again.'

She smiled down at him through her tears. How could she let him go? 'Yes, little warrior, we'll soon be home.' The emotion threatened to overcome her, and with it came a sudden anger. I *won't* let him go, she vowed. I'll fight tooth and nail to keep him! Damn you, Paul Savage! I'm going to stay! You can turn me out of your house, but you can't turn me out of your country! It's *my* home now! Mine!

CHAPTER TWENTY-THREE

HE HAD KNOWN of her coming, warned by the blowing of the conch-shell down-river long before they came into view. She was sitting proudly, one arm about the boy at her side. She was dust-streaked, splashed by the river, raven hair in an untidy knot at the nape of her neck—yet about her was an aura, a beauty, that caught at his throat, and in her eyes when she landed was a brilliance, an alive new kind of defiance he had never seen.

For Melody, seeing him standing on the bank, legs apart, hands on lean hips, fingers splayed downward in that familiarly challenging pose, it was like a battle-cry. At the same time her heart pounded at the very sight of that bronzed chest exposed by the open shirt and the muscular thighs encased in tight linen.

Both wanted with all their hearts to clasp the other and drown the agony of worry in the crush of flesh to flesh and mouth to mouth. Both hid their emotion in anger.

'Damn you, Melody! Don't ever do that to me again!' he shouted the moment she set foot on shore. 'David's my son, and if he's in danger, *I* shall deal with it!'

'You weren't there to deal with it!' she countered heatedly. 'And it wasn't you Luther Hogge wanted, anyway!'

'Papa, don't!' David begged, running to fling his arms round his father's waist, gazing up at him imploringly. 'Auntie Melody saved my life!'

Paul crushed his son to him, jaw tight, holding deep inside the kisses that a woman could smother the child with, for Paul Savage was all man—and the very strength that made him so was now his greatest weakness.

'He's right, old friend,' Te Whatitoa intervened. 'This

woman would have given her life for your son.'

'Yes, Papa,' David broke in. 'Auntie Melody said that she'd go back to England and be the Hog-man's slave if he'd let me go. How can a *pakeha* be a slave, Papa?'

Paul's face had gone deathly white, the scar blazing as he raised dark eyes to Melody's. 'Pray God you never know, son,' he said grimly.

'Well, anyway, Papa, this Mita Hogge he said that he'd take us both back to England to keep Auntie Melody . . . keep her . . . keep her . . .'

'Compliant,' Melody finished, holding that dark gaze.

Paul put the boy aside and turned away, unable to face any of them. 'My God!' he said quietly, the agony ripping through his words. 'I should have killed him when I had the chance.'

'That, too, has been taken care of,' the Maori said, and with many pauses—filled in by David with a great sense of the dramatic—they told him the whole story while making their way up to the *pa*. Paul walked in silence, and Melody's heart went out to him for the occasional touches as he reached out a rough hand to his son's shoulder or aimed a gentle punch at his arm in the only way he knew to signal his love. She saw his fists clench when David told how Hogge had tricked him into going with him, finding him when he had run into the woods.

'He was waiting. Just sitting there looking at the house,' David told them. 'He said that he had come to say he was sorry for hurting me, and asked me who I really was and where I was going.' The boy looked momentarily shamefaced, mumbling, 'I said that I was nobody because nobody wanted me, and that I was running away.' Melody felt the sob rise in her, but already the boy was continuing, 'He said that if I wanted everyone to come after me and say they were sorry, I should go with him. He said that he was Auntie Melody's friend, and he had bought a present for me that was so big he couldn't bring it with him. He said that I could stay in a lovely house in town and have as much candy as I wanted until she came to say she was sorry for not wanting me.'

'Oh, David!' Melody cried, 'I've always wanted you, from the very first!'

'I know that now, but I was very angry with you then. The Hog-man took me to a boat in Wanganui, not a nice house, and they gave me a nasty drink. I spitted it out. Then they hit me, so I drank it. Then I went to sleep. Then I woke up in the flax-barn. I tried to hit the Hog-man again, but he hit me back, so I stopped, and soon Auntie Melody came.' The breathless, disjointed monologue told them far more than his words ever could, and Paul's face was a terrible thing to see.

They reached the *pa*, and went to Te Whatitoa's *whare*, where a woman came to present them with pork and *tumara* cooked in the ground oven. They sat outside, since it was forbidden to eat inside the house, and each accepted the basket made of green woven flax although, at that time, not one of them felt hungry. David, rapidly recovered, had gone to play with his peers and enthral them with the story of his adventure. An awkward silence fell. Then, quietly, the chief said, 'There are times, old friend, when the talking has to stop and the thinking begin. Leave Rawiri here. I'll talk with him. He is safe now. The Hog-man will trouble no one again.' He turned to Melody, velvet-brown eyes meeting sapphire blue, though he still addressed himself to Paul. 'There is no honour great enough that I can pay this woman, but I can, in a small way, thank her for the life of Rawiri.'

He rose and left them, going into the dark shadows of the *whare*, but was back almost immediately, and over his arm was the most exquisite cloak that Melody had ever seen. It was blue and grey, and green and red, made up of tiny feathers from the *kakāriki*, the rainbow-hued parakeet. He smiled at Melody's gasp and the wonder in her eyes as she slowly got to her feet, unable to believe the vision before her.

Paul rose with her, torn between refusal and pride as the Maori asked, 'Will you accept this, Melody, Toa Iti?' calling her 'Little Warrior'. Carefully he laid the cloak about her shoulders. 'This can be worn only by the *ariki*,

who can trace their ancestors back to the First who
arrived in the Fleet, or the *rangatiri* like myself, who are
of noble birth and great courage. I do not think there is
a man here who would say that you should not wear
this.'

Melody did not attempt to brush aside the tears that
streamed down her cheeks as he bent and touched his
nose to hers. '*E hoa*, you are a new part of my country.
There will be others like you, who will find their heart
resting here even though they are of different blood and
different faith, but Paul was the first I met and you are
the second, so you must forgive an old warrior's gratitude.'

Melody smiled through her tears. 'Your country is my
country, Te Whatitoa. Maata taught me that in every
heart there is . . . ' she hesitated, then said fluently, '*Te
Taepaepatanga o' te rangi*.'

Paul's quiet voice translated, 'The place where the sky
reaches the horizon.' Then he said, 'Melody, I think we
should go now. We've some . . . thinking to do.'

Her level gaze met his. 'No, Paul, you have some
thinking to do. I have done mine.'

He saw her then, the feathered cloak sitting on shoulders
far too slender, her hair awry, face dusty and traced with
lines of strain and tiredness, yet more a woman than any
had a right to be. He gave a nod and a slight bow,
gesturing wordlessly toward the horses. Preceding him,
she turned for a moment to thank the woman who had
prepared the food, speaking to her in soft, fluent Maori.

'You're here to stay, aren't you?' he stated.

'This is my country now,' she answered, swinging
independently on to her horse and kicking ahead before
he could answer.

He followed her more slowly, seeing how she remembered the hardly discernible track through the thick bush.
A little up the trail he ventured, 'The *kakãriki* cloak . . . '

'I doubt that I'll wear it again.'

'It would be somewhat incongruous at a London soirée.'

'Yes . . . were I thinking of going back. I was simply

thinking it was too precious to clean the house or clear weeds in.'

'You are really not going to return?'

'No, Paul.'

They did not speak again until much later, as the trail touched the river bank and she reined in with a smile. 'Hear the kingfisher calling? He must be lost. He's much too far south at this time.'

'Far out of his territory,' Paul agreed. 'Like others I know.'

'He'll either find a way back or learn to adjust to his new environment . . . like others I know.'

The sun was setting before they came to the high bluff—breaking out of the tree-ferns and finding Windhaven below them. As on that first day, Melody reined in, drawing the view into her very soul.

'We're home,' he said, watching her.

'Yes.' But she was looking beyond, looking at the sun dropping like a stone into the sudden New Zealand night, leaving crimson and royal purple to cloak the land.

'Marry me, Melody,' he asked quietly, and saw her stiffen, but she would not look back at him. 'Melody . . . I'm sorry. I don't think I've ever said that to anyone before. I meant to tame you . . . tame you as I tamed the land. I wanted you from the first moment I saw you, yet saw nothing of you at all. I saw the fear that you hid beneath anger as rebellion, and your pride—that Savage pride that I should have known so well—as wilfulness. I saw your temper, but not your gentleness; your sensuality, but not the innocence beneath, and only when I destroyed that innocence did I begin to comprehend. I was wrong, so very wrong.'

'You were,' she agreed, only the slightest tremor in her voice.

'Yet, in spite of myself and . . . ye gods, woman, in spite of you . . . I've come to love you. I want you to stay. I want you to make this your home, I want you by my side, as my equal, as my wife.'

There was a moment in time, a heartbeat, when the sun

surrendered to the inevitable and Melody gave a deep
sigh. 'I'm not marrying you, Paul,' she declared in that
slightly husky voice that would stay with him for the rest
of his days.

He felt the mounting drumroll of his heart. He felt the
choking, clutching sensation at his throat. He had been
so sure! For an instant—the briefest instant before she
turned—he felt death close over his deepest untouched
soul. Then suddenly there was his future, all of it, reflected
in the marvellous sapphire of her smiling eyes. He saw
the dying sun cast fire from her hair as she gave him one
long look over her shoulder before turning back to the
land, deep velvet, untamed, and eternally mysterious
beneath the settling blanket of night.

'I shall *accept you*, Paul Savage,' she said. 'But it's New
Zealand I'm marrying . . . though . . . God help me
. . . I love you almost as much!' And, so saying, she
spurred down the slope—towards Home.